"Sometimes a story is almost too wonderful to be true. Thankfully, the bit of history at the heart of Gabhart's latest novel is absolutely true, providing the perfect platform for a tale of love and generosity that will restore the reader's faith in mankind. From the deeply compelling opening pages to the satisfying ending, readers will be inspired to examine their own lives and whether or not they 'pray believing.'"

Sarah Loudin Thomas, author of the
Appalachian Blessings series

"Ann H. Gabhart's *River to Redemption* will both capture your heart and bolster your spirits. Each of the well-drawn characters stepped off the pages and into my heart. This story will remain with you long after you've read the last page. A genuinely wonderful book."

Judith Miller, award-winning author of *The Chapel Car Bride*

"Ann Gabhart weaves a sympathetic tale set in pre–Civil War Kentucky. Rich in historical detail, *River to Redemption* reveals the heartbreaking reality of slavery in the first half of the nineteenth century, one young girl's dangerous quest to end it, and a slave's strong faith in God's timing and providence. You will fall in love with these unforgettable characters."

Jan Drexler, award-winning author of the
Journey to Pleasant Prairie series

Praise for *These Healing Hills*

"Gabhart paints an endearing portrait of WWII Appalachia in this enjoyable tale about two people trying to find their place in the world and discern what it means to truly be home. . . . Gabhart handles the Appalachian landscape and culture with skill, bringing them to vibrant life."

Publishers Weekly

"Humor, grace, and, of course, romance give the characters life and breath, and the message of faith is gently organic and sincere."

RT Book Reviews

"Based on the actual Frontier Nursing Service (FNS), which still serves parts of rural Kentucky, Gabhart's latest is a sweet historical romance set near the end of WWII that brings readers into the heart of the hills where Francine's traveling midwifery practice shapes a tale rich with themes of healing and identity. The tenacity and stalwart bravery that Gabhart so skillfully instills in her female lead in this rugged, heartwarming read are to be admired."

Booklist

"This novel vividly re-creates the world of postwar Appalachia. The compelling story line resonates long after the last page is turned."

Library Journal

RIVER *to* REDEMPTION

BOOK SOLD
NO LONGER R.H.P.L.
PROPERTY

BOOK SOLD
NO LONGER R.H.PL.
PROPERTY

RIVER *to* REDEMPTION

ANN H. GABHART

Revell

a division of Baker Publishing Group
Grand Rapids, Michigan

© 2018 by Ann H. Gabhart

Published by Revell
a division of Baker Publishing Group
PO Box 6287, Grand Rapids, MI 49516-6287
www.revellbooks.com

Printed in the United States of America

All rights reserved. No part of this publication may be reproduced, stored in a retrieval system, or transmitted in any form or by any means—for example, electronic, photocopy, recording—without the prior written permission of the publisher. The only exception is brief quotations in printed reviews.

Library of Congress Cataloging-in-Publication Data
Names: Gabhart, Ann H., 1947– author.
Title: River to redemption / Ann H. Gabhart.
Description: Grand Rapids, MI : Revell, a division of Baker Publishing Group,
   [2018]
Identifiers: LCCN 2018007141 | ISBN 9780800723644 (softcover : acid-free paper)
Subjects:| GSAFD: Christian fiction.
Classification: LCC PS3607.A23 R59 2018 | DDC 813/.6—dc23
LC record available at https://lccn.loc.gov/2018007141

ISBN 978-0-8007-3518-0 (casebound)

Scripture used in this book, whether quoted or paraphrased by the characters, is taken from the King James Version of the Bible.

This book is a work of historical fiction inspired by real people and events. All other characters and events, however, are products of the author's imagination, and any resemblance to actual persons, living or dead, is coincidental. Details that cannot be historically verified are purely products of the author's imagination.

Published in association with the Books & Such Literary Agency.

18   19   20   21   22   23   24   7   6   5   4   3   2   1

RICHMOND HILL PUBLIC LIBRARY
32972001307224   RH
River to redemption
Mar. 04. 2019

To my children:
Johnson & Leah, Tarasa & Gary, and Daniel & Carrie

One

JUNE 1833

Adria Starr didn't want her mother and little brother to stop breathing the way her father had. She wanted to take care of them.

She was seven. That was old enough to do things. She could draw water from the well and carry wood to the stove. She could even run for the doctor, like she did after her daddy came home sick, but a woman answered the door at the doctor's house to say he couldn't come. He was sick too. That it wouldn't matter anyway. Not with the cholera.

Adria had heard her father whisper that word to her mother. Adria didn't know what it meant, but her mother clutched the back of a chair and made a sound like somebody had hit her in the stomach. Then with her eyes too wide, she looked at Adria, and it was like somebody was squeezing Adria's heart.

"Leave." Adria's father told her mother. "Get away from the bad air here in town."

Even before her father quit breathing, her mother started packing a bag to go somewhere after Adria came back without the doctor. But how could they leave Daddy? Then Eddie got sick. Just like their father. He was only two and he cried until Adria wanted to put her hands over her ears. But when he stopped, everything was too quiet.

They didn't leave. Her mother couldn't stop shaking and she was very sick. Like her insides wanted to come out of her body. She leaned on Adria while she sat on the pot. She told Adria to go away, but if Adria hadn't held her, her mother would have fallen to the floor.

After Mama got through being sick, Adria helped her to the couch and laid Eddie down beside her. Adria kissed his cheek, but it didn't feel right. She didn't look at his chest. She didn't want to know if it had stopped moving up and down. She didn't look at her mother's chest either. Instead she carried the slop jar and basin into the sitting room in case her mother needed them again. Then she got a blanket and curled up on the floor beside the couch.

Her mother didn't need the basin, but Adria did. She must have breathed in that bad air too. After she was through being sick, she lay back down on the floor. The only sounds were the mantel clock ticking and more bad air ruffling the window curtains.

She fell asleep for a while. When she woke up, the clock wasn't ticking anymore. Her father was the one who always wound it. The air had stopped moving too. Maybe the bad air had moved away to another town. But Adria's stomach still hurt. She needed a drink of water, but she didn't think she could get up to go to the kitchen.

Adria reached up toward her mother but stayed her hand without touching her. Everything was so still. Nothing was moving. Usually their house was filled with sound. Eddie jabbering or crying. Her mother singing while she clattered pans in the kitchen. Her father coming in the door from work and grabbing Adria to swing her up in the air and then giving Eddie a turn. She didn't know which of them squealed the loudest.

But now silence wrapped around her. Nothing but her heart beating in her ears. She wanted to ask her mother if the bad air killed everybody, but she clamped her lips together and didn't let the words out. She was scared her mother wouldn't answer.

Adria squeezed her eyes shut. Where she'd been sick smelled bad. Really bad. She pinched her nose to block the odor, but then her breathing sounded too loud, like she'd been running or something. She pulled a pillow over her face.

She hoped it wouldn't hurt if the bad air killed her. Maybe her heart would just stop the way the clock had stopping ticking. She tried to remember whether the preacher ever said anything in his sermons about dying. But most of the stories she could remember were about Jesus feeding people or making them well. Maybe if she prayed, he would make her well, and Eddie and her parents too.

"Please," she whispered into the pillow. She tried to think of more words, but she was tired. So she just said the bedtime prayer her mother taught her. "Now I lay me down to sleep. I pray the Lord my soul to keep. And if I should die before I wake, I pray the Lord my soul to take."

She prayed that all the time, but she had never worried about not waking up. Not until now. What would happen if the Lord took her soul? Would it be silent like now, or noisy? Angels singing maybe. No, that was when Jesus was born. But heaven might be noisy. Lots of people there, and didn't they say something about crossing a river? She'd seen a river. The water was noisy. She really needed a drink.

The knock on the door made her jump. Her father had said something once about a person knocking on heaven's door, but this sounded more like their own front door. Maybe it was the doctor coming after all. When she pushed up off the floor, the room started spinning, and she cried out and fell back with a thump.

The door swung open and a deep voice called out, "Somebody in here needin' help?"

When the big man stepped around the couch, Adria let out another shriek, but her mother didn't make the first sound. The man stared down at Adria. Sweat made tracks down his black face and he looked like a giant looming over her. She scrambled away from him, but moving made her sick again. She tried to get to the basin, but she didn't make it.

Big gentle hands reached down to hold her. "There, there, missy. It's done gonna be all right." He stroked her hair sort of the way her daddy did sometimes when he was telling her good night.

When she was through being sick, the man wiped her mouth off with a handkerchief and gathered her up in his arms as though she wasn't any bigger than Eddie. She forgot about being afraid and laid her head against his chest. His heart was beating, steady and sure. It was a good sound, and even his sweaty smell was better than the smell from her being sick.

"What's your name, child?" he asked.

"Adria," she whispered, a little surprised the sound came out of her dry lips.

"Adria," he echoed her. "That's a fine name. I'm gonna take you back to Mr. George's hotel where we can see to you."

"What about Eddie?"

"That your little brother there?" The man's voice was soft. "You don't have to worry about him. I'll come back and do what needs doing."

Adria didn't want to, but she couldn't keep her eyes from peeking away from the man's chest toward Eddie beside her mother. He wasn't moving and her mother's eyes were staring up at the ceiling. "What needs doing?"

"Well, it ain't an easy thing for a little missy like you to know, but your mama and li'l brother done gone on to glory. All's can be done for them now is a proper burial. I been doing it for all them that got took by the cholera." He rubbed his hand up and down Adria's back and turned so she couldn't see her mother anymore. "What about your pappy?"

"He died first." Adria pointed toward the bedroom.

The man nodded. "It's a sorrowful thing."

"Am I going to go to glory too?" Glory seemed easier to say than die.

"Only the good Lord knows our appointed time to leave this old world, but I'm thinkin' that you might have to wait a while to see glory. Could be the Lord has more for you to do down here like he has for me."

"What's that?"

"Hard to say. But time will tell, missy. Time will tell. Now you just rest your head down on my shoulder and let ol' Louis take you on up the street. Matilda, she ain't bothered by the cholera, same as me, and she's got a healin' hand. Me and her, we'll do for you and chase that old cholera out of you."

"I want my mama." Adria was crying inside, but her tears had all dried up. Her eyes felt scratchy when she blinked.

"Ain't that the way of us all. To want our mammies." He carried her out the door.

Night was falling, or maybe day was breaking. Adria didn't know how long she had lain there by the couch afraid to look at her mother. And now she would never see her again. Not unless she went to glory.

She ought to want to go to glory along with her mother and father and Eddie. They were a family. Her mother said that all the time, and then she would pick up Eddie and pull Adria close to her in a hug at the same time. If Daddy was there, he'd put his arms around them all and make what he called a family sandwich with his children in the middle. That always made Adria giggle. She liked being in a family sandwich, and now that was gone. Unless she went back and lay down beside her mother to let the bad air get her too.

But she didn't want to do that. She was glad the big man was carrying her away from her house. Away from the bad air. She thought she ought to be sorry about that, and she was sorry. Very sorry and sad her family was gone, but she wasn't sorry she was still breathing. She wanted to believe it was like the big man said. That the Lord wasn't ready for her yet.

She thought she should tell the man she could walk. She was way past carrying age, but the man wasn't breathing hard and it felt good to let him take care of her.

"I prayed," she said. "Did God send you to my house?" That wasn't what she'd prayed for, but she heard the preacher say once that sometimes the Lord knew what you needed better than you did.

"That could be." The man's chest rumbled under Adria's ear as he chuckled at her words. "I reckon the good Lord has his ways of makin' things happen, but fact is, the doctor's wife told me you'd been there to get the doctor."

"She wouldn't let him come."

"Well, he couldn't rightly make it, child. The cholera has done laid him low too. Could be he'll make it through, but he can't be no use to nobody else till he does." The man's voice was soft and deep, with nothing scary about it.

"Are you an angel?" Adria had never thought about angels having black skin and smelling sweaty. She always thought about them floating around with wings and white robes, but could be that was all wrong.

The man's chest rumbled again. "That's something I never expected anybody to say about me. But no, missy, I ain't no angel. I reckon I should've tol' you who I is to rest your mind a bit. I'm Louis Sanderson, Mr. George Sanderson's man. He owns the hotel here on Main Street, and when the cholera come to call, he give me his keys and told me to carry on with things best I could. He aimed to get as far from the cholera as he could and I'm supposin' he did."

"Daddy wanted Mama to go, but Eddie got sick and then she got sick too."

"The cholera is a terrible thing."

"Why didn't you go too?"

"There's some wonderin' 'bout that, but whilst I ain't no angel, the good Lord had a job here for me to do. Folks to take care of. He somehow kept the bad air from botherin' ol' Louis and seemed to me he must have had a reason for that. Somethin' he expected me to do. The Lord gives you a job to do, then I reckon you'd best do it. Ain't that right, missy?"

She tried to listen and understand what he was saying, but she couldn't hold all his words in her ears. "I don't know."

Louis patted her back as he carried her up some steps to a door with painted glass. "Well, don't you never mind about that. Right now you just think on gettin' better. Matilda and me, we're gonna take good care of you."

Two

M atilda's black face had wrinkles all around her eyes and mouth, and her fingers felt hard and bony when she laid her hand on Adria's forehead. Adria could tell she aimed to be gentle, so she didn't jerk away from her.

Louis started up the stairs with Adria, but the old woman stopped him. "Don't be takin' the child up there where they're sicker. You bring her on back here to the cot in the room off'n the kitchen. That will work fine."

Louis hesitated before he turned around. "You sure about that, Matilda? Folks might not like us puttin' a white child in a slave room."

Matilda made a sound and waved her hand. "Ain't none of them around to know nothin' about it. They done all run out of town. And I ain't got energy to be runnin' up and down the stairs every five minutes to see about this child. You put her right here in that room so's I can make sure she gets the attention she needs." She patted Adria's cheek. "Don't you worry, child. We's gonna get you through this."

"I'm thirsty," Adria said.

"'Course you are, sweet child. Aunt Tilda is gonna see that you does fine."

She led the way through a big kitchen into a room that barely had space for the cot. It didn't have a window, but that was all right with Adria. Maybe that would keep the bad air from finding its way inside here.

Louis placed Adria on the cot after Matilda pulled back the cover. "What about Florella? Wasn't she in here?"

"She done got better enough that she went on back to see how her folks was doing." Matilda lifted up Adria's head to let her sip some water. "What about this one's folks? You bringing more of them here?"

Louis shook his head. "I got to head back there to take care of them."

Adria spoke up. "They've gone to glory."

Matilda's lips gentled into a sad smile. "Well, now that's a right good place to go when a body's time comes."

"I don't want to go yet," Adria said.

The woman nodded. "Ain't no need in hurryin' the trip."

"That's for sure." Louis smiled down at Adria. "This little missy says her name is Adria."

"Adria. Well, ain't that got a pretty sound?" Matilda pushed Adria's hair back from her face.

"I'd best be about what needs doin'. An'thing you need 'fore I go, Matilda? Do I need to see to them up the stairs?"

"They're all 'bout the same except Mr. Harrod. He's took a turn for the worse. Wouldn't even try to sip the water I give him." Matilda put the glass to Adria's lips again.

Adria held the water in her mouth for a few seconds before she swallowed. She didn't get sick.

Louis sighed. "I'll give him a look when I get back." The big man leaned over Adria. "I'll see you later, missy. You'll be fine with Aunt Tilda here. Like I tol' you. She's got healin' hands."

After Louis left, Matilda brought a pan of water and sat on a stool beside the cot to wash Adria like her mother did Eddie. Adria started to tell her she could do that herself, but she wasn't sure she could. Besides, she liked letting the woman take care of her. She didn't have to think. She just had to lie there and do whatever she said. Turn this way. Hold up her hand. Sip this water. Suck on this bit of ginger candy.

Matilda talked the whole time. Words upon words. Some of them sounded like they might be out of the Bible and then sometimes she sang a few words. Her voice wasn't pretty. Not like Adria's mother's voice when she sang while she worked in the kitchen. But there was a comfort to the sound, and while the old woman was washing her toes, Adria fell asleep. She knew she hadn't slipped off to glory because there in her dream Matilda's voice went on and on. It didn't sound a bit like an angel.

When Adria woke up, she didn't know what time of day it was. Without a window, it was hard to tell. A lamp burned on the table by the bed and the door was open into the kitchen. The kitchen had windows, but Adria couldn't see them from the cot. She thought about getting up, but her legs felt good there under the warm cover. She wasn't shaking any longer and her stomach wasn't hurting. Her heart still felt funny, but that might be because she wanted her mama and not have anything to do with the cholera.

Something was on the pillow beside her. Something soft. She sneaked a hand out from under the cover to pick it up. Callie. The doll her mother made for her. She had black yarn pigtails and light brown buttons for eyes. To match Adria's brown eyes and dark hair. The doll's dress was yellow, and Adria had a dress just the same until she got too big for it. Adria hugged the doll close and squeezed her eyes shut. A couple of tears slid out and down her cheeks anyway.

Voices drifted back to her from the kitchen. Matilda and Louis. Adria opened her eyes and shifted a little on her pillow until she could see Louis sitting at the table, his arms hanging down beside him. Her daddy looked like that sometimes when he came home from working at the sawmill. He said he had to rest up some before he could pick up a fork to eat.

"You looking worn to a frazzle, Louis." Matilda sat a bowl in front of the man. "Eat some of this stew. You got to keep your strength up."

When he didn't move, she went on. "You ain't getting sick, is you?"

He shook his head slowly. "No'm. But there's times I can't help but wonder if them that are laying out there on Cemetery Hill ain't the lucky ones."

"It's a sorrow burying all them folks. A burden on you." Matilda put her hand on the man's shoulder for a few seconds. "Digging all them graves. How many now?"

"Forty-eight counting this new one." He looked over his shoulder toward the little room where Adria lay, but she shut her eyes quick so he'd think she was sleeping. When she opened them again, he was staring down at the bowl in front of him on the table.

"Just one?"

Adria couldn't see Matilda now, but she could hear pans clanking.

"I wrapped them all up together and put them in one of the boxes Mr. Joseph made 'fore he left town. He didn't put no name on it and it seemed the thing to do. This way I can tell that little girl in yonder I done proper by them. Let them stay a family."

Adria held Callie tighter against her chest. Her heart hurt bad. Maybe she should be in the box too.

Louis picked up a spoon and ate a few bites. "How's she doing?"

"Sleeping. Normal like. Best thing for her. I'm thinking she weren't as sickly as most. Not like you and me and completely clear of it, but easing past it fine enough. I'm fixing some broth for her."

"I tol' her you had healin' hands."

A chair scooted on the floor in the kitchen and then Adria could see Matilda's arms on the table across from Louis. She couldn't see the woman's face.

"Is the dyin' letting up?"

"I'm thinkin' it might be." Louis blew out a long sigh. "Ain't that many left in town to die."

"But if it's lettin' up, then folks'll be comin' back to town when they hear the bad air is gone." Matilda's hands came across the table to take hold Louis's arms. When he looked up from his food, she lowered her voice, but Adria could still hear her. "Could be time for you to head out. Go find your freedom, Louis, whilst you have a chance."

"What you talkin' 'bout, Matilda? I ain't goin' nowhere."

"They say it ain't that far to the river and once you're across you're in freedom land. Easy as pie to get on up north where the slave hunters can't go. Me, I'm done too old to try it, what with my rheumatism and all, but you, Louis. You's young and strong."

Louis jerked back away from her. "You're talkin' nonsense. I do just fine here workin' for Massa George. He treats me right."

"You think because he give you the keys to this hotel here and told you to look after things whilst he took off to escape the cholera that he's treatin' you like a white man? He didn't know you wouldn't be bothered by the bad air here. I ain't sayin' he didn't hope you wouldn't die, but that ain't no credit to him. You're his slave. That's all. That man were to fall on hard times and need money, he'd sell you in a minute."

Louis put down his spoon and stared at the table, his shoulders slumped. Adria held her breath, waiting to see what he might say. She knew about slaves, even if her family didn't have any. Her mother said that was for rich people. Not them. But sometimes they paid Mrs. Simpson to let her slave, Viola, come over and scrub the floors. Most all the black people in Springfield belonged to somebody. So she wasn't surprised to know Louis did too.

When Louis started talking, Adria had to strain to hear what he said. "I ain't sayin' you ain't right, Matilda. And I ain't denyin' that freedom seems like a happy road that I might like to someday travel. But the Lord, he done tol' me to stay right here and do what needs doin' for all these folks, black and white. If'n I tried to run down that freedom road right now, I'd be goin' against the Lord, sure as anything. He kept me free of the cholera, and I reckon that's all the freedom I'll be gettin' right away."

Matilda's hand came back across the table to pat Louis's arm. "You is a good man, Louis Sanderson. I hope someday the Lord will reward you for what you is doing."

"I ain't an unhappy man. Leastways I wasn't 'fore ev'rybody went to dyin' around here. Good times'll come back to Springfield soon's we get past this hard spot."

"Maybe so. Maybe so." Matilda got up. Adria heard her stirring something, the spoon clacking against the side of an iron pot. "What we gonna do with that child in there? She got any other people?"

"I don't know."

"What if she don't?"

"Then the good Lord will help us figure out what to do. He won't desert a little child like that."

"He done took her parents."

"He'll supply. Ain't that what the Good Book says? The Lord will supply our needs." Louis pushed back from the table. "I got to go see to the horses."

When Adria heard Matilda coming toward her little room, she shut her eyes and pretended to be asleep, but she didn't fool Matilda.

The old woman sat down on the stool beside the cot. "You can stop squeezin' your eyes so tight shut, child. You don't have no reason to be fearful. Ain't nobody gonna hurt you with me and Louis around." She gently wiped a tear away from Adria's cheek. "Leastways no more'n you already been brought low by the cholera."

Adria opened her eyes then and looked straight into the old woman's brown eyes. "I'm an orphan, aren't I?" Her teacher at school, Mr. Harmon, had read them a story about an orphan last year. The story made her cry for the girl with nobody to love her.

"That's a sorrowful word, but not one you need to dwell on. Now eat some of this broth to get your strength back."

Adria sat up and let Matilda spoon the soup into her mouth. "I don't want to be sent away. Can't I just stay here with you?"

"Well, no, child. Folks wouldn't let that happen. A slave woman takin' in a white child. Besides, that wouldn't be no life for the likes of you."

"But what's going to happen to me?" Adria clutched her doll closer.

Matilda sat the bowl of broth down and moved closer to wrap her arms around Adria. "Now don't you fret. The Lord will provide."

"How?"

"I don't rightly know, but Louis, he said so, and that man has the good Lord's ear." Matilda settled Adria back on the pillow. "We'll just have to wait and see what's headed our way, but come tomorrow when you is back on your feet, you can help me make a cherry pie. That's the thing about God's sweet earth. Even when folks ain't doing well, the Lord keeps puttin' fruit on the trees and lettin' the beans in the garden grow."

"I like cherries."

"'Course you do. They's a sweet gift from the Lord to us." Matilda smoothed back Adria's hair with her bony hand, but somehow it was still a comfort. "Now, if'n you knows any prayers, you might be whisperin' some of them your own self. For a better tomorrow."

She waited until Matilda went back in the kitchen and then she held her doll up close to her mouth. "Now I lay me down to sleep. I pray the Lord my soul to keep," she whispered.

She stopped there. She didn't want to pray about dying before she woke.

Three

Ruth Harmon was in no hurry to go back to Springfield. The town held nothing for her now. Peter was gone. Dead at age twenty-five. Their dreams of a family gone with him. Red-headed, freckled-faced boys for him. Blue-eyed, blonde girls for her. She used to tease him that their daughters might have his red hair and the boys might be fair and blonde like her.

Peter would laugh at that and promise to love their babies even if they had no hair at all. Then he always added that he had no doubt at all their girls would be beauties like their mother. He did love her. And he loved children. He was a schoolteacher, after all, and so eager to have his own children to teach.

She felt the same. They'd been married a year, and every month she hoped to be with child. Then in May she had the first indication of that perhaps being true. Peter was so happy. He had picked pink roses out of who knows whose yard and brought them to her. They hadn't shared the news with anyone else. It seemed better to wait until her rounding figure gave proof of a child on the way. Even so, they were dancing on air. Their dream of a family was coming true.

But cholera turned their dream into a nightmare. The disease swept into town on the summer winds. Bad air, some said. Others blamed it on the rotting vegetables and fruits people pitched out of their kitchens. She supposed garbage could cause the bad air, but no matter what the town officials did, they couldn't stop it once the first person sickened in town. It swept through the houses, striking down young and old alike. Some lived. Many died.

The cholera wasn't only in Springfield. All across the state—all through the country, in fact—the grim reaper came in with the scourge. People ran from cholera, leaving towns deserted and the sick to manage however they could. Doctors died along with their patients. One after another. Quickly. Sometimes only a day after the severe symptoms set in. Hardly time to properly say goodbye.

Peter insisted she leave him and escape to the Springs Hotel on the other side of the county. The air would be good there. The waters healing. He could take care of himself, he said. He'd be there, recovered, when she came back. She had to think about the baby.

She hadn't left. Not until he went beyond her. Closed his eyes and refused to open them. Refused or couldn't. Once his breathing stopped, she did think of their baby. Heaven forgive her, but she hitched up their little buggy to the high-stepping pony Peter was so proud of and left her beloved husband stretched out on their bed. She did not hang black crepe over the windows and have a funeral for him. She didn't even see that he was properly buried.

She left him there and ran away to where the cholera wasn't. For the baby. Then the baby ran away from her. Gone in the fresh hours of the morning. Perhaps there had never been a baby. Only a dream. Now grief hung heavy over Springfield as people trickled back into town once they heard the cholera had run its course.

Some of them had more to come back for than Ruth. She had nothing. Only the rooms she and Peter were renting until they could get a house. A schoolteacher didn't make much money and often as not got paid in bartered goods. Jars of honey. A side of bacon. A sack of potatoes. The county officials sometimes made a big show of pitching in a few dollars to keep the school building in shape, but the families of the students were expected to support the teacher. Some did. Others with the means sent their boys away to schools in bigger towns and their girls to the Loretto School run by the nuns. Ruth had gone there herself. Maybe she should consider going there again. Converting to Catholicism and taking vows. But such vows were not to be taken simply because one had an empty heart.

As soon as she got back to Springfield, even before she went to their rooms, she drove her buggy out to Cemetery Hill. New mounds of dirt with grass only beginning to sprout on some of them lined the edge of the graveyard. Many more than she had expected in spite of the news reaching her at the hotel of this or that person succumbing to the cholera.

She'd also been told who had taken care of the dead. George Sanderson's slave, Louis. He'd been untouched by the cholera, but as she stared at the dozens of graves, she doubted that was true. He might not have come down with the sickness, but no one could be unaffected after digging graves for so many.

Her heart grew heavy when she saw no markers stuck up out of the fresh mounds of dirt. How would she know where her Peter lay? She wanted to tend his grave, plant flowers to show he was loved. And now he was just one of many. She bent her head and tried to pray. Peter would want her to pray. Before the cholera, she'd found whispering prayers easy, as natural as breathing.

Thank you, Father, for your blessings. Thank you, Lord, for the food we have. Praise you, Lord, for the beauty of your world.

But now, the prayers came hard, wrenched out of her heart with desperate tears. *Why, Lord, why? Peter was a good man. Why didn't you spare him? Why?*

She knew it was wrong to question the Lord. But *why* ran through her thoughts and would not be shut away. Surely it was better not to pray at all. Best to push aside the questions and get on with life. But she had no idea what to do next.

Her brother had a farm in Ohio. Her mother had gone to live

with him after Ruth married Peter. She promised to come back after Ruth had a house, but then she had died. Everybody died.

There was still her brother. He and his wife had three children, but they would make room for her. They were family. Even so, she would be a burden. She was too young to become a burden. Better to find a job to support herself. She was capably educated. Peter once told her she would make a better teacher than he. And now that she was single, she could get a teaching position. Go west perhaps and live with first one student's family and then another. That's how schools were on the frontier. Or perhaps she could go to Louisville or some other big city and find a position as a clerk.

Thinking about it all made her heart hurt. Made her feel empty. She was empty. She raised her head again and looked out over the graves. None empty. Each mound covering someone's loved one.

She was turning back to her buggy when a black man and a little girl came through the cemetery gate. The man held the child's hand. The girl had dark curly hair, but she wasn't black. The soft mumble of the man's voice drifted across the graveyard to Ruth, but she couldn't make out any words. Neither of them noticed Ruth there. The man kept his gaze locked on the child while the little girl stared straight ahead, obviously uneasy, even frightened, to be there among the dead.

A cemetery full of fresh graves was no place for a child, and a spark of anger flared inside Ruth. Where were the child's parents to allow such a thing?

When the man looked up and saw Ruth, he bent his head quickly, but not before she recognized him as George Sanderson's slave. The one who had buried the cholera victims when no one else could or would because they were too sick or had fled the town. Fled as she had.

The child looked up at the man when he stopped walking and turned loose of her hand. "Is this it?"

Ruth heard the distress in the words.

"No, missy, but there's another here we don't want to be a bother to. We'd best come back another time."

The child looked at Ruth and then back at the man beside her. "No. Show me now. She won't care." The girl stepped away from the man, closer to Ruth. "Will you, ma'am? Louis is going to show me where my parents and little brother are buried. That's important to know. Aunt Tilda says so."

Ruth knew the little girl, but her name wasn't coming. Poor child left alone in the world, the same as Ruth. "Yes, you should know."

The child stared up at Ruth. "You're the teacher's wife." When Ruth simply nodded, the child asked, "Did he go to glory too?"

"To glory?" Ruth said.

"That's what Louis said. That my family went to glory." The girl looked back at the black man. "That's easier to hear than—" She stopped and swallowed hard before she went on. "Than other things. Glory is heaven, you know."

"I know." Ruth's throat felt tight, but how could she cry in front of this child who was staring at her with dry eyes?

"Louis, he buried my parents and little brother all together. So they could stay a family. I was part of their family too, but I didn't go to glory. I got better."

"That's good." Ruth didn't know whether that was the best thing to say or not. Peter would have known. Peter said children appreciated honesty and knew if an adult was speaking down to them.

"Louis and Aunt Tilda, they helped me." The child looked out at the graves. "Which one belongs to Mr. Harmon?"

Ruth blinked away tears. "I don't know. There aren't any markers."

Louis had moved up behind the girl. "I'm some sorry about that, mistress, but I done the best I could to give folks a proper burial. I did say words over each and ev'ry one. I knowed the Lord heard me when I asked for him to comfort the hearts of them that were left behind."

"I understand, Louis. How many did you bury?"

"Fifty-seven, best I recall." He looked out over the hill.

"Do you remember Peter? My husband, Peter Harmon." Ruth couldn't keep the quaver out of her voice.

"I do. I remember each poor soul I laid to rest here. Let me think. The schoolteacher. He was tall, a fine-looking man in his prime. It was a sorrow havin' to put him in the ground." Louis shook his head. "He wasn't one of the first ones, but somewhere toward the middle."

Louis walked a little way down the row of graves and pointed. "That one there in the second row. See how it's some longer than them beside it. That's where your fine husband lies."

Ruth stepped between the graves to kneel in the grass beside the mound and couldn't stop the tears that slipped down her cheeks. The little girl followed her and put her hand on Ruth's shoulder.

"Aunt Tilda says it's good to cry, but sometimes I can't." Then she walked away with Louis.

They were talking, comfortable with one another now that they thought she wasn't paying any attention. The girl once more held the man's hand. Adria, Louis had called her. An unusual name. Maybe that was why Ruth remembered Peter talking about the child once or twice. The last name was different too. Starr. That was it. Adria Starr. Peter had said she was a bright child with a gift for words. When Ruth asked if that meant she was a chatterbox, Peter had laughed.

More tears flooded her eyes. Oh, how she was going to miss that laugh. To keep from falling completely apart, Ruth thought about the girl again. She remembered Adria's mother, a pretty woman with an easy smile. Now she was dead just like Peter. And her sweet little boy too. Just like all these others under her feet.

It would take someone with the faith of Job not to wonder why there was a disease like cholera. To rob her of her husband. To whisk that child's whole family away and leave her an orphan. Ruth pushed up off the ground and looked around. Every mound of dirt somebody's sorrow.

The child was standing in front of one of the mounds. Not crying. Just staring down at the dirt while Louis stood back, his hat in his hands and his head bowed. His mouth was moving, perhaps muttering a prayer. The girl didn't seem to hear him.

Ruth eased closer to hear what Louis was saying. She needed a prayer in her ears and had no words of her own for the Lord. Peter would have been able to pray. If it had been her in the ground and him standing here, he would have prayed for her soul. He would have looked to the Lord to somehow work things for good in spite of the bad. But how could any of this be good? Orphans and widows. Why? That was her only word.

"Yea, though I walk through the valley of the shadow of death, I ain't gonna be fearful. The good Lord's rod and staff, they guide me and knock away the evil. Blessed are the meek. Bless also them that mourn and those what stand in the need of your sweet blessings."

The man's words were a mishmash of Scripture strung together, but somehow the words sounded right when he spoke them. A man who loved the Lord. A man who had buried all these people and said words over their graves when their families couldn't. Slave or not, she owed him thanks for that.

When she stepped over behind him, he stopped praying and bent his head to stare at the ground again. He twisted his hat in his hands. "Me and the girl, we'll be leavin' now. Give you some alone time here. Come along, missy."

"That's all right, Louis. I'm leaving now myself. I simply wanted to thank you for what you've done here. For burying my husband." Her voice caught and she had to swallow down tears. "And all the others."

"'Tweren't nothin' you have to thank ol' Louis for, ma'am. The Lord, he give me the strength to do what needed doin'. That's all."

The girl turned away from the grave. "Aunt Tilda says Louis could have gone across the river and found freedom, but he didn't. 'Cause he had a job here to do."

"What you talkin' about, child? Aunt Tilda shouldn't a ought to tol' you that." Louis frowned.

"She didn't. I heard you talking when I was sick."

"Best you didn't talk about things you maybe dreamed up whilst you was feverish. Get me and Aunt Tilda in some trouble." His eyes flashed up to Ruth's face and quickly away. "I ain't never thought about goin' across the river."

"Louis is right." Ruth looked down at the child. She was so small. Ruth forced a smile. "Some things are better kept under our hats."

"I don't have on a hat." The girl touched her curly, dark brown hair. Her eyes were a lighter brown.

Ruth's smile came easier now. "No. No, you don't."

"But I can keep it under my hair." The girl looked over at the man. "Will that be good, Louis?"

"That be fine, missy. Come on now. We'd best go see what Aunt Tilda is fixin' us for supper." He didn't take the girl's hand as he turned toward the gate, but she ran up beside him and slipped her hand in his anyway.

He cast a nervous look back toward Ruth. "She be needin' somebody right now, you understand. What with losin' her folks and all."

"Yes."

She watched the two leave and wondered what would become of the girl. She wouldn't be able to stay with Louis. Perhaps she had relatives, or if not, some family would take her in as a servant. That seemed a hard road for such a small child. Ruth shook her head. She couldn't worry about the little girl. She had troubles enough without adding the poor child's to her own.

When she looked back at Peter's grave, he seemed to nudge her. She surely could say a prayer for the child even if she couldn't pray properly for herself.

She bent her head and whispered, "Lord, send someone to help Adria Starr. Thank you for Louis and what he did for her." She swallowed hard and went on. "And for my Peter."

Four

Adria cried when Aunt Tilda told her she'd have to start sleeping in one of the hotel rooms up the stairs instead of the little room beside the kitchen. She liked being close where she could get up and help Aunt Tilda fix things to eat. Not only that, but Aunt Tilda let her wash dishes in the big sink. They didn't have a sink like that at her house. Just pans of water. But Aunt Tilda's sink had a drain hole where the water swooshed away with a few gurgles and nobody had to carry it out the back door to sling it away.

In the dark of the morning, she could lie in her bed and hug Callie close while she listened to Louis and Aunt Tilda talking before anybody else was moving around. Adria's heart still hurt when she thought about her mother and father and little Eddie. It hurt so bad she tried not to think about them. That was easier to do when she was helping Aunt Tilda break green beans or chop up potatoes for soup.

Aunt Tilda had a way of putting her hand on Adria's curls that made her believe somehow everything was going to be all right. She combed her hair for her too and never fussed once about all the curls. Sometimes Aunt Tilda braided it up quick as anything to keep it out of Adria's eyes while she was helping cook.

Best of all, if she ever noticed Adria looking sad, she stopped whatever she was doing and pulled Adria right into her apron to hug her tight. She wasn't Adria's mama. Aunt Tilda's hugs didn't feel anything like her mother's. Her mama was soft and smelled like purple flowers. Adria forgot which kind, but her mother always put that smell in their soap. But even if Aunt Tilda was bony and old and smelled like onions sometimes, Adria still liked being folded in tight to her middle.

But when people started coming back to town, Louis carried her few clothes up the stairs to where the white people stayed. Adria told him she wanted to stay in the room by the kitchen, but Louis said that was Florella's room and things would be better if everybody stayed in their proper places.

"I don't have a proper place," Adria said.

"Now don't you think like that, missy. The Lord is gonna help us figure out all that in his good time."

Adria couldn't figure out anything. Not since she'd gone to the cemetery where Louis put her family. That had been too hard to think about—them under the ground together. A family. And her up above ground with no family. Only Louis and Aunt Tilda.

Louis said her parents weren't really there in the ground. Leastways not their spirits. She had to remember how they were in glory. That day as they stood by the grave, he'd asked her what she thought glory might be like.

"I don't know," she answered.

He looked down at her as they walked away from the cemetery. "You ain't never thought about glory?"

"Not till you said Mama and Eddie went there." She dragged her feet a little as she walked. She felt like she shouldn't leave them. "I did think about going to heaven and wondered if it would be noisy up there when, well, before you came and got me. Do you think it's noisy in glory?"

"In my mind glory is full of ev'ry good sound a body can imagine. Angels singing. Folks shoutin' hallelujah. And it's bright all the time with Jesus' light a-shinin' off those golden sidewalks and walls of jasper."

"What is jasper?"

"I don't rightly know, but I'm thinkin' it must be something mighty pretty. Maybe like the sparkly jewels rich ladies wear pinned to their dresses. Did your mama have any of those kinds of things?"

"We weren't rich. Mama said we weren't."

"Well then, missy, there's all kinds of ways to be rich, and I'm thinkin' afore your folks passed up to glory, you was plenty rich."

Adria wasn't sure what he meant by that, but she asked, "Are you rich, Louis?"

"Not by this old world's standards. Not at all. I ain't got nothing. Don't even belong to myself what with how Massa George, he owns me. But I got them other kind of riches. Them kind the Lord hands out. You can have those too. Every livin' soul can just for the askin'."

"I don't understand."

"You will when you're older, missy. Till then, just you don't worry your head about it and let the good Lord take care of you."

"Will he? Will he take care of me?"

"Yes, indeed, he will. Don't you never wonder about that."

But Adria did wonder about that. Especially after she had to start sleeping in the room upstairs. It was lonesome up there. And scary when she heard steps in the hallway outside the door that she knew weren't Aunt Tilda or Louis. At times like that, she hugged her doll close and hid under the covers, even if it did make her sweat in the summer heat.

Then Mr. George came back to the hotel. The man Louis called master. He wasn't anything like Louis. Or Adria's father. He looked bothered when he came in the kitchen. Louis was different with him in the room. Kept his eyes down the way he had that day at the cemetery when they saw the schoolteacher's wife.

Aunt Tilda didn't act any different than she always did. At

least not that Adria could tell. She kept on stirring the pots hung over the fire. But then she did give Adria a look. She didn't say a word, but Adria knew to sit still and not say anything. In fact, she wished she could just crawl under the big table and hide out till the master man went away. But she didn't do that either. She sat in her chair quiet as a spider in a web up next to the ceiling and hoped she'd be too little to notice.

For a while the man didn't seem to see her while he talked to Louis.

"You'll be rewarded for what you did here in Springfield, Louis. Keeping the hotel going and watching over the other businesses too while people were away. Everybody in town is talking about how you buried all those people. It was a fine thing and one we won't forget."

Aunt Tilda dropped a pan lid with a clatter and then murmured how she was sorry for the noise. But her back looked stiff like something was hurting her. She did say she had rheumatism, so maybe that was what had her looking sort of twisted, but something about how Aunt Tilda was standing made Adria wish she had Callie to hold on to. Instead she twisted her hands up in the apron Aunt Tilda had fixed for her to wear in the kitchen and tried to breathe quiet like Aunt Tilda's cat when it was ready to pounce on a mouse. Trouble was, Adria felt more like the mouse than the cat while she listened to Mr. George talk.

"And I understand completely how you had to let some of the sick people stay here at my hotel and why no rooms were rented. Nobody was going to come through here once they heard about the cholera." Mr. George looked even more bothered than he had when he first came in the kitchen as he blew out a long breath. "I've talked with those still here and they're willing enough to pay for the rooms they used. At least a portion of what they would owe. I guess that's the best I can hope to get. A portion."

Louis spoke then. "I didn't feel right turnin' anybody in need away, what with how things were."

"Completely right of you. What you should have done. People will long remember that and thank me for my generosity."

Aunt Tilda flashed a look around so quick Adria barely caught it. Then the old woman stirred the beans with a hard jerky motion that flipped some out on the hearth. She cleaned them up with her apron tail before they started smoking.

The man went on talking. "But now that the cholera has moved on, things will have to get back to normal with people paying full price for their rooms. Business will pick up. So we can't be giving rooms away."

That's when the man's eyes landed on Adria. He hadn't not seen her at all. He was simply waiting. "We'll have to find somewhere for the girl. She can't stay here without a proper guardian."

Adria wasn't sure what a guardian was. She sort of hoped it had something to do with a garden, but she didn't think it did. From the man's face, she feared it might have more to do with her not having any family after the cholera. She opened her mouth to say something, but Louis gave her a quick look. Not a mean look. Just one that said she'd best keep quiet.

"Her folks died and we hasn't been able to find out if she has more kinfolk around here." Louis kept his eyes low. "You wouldn't happen to know, would you, Massa? Her name is Adria Starr."

"Starr." The man rubbed his chin as he looked at Adria. "Seems I remember Edward Starr. Worked at the sawmill, didn't he?"

"Yessir, he did. They had a nice little house over on Elm Street."

"And he died?"

"Him and his wife and little boy. Missy Adria here is the only one to make it through the cholera, and she was sick awhile. Matilda took care of her, like as how she did some of the others."

"We thank you for that, Matilda."

"Weren't nothin' but what the Lord intended, Mr. George." Aunt Tilda looked around with something like a smile on her face, but it wasn't one Adria had seen before. She turned back to stir the beans again, but this time she didn't spill out any.

"True." The man let out another long breath.

Adria kept her head down and her gaze on the table, but she could feel the man's stare. The kitchen got too quiet except for Aunt Tilda's spoon stirring. The silence settled down on Adria the same as it had back at her house when the clock stopped ticking and her mother went to glory.

Finally the man started talking again. "I'll check around and see if I can find anybody kin to her. Maybe the preacher will know. They went to the Baptist church, I'm thinking."

"The Reverend Watkins, the cholera got him, but could be others in the church might know."

"If they don't, maybe one of them will have enough Christian charity to take her in. She's a little thing, but I'm sure even at her age, she could find ways to make herself useful."

Aunt Tilda spoke up then, her voice soft but determined somehow. "We'd want to make sure they were kindly."

"They'll be kindly if they take her in." The man sounded cross. "She can talk, can't she? She's not deaf and dumb. Might make things harder if she is."

"Oh, no sir, she's a fine girl." Louis smiled over at Adria. "Tell Massa George how you 'preciate him tryin' to help you."

She didn't want to, but since Louis looked like it was important, she did. "I'm glad I could come here and get well. Thank you." She hoped that sounded good enough.

He smiled at her then and put his hand on her head. She ducked away from his touch. She couldn't help herself, but she did smile at him. A smile something like Aunt Tilda's a little while ago. She didn't want to be handed off to just anybody. She wanted family. Like she'd had. Or like Louis and Aunt Tilda, but Aunt Tilda had already told her she couldn't stay with them. They were slaves. That meant they didn't have any freedom. She wouldn't have any freedom either if that man gave her to some family who took her in to do chores. She'd be an orphan slave until she got big enough to be on her own. How old would that be? Maybe she was old enough already. She had a house.

Nobody said anything for a good spell after the man left the kitchen. Aunt Tilda kept stirring the beans and Louis kept staring at the floor. Finally Adria said, "I want to go back to my house and stay there."

Aunt Tilda turned away from the stove. "You is too young to be on your own."

"I could sleep there and come over here every day to help you." Adria really wished she had her doll to hold.

Louis and Aunt Tilda looked at each other and then they both sat down at the table on either side of Adria. Louis reached over and laid his hand over Adria's. "That would be a fine thing if it could be, missy, but that ain't somethin' we can make happen. Massa George, he'll see to findin' you a place."

"What if it's a bad place? Somewhere I don't want to go. I'd have to go anyway, wouldn't I?" Adria looked at Louis.

"Now, that ain't likely to happen. Most folks is good folks, especially to pretty little girls like you. They might take you in like one of their own."

"And they might not." Aunt Tilda slapped her hand down on the table. "We can't just let this child go wherever. Better if we find a place for her our own selves. Like you're always saying, Louis. The Lord will provide."

Adria's heart lifted a little. If the Lord provided it, then it would be good and not somewhere where'd she have to sleep in the barn. She didn't know why she thought that. She never knew anybody who slept in the barn except the man who took care of the horses at the livery stable, and he had a regular room there with a bed and everything. She'd seen it once when she went with her daddy to borrow a horse and wagon to fetch home a table from her grand-mother's house. For a second, hope flared. She had a grandmother, but then she remembered she'd died. Everybody died.

Louis looked doubtful, but he said, "It could be we should think on it. Say a prayer and see where the Lord might lead us."

"And do it quick." Aunt Tilda's voice was firm. She looked at

Adria. "Tell me, child. Is there anybody you remember knowing? Anybody at all."

Adria tried to think. She knew people. Mrs. Hostetter from next door. Carlton, the boy who liked to chase her around the schoolyard. Mr. Riley who sat in front of them at church. The schoolteacher, Mr. Harmon. But then he was dead. She'd seen the schoolteacher's wife at the graveyard. The woman had been nice. She'd smiled at Adria through the tears she was shedding for her husband. She had been alone. Alone like Adria.

"The schoolteacher's wife. I know her," Adria said.

Louis looked over at Aunt Tilda. "We saw her at the cemetery the other day when I took the little missy to see where her family lay. The lady did look nice enough. Not much bigger than a minute, like she hadn't had anything good to eat for a spell."

"She looked all alone," Adria said. "Like I'm going to be if I can't stay here with you."

Again Aunt Tilda and Louis stared at one another for a long moment. Then Louis bent his head.

Aunt Tilda shushed Adria when she started to say something. "Better let Louis pray it out, child. Or pray with him."

Adria wasn't sure what to pray, but she shut her eyes and pulled up the memory of the schoolteacher's wife. She hadn't been very tall and, like Louis said, slim as a reed. She had pretty blonde hair tucked up under a black hat. Adria almost smiled remembering the woman telling her she should keep some things under her hat. Things like Louis and Aunt Tilda trying to figure out what to do with her and not leaving it all up to Mr. George.

Adria didn't say her prayer out loud. She didn't even put it into words in her head. She just sent up a longing to the Lord to find her a home with the schoolteacher's wife.

Then Louis looked up. "There's words somewhere in the Bible that says the reason we don't have is because we don't ask. I've heard preachers expoundin' on that very thing." Louis looked up at the ceiling. "So I'm askin', Lord."

"It's her, the schoolteacher's wife, you need to be askin'," Aunt Tilda said.

"What with both you and the Lord tellin' me that, I best be givin' it a try." Louis patted Adria's hand. "Run, get that doll of yours, missy, and we'll walk on over that way."

Five

A musty smell greeted Ruth when she pushed open the door of the schoolhouse. Little wonder since the place had been closed up for weeks. School hadn't been in session for several months, although Peter had often gone to the small building to plan for the coming term. Sometimes Ruth had come with him to clean away the cobwebs.

The building with only the one big room had been used as a school off and on for years, but the place had been vacant for a while before Peter came to teach here. Peter had recruited a few parents to help make the benches and long narrow tables that served as desks from planks donated by the sawmill just outside town. Ruth ran her hand across one of the planks. Roughly finished to be sure, but sturdy.

A slate lay on one of the benches, forgotten by a student last term. The slates were used to write their lessons with chalk. They could be erased and used over and over. Only a few of the older students used paper and pen. Not that Peter had many older students. After a certain age, his students generally bypassed school to stay home and help their parents. Much too young, Peter believed.

He had been proud to teach the boys and girls to read, write, and do basic arithmetic. He prayed daily for each of his students, even those who gave him the most trouble and especially the ones who had no interest in being at school.

"They think reading is something they will never need," Peter told Ruth. "They just want to work the land, they say. Once they can sign their names and add and subtract, they decide they have learned enough. Perhaps in the past that was enough, but the world is changing. In these modern times, we have newspapers and books available to rich and poor alike, but what good will that be if a person cannot read? It saddens me to think of what they'll miss. All for the lack of learning."

Ruth dusted off the chair behind Peter's desk and sat down. She was so proud to be married to Peter Harmon. A good man. He could have chosen any profession. A lawyer. A doctor. A man destined for political office perhaps. It wasn't beyond the realm of imagination to think he might have someday been governor if that was how his ambitions ran. But no, he wanted nothing more than to teach.

He had come to America from England while still in his teens and eventually found his place here in Springfield. Ruth had been attracted to him on sight, but Peter encouraged her to take her time. To think of the years ahead when, if she married a man with land, she could have a more secure and settled future. But Ruth's heart had already settled. Settled forever and now broken in bits.

When she opened up a book left on the desk, dust motes flew up to dance in the strip of sunshine coming through the window next to her. A reading primer with the words written in larger, dark print. The desk drawer grumbled as she pulled it out. A ruler. Scissors. A composition book. An empty inkpot and pens. She pulled out a sheet with a list of names. Last term's students. She wondered how many of them were still living after the cholera epidemic.

With a heavy sigh, she put the paper back in the drawer and shoved it closed. The wood squeaked even louder in protest going back in. A bit of beeswax could fix that. Not that it mattered. The school no longer had a teacher. The cholera epidemic had upset all of normal life.

She stood up and peered out the window at the street. Perhaps that wasn't true for everyone. Commerce appeared to be picking up in the town, with people going in and out of the businesses. The hotel was just up the street. She'd heard the owner, George Sanderson, was back in town. That made her think of his slave, Louis, who had buried Peter and all the dead. She couldn't help but wonder what happened to the girl she'd seen with him on Cemetery Hill. Adria Starr. Surely a relative had come for her. She'd have a home.

More than Ruth had. She had sold Peter's pony and the buggy. She doubted she got a fair price, but she was desperate. The hotel stay had taken all her cash and she had rent to pay while she searched for a job. She'd asked around town without any luck. Many of the businesses were family run, with more than enough relatives to fill any hiring needs. Ruth had no relatives in Springfield.

The night before, she had written to her brother to tell him about Peter, but she hadn't asked for his help. Not yet. First she would go to Louisville and seek employment. The thought frightened her. She'd never been to a big town. But in such a place with so many people, she would surely find work of some sort. A clerk or a family in need of a tutor. Failing that, a maid. She was in no position to be proud.

The day was hot, so she pushed up a couple of the windows. She should leave. Walk back to her rooms and continue sorting through the accumulations of her short life with Peter. Maybe she could bring his books here to the school building for the next teacher. The bookcase too. She couldn't take it or the books with her. She had a trunk for her clothes and some necessary household items in case she was able to rent a room. A few books, perhaps. Peter's Bible for certain and some of Nathaniel Hawthorne's works. A few slim volumes of poetry.

What dreams she'd once had of perhaps writing poetry herself.

Peter had encouraged her. A proper pursuit for a genteel woman while she raised her children. That along with needlework, for which she had never shown any aptitude. Her mother had despaired at her uneven stitches. Embroidery seemed such a terrible waste of time when she could be reading.

With a sigh, she turned to lower the windows and head back to her rooms. There was no reason to put off leaving Springfield. While she would miss the town, perhaps it would be good to make a fresh start. Away from all the memories rising up to surround her in this place.

At the same time she didn't want to surrender those memories. That must be why she lingered in the schoolhouse. She felt Peter so strongly here. His voice seemed caught in the air. Alive and happy. While at their rooms, she could think of nothing but how he'd looked stretched out on their bed, breathing his last ragged breaths.

As she pushed the second window down, she saw Harold Franklin, one of Washington County's justices of the peace, making his way purposefully toward the school. That was good. She could give him Peter's key. Finish this part of his life and hers.

"Mrs. Harmon." He came through the door without knocking, but then she supposed a person didn't have to knock to enter a school or a church.

"Mr. Franklin, how are you?" She picked up her reticule and moved through the benches toward him.

"Well, thankfully. So many weren't." The smile on his face, reddened by his walk down the street, disappeared. "You have my sincere condolences regarding the loss of your dear husband. Such a wonderful man. A fine teacher. The kind of citizen we need here in Springfield."

"Yes." She didn't trust herself to say more than that. To keep any stray tears at bay, she studied the man in front of her.

He was short, with a healthy girth and an effusive way. Always ready to shake a hand and point out the better parts of his town. He reveled in the role of justice of the peace. The governor appointed him to the position years ago, and fortunately for Justice Franklin, the appointments were for life. Other justices in the county served a while and resigned, but not Harold Franklin. Being a justice of the peace was his calling, he sometimes said, as though he were a preacher instead of an appointed official. But in spite of all that, Ruth was glad to see him looking well and hardy. It meant that something in Springfield was the same. Somebody hadn't died.

"Such a shame. All those lost to our town. But Springfield will recover. We will see that it does, and one of the things we need to make sure of is that we have educational opportunities for our children." Justice Franklin threw out his hand as if addressing a crowd instead of only Ruth. "While some think a parent can teach a child all that's necessary for life, you and I both know that's not true. Our children need to advance beyond us, to become better citizens in the future. Don't you agree, Mrs. Harmon?"

Ruth had somewhat tuned out the man's speech as she considered how to make a graceful exit. So the question and his direct stare caught her a bit off guard. "Yes," she said weakly with the hope she hadn't claimed to agree to something totally disagreeable.

"Of course you do." The justice smiled down at her and took a deep breath.

Ruth pulled the school's key out of her pocket and spoke up before the man could launch into another oratory barrage. "It's good that you dropped by. Here is Peter's key to give to the next schoolmaster."

He didn't take the key. "That's just it, Mrs. Harmon. It seems to us, those of us who know the most about our town, that you would be the perfect person to take your good husband's place as teacher. We hear you've been inquiring about this or that position around town, and so here is a needed position you are well qualified to fill. Your late husband told me himself what an invaluable help you were when he prepared his lessons. Your English skills are excellent, and if we're not mistaken, you received a well-rounded education at the Loretto School. Quite enough to qualify you completely for the position. So what do you say? Can we count on you to continue in the wake of your husband?"

"I . . ." Ruth searched for words.

"You don't have to answer right away. I understand this might be sudden."

Ruth gathered herself. "Are you saying that the town is willing to pay me for teaching?"

"As a matter of fact, we have considered the idea of supporting the school in such a way. That has not been an approved part of our town's budget. It still is not, but a few justices in addition to myself are willing to contribute to your salary. That with the necessary fees collected from the families of those children who attend will assure you a fair salary. I give you my word on that." He paused, and then like an archer who had saved his swiftest arrow for the last shot, he went on. "I do think Mr. Harmon would want you to step into his position and not let our Springfield children slide back into ignorance. He always seemed to care so much for his students."

She started to open her mouth and say she had no idea how to run a school, but then she seemed to almost feel Peter's hand on her shoulder. It was more his words than hers when she said, "Yes. I can be the teacher."

"Excellent." Justice Franklin beamed at her. "Excellent. We will leave it up to you to gather your students and decide when to commence school. Generally fall is a good time for those rural children near enough to come into town to school. That will give you some time to prepare. I am certain our county's citizens will be more than ready to come forth with the necessary fees for the betterment of their children."

Once back in her rooms, she realized while the man had spoken of a fair salary, he'd mentioned no numbers. If she could gather any students, she would have to convince the parents to pay. Many of them had been willing enough to pay Peter, but would they feel the same with her as teacher? A woman with no teaching experience.

Even if she did obtain enough students for the school term, how would she survive until school began in October? Peter had been in demand as a tutor between terms as some of the young men sought application into prestigious schools, but that would not be a path open to her.

Yet, in spite of the worries, the thought of stepping into Peter's place, the thought of teaching, stirred awake the first bit of excitement since cholera had stolen everything she held dear. She picked Peter's Bible up out of her trunk. A slip of paper he must have used to mark his place fluttered to the floor as the Bible fell open to Isaiah 40, where verse 31 was circled. *But they that wait upon the Lord shall renew their strength; they shall mount up with wings as eagles; they shall run, and not be weary; and they shall walk, and not faint.*

The verse was so like Peter, always charging forth in life, yet at the same time, ready to do exactly what the verse said and wait upon the Lord. Now she was the one who needed to renew her strength in order to face each day to come. Alone. No, not alone, Peter would say. With the Lord one was never alone. She had told him many times that he should have been a preacher, but he said teaching was a calling spoken of in the Bible, the same as preaching. A calling cut short. Could she step into that calling even if she trembled at the thought of failing?

She leaned down and picked up the paper that had fallen out of the Bible, and there in a steady hand, Peter had drawn an eagle in flight. Strong wings carrying it forward. Under it he had written Ruth's name.

Six

That afternoon, Ruth sat down at Mrs. Jackson's kitchen table to compose a letter to send out to potential students. Mrs. Jackson, who rented them the upstairs rooms in her house, had not returned to Springfield as yet after the cholera epidemic. She sent notice for the rent to be paid to her representative at the bank. She obviously didn't know about Peter, since she had addressed the letter to him, but Ruth saw no reason to inform her landlady about his death. Not as long as she could pay the rent.

Her throat tightened a bit at the thought. She had counted her remaining money before she came down to the kitchen to write the letter. Enough for two more months' rent if she was very careful about what she bought to eat. At least Mrs. Jackson had lowered the rent amount since she wouldn't be supplying their breakfasts and evening meals. She had told Ruth she was free to cook her own meals, but Ruth hadn't bothered to build a fire in the fireplace. She had little appetite, so the apple and cheese bought at the store on the way home from the schoolhouse would suffice.

She stared down at the sheet of paper in front of her. The letter was easy enough to write, but then what? She had the list in the drawer at the school but shrank from the idea of sending a missive out to parents of a child who may have succumbed to the cholera. Mrs. Jackson could have helped her. The woman seemed to know everyone in Springfield and their business, but according to her note, she didn't plan to return until September.

Justice Franklin might be able to help with the names. Or perhaps Louis, George Sanderson's slave, could tell her which children had not survived the cholera epidemic. When she saw him at the cemetery, he had claimed to remember each person he buried.

She shut her eyes and tried to recall some of the names on the list. The Starr child's name was there. She had survived, but who knew what her situation would be. She might not even stay in Springfield. Ruth pushed the thought of the girl away. She didn't want to remember how forlorn the child had looked, staring down at her family's grave. Ruth had prayed for her. She would remember to pray for her again. What more could she do?

She would have to fetch the list of names from the schoolhouse and then make a call on Justice Franklin. If he couldn't help, she would approach George Sanderson about speaking to Louis.

After she copied the letter ten times, she stretched her fingers to rest her hand. She wasn't sure how many copies she might need, but the list had held at least twenty-five names. She finished off the apple and wrapped up the remainder of the cheese. Perhaps tomorrow she could boil some cabbage for her dinner with a bit of cornbread. She could buy what she needed when she walked to the schoolhouse in the morning.

Using any of her coins brought on a bit of panic, but she did have to eat. Unless she wanted to lie down and die like Peter. Even with her heart heavy with grief, she didn't want to do that. Peter would say the Lord numbered a person's days.

Oh, Peter. Her every thought kept circling back to him. If only they had both managed to escape the cholera. But what good did it do to think "if only"? That changed nothing. She brushed away her tears and picked up the pen to copy another letter.

A knock on the back door made her jump and smudge the word she was writing. She blotted the ink before she stood up to answer the door. Someone looking for Mrs. Jackson, no doubt.

When she pulled open the door, Louis was standing on the small stoop, holding his hat with his eyes cast down respectfully.

"Louis." Ruth frowned a little. "Are you looking for Mrs. Jackson?" Perhaps he was bringing whatever he carried wrapped in a cloth to the woman.

"No, ma'am. I come to see you." He held out the parcel. "Matilda, she had an extra loaf of her raisin cinnamon bread and she thought, well, we thought you might have use for it. The little missy helped her make it."

Louis nodded his head toward the wooden fence that lined Mrs. Jackson's narrow backyard. Only then did Ruth notice the girl standing several feet behind Louis. She was clutching a rag doll to her chest and staring straight toward Ruth. When Ruth looked her way, the child stepped forward, but Louis held up his hand just a bit and she stopped.

Ruth took the bread and sat it on the cabinet inside the door. "I thank you and Matilda. And the child too." She kept her eyes on Louis and not the girl. Even so, Ruth could still feel her watching her.

"Adria," Louis said, as if he thought she needed to be reminded of the child's name. "Adria Starr." He didn't turn to leave.

"Yes." Ruth wasn't sure what the man expected her to do or say next. He just stood there as though waiting for something. "Is there something I can do for you, Louis?"

"I'm pleased you asked, ma'am. As a matter of fact we've come with a hope in our hearts."

"Oh?" She hesitated. She could tell him to leave. She should tell him to leave, but instead she asked, "What hope is that?"

"It's about little missy back there." Again he dipped his head toward the child. "She tells us, Matilda and me, that your husband, the schoolteacher, was kind and caring to her and all the children."

Ruth didn't say anything. Her throat suddenly felt too tight.

"Well, and then the news is goin' 'round town that you is gonna take his place. Teachin' and all. Folks is happy about that. Little missy is happy about that."

"That's good to know." Ruth swallowed back her tears and pushed out the words. "But that doesn't explain why you're here."

"No, ma'am, I guess it don't. I might as well be out with it. Massa George, he's saying Missy Adria can't be staying at the hotel no more. He's thinkin' on findin' her a place, but we're, Matilda and me, we're a mite worried that the place won't be one to the little missy's liking. She might end up little better than a slave like the two of us. Made to work for her keep."

Louis shot his eyes up to Ruth's face and as quickly back down. He twisted the rim of his hat and went on talking fast, as if he was afraid he wouldn't get the words out before Ruth stopped listening. "Not that the missy ain't a good worker. Even if she is just a slip of a girl. She's been a fine help to Matilda in the kitchen and does whatever anybody tells her. Don't hardly cry at all except at night when she don't think nobody can hear. Poor little thing. Ain't got nobody but that rag doll now."

"And you and Matilda," Ruth said.

"But that's just it. We've grown mighty fond of her in the time she's been with us, and we's hopin' to find her a place where we know she will be treated like a girl child should be treated. And so . . ." Louis let his voice die off.

Ruth stared at the top of the man's head. She couldn't take in the child. She couldn't. "Louis, I can't. I barely have enough to buy food for myself."

"I knows things is hard for you and that teachin' don't overstuff a body's pockets with money, but that's where the little missy can help you. Her family had a house. A right nice place over on

Elm Street not far from the schoolhouse. You could move in there with her and save whatever you're paying for these rooms here. I can bring you over some of the leavings from the hotel from time to time, and Matilda would be obliged if you let her come cook or clean for you now and again so's she could see the little missy. Matilda, she ain't owned by Massa George. She belongs to Mistress Williams, who hires her out to Massa George, but her mistress ain't countin' up every hour of the day for Matilda. She lets her take her ease now and again."

Ruth swallowed and told herself not to look at the girl, but she couldn't stop her gaze from sliding across the yard to the child. Adria Starr stared back at her. What was it Ruth had prayed at the cemetery? That the Lord would help the child. How many times had she heard Peter say that sometimes a person had to put feet to his prayers? Or her prayers.

Ruth looked back at Louis. "Why are you so intent on helping her?" She kept her voice low. "It would seem that you have enough worries of your own without taking on hers. Or mine. Trouble is all around us after the cholera."

"Ain't that the truth." He twisted his hat again and shuffled his feet. Then he surprised her by looking straight at her. "I ain't denyin' that plenty of folks is in need, but this little girl is the one the Lord set down in my path. I don't reckon he expects me to help ev'ry hurtin' body, but he does expect me to help them I can." He turned his eyes back down to the ground then. "So's I'm doin' what I can."

"The same as you buried all those people."

"It needed doing."

"So it did." Ruth shut her eyes again and blew out a long breath. Had the Lord shoved this child in her path? She opened her eyes and looked over Louis's head toward the girl again. "What does she want?"

"I guess you needs to ask her that." He turned to smile at the child and beckon her over to the door.

❧

Adria was almost afraid to breathe while Louis talked to the schoolteacher's wife. She listened hard, but she couldn't make out enough words to know what they were saying. She wanted to run to Louis and grab his hand. Somehow holding Louis's hand made her feel safer, but Louis told her she couldn't. Not even when they were walking over to where the schoolteacher lived. Louis said she needed to walk a little in front of him now that so many people were back on the street.

Her legs trembled, but she did what Louis said. Aunt Tilda said Louis always knew the best thing to do. That must be why Adria felt so safe when his big hand was wrapped around hers.

She'd been scared of him when she first saw him at her house, but as soon as he picked her up, she knew he meant her nothing but good.

He meant her nothing but good now too. That was why he was talking to Mrs. Harmon. Trying to see if she would take Adria's mother's place. Not that anybody could do that. Not ever. But Adria needed family. Or Mr. George would find her a place. A place, he said. Not a family. Just thinking about the look on Mr. George's face when he said it made Adria squeeze Callie a little closer.

She hoped the schoolteacher's wife needed family the same as Adria, but the woman didn't smile when she looked across the yard at Adria. The schoolteacher, Mr. Harmon, had always been smiling. He was like Louis. You knew he meant good for you. But maybe Mrs. Harmon wasn't that way. Maybe she didn't like children. Maybe she wouldn't like Adria.

Where before she had wanted to run the short distance over to where Louis stood in front of the woman, now her feet were like clumsy bricks.

"Come along, missy." Louis held out his hand toward her.

"Is she afraid of me?" The woman sounded surprised.

"Not of you. More of tomorrow."

Adria wasn't sure what Louis meant by that, but she felt braver when his big hand wrapped around hers. Brave enough to look back up at the schoolteacher's wife.

"I'm not afraid." The words came out weaker than Adria expected. She did sound afraid. She swallowed hard and repeated. "I'm not afraid."

"'Course not. Mistress Harmon is wantin' to ask you something." Louis tightened his grip on Adria's hand a bit. "You answer her right."

Adria hoped she would know the right answer as she looked up at the schoolteacher's wife, who still wasn't smiling. Maybe that was because she was missing the schoolteacher the way Adria missed her mother and father. That could make it hard to smile. Especially if she didn't have anybody's hand to hold. Adria hesitated, but then she laid her doll down beside her feet and reached over for the schoolteacher's wife's hand. At first the woman's fingers were stiff, as though she couldn't bend them, but Adria just kept her fingers wrapped softly around her hand. After a minute, the woman's hand curled around Adria's.

"Louis said you wanted to ask me something. Did you forget what it was?"

"No, I didn't forget."

The schoolteacher's wife stared down at Adria as though she were searching for an answer without asking a question. Adria's heart started beating a little faster. The woman still wasn't smiling. The question was going to be hard.

"What do you want, Adria?"

At first, Adria thought the question wasn't hard after all, but then the answer that came swelled up out of her sad heart. "I want my mama." That looked like it scared the schoolteacher's wife, so Adria blinked away her tears and added, "But I know I can't have her. She's gone on to glory."

"That's right, missy." Louis squeezed Adria's hand. "So what is it you want now?"

Adria looked up at Louis and then over at the schoolteacher's wife. "I want family. Aunt Tilda and Louis say they can't be my family no matter how much I wish they could. Because I'm white." The woman just kept looking at her without saying anything. Adria pulled in a breath for courage. "Will you be my family?"

Seven

I can try. Ruth's words echoed in her head as she watched Louis and the child walk away from her door. They would be back later that day. Louis to help her move her things to this house on Elm Street. The child to stay with her after telling the slave Matilda goodbye.

After softly closing the door, Ruth leaned against it. Heaven help her, why had she said those words? Not exactly yes, but the same as. But then, what else could she say, with the child clutching her hand and staring up at her with those forlorn brown eyes? After Ruth said she'd try, the child's smile had transformed her eyes. Made them come to life. Ruth had the feeling her own pale blue eyes looked more forlorn than ever, but neither Louis nor the child seemed to notice. Adria. Ruth needed to stop pushing her away as a child she had nothing to do with and call her by her name. If she was going to be family.

Ruth had wanted family desperately with Peter, but that dream had died. She couldn't replace it with an orphaned child. She couldn't.

It was the Christian thing to do. Peter's words were in her head as she trudged back up the steps to their rooms. He'd said that to her more than once when he would allow a child to come to school even when the parents didn't pay the fee. Or when he put extra money they didn't have to spare in the offering plate if the preacher spoke of a need in the church. The Christian thing to do. A person couldn't sit on a church pew claiming the title Christian if that person didn't allow Christ to work through him. Peter lived his beliefs.

Ruth paced back and forth across the narrow room. If Peter were still alive, then perhaps she could take in the child, but alone she couldn't do it. Louis would have to shove the child into someone else's path. Her gaze fell on Peter's Bible she'd left out on the chair. The Bible instructed Christians to care for orphans. Widows and orphans, actually. She was a widow.

She stared up at the ceiling and spoke aloud. "Who is taking care of me?"

The question bounced back at her. She stopped pacing and stared at the trunk she had begun to unpack after Justice Franklin's offer of the schoolteacher position. Her purse, with its scarcity of money, lay on the end of the bed. But now she would have a house and no worry about paying rent. In shame, she bent her head and stood silent in the middle of the room.

"Forgive me," she whispered, whether to Peter or the Lord she wasn't sure. Perhaps to both. "I will try."

She didn't have to be the child's mother. She couldn't be that. But family. That she could do. With the Lord's help. The child would understand. Ruth stopped herself. Not the child. Adria. Adria would understand. She wasn't a baby.

Ruth regretted the word as soon as it crossed her thoughts. She put her hands on her abdomen. So empty.

She shook herself a little. Yesterdays couldn't be changed. She needed to move on into her tomorrows. What was it Louis had said? That the child, Adria, was not fearful of Ruth but of tomorrow. But she had put down her doll and taken Ruth's hand. Hoping for a tomorrow with her.

How hard would it be to take care of one little girl's needs? Meals and clothes. After all, wasn't she planning to gather a whole school-house full of children and take care of their need for education? She would put away her bitterness and wait upon the Lord to renew her strength. Wings of eagles. She could pray for wings like that.

By the time Louis returned a few hours later with another man to help, she had the trunk packed once more. The furniture all belonged to Mrs. Jackson except for Peter's bookcase and desk, so there wasn't a great deal to carry down the steps and out to the wagon the livery man had loaned without charge. He had children in need of schooling, Louis said.

The child. Ruth shook her head and corrected her thinking again. Not the child. Adria. Louis said Adria had gone ahead to her house with Matilda. To open the windows and air out the place. To get ready for Ruth. Matilda couldn't stay long. She had to be back at the hotel to cook the evening meal.

Ruth grabbed the rest of her block of cheese and Matilda's bread on the way out the door. At least they'd have something for a light meal. Then she'd have to lay in some supplies. The child—Adria—was small but even so, a growing girl. She would need proper food. As did Ruth if she were to have the energy to keep a roomful of children in line and motivated to learn.

"I will try." She whispered the words as she climbed into the wagon and looked back at Mrs. Jackson's house. She had been so happy there with Peter, but now she had little choice but to close the door on that part of her life. Not that she wouldn't take Peter with her. He would always be part of her, but at the same time it might be good to start over in a new place. Make new memories. She turned to face forward toward the house on Elm Street.

But what about Adria? She would be surrounded by memories in her house where her family died. Would she be able to accept a new person living there with her? It could be that she would have to try too.

Adria wanted to go home to her own house. She did, but the closer she got to the front door, the harder it was to keep walking. Aunt Tilda was talking to her. She could hear her voice, but she couldn't concentrate on her words. Instead she kept thinking about how her mother wouldn't be there to call out a cheery greeting when she ran inside. She wouldn't be in her favorite chair, rocking Eddie back and forth to get him to take a nap. She wouldn't hold out her hand to invite Adria to come close and tell her all the things she'd been doing.

She would have much to tell. About Louis and Aunt Tilda. About the schoolteacher's wife. Adria didn't know what to call her. Maybe Mrs. Harmon until she knew her better.

She had looked kind when they talked to her earlier, but although Adria had watched closely, she hadn't smiled. Smiles didn't matter all that much, Aunt Tilda said when Adria told her that.

In fact, Aunt Tilda didn't smile much either. Never big happy smiles like Adria's mother, but she did sometimes get a look on her face that softened her lips and made the wrinkles between her eyes go away. That was when she would smooth down Adria's curly hair or give her shoulder an easy squeeze as if they were sharing some secret no one else knew.

Aunt Tilda didn't have that soft look on her face now. She had her firm look as she opened the front door and stepped behind Adria to push her through.

"Ain't nobody here, child. Them you loved is done gone to glory where they is lookin' down on you and wantin' good things for you."

"How do you know?" Adria asked.

"I just do." Aunt Tilda sounded very sure. "Now we ain't got but a little while to have this place all shiny before that new schoolteacher gets here." She pulled a feather duster out of the bag she had brought from the hotel.

"What if she doesn't like it?"

Aunt Tilda frowned as she handed the feather duster to Adria. "And why wouldn't she like it?" She looked around. "Appears to be a fine house." She opened up the front windows.

Adria slipped her gaze over to the couch where she'd last seen her mother and Eddie. It was empty now, with the cushions her mother had made arranged the way they were supposed to be. Eddie's baby blanket that he liked to hold when he was going to sleep was nowhere in sight.

She wasn't going to cry. Not here in the middle of the day. Better to wait until night for that when she could hold Callie close and not bother anybody with her tears. She swallowed and pulled in a shaky breath. "What if she doesn't like me?"

"Now what on earth put that thought in your head?" Aunt Tilda reached down and put her fingers under Adria's chin to make her look up at her.

"Louis says she was never a mother. Maybe she won't know how to be family."

"Don't you worry none about that. The good Lord has put a motherin' feel in most ev'ry woman I ever knew. I'm guessin' this woman ain't no different, whether she's had her own babies or not." Aunt Tilda turned loose of Adria's chin. "Now where can I find a broom?"

"Behind the kitchen door." That's where Adria's mother kept it. Handy, she said.

Adria moved the feather duster over the table and chairs. Her mother always just gave her a rag for dusting, but the feather duster was more fun to use.

Aunt Tilda started sweeping. "This woman, she might not do things like you remember your mama doing them, but it'll all work out fine. You just have to do what she says and not be thinkin' your egg has to be cooked a certain way come morning."

"If she wants me to, I can cook her egg."

"So you can." Aunt Tilda paused in her sweeping to give Adria one of those soft looks. "You're a right good hand at cookin'. It's a blessin' to have a helpful child around. A body don't have to have a baby to understand that."

"Did you ever have babies?" Adria couldn't imagine Aunt Tilda with a little baby of her own. She was too gray and wrinkled, but she could be a grandmother. A woman couldn't be a grandmother unless she was a mother first. That was just how it worked.

Adria used to have a grandmother, but then Mama said she went to heaven to get things ready for when they might come. Mama said Adria's grandmother was a great one for getting things ready. Adria shut her eyes and imagined them all sitting down at a shining table to eat. That had to be good.

Aunt Tilda was quiet so long Adria almost forgot what she'd asked her after her mind ran off to her family in heaven. But when Aunt Tilda started talking in a voice that sounded too quiet, she remembered.

"I did have babies. A long time back." She leaned on the broom. "How I did love those sweet bundles. That motherin' feel I spoke about from the Lord was strong inside me. That can be more of a curse than a blessin' for a slave like me." She waved her hand and began sweeping again. "But ain't no need burdenin' your young mind with any of that. Things won't never be that way for you."

She knew Aunt Tilda didn't want to talk about it anymore from the way her shoulders were stiff as she swept, but Adria asked anyway. "Where are they now?"

"Hard to say, child. They'd be older than Louis now."

She looked so sad that Adria moved over in front of her. "They could have gone across that river you told Louis about. Not the one to glory but that other one to freedom."

Again Aunt Tilda stopped sweeping. She shut her eyes a second while a hint of a smile played across her lips. "That's how I think about them, child. Done run up to freedom land. I'm thinkin' they might have made it. I whispered the want-to in their ears while I was nursin' them on my breast."

"Why didn't you go find that river, Aunt Tilda?"

She blew out a long breath. "Too fearful when I was young. Too old when the fear left me."

"Is Louis afraid too?"

"These is things you can't understand, child. Hard things. But Louis ain't your regular man. He walks on the Lord's path and I don't reckon that path has ever took him toward that river you're thinkin' on." She started sweeping again, slow, measured strokes. "Could be the Lord will reward him for that someday, whether here on God's green earth or in the heavenly realm. We're all measured and weighed by the Lord's scales."

Adria started to say something more, but Aunt Tilda held up her hand to stop her. "We ain't a-gonna talk about this no more. Ever. You understand?"

Adria nodded a little.

"Good. And don't be talkin' 'bout that river to nobody else either. That wouldn't do nothin' but bring trouble down on us all. You is ready to start a new life where you don't never have to worry about findin' no river to cross to freedom."

"Will I ever see you again? Or Louis?" Adria squeezed the feather duster up against her chest as though it were her doll, Callie.

The hard look faded off Aunt Tilda's face. "Ain't none of us goin' anywhere, and I'll be back to help the schoolteacher woman here at your house from time to time. We ain't throwin' you aside, child. We just doin' what has to be done and you is gonna be fine."

She reached a hand toward Adria and that was all the invitation Adria needed to wrap her arms around Aunt Tilda's waist and bury her face against the woman's apron.

Aunt Tilda stroked her hair. "There, there, child. I done told you. You has had some hard times, but things is gonna get better now that this schoolteacher lady is comin' to stay with you. Louis and me, we prayed and this is the answer we got." She pushed Adria away from her and bent down to look straight in her face. "And the Lord's answers are always the best answers. You understand that?"

Adria nodded her head.

"Then you wipe away them tears and get back to usin' that feather duster. Louis'll be here with that schoolteacher lady anytime now."

When Louis got there with the schoolteacher's wife and her trunk, everybody was busy putting things here or there. Then Aunt Tilda had to go back to the hotel. Not long after that, Louis and the other man helping him finished carrying things in and they left too. Adria and the schoolteacher's wife were alone with neither one of them seeming to know exactly what to do next.

They ate at the table where Adria had last sat with her mother and father and Eddie. She tried not to think about that, but it was hard not to. Everything about the kitchen made her think of her mama. The schoolteacher's wife sat across the table from Adria and did more stirring of the soup Aunt Tilda had given them than eating. She did smile, but something about it wasn't right. Adria smiled back and wondered if something wasn't right about her smile too.

"Aren't you hungry?" the schoolteacher's wife asked.

Adria looked down at her soup. She'd barely eaten any. "I guess not."

"You need to eat." The woman looked worried.

"Yes, ma'am." Adria ate a spoonful. Aunt Tilda told her to try to do whatever the schoolteacher's wife wanted her to do. She thought about telling the woman she needed to eat too. She was even skinnier than Aunt Tilda and she looked kind of pale. "Are you sick?"

The woman looked surprised. "No. Why would you ask that?"

"I don't know." Adria shrugged a little. "I just didn't want you to be sick."

The woman's face changed, got softer the way Aunt Tilda's did, even though she didn't have any wrinkles to ease out.

"I'm not sick." The schoolteacher's wife reached across the table and put her hand over Adria's. "Listen, Adria. This is a little strange for the two of us. But if we both try, I think we'll be all right. You can tell me what you need and I'll do my best to help you."

Adria wasn't sure what to say. She needed her mama, but this woman couldn't make that happen. Nobody could.

When Adria didn't answer right away, the woman said, "We just need time to get to know each other. Then it will be fine."

Aunt Tilda's words echoed in Adria's head. *You is gonna be fine.* "Yes, ma'am."

"So you ask me something and then I'll ask you something." The woman squeezed Adria's hand when Adria hesitated. "Ask anything you like."

Adria moistened her lips. "What should I call you? Mrs. Harmon?" That might be better than "the schoolteacher's wife" that kept being in Adria's head.

"Oh no. That's much too formal."

"Do you want me to call you Mother?" She had never called her mother that, only Mama.

The woman flinched a little and pulled her hand away from Adria's. "No. Best you keep that name for the memory of your real mother." She took a deep breath. "I could be your sister and you could simply call me Ruth, but others might think that wasn't proper. Not that we have to worry about what others think, but if I'm going to be the schoolteacher, I need to keep the opinions of my students' parents in mind."

"You could be my aunt like Aunt Tilda."

The schoolteacher's wife smiled. A real smile that went all the way up to her eyes. "I think that would work. Aunt Ruth. Do you want to try it out?"

"Aunt Ruth." Adria tried a smile out on the woman too. On Aunt Ruth.

She reached back over to touch Adria's hand. "Good."

"Now it's your turn to ask me something," Adria said.

"So it is." Aunt Ruth let her eyes wander all around the kitchen and then back to Adria's face. She looked uneasy again. "What would you like to do next? After we eat."

Adria remembered all the books Louis had carried in for Aunt

Ruth. "Could you read me a story out of one of your books before I go to bed?"

So later, they sat close together on the couch where Adria's mother had died while Aunt Ruth read from *Gulliver's Travels*. Her voice was strong and carried Adria into the story. While she was reading, Adria didn't think about her mother. Finally Aunt Ruth marked their place and promised to read more the next night, but even then they just sat there together a moment.

"I liked that. Mama used to tell me stories, but we didn't have any books but the Bible." Adria leaned her head against Aunt Ruth.

"The Bible has good stories. We'll read it sometimes too." Aunt Ruth eased her arm out and around Adria.

"I'm glad you're here, Aunt Ruth." Her name was beginning to be as easy to say as Aunt Tilda.

"I am too. We're going to be fine," Aunt Ruth said, and Adria believed her.

Eight

I'm not going to wait on you forever, Adria Starr." Carlton
Damon ran his hand through his hair, mussing it even more
than usual. He had a couple of cowlicks that only going bald
was apt to tame, but with his thick brown hair, that looked a long
time away.

Adria tried not to sigh, but she couldn't help it. Usually she
could tease Carlton out of talking marriage, but tonight she was
tired. Ruth had been baking all day. Pies and cakes. Adria had
helped her as soon as she got home from work. A few cakes were
still cooling before they could frost them. Adria was sick to death
of sugar icing. Why couldn't people just want bread? She liked to
make bread. But Ruth said desserts sold better, and when school
wasn't in session, they needed the extra money.

That wasn't quite as vital as it used to be since Adria started
working at Billiter's Mercantile. All day long she had waited on
customers, smiling whether she felt like it or not, and then came
home to get elbow deep in sugar. That hadn't made her the first bit
sweeter when Carlton showed up to complain about her working

at the store. He didn't like her waiting on the drovers and wagoners who came through town. A lady didn't need to be exposed to that kind of riffraff. Especially his girl.

Carlton was always pushing her to quit her job and get married. Everybody in Springfield thought they were headed to the altar. Everybody. Even Adria most of the time, but she still hadn't said yes. She hadn't said no, but tonight she was wondering if maybe she should.

They'd known each other forever. Carlton started following her around before they got out of primary school and then asked Ruth if he could come calling on Adria when she turned sixteen. Ruth thought that showed proper manners, but he should have asked Adria, not her aunt. She was the one who could decide what she wanted to do when it came to romance.

Ruth had never really told Adria what to do. About romance or anything else. Not even when Adria was just a kid and started living with her after the cholera. Ruth seemed to assume Adria could figure things out for herself. Not that she didn't take care of Adria. She did. She put food on the table for Adria, heated water for her baths until Adria was old enough to do that herself, and saw that her clothes were clean and suitable for the occasion, whether that was school or church or baking pies.

She and Ruth had worked things out step by step, two strangers thrown together by need. Ruth was kind to Adria, but sometimes Adria felt like she was living with her schoolteacher instead of family.

Adria smiled at the thought. She *was* living with her schoolteacher, and she was glad about that. But sometimes she longed for a family like the one she'd lost in the cholera epidemic.

That made her not jumping at the chance to get married even odder. Here was Carlton right in front of her, ready to be family. Ready to start a family with her. He wanted sons and daughters. A houseful, he sometimes said. She had always assumed she would get married, probably to Carlton, and have children someday, but that day hadn't come yet.

She summoned up her sweetest smile to make Carlton forget her unfortunate sigh. His lips were pressed firmly together, as though he was trying to keep the wrong words from exploding out of his mouth. She ran her hand up and down his arm. "Why are you in such a hurry?"

"You're nineteen. My mother had two babies by the time she was nineteen."

"I'm not your mother." Adria tried to keep her voice soft, but an edge of irritation came through. Carlton's mother was great. Adria liked her, but she didn't want to be her. She wanted something more. The problem was, she wasn't quite sure what the more was.

"You need to get your nose out of storybooks and start seeing what's right in front of you."

It was useless. She was too tired to dance around and pull up sweet words. Not when he was attacking her love of books. "Maybe you should try reading a few books."

"I do read books. History books. The Bible. What's real. Not romantic nonsense that keeps your head in the clouds all the time."

"Sometimes the view is better from up in the clouds. Better than what's right in front of my eyes anyway." Adria planted her fists on her hips and glared at Carlton.

Nothing was wrong with reading books. Ruth would back her up on that. Reading was what had helped the two of them find a common ground. From the very first night they had lived together, they had ended almost every day by reading to one another. So many stories through the years. And the Bible too.

She was sorry she thought of the Bible. That brought to mind all that James wrote about how your tongue could get you in trouble. Aunt Tilda had made her memorize that one about being swift to hear and slow to speak. Slow to wrath.

Dear Aunt Tilda. She had tried to step in and be the mother Ruth seemed unable to be. Aunt Tilda didn't let Adria get away with anything and she taught her so much. Ruth too. Not about mothering, but she taught Ruth to cook and shared her recipes for cakes and pies. Any time Aunt Tilda could steal a few minutes away from her work at the hotel or her mistress, she was in their kitchen, helping Ruth and making sure Adria behaved.

"You're free, child. You can do anything you want. But it ain't good to want to do what ain't right. Or to lose your temper over ev'ry little thing. Best remember that slow to wrath verse in the Good Book. You understand that?"

Sometimes Adria wondered what Aunt Tilda would think about her hesitating on the edge of matrimony. She wished she could ask her, but Aunt Tilda had gone on to glory four years ago. Happily. Rejoicing in the thought that in heaven she wouldn't be a slave. She would finally find freedom in eternity.

The black woman was buried toward the back of Cemetery Hill with other slaves, but Adria kept the place in mind and carried flowers there whenever she and Ruth visited the cemetery.

With Aunt Tilda's words whispering through her mind, Adria shut her eyes and drew in a deep breath. "Look, Carlton. I don't want to fight with you."

"Then don't. Kiss me instead." Carlton put his hands on her shoulders and pulled her toward him.

Adria jerked back from him. She could never understand how Carlton could say things that made her mad enough to spit and then the next instant expect her to kiss him. She might not want to fight, but she didn't want to make up either. Tomorrow, if he came around talking nice, might be a different story. Then she might entertain the idea of a kiss.

"Why don't you just go home?" Adria said.

"Maybe I will." Carlton dropped his hands back to his side. "And maybe I won't come back."

"Fine with me."

Ruth stepped out onto the back porch behind Adria. "Whatever are you two fighting about now?"

"She won't listen to reason, Miss Ruth." Carlton dropped his head to stare down at the ground. He looked something like his nine-year-old self from their school days.

"And what reason is that?" Ruth asked.

That was one thing about Ruth. She didn't let a person slide past an explanation. A person needed clarity of thought, she was fond of saying. In the schoolroom, the answer "I don't know" would get her ruler pointed toward your forehead. Think, she would say. Think. She wanted her students to figure out more than an answer but the reason behind it.

Instead of a ruler, she pointed the spoon she held at Carlton. Once a student of Miss Ruth, always a student, no matter how long it might have been since he sat on the schoolhouse benches.

"You know she should marry me. You said so yourself." Carlton glanced up at Ruth.

The whine in his voice made Adria want to grab him and shake him. She supposed he couldn't help it if he was the youngest child in a family with money where he got nearly anything he wanted. His father ran the town haberdashery, making silk top hats along with the slouch hats. A booming business, but Carlton wanted to have a plantation like his mother's family, with slaves doing the work. Another reason Adria had not said yes. She couldn't abide the thought of owning slaves. Not after loving Aunt Tilda.

When Adria frowned and opened her mouth, Ruth held up the spoon to silence her. She turned back to Carlton. "Wait right there, Carlton. I think you have added to what I actually said. I said you could ask her to see what she said. I certainly would not answer for her. Adria makes her own decisions."

"She makes the wrong ones," Carlton said.

Adria's frown grew fiercer. If they were simply going to talk about her as if she wasn't there, then she wasn't going to be there. "I've got cakes to frost." Without looking at either of them, she whirled around and went in the kitchen.

The icing was simmering on the back of the stove. Adria pulled it to the front and stirred it. That was what Aunt Tilda said made the difference. The stirring. A person wanted it to be right, she couldn't worry about her arm getting tired. She had to keep stirring and waiting. She said there wasn't any way to rush things up. That a good cook had to learn to wait until things were right.

As Adria stirred the sweet concoction, she remembered asking Aunt Tilda how she could know when it was right.

"You just know. It's something you can feel in your arm whilst you're stirring."

Adria took the pan off the stove and beat the sweet mixture. Was love like that? Something a person just knew when it was right? Or maybe she was simply waiting for a feeling that would never happen, like frosting taken off the fire too soon. You could beat it until your arm fell off and it still wouldn't thicken up.

This caramel batch was perfect. With a knife, she smoothed it on the cake while out on the porch Ruth tried to smooth down Carlton's ruffled feathers. Her words drifted through the open window into the kitchen.

"You can't push her. You should know that by now."

"But I love her, Miss Ruth."

Now that Adria wasn't facing off with Carlton, the longing in his voice touched something inside her. Maybe she was wrong to want more.

"I know that. But do you love her enough to give her the time she needs?"

"I've given her plenty of time." He sounded cross again.

Then nobody said anything. Adria almost smiled, thinking about how Ruth was surely staring at Carlton with her teacher look that could make a person squirm. Adria knew that look well.

After a moment, Carlton started talking again. "What if we're wasting the time we have? Something could happen. Like it did with the cholera in '33."

"Indeed."

Adria stilled her knife and barely breathed as she listened for more. Carlton's words would have stabbed through Ruth and brought back the loss of her husband and how the cholera epidemic had stolen so much from her. As it had Adria, but Adria hadn't clung to her grief. She wished her parents had lived, but at the same time, they had faded in her memory. It wasn't that way with Ruth. She claimed not a day went by that she didn't think of Peter and wish things were different. She had never once entertained any of the suitors who came to her door. None of them could compare to her Peter.

"There are other girls in Springfield." Carlton's voice got a little louder, as if he knew Adria was listening to his every word on the other side of the door.

"So there are. Some very nice girls," Ruth said quietly.

For a second, Adria held her breath. She imagined Carlton not at her door but stepping up to Janie Smith's door. She'd seen Janie eyeing Carlton at church. Janie would run to the altar with him. Outside, Carlton mumbled something she couldn't quite hear, and then Ruth was coming back into the kitchen.

Adria very carefully made swirls in the caramel frosting on the cake and didn't look at Ruth.

"That looks pretty." Ruth brought another small cake over from the cabinet. "Do you have enough frosting to cover this little cake? I thought maybe you could take it to Louis tomorrow. He does love Matilda's jam cake."

"Everybody loves Aunt Tilda's jam cake." Adria scraped the sides of the pan to get out every bit of frosting. "Except me. I wouldn't care if I never saw another cake."

Ruth smiled. "I guess we can be thankful the people here in town don't feel the same."

"I know. You should put up a sign out front. Ruth's Bakery. You could make more selling cakes and pies than you do teaching."

"Baking is fine, but I love teaching."

"I wish I knew what I loved."

"Or who?" Ruth gave her a look that demanded she think about the question.

"Or who." Adria blew out a breath as she managed to spoon out enough frosting to cover the little cake. "Tell me, Aunt Ruth. How do you know if you've met the right man? That you're in love?"

"If you have to ask, then you may not have met the right person."

"Did you know right away with your Peter?"

Ruth paused in putting the cakes and pies in boxes to deliver the next day. "While I did feel an immediate attraction the first time I saw him, I don't know whether I could say that was love right away. He was so handsome I had to keep sneaking looks at him when he showed up at church. He had moved here from Lexington to teach school. He was tall, with wonderful eyes that were an interesting gray color but at times flashed blue. But the best thing about him was his smile. He smiled at everybody and you could tell it wasn't forced. He liked people."

"And especially you." Adria raised her eyebrows at Ruth.

A blush warmed Ruth's cheeks as she laughed. "Yes, I think especially me. A year later we were married." The laughter went out of her eyes. "We had so little time together. And I did so want to have a baby, but it wasn't to be."

"You're not too old to marry and have a baby now."

Ruth gathered up the dirty spoons and dropped them into the dishpan. "That takes a husband."

"You've had opportunities there too."

"Stop it, Adria." She softened her stern words with a smile. "I'm not the one looking for romance. That's you."

"Am I, Aunt Ruth? Sometimes I don't know what I'm looking for. Maybe something more than romance. Like I should do something important with my life since I'm all that remains of my family."

"And what's that?"

"I don't know."

"If you want to go on to school, we'll find a way. I've been saving some of our baking money."

"But all those finishing schools teach you is how to catch a man. I don't care about how to swish my skirts or fill out my dance card.

I want to do something that matters. Fight for women's rights. End slavery."

"Matilda taught you well there."

"Well, it's not right that she was never free. That her children were sold away from her."

"What about Louis? He doesn't seem to be angry over being a slave."

"Aunt Tilda always said Louis was an uncommon man, but don't you think he would rather be free? Wouldn't anybody rather be free?"

Ruth reached over to touch Adria's cheek. "My young firebrand. You'll have the whole town against you if you keep preaching that sermon."

"Another thing a woman can't be. A preacher."

"True enough. But you could be the mother of a preacher or perhaps raise your own revolutionary sons."

Adria stared down at her hands. She had caramel on her fingers. "You think I should marry Carlton, don't you?"

"You know I've never tried to make decisions for you." Ruth dropped her hand away from Adria's cheek. "But if you keep putting him off, you might lose him."

"Yes."

"He's a nice boy from a good family. You'd never want for anything."

Except the wants she couldn't name.

Nine

Ruth's customers started picking up their cakes and pies after breakfast the next day. She would never be able to deliver all the orders. She hadn't had a buggy since she'd sold Peter's pony after the cholera epidemic. Everything they needed in Springfield was within walking distance, although a buggy at times would be nice.

When Adria was ten, she had wished and wished for a horse. Or a dog. Ruth smiled, remembering how Matilda told Adria if wishes were horses, beggars would ride. And then she showed up the next day with a kitten Adria had named Gulliver. He was a good cat except that, like his namesake, he did take travels from time to time, but he periodically showed up again to catch the mice in the shed out back and let Adria pet him for a while.

Ruth missed Matilda. She had filled a void in Adria's life that Ruth couldn't. Ruth had tried. She just didn't know how to be the family Adria needed when she was a little girl. Ruth could teach Adria. She could read to her. But she had trouble hugging her when the pain was leaking out of the sad places inside the child. Perhaps she had too many of her own sad places.

She should have cried with Adria, but instead Ruth locked away her own grief to keep it from overwhelming her. It was an ongoing grief. Not only the loss of Peter but the chance to be a mother. A natural mother and not merely one arranged out of need and accepted because it was her Christian duty. A duty she had fulfilled. She'd taken care of Adria and not regretted her acceptance of the child into her life. But Adria had never been her baby.

Just yesterday Adria had pointed out that Ruth wasn't too old for babies, but at thirty-two she felt too old. Yet, when she looked at it squarely, she realized Adria was right. She was not past childbearing years. Perhaps what she was past was opening her heart up to love. And to loss.

Best not to stumble into love and have it stolen away from her again. She was content with her single life as a schoolteacher. She had no necessity to consider a marriage for convenience. She and Adria managed without having a man in their lives, but now Adria was of age to consider marriage herself.

Poor Carlton. Ruth liked the boy, but he had no idea how to properly court an independent girl like Adria. He thought every woman was merely waiting for a man to rescue her from spinsterhood. Plus there was the problem of his family's slaves. If Springfield had an abolitionist group, Adria would be right in the middle of it. Sometimes Ruth worried that Adria would attempt to start such a group.

Ruth sighed as she packed her delivery basket with a pie and a loaf of bread for Leoda Gregory, who claimed she had no way to come pick up her order. Ruth put in another pie for the new pastor. He had preached his first sermon last Sunday, and a pie would be a nice way to welcome him to the community. Perhaps he would become a customer. Not that such was her intent. Generosity was its own reward, a lesson she tried to get across to her students. One should not always be looking for a return when a gift was given.

It could be she should have let Adria take the pie to Reverend Robertson. Ruth wouldn't want him or anyone in Springfield getting the wrong idea about her gift. After all, he looked to be about

Ruth's age and a widower. Tongues did have a way of wagging in Springfield. Over the years, she had been matched up with various eligible men by the town gossips.

Ruth sighed. She tried not to let being the subject of gossip concern her when she knew she had done nothing to incite the talk, but a schoolteacher needed to be above reproach. So yes, she should have asked Adria to take the pie to Reverend Robertson as she went to work that morning. But she had the little cake to take to Louis.

Another worry. Ruth did hope giving Louis the cake wouldn't cause problems for the slave. Of course, they took him sweets all the time, and his owner, George Sanderson at the hotel, never seemed bothered by that. He even allowed Louis to come help Ruth when the porch on the front of the house started sagging last spring. Ruth paid Mr. Sanderson a fair wage for Louis's work. That infuriated Adria. She thought they should pay Louis, but Louis told her that was just how things were.

"Now don't get all riled up, missy." Louis still called Adria that the same as he had when he'd brought her to Ruth's doorstep twelve years ago. "Massa George, he don't treat us bad long as we tend to our work."

Adria just couldn't accept that. She hated slavery. Ruth didn't like it either. For one thing, the teacher in her wanted to give every child the gift of reading. And some of the slave children wanted to learn. She could see the hunger in their eyes when, at times, they dared a peek in the school windows, but she wasn't allowed to teach black children. That was simply how things were. Adria couldn't change that nor could the northern abolitionists.

Yet another concern. Adria read those seditious abolitionist newspapers. She even copied bits from some of them and added her own words to send to the Lexington newspapers. She signed a fake name, but she could still be found out. Abolitionist thinking was not welcome in Springfield. Ruth could lose her students if the townspeople thought she was campaigning for the end of slavery. Not that she was, but she would be held responsible for Adria developing such inflammatory ideas.

Ruth shoved her worries aside as she went up Mrs. Gregory's rock walkway. Already the day was growing warm and she wished she'd left off one of her petticoats. The things a woman had to wear to be considered decent. At least she'd put on a small hat instead of a bonnet. Bonnets not only suffocated her, they made her feel as though she were wearing blinders. But she couldn't go out bareheaded. That wasn't done.

She hoped Adria had remembered to pin up her hair and wear her hat. She was up and gone very early this morning before Ruth was dressed. The girl was often careless with her hair and let her dark curls hang unhindered on her shoulders and down her back. Ruth touched her own neat coil of blonde hair on the back of her head. Peter had loved her fine blonde hair and often said he hoped their children would have hair like hers instead of his flaming red.

No, she wouldn't think about that. Those babies would never be. Instead she had a fiery dark-headed sister/daughter who had no idea how beautiful she was. Standing next to her at times, Ruth felt like a wilting flower. A head shorter than Adria and pale and blonde next to Adria's dark hair and rosy skin. Ruth supposed she had faded from when she was the belle of the town before she met Peter. Now she was a woman moving past her prime who should no longer be concerned about how she looked.

Neat was all that mattered, and she managed that with her blue skirt and crisp white blouse. Her schoolmarm outfit, but it serviced well for her deliveries too. Certainly nothing with which Mrs. Gregory could find fault. Leoda Gregory had a sharp eye and a way of noticing everything. She said that was all an old woman like her could do. Watch what was happening in the town. What she saw often found its way to other ears.

As she knocked on Mrs. Gregory's door, Ruth caught sight of her reflection in the narrow windows in the door. Her eyes didn't look so faded. She had plenty of spark yet to keep her students in line.

"My dear Ruth." Mrs. Gregory opened the door and reached to grasp Ruth's arm and pull her inside. "You must come have a cup of tea with me. And perhaps a piece of that cinnamon bread. You did bring me a loaf of it along with the chess pie, didn't you?"

"Don't I always." Ruth smiled at the old woman, whose shoulders were rounded as though her years had gotten too much to carry. "But I've already had my breakfast."

The woman twisted her head to peer up at Ruth. "As have I, but is that any reason not to enjoy a bit more?" Mrs. Gregory laughed and led the way to her parlor where she already had a tea tray ready.

Ruth would have preferred to go on about her chores. Her desk at home called to her. With Adria at the store and the baking done for the week, Ruth looked forward to some quiet time to work on her poetry. But a person couldn't say no to Mrs. Gregory. Before he passed on, Mr. Gregory was one of the justices of the peace appointed by the governor to handle the business of the county. The cholera hadn't stolen him. He died several years prior to the epidemic, so Mrs. Gregory had been a widow longer than Ruth. Sometimes she appeared to enjoy the role.

"We had been married these many years. I was quite used to Mr. Gregory," she had told Ruth on one of her first visits. "But there are times when the morning is more pleasant when one is by one's self. Don't you agree?"

At the time Ruth did not know Mrs. Gregory well and she had stuttered out some sort of answer.

That had amused Mrs. Gregory greatly. "I seem to have you tongue-tied, my dear, but you do surely know how men can be such a problem, with always wanting something. Food or drink or a clean shirt. If a woman has servants to do all the work, that's one thing, but then the woman has to see to the servants to be sure everyone is doing as they should and they never are. Trust me on that. They never are. But if you have only yourself to please, then the task gets decidedly easier."

"But you do have a maid, don't you?" Ruth looked around the old woman's spotless house. She knew that was not easy even if one did live alone or nearly so.

"Oh yes. Sally is a treasure. There's no way I could scrub the floors or get to the dust in all these hidden places." Mrs. Gregory waved her hand toward a table full of bric-a-brac. "You are young, so such is not a problem for you, and you have that dear little Adria to help you."

That had been when Ruth first began baking her desserts, when dear little Adria would rather read than dust. She still would, the same as Ruth. So books were all that decorated their tables.

Now Ruth poured the tea for them both. As she handed Mrs. Gregory a cup, she attempted to divert her from sharing the latest gossip by asking, "Have you heard from your children?"

"No, no. Sometimes I think they've completely forgotten their old mother." Mrs. Gregory sipped her tea and then sighed. "I raised three boys to adulthood, and trust me, that wasn't easy. Boys can be a handful. Not like your dear Adria. Then what do they do but take off for the frontier, as though nothing in Springfield was good enough for them. And after we sent them to the best schools. I don't know how many times I told Mr. Gregory that was our mistake. Those teachers led them astray. I'm sure of it."

Mrs. Gregory set her cup back on the saucer. "Oh dear, I suppose I shouldn't have said that about teachers, but I certainly wasn't speaking of you. All of us here in Springfield know we can count on you to not lead our children down any wrong roads."

"That's nice to know." Ruth had learned long ago to keep smiling no matter what Mrs. Gregory might say.

"But children do go off on their own in spite of anything we might do. As the good Lord intended, I suppose. Even so, it might have been nice if one of my boys had settled here in town to supply me with grandchildren close enough to run in and out of my house." She peered over her cup at Ruth. "You may be more fortunate in that with your dear Adria. I hear Carlton Damon is interested in making her his bride."

"They've been friends for a long time." Ruth avoided confirming or denying Carlton's courtship of Adria, but it was little use. Mrs. Gregory already had facts in hand.

"True enough, but will that friendship lead to a happy marriage? I've been told Adria is not exactly encouraging the young man."

"Young people have to set their own courses." Ruth set down her cup. "Thank you so much for the tea, but I really must finish my deliveries."

"Yes, of course. I noted that you had yet another pie in your basket." Mrs. Gregory stood up and fished several coins out of her pocket to hand to Ruth. "You keep the extra for delivering your goodies to me. I appreciate your kindness to this old lady. Perhaps a custard pie next week or even better, some of those delectable meringues you make."

"The meringues do cost a bit more than a pie," Ruth warned as she took the money.

"And worth every penny, my dear. Worth every penny. Those children of mine are going to have to become much more attentive if they expect me to give up my desserts to save their inheritance." Mrs. Gregory laughed, a tinkling sound that Ruth wondered if she had once practiced.

Ruth scooted the remaining pie to the middle of her basket before she picked it up.

"And who is the fortunate person getting your other pie?" Mrs. Gregory led the way through her hallway to open the door for Ruth. She turned with a sly smile. "I'm guessing it's for our new preacher. And what a nice thing for you to do."

Ruth was surprised by her accurate guess. "A welcome gift. That's all."

"Excellent. It's so good to have a new preacher and one so young. We can only hope he'll bring new enthusiasm to our church." The old woman peered up at Ruth. "What do you think? That he might be about your age? I certainly wouldn't be so bold to ask, but one can't help being curious, can one?"

"No, I suppose not, but I have no guess as to his age."

"A good-looking man for a preacher." Mrs. Gregory laughed and covered her mouth for a second. "Shame on me. That wasn't a very kind thing to say, but it does seem that many of the preachers in our pulpit have been old, with ears too big or noses too long."

"We only have the looks the Lord gives us."

"So true, my dear. I was once quite blessed in the looks department myself." Mrs. Gregory ran her fingers over her cheek.

"You're still beautiful." Ruth smiled.

"What a sweet liar you are." Again the tinkling laugh. "I don't have to tell a falsehood to say you are still every bit as lovely as the day I met you. Our young Pastor Robertson will surely note that fact too."

"Come, come, Mrs. Gregory. I'm only taking him a pie."

"And I'm sure he'll be thrilled to get it. Poor man. They tell me his wife died in childbirth a couple of years ago and that's why he changed churches. Too many memories, I suppose, in his old church. Somewhere up toward Danville."

"Did the baby die too?" Ruth's heart lurched, unable to keep from remembering losing Peter and then her hope of a baby.

"No, the baby lived. A little girl. But what could a man alone do with a baby? He gave the child to his sister to raise, or so I've been told."

"How very sad," Ruth murmured.

"Sad, but I suppose sensible. It does seem strange that he would be so eager to move away from where he could see the child now and again."

"Perhaps he thought it would be confusing for them all," Ruth suggested as she waited for Mrs. Gregory to open the door. She would have opened it herself to escape the conversation, but the old woman had her hand on the doorknob.

"Nonsense. Children adjust to situations such as that with ease. What the man should have done was find a new wife to be the child's mother. Then all would have been well."

"He could have been too brokenhearted."

"You young people are such romantics. I only suggest a marriage of convenience. A woman needing a husband. A man needing a mother for his child. Need can often trump love. Such arrangements abound in our world." Finally Mrs. Gregory turned the knob to pull open the door. "You made such an arrangement yourself with your dear Adria, did you not? One encouraged by George Sanderson's servant, I've heard."

"But that wasn't marriage. I merely stepped in to give a child a home."

"The same could have happened for our young preacher. A willing woman stepping in to give a child a place with her natural father."

Ruth pretended she didn't know the thought behind Mrs. Gregory's words. "I suppose that could have happened." She stepped out the door. "Thank you so much for the tea and I'll see you next week. Meringues, right?"

"Oh yes. Meringues. And do tell Pastor Robertson if he needs anything, anything at all, to not hesitate to call upon me."

"Anything at all?" Ruth smiled over her shoulder at the old woman before she started down the porch steps. "Even a marriage of convenience?"

"If only I were a few years younger."

Mrs. Gregory laughed and closed the door, but Ruth had no doubt she watched out the window to see which way Ruth turned at the end of the walkway. She considered forgetting her generosity and heading back to her house. She could find another customer for the pie. But no, she wasn't doing anything wrong and the gossips were going to talk at any rate.

She'd made a pie for their new preacher. She'd have done the same if he was an old man with those big ears and a long nose Mrs. Gregory mentioned. His looks and age had nothing to do with her taking him a pie. She was definitely not looking for a marriage of convenience.

Ten

Will Robertson stared at his Bible, open to Psalm 71 in front of him. He'd read the chapter five times over, but the words weren't sinking into his spirit this day. He looked at the first verse again. *In thee, O LORD, do I put my trust; let me never be put to confusion.*

If only he could make that true. He did trust the Lord. Hadn't he given his life to preaching his Word? But the confusion was there. He couldn't deny it. His eyes slid down through the verses. *O God, be not far from me.*

He shut his eyes, unable to bear reading the truth in front of him. Words written by a man, King David perhaps, who had leaned on the Lord. Who had been tested. Who had been through great and sore trials and yet continued to rejoice in the Lord.

Will stood up and paced across the room and back again. The truth followed him that if he felt far from God, it wasn't God who had stepped back. It was Will.

He had hoped coming to a different town, another church, would help him make a new start and shed at least some of the sorrow that had been his since Mary had died giving him a child. They had such hopes for a family. And then through the first ten years of their marriage, one disappointment followed another as

Mary was unable to carry a child past the first few months of pregnancy. And then she had. Borne him a beautiful girl child. A week later Mary was dead of puerperal fever.

He had trusted God, put his hope continually in him, served him through every disappointment, but losing Mary sent him into a downward spiral. He kept up appearances. He preached. He spoke words of prayer. He said the things everyone expected him to say. *God's will. The Lord giveth and the Lord taketh away. She's gone on to a better place.* But inside, his heart was shriveling.

His sister came and got the baby. She had a baby of her own six months older, but she claimed no difficulty also nursing little Willeena. What choice did he have? He had no way to care for a baby. Hazel understood that, but she also knew his sorrow. "I won't keep her forever, Will. Just until she's older or you find another wife."

"Wives aren't something you go looking for under rocks." Her words had made him angry. Watching her hold his baby had been painful when he so wanted it to be Mary rocking their child.

"No, of course not." Hazel had kept her voice calm. She had never liked arguing and had always given in to whatever he wanted to do while they were children. But she didn't give in this time. "I'll love her for you, and you can come see her as often as you are able. So she will know her father."

He had tried. The Lord knew he had tried. Will looked up at the ceiling as though for some sign that was true. But here he was miles from Hazel's house. Miles from his daughter. The baby's eyes had been so blue at first, but now that she was over two, they had turned a hazel green. Just like Mary's. Taffy-colored hair like Mary's. A chin that quivered like Mary's when she was unhappy.

He rubbed his hand across his own chin to still its tremble. "When will the sorrow end?" He spoke the words aloud into the air, but the same as in all the months since Mary died, no answer came. Only silence in his ears and in his heart.

The truth was, he had run away from his daughter. A shameful thought. A shameful act. But every time he looked in the child's face he saw Mary and his heart crumbled inside him. There were only so many times a man could gather up the pieces and put on a brave face for the world.

He should give the pieces of his broken heart to God. What man cannot do, God can. How many times had he glibly told those very words to his parishioners? *Give it to the Lord. He can mend your heart. He will never send you more than you can handle. That promise is in the Scripture.* And yet. Now the words bounced off his own ears.

Hazel hadn't understood, although he tried to explain when he went to tell her he was moving to Springfield. "I can't bear seeing Mary's smile every time I look at Willeena."

"You should be glad she looks like your Mary. This child is abiding proof of your love."

They had been standing in the middle of Hazel's yard while Willeena ran about, chasing after first one wonder and then another. She tripped on a rock and fell, but instead of crying, the child jumped up, brushed her hands against her dress, and ran off toward another flower or whatever caught her eye. Determined to enjoy life, like her mother.

After several miscarriages, Will had wanted to quit trying for a child. He was willing to live a celibate life to keep Mary from experiencing the pain of hoping for a child and then being devastated when she was unable to carry the baby more than a few months. Mary wouldn't hear of it. She was determined to share his bed, to continue to pray for the Lord's favor.

"If the Lord granted barren Hannah a baby and Sarah a son in her old age, then he might still answer our fervent prayers for a child," Mary had told him.

He wanted to believe her, wanted to continue to hold Mary in his arms, and then their prayer had been answered, but at what cost? That was what Hazel couldn't understand. The price he paid every time he looked at his and Mary's child. Hazel was angry with him. She tried to hide it, but she was his sister. He knew her too well. But he couldn't walk the path she thought he should.

"I won't forget her." When he said that to Hazel, he wasn't sure whether he spoke of Mary or Willeena. Hazel must have felt the same, because deep lines furrowed her brow as he went on. "I'll send money and I'll be back to visit. Springfield is only a few hours away."

"A child her age forgets quickly." Hazel spoke the words very softly as she let her gaze drift over to the little girl.

"You know I must follow wherever the Lord leads me." He tried to say the words stoutly as if they were true. As if the Lord had said to "get thee up and go hither to a new place."

Hazel stared back at him, not believing his words. That was the trouble with sisters. They accepted no lies. After a moment, she said, "My Andrew may replace you in her heart."

"Then that will be as the Lord intends." And this time he knew the words to be true. He was giving up his child. For the good of them both. But it hadn't felt good when he picked up the little girl, his daughter, and breathed in her earthy smell as he held her close. She giggled in his ear and he swallowed back tears and told himself it was right what he was doing. Whatever the reason.

He told himself the same now. The Lord could take a man's feeblest efforts and turn it into good. Will believed that. Or at one time he had believed that. Now he wasn't sure what he believed. He wanted to trust. He had to trust. To keep sending up prayers even when his heart felt empty. To keep believing the Lord would once again fill his heart.

The church here in Springfield deserved a preacher who did more than mouth the proper words. The people who had sat in the pews and welcomed him with smiles deserved his best. No, they deserved the Lord's best through him. Perhaps if he kept walking the walk, kept reading the Word, kept bending his knees to pray, the Lord would renew his spirit. Renew his calling. For without his calling, he had nothing left.

Will sat down at his desk and read the psalm through yet again. He would study and find a sermon for the people. He could continue to preach each Sunday. His heart feeling empty didn't change the truths he could share from the Bible. He would blow on the embers of his faith and surely come up with enough fire to share the gospel. Whatever else he doubted, he did not doubt that every man, woman, and child needed to hear the gospel. Perhaps those who were walking through a despairing, empty valley the most of all.

A knock on the door disturbed his study. He wasn't expecting visitors, but then a preacher could not keep a locked door to his people. He ran his hand through his light brown hair to try to put it back in some semblance of order before he stood up and went to see who had come to call. He pushed a smile across his face and opened the door.

A lovely, blonde woman with a small straw hat perched on her head stood on his porch, a large basket draped over her arm. He'd seen her in the congregation on Sunday and had shaken her hand as she went out, but her name escaped him now. So many names to remember. He did remember she sat next to a dark-haired younger woman who didn't favor her at all, but they seemed to belong together. The young woman was nearly a head taller than this woman, who surely stood barely five foot.

Now she gave him a tentative smile. "I hope you will forgive me for disturbing you, Pastor Robertson." Her light blue eyes showed obvious intelligence, and that made him recall the person following her out last Sunday telling him she was a local teacher.

"No problem at all, madam, but you will have to forgive me, for I have let your name slip out of my memory."

Her smile looked easier. "That's understandable. You can't be expected to remember all your members' names after only one week. I'm Ruth Harmon."

"Of course, Mrs. Harmon. I do remember meeting you last Sunday even if I failed to properly remember your name. It is Mrs., isn't it?" No husband had been with her on the pew, but not every couple was equally yoked with regard to spiritual belief.

"Yes, I was married." Sadness flashed through her eyes, but she kept her smile firmly in place.

He didn't inquire about her use of past tense. Such information could wait. He did hope she hadn't come calling in hopes of changing that to a present tense. In spite of Hazel continually saying he needed to find a wife, he had no plans to do so. Not and open up his heart to pain again.

"How may I be of service to you today?" he asked. "Have you a prayer need?"

"Oh no." A bit of color stained her pale cheeks as she rushed out her words. "I brought you a pie. To welcome you to our town. Our church." She sat her basket down and lifted out the pie. "I hope you like cherries."

"Who doesn't like cherry pie? How very kind of you." He took it from her. "It looks delicious."

"Thank you," she murmured while picking up her basket.

He berated himself for his lack of hospitality. "Would you like to come in and have a piece with me?"

"I don't think that would be a good idea. We are a small town with many eyes that watch. I would not want to be the cause of gossip about the new pastor in town. Or about me." She looked straight at him and didn't shy away from the directness of her words. "However, I do make pies each week should you need to satisfy your sweet tooth in the weeks to come."

"Someone told me you were a teacher."

"Teachers can bake." Laughter lit up her eyes. "The school term is short and a teacher has to find ways to supplement her income. Fortunately for you, church goes on year around."

His answering laugh sounded a bit strange in his ears. He had rarely found reason to laugh in the last few months. "You are correct, madam. And I will keep you in mind should I need another pie."

"Oh dear, that sounded as if I was drumming up business."

Her cheeks were scarlet now, but the color made her even more attractive. "I truly wasn't, Reverend."

"Worry not, Mrs. Harmon." He balanced the pie in one hand and touched her arm. "I am grateful for your kind thoughts and generosity."

She stepped back, perhaps as surprised by his touch as he was surprised to have laid his hand on her. He should have simply smiled to reassure her.

"You're welcome," she stammered as she turned and started down the porch steps.

To try to dispel the awkwardness his touch had caused, he called after her. "I hope to see you Sunday morning. And your daughter."

She hesitated as though to say something, but then she merely smiled over her shoulder at him as she hurried toward the street. He watched her out of sight and then took the pie into the kitchen.

Ruth Harmon. He sat at the table and wrote her name down in a ledger book. He added every other name he remembered of those he'd met in Springfield. A good pastor remembered names and learned about his congregation. Every name on the page had a story. His gaze lingered on Ruth Harmon's name as he wondered what her story might be.

He dipped a finger into the pie and licked the sweet cherry syrup off his finger. Then he got a fork and ate pie for lunch.

Eleven

Adria liked clerking at the store well enough, but she couldn't imagine working there forever. If only she knew what she did want to do forever. She knew what she was supposed to want. Marriage and children. Sometimes that sounded right. She liked children, and she often considered accepting Carlton's proposal and becoming Mrs. Carlton Damon. But then he would do something to infuriate her the way he had last night and she would be almost ready to point him toward Janie Smith's house.

Ruth said that they knew each other too well. That familiarity blinded Adria to Carlton's good qualities. Perhaps she did expect too much. Still, if a person was going to pledge her love and life to one man, shouldn't she expect much? Love. Understanding. Support. Adria could almost hear Ruth reminding her Carlton would expect as much in return, which was reasonable. But the problem was, Adria kept getting the idea that Carlton thought what he expected trumped anything she might expect.

That morning Adria had gotten up extra early to slip out into the dawning light. The streets were nearly empty, with only a few shopkeepers unlocking their doors to prepare for the day. Lamps shone dimly through some of the windows. Soon the town would be astir, but Adria liked being out and about before that happened.

For one thing, she had the cake for Louis, and that was easier to deliver before the hotel guests were up and moving. Bet could usually point Adria to wherever Louis was working. Bet had become the hotel cook after Aunt Tilda died. She was used to Adria and didn't mind at all when she showed up at the kitchen door.

Sometimes Adria thought Bet was making eyes at Louis, but if she teased Louis about it, he just laughed and shook his head. "Now you know there ain't no truth to that, missy."

Today, Bet met her at the back door. "Miss Adria, you bringin' something for that ol' Louis again? Now if he ain't the lucky one."

"It's just a little cake," Adria said. "If he's not around, I'll leave it here."

"Best not do that. I'll have it all et before the sun comes up. You and Missus Ruth make fine cakes."

"It's Aunt Tilda's recipe."

"I'm knowin' it is, but somehow I can't get all them ingredients to line up right in my cakes. Massa George tells me to stick to cornbread and biscuits and he'll buy cakes from Missus Harmon." Bet's smile disappeared. "The mister is sick. Louis tol' me he feared Massa George done took a turn for the worse this day."

"Oh? I'm sorry to hear that. Nothing too serious, I hope."

"Appears to be plenty serious. Done had two doctors in. Massa George's son come home from Louisville yesterday." Bet looked over her shoulder toward the front of the building. "Might be for the best if that one don't catch you in here. He's not like Massa George. He's all the time talkin' about how much ever'thing is worth, and I do mean ever'thing."

"Maybe Mr. George will get better and his son will head back to Louisville."

"I've been prayin' it so." Bet rubbed her hands on her apron. "I 'spect you can find Louis out in the buggy house. Always somethin' out there needin' shinin' up or fixin'."

Louis was happy to get the cake, but it was plain he was as worried as Bet about Mr. Sanderson.

"I been prayin', but things ain't lookin' good for Massa George. A person seen as much as me, they get a feelin' for that kind of thing."

"Bet said they had two doctors in."

"Doctors can't cure ever' ill that ails a body."

"It's not cholera, is it?" Adria lived in dread of another cholera epidemic.

"You can rest easy about that." Louis patted Adria's hand. "Nary a sign of the cholera. Looks to be his heart failin' him. He ain't a young man."

"Then maybe it's his time to go."

"That's what I'm feared of. Things is liable to be turned upside down 'round here if Massa George passes on to glory." Deep lines formed between Louis's eyebrows.

"Whoever takes over the hotel will still need you."

Louis shook his head. "Hard to know about that. I reckon I'll just have to depend on the Lord the way I've always done, no matter what comes my way. Ain't no need you worryin' your head over it anyhow. You need to get on to the store and I need to get back to work. You tell Mistress Harmon I appreciates the cake."

"What about me? I was the one who did the frosting. Just the way Aunt Tilda taught me." Adria gave him a mock frown. "And carried it over here to you."

"Now you knows you rememberin' ol' Louis always makes me happy."

"You're not old." Adria had thought him old when she first knew him. That had been because she was so young, but now she had clearer eyes. Louis didn't have the first gray hair, and his shoulders were just as broad and strong as the day he'd carried her to the hotel after her family died.

"Turned thirty-nine in January, best I can figure. Not but a short step to forty."

"That's not all that old. You're still in the prime of life."

"Maybe so, but that can be a good thing for a man like me or a bad thing, accordin' to what else is goin' on." His smile disappeared.

Adria didn't try to get him to explain what he meant. Even if he told her what had put the worry in his eyes, she had no way to make it disappear. All she could do was bring him some sweets now and again, and that did no good at all for the real problem. Him being a slave. She had told him more than once that she'd heard of people willing to spirit slaves to freedom, even if doing so was against the law.

But Louis refused to listen. He always waved away any mention of heading toward that river Aunt Tilda had talked about. Adria knew now she'd meant the Ohio River that, once crossed, meant a better chance for freedom in the northern states that didn't allow slavery.

"Matilda shouldn't have filled your head with her freedom talk," Louis had told her once.

"Don't you want to be free?" Adria asked.

"I reckon a man can't help but think on freedom now and again." A look of yearning flashed across his face before he rubbed his hands hard over his cheeks. A frown made furrows on his forehead then. "But some things ain't meant to be, and I'm just thankful not to be shipped down the river where a slave ain't nothin' but hands to pick cotton in the hot sun all the livelong day."

"Mr. Sanderson wouldn't do that after all you've done for him. During the cholera and all."

"Sometimes it's best to depend on nobody but the Lord. You can be sure he won't never do you wrong." Louis had dipped his chin and looked at her through lowered eyebrows. "Now no more of this kind of talk before you gets the both of us in a heap of trouble."

Trouble. Ruth told her the same. Trouble not just for Adria but for Ruth too. She worried that if the Springfield citizens heard Adria speak out against slavery or knew she wrote anti-slavery letters to the papers, they would withdraw their children from Ruth's school. Sadly, that was probably true, but it was also true that few people cared what any woman said. Even the northern abolitionist groups refused to let women speak at their conventions. Some free-thinking women formed their own groups, but when they met, people stirred up protests against women speaking in public that led to riots in the streets.

So even if Adria did speak out and stop hiding her written words behind a fake name in letters to the city newspapers, nobody would listen. Women were supposed to let men do the thinking for them. As Ruth often cautioned her, it was a man's world. A woman couldn't vote to change things. A woman was expected to stay in her place and agree with whatever her father or her husband said.

Adria supposed living with Ruth with no men in their lives since the cholera epidemic had skewed her thinking. Made her believe a woman could make her way without a man. But did she want that? Surely it was better to have love and a family. She remembered how her mother had laughed and sung while taking care of her family. She saw how sad Ruth was when she sometimes picked up her husband's Bible and held it as though she were still holding him.

Yet, was it too much to hope for a man to accept you as you were instead of as he thought you should be?

The streets were beginning to fill as she hurried toward the store. Dust rose up from a line of wagons leaving town on their way to Louisville. She waved her hand in front of her face and was glad to step into Billiter's Mercantile Store. Not that some of the dust didn't seep into the store or fly in whenever the door opened. Plus, the wagoners and drovers carried plenty in with them when they came to buy supplies for their journey.

Ruth worried about her being around the rough drovers, and Carlton was forever after her to quit. It wasn't a place for a lady, he said. She needed a job, she told him. She wouldn't if she'd come to her senses and marry him, he said. She supposed that was true, but she rarely had trouble with any of the men at the store. Mr. Billiter didn't abide rough talk or actions in his store, and he showed them the door out if they appeared to have partaken of too much of the wares from the taverns down the street.

But he wasn't about to bar them completely from the store. They brought ready money and he never had to worry with them asking to put their purchases on the books until they could pay. The drovers were here today and gone tomorrow. A different bunch coming through town each day in the summer. The new road built a few years ago with bridges over the Salt River made Springfield a convenient stop during the hauling seasons for wagons going to or from Louisville.

Adria didn't mind totaling up the men's purchases. They might be rough, unshaven, and not too clean from the dusty road, but at the same time, they appeared to be so free, ready to go wherever the road took them, with nothing to tie them down. Now and again a woman rode in one of the wagons with a man, but most of the men seemed to have few attachments to anyone or any place.

It was a busy day for the wagons, and by the time Adria headed home after the store closed down, the dust was so thick it almost choked her. She could feel it settling in her hair and on her dress. She was anxious to leave Main Street and the wagons behind and head down Elm toward her house where the air would be clearer.

She was halfway across Main when men began shouting. She froze at the sound of thundering hooves coming straight toward her through clouds of dust. All at once, somebody barreled into her, shoving her out of the way. She hit the ground hard next to the hitching posts as horses and a wagon pounded past. The horses' heavy breathing, the creak of the wagon, and the shouts of the wagoner seemed almost on top of her. Adria tried to scramble away, but she couldn't move. Whoever had pushed her out of the road was now a dead weight on her back, pressing her down into the dirt.

The man groaned and rolled away from her. Adria sat up and tried to see him through the thick dust stirred up by the horses and wagon.

"Are you all right?" she asked as she got to her feet and leaned down to look at the man. She didn't know him. He must be one of the drovers.

"That's what I should be asking you." He sat up, holding his head. "I thought you were going to be run down by that cart for sure and certain. Old Mac let his team get away from him."

"I would have gotten out of the way." Adria brushed off her skirt. It was useless. She was covered with dirt head to toe. Some even in her mouth. And her hat was completely gone, lost with her hairpins somewhere in the dust.

"Didn't look like that to me, my lady."

The dust cleared a little and she could see blood oozing between the fingers he held to his forehead. "You're hurt."

"Appears I might have cracked my head on the hitching post there." He grinned at her as he got to his feet. "A small price to pay for keeping such a beautiful lady from being trampled, because whatever you say, you were about to get run down and meet your Maker."

Adria pulled a handkerchief from her pocket. She wanted to use it to wipe the dust out of her mouth, but instead she offered it to the man. He was young and still smiling in spite of the blood trickling down his face. "Here. Use this to stop the bleeding."

"Bleeding, am I? Won't be the first time, I can assure you. My mother used to say I could find a way to bang myself up in a church pew." He laughed and waved away the handkerchief. "But she'd have had nothing bad to say about me banging up my head helping out a lady such as yourself."

"Take it." Adria pushed it into his free hand. "And come with me. Our house is right down the street. That wound needs to be cleaned up to see if you should find a doctor."

He took the handkerchief and held it to his forehead. "Our

house? Could be your husband won't appreciate you dragging home a piece of road trash."

"Could be." Adria wasn't about to tell this man she wasn't married. "But it's the least I can do after you saved me from what you thought was sure death."

"I did, didn't I? Very well. Lead the way. A drink of water will be welcome at any rate to wash away the dust." He walked beside her away from Main toward her house. "Logan Farrell at your service, ma'am."

He waited for her to say her name back, but she saw no reason to tell him that. She was going to wash out his cut and send him on his way. He was a drover. He wouldn't be in town more than a day.

After a minute, he said, "I guess it isn't exactly proper for a lady like you to share your name with the likes of me. Even if we have been down in the dirt together."

"I think you should choose your words a bit more carefully, Mr. Farrell." She gave him a hard look.

"Indeed. Forgive me. That was ungentlemanly of me, but then no one's accused me of being a gentleman for a while now. Not since I took to the road."

His words made Adria curious. "Were you once a gentleman?" She gave him a closer look. Under the dust, his features lined up nicely with a generous mouth that hadn't quit smiling since he sat up out of the dust. His blue eyes sparkled with amusement. She had no idea what color his hair might be, since somehow he hadn't lost his hat. She touched her head. She should have looked for her hat.

"Being a gentleman is way overrated. Trust me on that, my lady. Do you think your husband will mind me calling you my lady?"

"I doubt that will be a problem." She wouldn't think about what Carlton would say if he saw her taking this drifter into her house.

She went through the gate into their yard and led him around to the back door. No sense tracking through the sitting room. She stopped before she stepped up on the porch to knock as much dust as possible off her dress. With his free hand, the man took off his hat and hit it against his pants. In spite of herself, she couldn't keep from laughing at the cloud of dust they were raising.

"The only thing better to see than a beautiful woman is a beautiful woman with a smile on her face." Logan Farrell laughed with her as he corralled his dark blond curls under his hat again.

Twelve

I n the years she'd been with Ruth, Adria had brought home plenty of strays. A few dogs that eventually found their way back to their owners. A bird with a broken wing once. Somehow they kept it alive until its wing healed and it flew away. A minor miracle. Then the children around town had learned if they followed Adria to the house, she'd give them a cookie. So it wasn't unusual to see eager young faces, both white and black, peering through their kitchen door.

To Ruth's relief, Adria had not yet brought home a runaway slave, but Ruth worried she might someday. Should that happen, Ruth would pray for divine guidance. Or maybe another miracle, one far from minor.

All that should have prepared Ruth for the stranger at their table pressing a bloody handkerchief to his forehead, but it didn't.

"I didn't know we had a visitor." Ruth stopped in the kitchen doorway and looked from the man to Adria and back to the man.

He looked up at Ruth with a smile that flashed teeth in his dust-covered face. He was a young man, with eyes that made Ruth take a second look. Very blue with that sparkle she often noted in her most mischievous students. This man was hardly a boy. Or anyone they knew. A drifter. Maybe one of the rough drovers who disturbed the peace of the town during hauling season. She wouldn't be surprised if his bright eyes were because he had imbibed too many spirits, but she didn't smell alcohol on him.

"Sorry, ma'am, but my lady here insisted I come with her so she could tend to my head." His smile was infectious, and in spite of reservations about him being in her kitchen, an answering smile curled up Ruth's lips.

With a shrug, Adria turned from the wash pan where she had pumped out water to dampen a cloth. "He insists he saved my life and in the process knocked his head against a hitching post. The least I could do was bring him home to see how badly he's hurt."

"Very kind of her too." The man flashed those eyes Ruth's way again and then back at Adria. "And I did without a doubt save her from being run down by Mac Ritchey's horses. That scalawag Mac can't handle that team, and your sister here must have been blinded by the dust and didn't realize how near she was to death. No way could I stand idly by and watch her trampled."

Nothing was really wrong with his words, and yet there was, as he sat brazenly at their small table. Adria could be foolhardy at times. Opening their door to a complete stranger was proof of that. Ruth had to wonder who the really dangerous scalawag was. Mac with the horses or this man in front of her. He was indeed a charmer. She had noted how he named her sister instead of mother.

"Whether that was true or not, we will never know." Adria folded the cloth and waited for the man to move his hand away from his head. "But, at any rate, we both ended up rolling in the dirt. My dress is quite ruined and who knows what happened to my hat."

The front of Adria's dress was smeared brown with perhaps more than mere dirt. The roads could be dreadful when the wagons were going through town. Not only that, her hair was in a shambles, with dark curls tumbling around her shoulders. Adria rarely gave proper thought to appearances, but this was definitely a scene that would greatly upset Carlton if he were to appear at their door.

Adria was in a far too intimate and familiar position with this stranger. In spite of the blood on his face, the man appeared very pleased with her attention. Ruth didn't care at all for the way his eyes kept settling on Adria. She was a beautiful girl, but his gaze upon her lacked the proper reserve of a gentleman. Not that a drover could ever claim gentleman status.

Ruth stepped into the kitchen and moved in front of Adria. "You best let me do that." She reached for the wet cloth. As a schoolmarm, Ruth had tended to many scrapes and bruises over the years. She needed to take care of this situation efficiently and get this man on his way.

"Kind of you, ma'am." The man moved his hand to reveal a gash that was still leaking blood. "Logan Farrell at your service. Or I suppose you are the one helping me and for that I am grateful." He took off his hat, and curls that might be blonde if clean tumbled down over his forehead. He pushed them back out of the way.

"Sit still." Ruth kept her voice brisk but her hand gentle as she swabbed the wound. "You need to let Dr. Adams stitch this up." She looked over at Adria. "You should have sent him straight there."

Adria turned a little pale as she peered at the wound. "I knew it was bleeding, but I didn't see it until now. His hand was over it."

"Hey, no fair swooning, my lady. Not now." He reached to feel the cut. "It can't be that bad."

Ruth shoved his hand away. "Don't touch it. Your hand is filthy."

"My face too, I'm sure." His grin was back. "Don't worry yourself, ma'am. I'll wrap a rag around my head and be fine in a few days. That is, if I don't die of thirst first. I hate to put you to any trouble, but I'd be mighty appreciative of a tall glass of water to wash this dust out of my mouth."

"Of course." Adria got a glass out of the cabinet and filled it with water.

Ruth stopped pressing the cloth against the cut while he chugged down the whole glass.

"Could I have another where that came from?" He handed the glass back to Adria.

Blood dribbled down through his eyebrow and Ruth reached to wipe it away. "It's not going to stop bleeding if you don't get it stitched up."

He shivered as he reached for the water. "I don't like sawbones. They get hold of you and kill you with their lances."

"I don't think Dr. Adams will bleed you. You appear to be doing enough of that as it is. And surely you're not afraid of a few stitches to hold your face together."

"Ugly scars make a man look tough."

"Or cowardly if that man is afraid of proper treatment." Ruth refolded the cloth and pressed it hard against the man's head.

"No one has ever accused me of cowardice, ma'am." Logan Farrell flinched and his smile slid off his face. "Foolishness, at times. Carelessness more often than that, but not cowardice."

"Nor was I, Mr. Farrell. I was merely making an observation." Ruth turned to Adria. "Tear some strips off a clean dish towel and we will get Mr. Farrell on his way. I'm sure he has business to attend to here in town."

"No, I'm free as a bird." His smile was back.

"Aren't you one of the drovers?" Adria asked as she handed Ruth the cloth strips.

"Do I look like one of those rough characters?" He held up his hand with a laugh. "Don't answer that. Just believe me when I say I haven't always kept such coarse company, but a man's situation can change in a flash. I needed a job. They needed a drover, but then the man in the lead wagon decided they had one drover too many. So here I am, as I said, free as a bird."

Ruth considered asking him what situation changed so quickly for him, but then decided some things were better unknown. She folded one of the cloth strips into a square and put it over the cut. "Hold that in place."

"I thought my hands were filthy."

"They are, but you're touching the cloth, not the wound, and I can't hold it there while I tie the bandage in place."

"Her hands might be cleaner." He tilted his head toward Adria.

"I should hope so." Ruth shot Adria a look and the girl backed away from the table. "But you holding it will work fine."

"I promise I wouldn't bite." His infectious smile flashed across his face again.

"That's good to know." Ruth wrapped one of the strips around his head and tied it in place as tightly as she could. "Wagons come through all the time. I'm sure you can get another job without a problem."

"That could be, but I'm thinking on sticking around here awhile. I thought being a drover traveling all through the countryside would make for adventure, but believe me, it's nothing but hard work, a bed on the ground, and dust and mud. So since I hear Springfield is a town of opportunities, I thought I'd try my luck here for a while until adventure calls from some other direction."

"You don't have family?" Adria sounded sorry for him. She wanted everyone to have family. That was what she had first asked Ruth to be. Her family.

"A man can't lean on family forever. There comes a time when he has to strike out on his own. See what he's made of."

"Well, we wish you luck finding a job, Mr. Farrell." Ruth kept her voice cool. "Springfield has a hat factory, a hemp walk, a couple of slaughterhouses. Many stores. As you say, opportunity."

"I can't see me making hats, but I'm sure something will jump out at me before I run completely out of coin." He drank the last of the water in the glass Adria had handed him and stood up. The blood was already seeping through his bandage.

"You really need to see a doctor. Dr. Adams is a couple of blocks away on Cross Main." Ruth went over to the sink and pumped out water to wash her hands. She needed to get this man on his way.

That needed to be soon, with how Adria's face had changed while the man talked. She was curious about him now, and that could only lead to trouble. A drifter spouting about freedom. Adria would be hearing more than he was saying. But the man appeared to be in no hurry to leave.

"You could be right, ma'am. I am feeling a little wobbly on my feet. Guess I cracked my head harder than I thought." He grabbed the back of the chair.

"Maybe you should sit back down," Adria said.

"Adria, I think it best if we let Mr. Farrell go find a doctor." Ruth used her sternest voice.

"Adria." The man flashed his smile. "A lovely name for a lovely lady."

A blush warmed Adria's cheeks as she met the man's gaze. Ruth could practically see sparks flying between them. Not at all what she wanted to see. Adria often let her emotions get carried away, but Ruth needed to nip this in the bud. She stepped between the two. "As I said, the doctor is on Cross Main. Not far, but if you have difficulty finding the doctor's house, anyone on the street can direct you."

"But what if I stagger into another post?" He looked over Ruth's head toward Adria. "I might knock myself unconscious."

Ruth was having none of it. "Then I'm sure some kind Good Samaritan will help you up." She pointed toward the door. "Good day, Mr. Farrell."

He stayed where he was. "But I thought I'd already met that Good Samaritan. Perhaps Adria could walk with me to ensure I don't stumble."

Adria started to say something, but Ruth spoke first in her best schoolmarm voice. "I think not. Time for you to be on your way. Now." She stepped over and opened the door.

"Yes, ma'am. I wouldn't want to outstay my welcome." He put

on his hat and finally stepped toward the door. There he stopped and tipped his hat at Ruth. "Your kindness is much appreciated."

Ruth inclined her head a bit in acknowledgment.

Then the man looked at Adria. "Perhaps we'll meet again, Adria, in circumstances more in keeping with a lady's sensibilities."

"That could be," Adria murmured.

Ruth shut the door behind the man, glad to see him gone. She turned to face Adria. "A man like that is nothing but trouble."

"I thought him very charming."

"Indeed. And he as well thought he was very charming." Ruth frowned. "It was a game with him seeing if he could engage your feelings. A game I fear he was altogether too good at playing."

"Don't worry, Aunt Ruth. I'm not so foolish as to let my emotions run after a man I've only just met. But how do you think it would feel to be so free?" Adria stared toward the door with a sigh. "Able to do or go wherever your whim took you."

"Whims can lead you astray. Best to think things through. Especially for a young woman like you or even an older woman like me. A lady has to consider appearances if she doesn't want to spoil her chances for a good life."

"But what is a good life? Having to fit yourself in the mold some man prepares for you? A mold that you don't like?" A slight frown wrinkled the skin between Adria's eyebrows as it always did when she was trying to understand something.

"No, my dear. Not at all. Love makes the mold you want to fit."

"Was it that way with your Peter?"

"Yes. Yes, it was." Ruth closed her eyes for a moment. It was harder and harder to bring up Peter's image in her mind, but she had no trouble at all remembering their love. She opened her eyes and looked at Adria. "I wanted nothing more than to be his wife and the mother of his children."

"And what did he want?"

Ruth hesitated. She had wrapped her wants so completely around him in her memory that she wasn't sure exactly how to answer. What had Peter wanted? "To live, but he was cheated of that chance by the cholera. But he did love me and shared my desire for children. We would have had a beautiful life together. I have no doubt of that."

"If he loved you so much, wouldn't he want you to be happy now?"

"Of course. I am happy."

"Are you?" Adria kept her eyes on Ruth. "Really happy?"

"No one can be happy every moment of life. You know that."

"But shouldn't we try for that kind of happiness?"

"I think we do try, don't you?" Ruth said.

Adria was silent for a moment as if searching for the right words before she spoke. "You should have married again. Had the babies you so wanted and that I couldn't be for you."

"I'm thankful for you being in my life, Adria."

"Yes, I know. And I'll be forever grateful for what you did for me. You were my Good Samaritan when I most needed help."

"I'm still here for you." Ruth reached to touch Adria's hand. She started to step nearer to hug her, but they had never shared that many hugs, even when Adria was young.

"But I'm an adult now, and I have to find my own way."

"That doesn't mean I must stand by and watch you make wrong decisions without trying to help you see more clearly what your future should hold."

"And I will listen." Adria leaned over and kissed Ruth's cheek. "I will always listen, but you might have to listen to me too."

Ruth squeezed Adria's hand. She chose her next words carefully. "I promise to try. I want only the best for you."

Adria smiled then. "I suppose right now the best for me would be a bath. As Mr. Farrell so ungallantly put it, we did roll in the dust and who knows what else."

"I'll put some water on to heat." Ruth turned to pump water into a kettle. She felt better when doing something for Adria. Taking care of her physical needs. Reading to her. Teaching her. That was easier than talking about being a Good Samaritan. But then hadn't the Good Samaritan been a man of action?

Thirteen

Ruth was right about Logan Farrell. He had been much too forward. Calling Adria "my lady." She wasn't his lady. Far from it. She had refused to even tell him her name, although Ruth had let that slip. Ruth hadn't aimed to let the man know anything about them. She was not at all pleased that Adria invited the man into their kitchen.

Invited might not be the right word, Adria thought as she headed down the street toward the store on Saturday morning. *Allowed.* She had allowed the man to come into their house.

Ruth could be a stickler about using the right word. Sometimes when they were reading to one another at night, she would stop the story to point out that this or that word would be better. Not only better, but more accurate. That came from writing poetry, Adria supposed. Ruth loved words. She had instilled that love in Adria too, except Adria was more interested in the power of words instead of the poetry of their sounds.

She was continually searching for the strongest words to use in her letters condemning slavery. She sent her missives in plain envelopes to a woman in Boston so no one would suspect that she was involved with an abolitionist group. For all the postman knew, she and Abigail Summers were doing no more than corresponding about the latest fashions and their marriage prospects. Abigail clipped articles from the papers and sent them to Adria. An abolitionist newspaper would never make it out of the Springfield post office.

The fact that Adria was corresponding with the abolitionists worried Ruth. Adria seemed to be good at that. Worrying Ruth. Just like with Logan Farrell. Ruth was right. Adria shouldn't have brought him to their house. She should have pointed him toward the doctor, but she really hadn't expected him to have such a gash in his head. She thought it would be a mere scrape, easily cleaned and bandaged.

As Ruth often reminded her, she forgot to think about appearances or the consequences of ignoring those appearances. Ruth was right about that too. Carlton would be upset if he heard about her encounter on the street with a drifter. Not if. When. Nothing that happened in the middle of Springfield's Main Street had much chance of being unnoticed or, once noticed, not remarked upon.

Carlton wouldn't believe the man was saving her life. She didn't believe the man had saved her life, although when she thought about it, those horses' hooves were very close when they thundered past after Logan knocked her down. Perhaps she could have been trampled. Even killed. She needed to keep that thought and an attitude of gratitude when she told Carlton about what happened. Ruth thought she should tell him. First. Before the gossips made the story even better than it was.

Perhaps she could forget to mention taking Logan Farrell home with her to dress his wound. She supposed it was wrong to keep secrets from a man she was considering marrying. But she was already doing that with her letters in support of the abolitionist cause. Carlton roundly condemned the northerners who wanted to free the slaves. If she married Carlton, he would demand she cut all ties with the abolitionists. But she wasn't standing at any marriage altars yet. She was still free to do as she pleased. Maybe not free as a bird, the way Logan Farrell had claimed, but free.

Free as a bird. A sparrow flew past her with a bit of straw in its beak. Birds seemed free, flying here and there and not tied to the earth, but how free were they? They were always busy building nests, feeding their baby birds, searching for the next worm. Not that much different than people. Busy taking care of needs. Maybe it would be better to say free as a cat.

That made Adria smile. Her Gulliver had been a free spirit as soon as he was old enough to roam. That cat would come stay with them in the winter, and as soon as the days warmed to spring, off he'd go. Out hunting new mama cats to charm, new mice to catch. Doing whatever he wanted, when he wanted.

"My lady looks pleased with the world this day." Logan Farrell stepped out onto the walkway in front of her.

"Oh, you startled me." Adria put her hand to her chest. She had been so wrapped up in her thoughts she hadn't noticed him waiting there. Obviously watching for her. "I fear I was lost in thought."

"Happy thoughts it seems."

"The best kind." She let her smile stay. In spite of his bandaged head and black eye, the man looked more presentable this morning. No blood and dirt smeared his face. His straw-colored curls looked freshly washed when he took off his hat and tipped his head toward her in greeting. His clothes were worn, but clean.

The one thing not changed was the way his blue eyes seemed to demand she notice him as he tried to charm her with his words. "The only kind. Just looking at you brings a smile to my face."

She supposed she did look much better herself, with a fresh white blouse and brown skirt and her hair properly pinned up. The requisite hat perched on her head. It was a bit frayed around the brim, but it would have to do until she could get another since she'd lost her newest hat in the dirt yesterday.

"I'm sorry about your eye," she said. "Did you find the doctor's house without trouble?"

"I did. Managed to survive his administrations. He suggested I put a steak on my eye, but I told him I'd much prefer eating a steak rather than wearing one." The man laughed. "He was a talkative old gent. Filled me in on a number of things in Springfield."

"Job opportunities, I hope." Adria did hope that, but she feared the old doctor had let Logan pump him about her own situation. Dr. Adams, the same as most everybody else in town, thought it was well past time Adria accepted her proper feminine role and married Carlton.

"Among other things."

"Dr. Adams can be quite the talker when he's working on a patient. It's his way of putting a person at ease. He's liable to say most anything then." Adria pushed a smile back across her face. "It's been pleasant talking with you, but I must be on my way." She started to move past him. She had already noted several curious glances toward them from others on the street. She hoped Carlton was at work at his father's hat factory, far from any windows.

"Wait." He touched her arm to stop her. "I have something of yours." He pulled his other hand out from behind his back and there was her hat.

"My hat!"

"I cleaned it up as best I could, but I'm afraid it's a bit battered." He brushed at the torn yellow ribbon before he handed it to her.

"But amazingly it seems all of a piece." Adria held it up to examine it. "The ribbon can be replaced." She looked back at Logan, smiling this time with no reservations or worry of what those passing by might think. "I can't thank you enough. I hated losing this hat."

"Hats are useful." He knocked the brim of his own hat up to a jaunty angle. "To keep our brains from getting fried."

Adria laughed. "Yes, or frozen according to the season. Now I do need to get to work, Mr. Farrell."

"If you will allow me, Miss Starr, I'll walk with you. I was going that way."

"Which way?"

"Whichever way you are going." His eyes flashed with a smile again.

She gave in gracefully. What else could she do? A few more steps down the walk with him would hardly matter after they'd been talking together for several minutes. Besides, Carlton didn't own her. She hadn't promised him anything. He was the one always doing the promising. Unlike this Mr. Farrell. She doubted he'd ever promised any girl anything. He let that smile and those eyes do the promising for him. Promises that probably disappeared on the wind as soon as he tired of whatever town he was in. She needed to remember that free as a bird to him had nothing to do with building nests.

Even so, she could feel her pulse accelerating as he matched his pace to hers and told her how he found her hat thrown over next to the walkways and thus safe from the wagons and horses. How long had it been since she and Carlton could talk this long without some disagreement rearing up between them?

She tried to think back. Maybe it was that picnic last October. A beautiful fall day. A basket full of ham sandwiches, apples, and Carlton's favorite raisin pie. A buggy ride out to a flat field on his grandparents' farm that backed up to a creek that fed into the Salt River. The day had been warm. The creek low. They had shed their shoes and Carlton rolled up his pants while she modestly stripped off her stockings without showing an undue amount of leg. She didn't remember who had started splashing the other one first, but soon they were both soaked. And laughing.

Carlton had caught her to him and kissed her there in the middle of the creek. And she, forgetting Aunt Ruth's warnings about being reckless when alone with a man, had kissed him back with abandon. The sun, the water, the laughter. It was like rolling down a hill. She had come to her senses and pushed him away. Shoved him actually. So hard that he fell backward into the water, but he had merely laughed again.

He got to his feet and followed her out of the creek where they sat in the sun to dry off. He didn't try to kiss her again, but he had a different light in his eyes when he looked at her. And in the buggy on the way home he talked about where they would build their house. As though the kiss had settled everything, when all it had done was unsettle Adria.

This man beside her was unsettling her too, even as she only half listened to him going on and on about the friendliness of the people here. She knew his name and nothing else except that his smile and those eyes were making her heart beat faster. Not that she'd let him know that. Now or ever.

When he paused, she murmured a few words of agreement. She would be glad to get to the store where she could settle behind the counter and attend to her job of waiting on customers. Even if Logan Farrell came in to buy something, he'd simply be another customer then. Some of the men tried to flirt with her from time to time, but she paid them no attention. She knew it didn't mean anything. They knew it didn't mean anything. But walking with Logan felt different out here on the street.

They were almost to the store when pounding footsteps sounded behind them. Even before she glanced back, Adria knew it would be Carlton running after them.

"Uh-oh," Logan said. "Whoever that is bearing down on us does not look happy. Wouldn't happen to be your fellow, would it?"

"Whether he is or isn't, that is hardly any of your concern, Mr. Farrell." Adria kept her voice level.

"Maybe not, but from the look on his face, I think maybe he's got some concerns. I better head on down the street before I get another black eye." But he was still smiling. "My mother always told me beautiful women could be dangerous."

"Was your mother beautiful?" Adria knew Carlton was only a few steps away, but she refused to look back at him.

"Actually she was. And wise as well."

"Adria." Carlton spoke behind them.

Adria turned toward him with a swish of her skirt. "Good morning, Carlton."

She gave him her sweetest smile, even though, from the color in his cheeks, he looked ready to explode. He was breathing hard from the run to catch up with them. Somebody must have gone into the hat factory and reported on her. As if she couldn't walk with whomever she pleased on the streets.

She took a breath to keep her anger from rising to match Carlton's. "Have you met Mr. Farrell? He's new to town." She looked over at Logan. "Mr. Farrell, Mr. Damon. Mr. Damon's father owns the hat factory. Perhaps you could find a position there." Adria looked back at Carlton, her smile still firmly in place. "Mr. Farrell is hoping to find a job here in town."

"We're not hiring." Carlton almost spit out the words. He obviously wasn't going to be placated with smiles.

"No worries. Hat making isn't for me anyway." Logan held out his hand toward Carlton. "But good to meet you, Mr. Damon."

"I wish I could say the same." Carlton ignored Logan's hand, and after a couple of seconds Logan let his hand fall back down to his side.

Rude. That was what Carlton was being. And unreasonable. Logan hadn't done anything to him or to her. Except perhaps save her life.

Adria pretended Carlton hadn't spoken. "Mr. Farrell fortuitously knocked me out of the path of a team of runaway horses yesterday afternoon. And got a nasty bump on the head in the process. And then this morning he found my hat that I lost when I fell and was kind enough to return it." She saw no need in describing how Logan landed on top of her. Perhaps the roiling dust from the wagons and horses had kept others on the street from catching sight of that unseemly result of their collision.

Carlton just stared at her, his frown growing darker. Surely he wouldn't rather she had been trampled than rescued by this stranger. That stirred her anger to match his. He was being worse than unreasonable.

"Look, fellow, we were just talking. No harm done." Logan held up his hands in surrender. "I'll just be on down the street."

Carlton grabbed Logan's shirt and stepped closer to him, face-to-face. "You stay down that street and away from my girl."

"Carlton!" Adria grabbed his arm. "Stop it! You're acting like an idiot."

"Keep quiet, Adria." Carlton shot a look over at her. "I'll handle this."

"You don't really want to mess with me, fellow." Logan's smile was completely gone as he stood very still, staring back at Carlton. "Really you don't. I already told you, the lady and I were having an easy conversation. Nothing for you to get riled up about. But now I suggest you let go of my shirt."

They stared at each other a moment longer, and then Carlton turned loose of the man and stepped back. "Just so you understand."

Logan smoothed down his shirt front. "I think I might be understanding more than you." He turned toward Adria, his smile flashing through his eyes again as if the whole episode had been no more than a joke. "Good day, Miss Starr."

"Good day, Mr. Farrell."

She waited until he turned and walked away before she looked at Carlton. "You don't own me, Carlton Damon. I can talk to whomever I please, and if you ever make a scene like that again, you will be the one I'm not talking to."

"But Adria, that man is nothing but trouble. Anybody can see that."

"He wasn't the one making the trouble." She gave him a hard look. "Good day, Mr. Damon."

He started to say something, but she didn't listen. She turned and went inside the store. Mr. Billiter and a customer scooted away from the window when she came in. She and the two men had obviously been the morning entertainment.

Fourteen

Keeping a deathbed vigil was not Will's favorite part of pastoring a church. Even less so since he had kept a vigil at his own beloved wife's bedside and prayed fervently for a miracle that didn't come. However, in his years as a pastor, he had attended many deaths. A duty as necessary in serving a church as preaching from the pulpit on Sunday mornings.

Births and deaths, opposite spectrums of life, but sometimes joy and sorrow joined, as they had for Mary. Entering the birthing process was a walk through the shadow of death for women. To continue the Bible directive to go forth and be fruitful often meant men must marry more than once. As Hazel told him he should.

Will pushed such thoughts aside. He must stop dwelling on his own losses and consider the joys and sorrows of his new church members. Nothing in this deathbed visit was remotely similar to his last moments with Mary. This man, George Sanderson, wasn't even a member of his church. He was of the Catholic faith. Springfield seemed to be divided down the middle. Protestants in the eastern side of town, Catholics in the west. Some said the line of demarcation was the courthouse. When Will arrived at the sickroom, the parish priest was already in attendance, prepared to give the man his last rites should the need arise.

Father Jeffers pulled Will aside when he entered the sickroom to quietly assure him of his welcome and relieve Will of any concern that his presence might prove awkward.

"Prayer, yours and mine, can be a comfort to the family." Father Jeffers kept his voice low. "Mr. Sanderson's children are growing weary. Their father has lingered longer than the doctors expected."

"I see." The man on the bed showed no sign of life except his labored breathing. His time was short. Will had seen the same scene too many times, but when it was an older man, as Mr. Sanderson appeared to be, the sadness wasn't quite as palpable.

The priest introduced the two men in the room as sons. One man turned from staring out the window to nod toward Will and the other one paused in pacing the room to shake his hand. Both men looked very ready for the ordeal to be over. A woman sat in a chair close to the bed, her hand on the sheet that covered the man. The priest indicated she was a daughter. She appeared to be the only grief-stricken person in the room.

When she looked up at Will, dark smudges under her eyes indicated she had been watching her father die for many hours. "Please pray for Father."

So Will stepped up to the man's bed and put a hand on his shoulder. He prayed for healing although he had no faith that would be. The stink of death was already in the room, and though the man continued to breathe, his spirit seemed to have abandoned his body. Will pulled up more prayer words, asking comfort for those around the man and for God's will to be done. He had never been able to speak or even think that prayer while his Mary lay dying. He saw no reason for God to take his Mary, but mortal man could not understand God's ways.

He spoke his prayer aloud and then, after his amen, silently added a plea for this man to surrender to death and end his suffering while delivering his daughter from the hope that flickered vainly in her eyes.

Will hadn't stayed at the man's bedside long. Father Jeffers was their under-shepherd. Not Will. He'd done his duty as requested. Offered his comfort. The people couldn't see how dry his own spirit was. The proper words had come from his mouth.

Later, before he retired to bed, he included the man and his daughter and sons in his nightly prayers.

Hear my cry, O God; attend unto my prayer.

He used to pray with every confidence that such would be the case. Now he didn't have that same assurance, but didn't the Bible say that God answered the prayer of faith? Jesus said such faith could move mountains if a man did not doubt in his heart but believed that whatever he prayed should come to pass. Will did not believe George Sanderson was going to rise up from his sickbed and be whole again. He had believed Mary would. Had some sliver of doubt sneaked into his prayers that took his Mary from him?

The next morning when he got to church, he was not surprised to hear George Sanderson had slipped into eternity during the night. The church was abuzz with the news, but he supposed that was normal. Springfield was not a large town. George Sanderson was a respected businessman whose hotel near the courthouse had long been a focal point in the town.

Will considered changing his prepared sermon on the Great Commission to one of comfort from the Psalms. But no, better to stay with the Great Commission sermon to assure these people he would work for church growth. Didn't all Christians want their churches bigger and better? And even in this season of doubt, Will felt no less compelled to share the gospel. Yet, at the same time, he felt akin to Peter, who had been warned by Jesus that Satan desired to sift him as wheat.

Will had helped his father thresh wheat on their farm. The wheat stalks were broken, beaten and stomped to release the grain. In the

Bible, Jesus had prayed for Peter's faith to be strong. But each man faced his own time of sifting. Would that the Lord was praying for Will to keep him from ending up broken and of no use on the threshing room floor.

When he stood behind a pulpit, he wanted the fire of belief in his words. He desired to be the Lord's servant to his people. Whatever else was bedeviling him, the love for his people had not lessened, even these he was only beginning to know. Now, as he sat in the pastor's chair behind the pulpit while the congregation sang a hymn, he looked out over the ones clustered in the pews in front of him and wanted to care for these sheep the Lord had sent him to shepherd. To keep them safe in the fold.

Forty-seven people looked back at him expectantly. Some watched him warily, as though withholding their approval until he proved worthy. Others stared up at him with childlike trust that the Lord had sent them the very man their church needed. Before Mary died, he would have been confident that was true. Now, with the devil sifting his beliefs, Will's faith was being tried as surely as Peter's had been when he had denied knowing Jesus thrice before the cock crowed. And yet even as Peter was rejecting him, Jesus was praying for him.

Will looked up toward the ceiling as they came to the end of the hymn. He knew the words so well he had no need of a book to sing. "Rock of Ages cleft for me." A prayer rose in his heart that he would find his way through this dry-bone valley with doubts rising like tares all around him. Not doubts of God's existence. He could have no doubts there, but what of his own calling to preach? Perhaps he had merely been puffed up by his skill in oratory. His mother had been so proud when he surrendered to preach. Perhaps he had basked in that pride too much. The Bible stated quite clearly that pride goeth before a fall.

He shoved such thoughts aside. A true calling or not, he was here in this pulpit with a gospel message for the people waiting so expectantly for him to speak. Whatever his failings, the Lord could take his words and empower them in the ears of those listening. That too was in the Bible.

The congregation settled back into their pews as the deacons came forward to pass the offering plates. Mr. Manderly continued to pump and play the organ. A hymn Will did not know, or perhaps the man merely lacked the skill to make the song recognizable. Mr. Manderly had donated the organ, and Will had been assured that most of the time the man hit enough right notes to enable the congregation to get through a couple of hymns each service.

Will kept his eyes on his Bible in an attitude of prayer. He never felt he should watch the offering plates being passed. What the people gave was between them and the Lord. In the church he'd led in Danville, the offering was always sufficient for the needs of the church, although now and again the deacons had insisted he preach on the blessings of tithing. Such a need might arise here as well, but no one would be ready to hear such a message from a preacher on his second Sunday.

At the clatter of the metal plates being placed on the table to the side of the church, Will stood up and approached the pulpit. He held its sides and studied the people while Mr. Manderly pumped on through the song. Will knew a few of the names now. The four deacons. Their wives. The children. He had always been good at recalling children's names. They were so pleased when he spoke their names, as though he'd given them a gift by recognizing them.

On the fifth pew was the lady who had brought him the cherry pie on Friday. A delicious pie. He must remember to properly thank her after the service. Not a hard duty at all. If she was a schoolteacher as he'd been told, she was a much more attractive teacher than any he'd had as a youth. Today, the same as the day she'd brought the pie, her blonde hair was neatly tucked under a proper hat. While he wasn't near enough to see her eyes now, he remembered they were a lovely light blue. He would not at all mind engaging her in conversation to thank her for the pie. Perhaps, according to the offering just collected, he could order another one. He kept his gaze away from the offering plates.

The young woman next to the schoolteacher was an opposite in looks. Curls of her dark hair escaped the small hat perched on her head. She did have her hair tucked up, but it appeared to be a bit unruly. A beautiful young woman, but right now, she appeared somewhat ill at ease as the music continued.

Perhaps that was due to the handsome man sitting in the pew behind her with a smile that seemed to brand him as carefree as a cowbird. Those were the birds that didn't bother building their own nests but instead waited for the opportune time to lay their eggs in another bird's nest. That left the cowbird with nothing to do but whistle through the spring while other birds worked to feed their hatchlings.

On the opposite side of the church, another young man kept peering across the aisle at the young woman. Carlton Damon. His father owned the hat factory, and a few of the deacons had impressed upon Will that this was a family he should do everything in his power to keep happy. Carlton Damon had squired a different girl into the church, but he was paying her little attention now as he stared at the woman beside Ruth Harmon.

Adria Starr—yes, that was the name Mrs. Gregory had told him for the young woman—didn't appear to notice Damon. She was looking toward the rear of the church where the black servants of some of the members were assembled. Ruth Harmon put her hand on Adria's arm, and the girl turned back toward the front, but she did appear very agitated as she shifted in the pew. He must give her a chance to talk with him after the service to see if she wanted to share her troubling thoughts.

She was an orphan. Mrs. Gregory had told him that. The elderly woman sat in the second pew, looking calm, almost beatific as she watched him. She had sent a note around to him the day before, almost demanding he come visit. Will knew better than to ignore such a summons. He needed the support of the likes of Leoda Gregory if he was going to succeed as pastor here.

Mrs. Gregory had been a wealth of information about the church members. She had much to say about Ruth Harmon and her adopted daughter, Adria Starr. More times than necessary, many more times, she had stressed that she and Mrs. Harmon were both widowed. But while Mrs. Gregory was happy in her widowhood, she suggested Mrs. Harmon surely wasn't, even though it had been years since Mrs. Harmon's husband had succumbed in the cholera epidemic of 1833.

That was when Miss Starr had lost her family too. Mrs. Gregory had clucked her tongue and noted what a tragedy that was.

"I do believe it affected the child. That and, I suppose, growing up in a house without a father figure in residence." Mrs. Gregory had dabbed at her eyes with her handkerchief. "But the girl seems to be harboring all sorts of ill-conceived ideas about what a woman should or shouldn't do. She needs to settle down and marry that nice Carlton Damon."

Her words echoing in his head reminded him of the connection between young Damon and Miss Starr. He had not encouraged Mrs. Gregory to continue with her gossip about the two women, but he might as well have tried to stop the nearby Salt River from flowing. As she continued to extol Mrs. Harmon's Christian kindness in taking in the girl and how capable she was as a teacher, it occurred to Will the old lady might be doing a bit of matchmaking. It was little wonder Mrs. Harmon had been so uneasy when she'd brought him the pie.

He thought back on their encounter. She'd given no sign she was trying to endear herself to him. She had merely welcomed her new pastor by baking him a pie. He knew the signs of flirtation, since several women in his last church seemed all too ready to be a pastor's wife. He could tell them it was not always an easy position. Mary had done it well, but she had been called to the position the same as he. Even more reason to question why the Lord stole her away too soon.

He repressed a sigh as finally Mr. Manderly allowed the organ to wheeze to silence. He waited until the man stood and then settled on the front pew. With a silent prayer that the Lord would give him words with power, he opened his Bible and began to read from Matthew 28.

Fifteen

We have to do something. I have to do something," Adria had whispered as she slid into the pew beside Ruth at the beginning of the service. "Mr. Sanderson died."
They had heard about George Sanderson's death when they arrived at church. Ruth wished the news had been kept in the dark until after the church service. It hardly seemed fair to the new preacher for the members to be so distracted by a death that actually had little to do with their church. Mr. Sanderson was Catholic. He may have passed over the threshold of this church from time to time, but his death would in no way affect Mount Moriah Church except for his slaves that he allowed to attend services here if they so desired. That included Louis.

Of course, Louis was why Adria was in such a state of agitation. She loved him like a family member. Adria hated that Louis was a slave. She hated all slavery and would have led every Springfield slave out of town and to freedom across the Ohio River if she could. But she couldn't. That was what Adria didn't want to believe. Right or wrong, slavery was entrenched in the South, and Springfield was part of it.

"Shh," Ruth whispered. "We can talk about it after the service."
They had talked about it already. The night before. Bet had told

Adria that if Mr. Sanderson died, they were all to be sold. All. It didn't matter about years of faithful service. They were no more than property. Valuable property. A skilled slave like Louis in the prime of his life would bring hundreds of dollars.

Ruth's heart constricted at the thought of Louis being put on an auction block, or Bet either. The very idea of such commerce in human beings was a blight on their land. Yet, good people, people who were sitting in pews under this same church roof as she, saw no wrong in the institution of slavery. Others, like Ruth, pushed thoughts about slavery aside as something that had always been and that they could do nothing to change.

Adria was not so passive. Ruth could feel her tension and worried she might rise up out of the pew and to start preaching before the new pastor could begin his sermon. The girl was so troubled, she hadn't even noticed when Logan Farrell came into the church and took a seat in the pew directly behind her. Ruth had not been so unobservant.

The man was evidently determined to court Adria's favor. His confrontation with Carlton Damon had been the talk of the town yesterday afternoon, although Adria had waved her hand and dismissed it as nothing when Ruth asked her about it.

Obviously, Carlton did not agree, as he had come into the church with Janie Smith clinging to his arm. Now he was continually staring over at Adria. If he had hoped to inspire her jealousy, he had picked a bad morning for it. Adria could think of nothing but George Sanderson's unfortunate slaves.

Louis was not at church. Nor was Bet, who generally came with him. The black members of the church sat on the back rows. Free to worship as long as they remembered their place. But wasn't the same also true of women, black or white, who were expected to keep their silence in church?

Ruth said a quick prayer Adria would abide by that rule this day. She certainly didn't wish for the girl to be unchurched, her membership revoked. For if such happened, Ruth could do no different than stand with Adria, whatever the cost. But it was a cost she preferred not to have to pay.

She could feel the girl practically trembling beside her. Perhaps they should claim illness and depart. But instead Ruth laid a steadying hand on Adria's arm. "Pray."

The word was barely a whisper. One Ruth wasn't sure was meant for Adria or herself, but Adria bent her head and became very still. Ruth's prayer answered. Pray God, that he would answer Adria's prayer for Louis as well. But how, Ruth couldn't imagine. Nevertheless, she could add her prayer to Adria's. The Lord attended to the prayer of the faithful.

And who had been more faithful in his Christian walk than Louis? Taking care of the whole town of Springfield while all who were able fled the cholera. Digging grave after grave. Her Peter's grave. Adria's family's grave. Nursing the sick with the help of Matilda. Taking care of Adria when the child had no one. Bringing the child to Ruth. Together she and Adria had weathered many storms, but a formidable storm like the one threatening to engulf them now needed divine intervention.

Show us a way, dear Lord.

The prayer slipped through her thoughts as the pastor began to read from his Scripture.

"'And Jesus came and spake unto them, saying, All power is given unto me in heaven and in earth.'" The preacher made the words of the Bible resound in the church. His voice was strong and deep.

He continued to read, but Ruth stopped listening and dwelt on the words of that one verse. All power. She wanted to lean over to Adria and whisper those words to her. All power. The Lord would help them find a way.

But it was not good to whisper while the preacher was delivering his sermon. Pastor Robertson looked much more presentable today than he had the day she'd taken him the pie. That day his hair had been standing on end, and his eyes had looked anything but calm. She had caught him at a bad time, but now he looked the part of a preacher. Brown hair combed neatly back from his forehead. Expression serene as he read from the Bible and then began his sermon. He didn't pound the pulpit as the previous preacher had been fond of doing to emphasize his words. Pastor Robertson spoke the words as though receiving them straight from the Lord to hand out to the people the way one might a plate of nourishing food. Here, this is what you need.

Ruth was caught up by his voice, her spirit touched. He appeared to hunger for the words as much as his listeners did.

She knew he had lost his wife to childbirth fever a couple of years prior and had not yet remarried. Mrs. Gregory had made sure to tell her so. Not that Ruth was the least concerned with his marital state. She was not looking for a husband. But Adria's words about how she should have remarried had tickled awake something inside Ruth. She wasn't too old to bear a child. If she were married.

Right on cue, a baby whimpered behind her. Probably the new Johnson baby, only two months old. Mrs. Johnson was several years older than Ruth, and she held a new baby, her tenth.

Did Ruth still desire to hold her own baby in her arms? That was such a long-ago dream. One she shared with a man she loved. She had no such man in her life now and wasn't looking for one, in spite of Mrs. Gregory's matchmaking efforts.

Pushing those thoughts away, Ruth fastened her eyes on the preacher and concentrated on his words, not on his looks. But even though she was in church, she did notice him as more than a preacher in the pulpit. Something about the sad look she re-membered in his eyes when she took him the pie made her want to know more about him. Not just as her new preacher, but as a man. That uncomfortable feeling had her shifting in the pew, as uneasy as Adria beside her.

After the services, Logan Farrell stepped in front of Adria and Ruth before they could make their way up the aisle to the door.

Ruth had to step in with polite remarks since Adria was too distracted by her worries to converse properly.

"So nice to see you here at Mount Moriah this morning, Mr. Farrell," Ruth said, even though his motives for being there were suspect. She had no desire to see Adria interested in Logan. He was not steady and dependable the way Carlton was, although Carlton wasn't exactly demonstrating maturity this day, showing up with Janie Smith on his arm and then watching Adria all morning. Sometimes young people could be so foolish.

"My mother always said a man couldn't go wrong by starting out his week in church." Logan flashed his smile that had surely made many girls' hearts flutter.

Adria hardly noticed. She did give him a weak smile before she looked past him to the door. "It's good to see you, but we really need to be going." She put her hand under Ruth's elbow to encourage her to keep moving past people.

Ruth almost smiled at the look on Logan's face. He was not used to girls brushing past him. He would be even more surprised if he knew the reason. Stepping out of a pew across from them, Carlton had the look of a dog in search of a fight. He moved away from poor Janie Smith toward Adria. Ruth, with her schoolteacher's knack of waylaying trouble, moved to Adria's other side to intercept Carlton.

"Now is not a good time or the proper place, Carlton. I suggest you accompany Miss Smith out of the church as you accompanied her in."

Ruth's words found the mark with Carlton. He looked like a whipped dog as he dropped his head and muttered, "Yes, ma'am."

Adria surprised Ruth by stopping in her rush up the aisle to look at Carlton. "I'm sorry, Carlton, but we really are in a bit of a rush." She smiled at Janie. "Hello, Janie. It's good to see you."

Carlton looked totally thrown off-kilter by Adria's smile at Janie. His attempt to make Adria jealous had failed royally. Instead, Carlton was the one beset by jealousy at the sight of Logan Farrell. Ruth couldn't keep from feeling a little sorry for Carlton. He did so want proof that Adria loved him, but romance wasn't a problem Ruth could solve for Carlton or for Adria. As for Logan Farrell, she doubted he needed anybody to help him solve anything.

She was relieved to reach the back of the church, where Pastor Robertson smiled as he took her hand. "Mrs. Harmon, thank you for coming and thank you so much for that delicious pie. I don't think I've had a cherry pie that tasty since my grandmother passed away."

"I'm glad you enjoyed it, Reverend." Ruth returned his smile. "Your sermon was very effective and the message much needed."

He turned loose of Ruth's hand and reached toward Adria. "And good to see you too, Miss Starr." He managed to capture her hand. "I couldn't help noticing that you appear concerned about something. Can I be of help? As your pastor."

Adria's eyes widened a bit, obviously surprised her unease was so evident. "That's kind of you, Pastor, but I'm fine."

Without a backward look at Ruth, she pulled her hand from the preacher's grip and escaped out the door. Logan Farrell edged past Ruth to follow her. That concerned Ruth, but she could hardly chase after them. Not with the preacher still talking to her.

"If you are going to be home this afternoon, Mrs. Harmon, I would like to come by to talk to you and Miss Starr."

Ruth wasn't sure what to say to that. She could almost feel Mrs. Gregory's eyes on her from where she stood in the church aisle behind Ruth.

Pastor Robertson must have noted her hesitation as he went on. "I hope to visit all the members. To speak of how the church can better serve our community. Would today be a good time for you?"

What could she do but smile and acquiesce. "Of course, Reverend.

Whenever it pleases you to come. We want to help the church any way we can."

"And I want to help my members with whatever needs they may have." The preacher smiled at her and finally turned to the next person in line, releasing Ruth to go after Adria and hope that Carlton and Logan Farrell weren't squaring off in the churchyard.

All appeared peaceful. Carlton was nowhere in sight. She supposed he had properly escorted Janie Smith home. Logan Farrell was attempting to talk to Adria, but she appeared to be paying scant attention to his words. As soon as she saw Ruth come out of the church, she turned away from him and hurried to Ruth's side.

"I need to go by the hotel to see Louis. They couldn't have sold him this quickly, could they?"

"No, dear. If it's an estate sale, it could be weeks, perhaps months. They will want to advertise the sale."

"It's ungodly to advertise the sale of another human being." Adria was ready to explode.

"Keep your voice down. Remember where you are."

"I do remember." But she did lower her voice as she led the way out of the churchyard. "I'm at church, an institution that is completely failing to take the proper stand in regard to this issue."

"You have to remember that many of the most influential members own slaves."

"You mean the rich members." Adria shot a look back over her shoulder toward where some of the people were clustered in front of the church, perhaps still talking about the death of George Sanderson.

"Generally, yes."

"That doesn't include us."

"Indeed not." Ruth put her hand on Adria's arm to encourage her to keep moving away from the church. She didn't want anyone to overhear their conversation. "But we're all children of God."

"So are Louis and Bet." Adria gave Ruth a beseeching look. "I have to talk to Louis."

"Yes. You should, as long as you don't cause him a problem with your abolitionist talk."

Louis was levelheaded. He would help Adria calm down. But then maybe Adria was right. Maybe none of them should calm down. Not if staying calm and letting things happen as they had always happened meant a good man would be sold down the river. Ruth shivered at the thought as Adria hurried away, not content to walk at Ruth's slower pace.

Adria wouldn't be happy about the pastor coming to call. Not today, but what else could Ruth have said? If a preacher asked to come visit, one could hardly refuse. Even if the man didn't seem to realize the gossip such a visit to a widow woman might engender.

People would talk, but she didn't have to listen. She hurried her steps. She needed to get home to see if the front room was presentable without too many stray books or papers scattered around. Especially Adria's abolitionist papers. She was supposed to keep them hidden in her bedroom, but sometimes she forgot. So far, Ruth had been able to spirit them out of sight before any visitors noticed. Even Carlton had no idea that Adria was so involved with the northern abolitionists. Perhaps it would be good if he continued to squire Janie Smith around and forgot about Adria. Off and on, the two of them, Carlton and Adria, imagined that they were in love, but if it was really love, shouldn't it be on all the time?

Ruth sighed. She had to step back and let Adria make her own decisions about love.

When she went in the kitchen door, Ruth was glad to see the applesauce cake one of her customers had failed to pick up yesterday. She had planned to let Adria take it to the store on Monday to sell by the piece, but a slice of cake along with tea or coffee would be the very thing to entertain the pastor.

She had no reason to be apprehensive about his visit. Adria would be back by then. Everything would be proper.

As she took off her hat and then began to straighten the books scattered on the sitting room tables, she wondered if Reverend Robertson read only the Bible or if he had varied interests in books. It might be good to converse with an educated man.

Sixteen

Adria walked fast away from church. She didn't run. Ladies didn't run through town. Another of those unspoken rules about a woman's behavior. Perhaps a good one. She might trip over all the required petticoats and fall flat on her face. Not to mention that a running woman would attract entirely too much attention.

Just as standing up in church and demanding people do something to stop George Sanderson's family from selling Louis would have brought disbelief and censure. A woman standing up in church and demanding anything would surely bring down the roof. Sometimes Adria thought it might be good to bring down some church roofs, to make some changes, but Ruth was always there to pull her back and make her consider the results of her impetuous leanings.

Bringing down the church roof would do nothing more than mess up the church and embarrass Ruth. Nobody would listen. Not even the new pastor, in spite of how he acted as though he wanted to help with whatever was bothering her. He didn't know what that was. He didn't realize she was ready to go against the whole town, even against the law, to save Louis from being sold down the river.

Louis wouldn't go against the law. She knew that as surely as she knew money was the reason people didn't want to consider the evils of slavery. Money. Maybe that was the answer. She could buy Louis. Ruth said they had a little money saved. Adria had a job. They could mortgage the house. Even with all that, it probably wouldn't be enough. Not for a man like Louis.

Adria was so caught up in the whirlwind of her thoughts that she almost walked past the hotel. She looked at the front entrance but then headed down the alley to the back of the hotel. At this time of day, Bet would be in the kitchen serving up the midday meal. Ruth was probably fixing dinner for them at home, but she wouldn't worry if Adria was late. At least not about her missing dinner. More likely she would be worrying about what trouble Adria might stir up while she missed dinner.

Bet came to the back door when Adria knocked. "Missus Starr, what are you doing here on a Sunday?" She slid her eyes to the side without moving her head to let Adria know they weren't alone. "Were you comin' to see what cakes we might be needin' for the funeral meal?"

A tall man stepped up behind Bet to stare at Adria. One of George Sanderson's sons. "You should come to the front desk to make inquiries," he said.

"I suppose that might have been best," Adria said quickly. "But I usually brought whatever Mr. Sanderson ordered from my aunt to the kitchen."

Ruth was always warning her she was going to get in trouble for not keeping the proper social conventions. White people in the front doors. Black people in the back doors. The man's frown got darker.

Adria grabbed at words to lessen the tension in the air. "I, my aunt and I, were both very sorry to hear of your father's passing. He was a fine man. Springfield will miss him." Adria pushed a sympathetic smile across her face. "We want to offer a couple of cakes to show we're thinking of you and all his family. I hoped Bet would know what kind might be best."

"I see." The man's face didn't soften.

Adria began to wonder if it ever did, but perhaps she was being unfair. The man had just lost his father. "I can bring them over in the morning, or if you want them this evening, you could send one of your servants to get them. Louis knows where we live."

The man's face changed, lightened a bit. "I remember you now. You're that little girl Louis brought here during the cholera epidemic after your parents died. My father told me how he found you a place with a schoolteacher."

Adria bit the inside of her lip. George Sanderson had nothing to do with her finding a home with Ruth. She very well remembered the conversation right here in this kitchen with George Sanderson ready to send her off anywhere to get her out of his hotel. Louis and Aunt Tilda had been the ones who made sure she got a good home. But it did no good to pull that memory out into the open.

"Yes, he was very kind." Adria dipped her head a little.

"Where is Louis anyway?" The man's frown came back as he looked around.

"Don't you remember, sir?" Bet spoke up. "He wanted to go start diggin' Massa George's grave. Said it was the last service he could do for him."

"Yes, he did ask me about that." The man rubbed his forehead and then looked at Adria. Finally a small smile lifted the corners of his lips. "So many arrangements to make and not enough sleep. Louis has kept things going around here while Father was sick."

"He kept things going for your father during the cholera epidemic too. Were you in Springfield then?" Adria asked.

"No, but it hit hard in Louisville too. My family and I fortunately were summering in the country at the time." He pulled his watch out of his pocket and looked at it. He was obviously ready to be through with their conversation. "Bring whatever kind of cakes you like, Miss Starr, but you'll have to deliver them. If Louis is digging Father's grave, he'll be too busy to pick them up."

"You know he dug all the graves for the victims of the cholera epidemic. More than fifty people. Your father appreciated that. The whole town did." Adria wanted to make sure the man knew how valuable Louis had been to the town.

The man had turned partially away, but now he looked back at Adria. "Were you old enough to remember much about that time?"

"A person remembers when she loses her parents."

"I suppose so, but I'd just as soon forget this week and remember my father in happier times."

"You have my sympathy, sir."

He acknowledged her words with a lift of his hand as he left the kitchen.

Adria waited until she couldn't hear his footsteps in the hallway. Then she put her hand on Bet's arm. "Are you all right?"

"Ain't no way to be all right with what's goin' on here. Doom hangin' over all our heads."

"I'm sorry, Bet."

"I knows you are, Miss Adria. You best be gone 'fore that mister comes on back about somethin' or other. You be wantin' to see Louis anyhow. But I tell you, he just like always. He don't let nothin' bother him. Says it ain't no use worryin' what we can't change, but I shore enough is worryin' plenty for him and me too."

"Whoever buys the hotel will need a cook."

"I be obligin' if you pray that's so, Miss Adria. I like it here where I knows folks and I ain't thinkin' I'll like standin' on an auction block for who knows who to be pinchin' and proddin' on me to see what kind of shape I be in."

Adria said she was sorry again. Nothing but words that didn't help anything. Bet just shook her head and closed the door.

It wasn't far back to the cemetery. And she had to see Louis. He had to know she wasn't going to stand idly by and do nothing to help him. What she might do remained a mystery, but mysteries could be solved. Ruth would help. As long as it didn't threaten her schoolteacher reputation. As long as it wasn't illegal.

Illegal. Slavery was what should be illegal. People agreed with her and they weren't all in the north. Some were surely here in Springfield too, but just afraid to speak up the same as she was.

She had no doubt that if she did ever have the nerve to speak up, George Sanderson's son wouldn't be the only one staring at her as though she were some kind of miscreant.

She hadn't liked him. On sight. Not exactly a Christian attitude for someone who just came from church, but no use pretending. The Lord could see right through any kind of smoke screen straight into a person's heart.

She started walking faster. She was smothering in her church dress with sleeves to her wrists and two petticoats under the full skirt. Its dark umber color soaked in the heat of the sun. Perhaps she should slip by the house and change into something more suited to the late June day. But no, if Louis finished digging the grave and headed back to the hotel, she might miss him. She couldn't very well show up at the hotel again.

At least not until she had cakes in hand. They did have that applesauce cake no one had picked up yesterday, but that still left one to bake. She shouldn't have promised two. Ruth wouldn't be pleased about baking on a Sunday afternoon.

A man stepped in front of her. Logan Farrell. This was getting to be a habit, one that she wasn't at all happy about at the moment.

"Where are you off to in such a hurry?"

The smile he flashed at her didn't have the same effect on her as it had the day before. She really couldn't be bothered with him right now. "Mr. Farrell, you do have a way of surprising a person. But you are right. I am in a hurry, so if you'll excuse me." She softened the words with a smile.

"Late to Sunday dinner, are you? If so, it appears you're heading in the wrong direction. Your house is that way." He pointed back toward Elm Street.

"Thank you for the reminder, but I do know where my house is." She moved past him.

He fell into step beside her. "I was heading this way. Mind if I walk along?"

"It's a free country," she said, then muttered. "At least for some people."

"So it is." He walked along a ways without saying more. "You seem upset. You aren't holding it against me that your boyfriend came to church with another girl on his arm? I mean after our little set-to yesterday."

"I haven't given you a thought." At least she hadn't since she heard George Sanderson died. Before that, she had given this drifter too much thought.

"You know how to hurt a fellow." He laughed a little. "But whether you've given me any thought or not, I've been thinking plenty about you. I can't say I was sorry to see your fellow squiring a different girl to church this day. Figured that might free you up to take a new look around. See if you might do better than Damon."

"It would be hard to do better than Carlton Damon. His family is very influential in this area."

"So why aren't you married then? If he's such a catch. Unless I'm reading the signs wrong, I'm guessing he'd be more than glad to make you Mrs. Damon."

"Really, Mr. Farrell, that's none of your concern." She frowned to let him know he had crossed the line of politeness.

He didn't seem to care. "True, but I'm just a little curious about it all. The way he was mad enough to spit nails yesterday when he saw you walking with me. He was ready to fight."

"But no punches flew." She didn't look at him as she kept walking.

"That didn't mean he didn't want to knock me silly. Then at church this morning he was hoping you'd be that mad at him, but seeing him with that other girl didn't appear to bother you in the least."

"Carlton is free to escort whomever he wishes to church." Adria kept her voice cool.

"That may be, but I can tell you he didn't have the girl he wanted on his arm today." His smile was back as though amused by the whole situation.

"Do you laugh about everything?" Adria didn't try to hide her irritation as she looked over at him. Dark stitches laced together the cut on his head that he hadn't bothered to cover with a bandage, and the skin around his eye was a motley green and black. "Even black eyes?"

"Not the first shiner I ever had." His smile didn't fade as he gingerly touched his eye. "But I didn't have to fight for this one. This colorful eye is a badge of honor, since it resulted from me saving the life of one beautiful woman, my lady." He made a little bow toward her.

She didn't bother insisting again that she would have gotten out of the way of the horses without ending up facedown in the dirt with him. Instead she said, "It looks like it would hurt. Especially when you smile."

"You've never smiled even when something hurts?" He didn't wait for her to answer. "Trust me, it's better to keep smiling. I learned a long time ago that you can stew through life or you can glide along on a smile."

"But there are many reasons not to smile in life. Sorrows. Injustices. Troubles of all kinds." She stopped to look directly at him.

"I can't deny that, and you can believe I've seen my share." His mouth stopped smiling, but the smile lurked in his eyes. "But I never saw the need to wallow in them. Best move on to an easier time."

"What if you can't? What then?"

"I guess I haven't run up on any of those kinds of times." His smile came back.

"Then you must be a very fortunate man." She began walking again. She needed to get on to the cemetery.

"Some men have to make their own fortune."

"With a smile, I suppose."

"Why not?" He looked around at the buildings they were passing. They had moved away from the storefronts to pass by a hog slaughtering place. "Are you sure you haven't lost your way?"

The smell was less than pleasant, and the hogs squealing in pens waiting their turn to be turned into bacon and hams the next day made Adria anxious to be past them and on up the hill to the cemetery. She pulled a scented handkerchief from her pocket to dab her nose.

"I haven't lost my way at all, Mr. Farrell. If you must know, I am heading to the cemetery here on the edge of town to visit my parents' grave. Something I prefer to do alone. I'm sure you understand."

The smile did leave his face then. "I do. Watched my own dear mother buried last year. She never gave up on me once, even though there were plenty of times my stepfather thought she should."

"I'm sorry." Adria seemed to be saying that a lot, but the sorrow in his eyes touched her more than his smile. A man still grieving for his mother didn't seem to be such a carefree drifter.

"That's kind of you. She did her best by me, but after my father died when I was five, we had some struggles. Barely remember my pa, but I do remember the hard times. I didn't blame her for marrying again, but my stepfather never took to me. I used to worry he'd take me to the river and drown me like an unwanted pup. I figured Ma must have kept him from it. Could be that's when I learned to keep a smile on my face."

"To fool the world."

His smile came back. "You know, it did start out that way, but after a few years it changed. The smile made a difference in how I looked at life. Gave me a leg up." He cocked his eyebrow at her. "You should try it."

"It's hard to smile when a person is on the way to the cemetery."

"We're all on the way to the cemetery, Miss Starr. Some of us are taking a longer road there than others, but long or short, a person might as well enjoy the trip."

"That's profound. Are you sure you're not a philosopher instead of a drover?"

"I'm whoever I want to be. Philosopher. Drover. Escort of a beautiful lady." His smile was practically bouncing in his eyes.

"You're irrepressible." Adria laughed. The man did have a way about him. A dangerous way, she could almost hear Ruth warning her.

"So I am, but I did make you laugh. Are you sure you don't want me to accompany you the rest of the way to the cemetery? This part of town looks a little rough."

"I'll be fine. I come this way all the time." Adria gave him a real smile. "Now, good day, Mr. Farrell. Perhaps our paths will cross again on another day."

"What day is that?"

Adria stepped away from him and looked back over her shoulder. "I suppose we'll have to wait and see."

"I like a woman who keeps me guessing," Logan called after her.

A smile played around Adria's lips as she continued on up the hill. She couldn't keep from liking Logan Farrell. He was as different from Carlton Damon as night from day. Not that there was anything wrong with Carlton. At least nothing that Adria hadn't caused with her reluctance to set a wedding date when Carlton was so ready to get married.

They used to have fun together, with Carlton in and out of their house all the time. When they were kids, they climbed the big old oak in the backyard and got a bird's-eye view of the world. They played in the field behind his house, where she liked to catch toads and make up stories about them. That would make Carlton laugh, and in turn, she laughed at the stories he told about the people who bought hats from his father.

Ruth used to say that Carlton's feet were surely under their dinner table more than his mother's. But that was before Carlton decided it was time they got their own dinner table. His eagerness to make that happen and Adria's hesitation had them forever at odds now.

Then here was Logan Farrell with his smiling eyes to play with Adria's emotions. He had a way of making her heart beat faster in a way Carlton didn't. A way she liked.

Ruth wouldn't be happy that she'd let Logan walk with her. She would tell Adria all the reasons she should be wary of a man like Logan Farrell. But what could it hurt to get to know the man better? It might make Adria appreciate Carlton's steadiness more.

Seventeen

Adria had the feeling Logan watched her walk on up the hill to the cemetery, but she didn't look back at him. Perhaps he was being chivalrous, making sure she made it to her destination safely. More likely, her behavior simply awakened his curiosity.

No time to worry about that now. She had to think about Louis. She paused at the entrance to the cemetery and looked around. The grass had been knocked down with a scythe. Adria wondered if Louis had done that too. To make the place presentable for the burying.

He was working up toward the middle of the cemetery. A tall stone monument marked the grave of George Sanderson's wife there. Nearly the whole town had been in attendance at her interment. Not like all these townspeople buried in unmarked graves from the cholera epidemic. They had lonely burials, perhaps attended by only one person—Louis.

At her parents' and little brother's grave, she paused and shut her eyes, but try as she might, she couldn't pull up clear images of their faces. They'd been gone so long now, they seemed no more than the fragments of a dream she couldn't quite capture. The family love was there. That memory was secure in her heart.

When she married, she wanted to be happy the way her mother had been. She had so loved her family.

She left their grave and passed by Ruth's husband's final resting place. She said a quick prayer for him or really more for Ruth. That she would find love again. Now that Adria was older, she sometimes wondered if taking her in had spoiled Ruth's chances for more happiness. But it wasn't Adria who had sent the potential suitors away.

At last she stood by Aunt Tilda's grave along the back of the cemetery. Thinking about Aunt Tilda always strengthened Adria's resolve. The old black woman may have been a slave, but she had never lacked courage. Whispering freedom to her babies. Whispering freedom to Adria. Of course, Adria was free, or as free as a woman could be in a man's world. But Aunt Tilda had given Adria a vision of freedom for her. For Louis. For all who were enslaved.

"You're up there with the Lord." Adria looked up at the sky and whispered the words. "Beg him for me, to help Louis find his way to freedom. You know Louis won't slip away in the night, and as much as I want to make things right for him, I'm just one person."

But you are one. One plus the Lord can do mighty things now and again. That's what Louis said back when he was digging all those graves. You remember that and make everybody else remember that too.

Aunt Tilda's words seemed to echo in Adria's head. One plus the Lord. She squared her shoulders and headed over to where Louis was climbing out of the grave he'd dug.

"What you doin' here, missy?" Louis pulled out a big square handkerchief to wipe the sweat off his face.

"I came to see you."

"Don't come too close." He held his palm out toward her to keep her away. "You might ruin your Sunday finery. Grave digging is dirty work."

"Work you've done time and again."

"Only when it needs doing. I owed Massa George this last service." He looked around at the hole behind him.

"You didn't owe him anything. He owed you. He should have set you free before he died." Adria picked up a dirt clod and threw it across the graveyard.

"Now, don't take on, missy. Things will work out." He stared down at the ground and after a moment added, "Somehow."

Adria had never heard him sound so defeated. "How, Louis?"

He didn't look up at her. "I don't rightly know. I guess I'll just have to trust in the Lord's provision." He picked up his shovel, shoved the blade into the ground, and leaned on the handle.

"Tell me, Louis, if you could ask the Lord for the provision you most wanted, what would it be? Freedom first, but then what?"

"Freedom. That would be a wonder in itself." He looked up at the sky as though counting the few white clouds that dotted the blue. "It ain't something I ever much let my mind linger on."

"But you have thought about it, haven't you?"

"Ain't no denyin' that. I reckon you're old enough to know that now." He touched his gaze on her face and then stared back down at the ground. "I never wanted you to worry your head over ol' Louis. Not so long as things was goin' along pretty fair."

"And now they're not."

"It's some troublin' with how Massa George's sons is talkin'."

"We'll think of something."

"I ain't one to be runnin' away." He looked directly at her then.

"I know that." She met his look. "But you didn't tell me what you'd like to do once we get your freedom."

"You do make a man hopeful." A smile slipped across his face as he looked back down toward the town. "I wouldn't mind workin' at shapin' iron. Shoein' horses and making plows and such. You know how Massa George sometimes hired me out to Mister Elias, the smithy over on Walnut, when he didn't have enough work around the hotel for me. Mister Elias says I has a knack for hittin' the hammer right on the hot iron."

"Then that's what we'll pray will happen. You free with your own blacksmith shop."

Louis smiled, but he looked sad as he shook his head. "That sounds fine, but I'm thinkin' it's about as likely as the sun reversing directions and going down in the east."

"The Lord could make that happen if he wanted to, couldn't he? Doesn't it say in the Bible that the sun stood still in the heavens for a whole day so the Israelites could win a battle?"

"Seems there is a story like that somewhere in the Good Book." Louis chuckled. "But I ain't thinkin' the Lord would do that for ol' Louis. Best to look at things straight on. Get yourself prepared for what is gonna happen." His smile disappeared.

"Do you remember when you and Aunt Tilda prayed for me? After Mr. Sanderson said I had to leave the hotel. I was scared, but then you prayed. And Aunt Tilda said when you prayed the Lord listened."

"He listens to everybody who has a mind to pray. You best be sure of that."

Adria watched him a minute without saying anything. His hands were restless on the shovel handle. "Are you scared, Louis?"

He blew out a breath. "Don't know that scared is the exact right word. But uneasy for sure. Only natural when things is changin'."

"You know what made me feel safest after my parents died?"

He looked up with a smile. "I expect it was huggin' that little rag doll you had. The one your mama made for you."

"That was good, but this was better." Adria stepped closer to him and took his hand. "I always knew I was safe when you were holding my hand."

His fingers curled around her hand. "You was the sweetest li'l child. When I first laid eyes on you that day a-layin' there by your mama's body and you looked up at me, your big brown eyes went straight to my heart. I knowed the Lord aimed for me to take care of you."

"Now he wants me to take care of you. The two of us, we'll

pray the way you did for me when I was a little girl, and the Lord will show us a way."

"The Good Book does say that if you pray believin', you can make a mountain move from this spot here to somewhere over there."

"I want to pray like that, but sometimes it's hard to have that sure belief my prayers are going to be answered," Adria said.

"The Lord, he always answers if you pray believin'." No doubt leaked into his words.

"Then we'll pray believing." Adria tightened her hand around his and looked up at the sky. The only prayers she'd spoken aloud in front of anyone had been simple bedtime prayers when she was a little girl or grace before a meal with Ruth. But now she kept her eyes open and pushed her words up toward heaven. "Lord, we look to you for help."

She paused, not sure what else to say, but when Louis said amen, no more words seemed necessary. Not even goodbyes. They just looked at each other for a couple of seconds. Then he let go of her hand and turned back to the grave to scrape loose dirt away from the opening.

Pray believing. All the way down the hill and back through town toward her house, those words echoed in her mind. But what exactly should she pray? Could she be bold enough to not only pray for Louis to be free but also to have his own blacksmith shop? Such a prayer seemed too much to ask. Going up the hill to talk to Louis, she had merely wanted to think of a way to give Louis his freedom. She hadn't given a thought to what he would do then.

Springfield was home to some free blacks. She looked over to the north. They lived clustered on one street in behind town. Free, but all doors weren't open to them.

Adria hurried her steps past the slaughterhouse and back to Main Street. She passed a blacksmith shop, the fire in its forge banked and waiting for Monday when the hammer would ring down on the hot iron. She paused a moment and stared toward the shop and tried to imagine Louis as the one swinging the hammer.

"Dear Lord, help me believe that can be true." She barely breathed the words aloud, but a man gave her an odd look as he passed her on the street.

Time to start acting like a proper lady and stop walking unescorted on the street. Her dress was sticking to her back and sweat rivulets were sliding down under her arms. She wondered how it would be to never have to worry about what others thought. To not have to continually consider appearances.

Like now. She wanted nothing more than to strip off her hat and take the pins out of hair to let it hang loose. To shed her much-too-warm Sunday bodice and walk around in her chemise. That was too scandalous to even consider. Only women of the night did such things. But she could change into something lighter with puff sleeves and leave off at least one petticoat when she got to the house. Then she would have to heat up the kitchen baking that cake she'd promised. Ruth was not going to be happy, but Adria had to tell the Sanderson man something.

Subterfuge. That would be the perfect word Ruth would use to describe Adria's actions. She wouldn't exactly be taking Adria to task. She was always understated with her corrections, but Adria would know she was displeased. That was the way it had always been. Ruth never got really angry at Adria. She didn't use a switch on her. Maybe that was because as a child Adria had tried so hard to be no trouble for Ruth. Especially at first. Adria lived in fear that Ruth would change her mind about taking care of her. Sometimes Adria would catch Ruth looking at her as though the very sight of Adria sitting across the table from her was still something she didn't quite expect to see.

When Adria worried about that to Aunt Tilda, the old black woman had frowned. "Now, don't you be stirrin' up trouble with that sweet Miss Ruth. She done took you in."

"But I think maybe she wishes she hadn't. She doesn't love me."

Adria had been with Ruth almost a year then. "Not like Mama did. Not like you."

Aunt Tilda's face had softened even as she leaned down to look straight in Adria's face the way she did sometimes when she was fussing at her. "Now, you listen, missy, and you listen good. There's all kinds of ways of lovin' somebody. Miss Ruth ain't your mama, so maybe she can't love you like that. You is worryin' 'bout something that ain't no worry. What the two of you, Miss Ruth and you, has might be more sister love. Sister love is a good kind of loving. It's gonna last for you."

"I just want family."

"Sisters is family." Aunt Tilda stood up and held out her arms to Adria. "Come here, child."

Adria stepped into her embrace and felt better as the old woman smoothed down her hair.

"It's all gonna work out. Long as you remember that part 'bout all kinds of lovin' ways. Miss Ruth, she lovin' you each and ev'ry time she fixes you something to eat or reads to you or takes you to church so you can learn right from wrong. And you is lovin' her when you do what she says and don't cause her no trouble."

Adria had done that for years. Tried hard to do all the right things, but now she was doing nothing but making worry lines on Ruth's face with the way she wanted to ignore the social conventions of ladylike behavior. Bad as that was, her continued support of abolitionist causes was worse. Ruth surely wished Adria would tell Carlton Damon yes and settle down into a proper southern wife's role.

She could do that. She hadn't ruled it out. But. There was always that but. And now she was thinking too much about Logan Farrell. Not as a serious suitor. She doubted Logan Farrell knew how to be a serious suitor. Perhaps that was what appealed to Adria. His cavalier attitude. That sense of total freedom.

When at last she turned down Elm, she groaned aloud at the sight of a horse and buggy stopped at their yard gate. That slowed her steps. She looked up at the sun, already dipping to the west toward mid-afternoon. She was later back to the house than she'd expected, and now she would have to summon up her manners and deal with callers.

At least it wasn't Carlton. Not unless he'd bought a new horse and buggy. That wasn't a good way to think about a man she might marry, but it was true. She had no patience for placating Carlton right now by pretending to be someone she wasn't. Again she thought of Logan Farrell. She hadn't bothered to pretend with him.

It could be the person was merely picking up the cake he hadn't had time to get yesterday. In that case, they'd have to bake two. More trouble on a Sunday, but baking another cake sounded more appealing than making polite conversation.

She slipped past the horse waiting patiently in the shade of a maple tree to go around the house to the kitchen door. That would give her a minute to get a drink, take off her fetched hat, and dab her face with a cool rag, if it was a caller instead of simply someone picking up the cake.

Adria was surprised to hear Ruth laughing when she stepped inside. An easy laugh. The kind they sometimes shared when they were reading to each other at night after a day of baking. The sound brought a smile to Adria's face.

Ruth must have heard the back door open because she called from the sitting room. "Adria, we have company. Pastor Robertson has come to call."

The preacher. That gave Adria a moment's pause as she pulled the pin free from her hat. But he had said he wanted to help, and who better to show her how to pray believing the way the Bible said.

"Coming, Aunt Ruth."

Eighteen

Ruth was relieved to hear Adria come in. As an unmarried woman, it was hardly proper to entertain a single man in her parlor without someone else there with them. Even if he was her preacher. Town gossips were ever ready to imagine the worst.

Not that she hadn't enjoyed talking with Pastor Robertson. They had shared a lively conversation regarding William Wordsworth's poetry. Ruth had smiled so much her cheeks hurt.

She brushed her hand across her face to smooth away her smile, but the pastor seemed content to leave his smile in place. And surely there was no sin in enjoying a pastor's visit.

He stood when Adria came in the room. "Miss Starr, your aunt said you would be here soon."

He was tall and very slim. Ruth supposed that might be expected for a man on his own who lacked someone to cook for him. Perhaps she should make him another pie. He had certainly tucked into the applesauce cake with enthusiasm. He had eaten three pieces without slowing down.

"I was delayed in my errand longer than I expected." Adria shot a look over at Ruth. "I'm sorry, Aunt Ruth, and I hope you weren't waiting on me, Pastor. I wouldn't want to delay you if you have other visits to make." Adria perched on the edge of the couch. Her face was flushed with the heat and her obvious hurry.

"No, indeed." Pastor Robertson sat back down in his chair. "Your aunt and I have been discussing poetry."

Adria smiled. "I'm sure Aunt Ruth enjoyed that. Did she tell you that she writes poetry of her own?"

A blush rose in Ruth's cheeks. Sometimes Adria could divulge too much information too quickly. "Adria, Pastor Robertson isn't interested in that."

"But of course I am. It's always a pleasure to discover talented members among my congregation. I'm very impressed, but hardly surprised." His smile got broader as he looked toward Ruth. "What sort of poetry do you write, Mrs. Harmon?"

He was really quite handsome when he smiled. No too-big nose or ears as Mrs. Gregory had claimed most preachers sported. The sad lines around his eyes were still there, but softened. Ruth's heart began to beat a little faster. She assured herself that had nothing to do with the preacher's handsome face but was only due to his expectant look as he waited for her to tell him about her poetry. She was never comfortable speaking about her writing.

"I merely dabble in verse." Now why had she said that? She took her poetry very seriously.

"She's too modest, Pastor." Adria spoke up. "The pieces she has allowed me to read are beautifully inspiring. Some have been printed in the city newspapers."

"That is impressive."

The pastor beamed at Ruth and her heart gave a funny jerk. Merely because they were discussing her poetry. She would have to speak to Adria after Pastor Robertson left. Some things didn't need to be shared so openly.

He went on. "You do know that several of the books in the Bible were written as poetry. Words can be musical." He was still smiling at her. "Perhaps you will allow me to read one of your poems sometime."

"Perhaps." Ruth stared down at her hands. She was being completely too carried away by this man. It was time to shift the conversation. "Would you care for more cake, Pastor? Adria?"

Adria seemed to notice the cake on the side table for the first time. "Cakes. Oh dear. I really should excuse myself to change." She sent the preacher an apologetic look. "I know it is Sunday, Reverend, but I promised the Sanderson family two cakes for their funeral meal tomorrow. Does that qualify as an ox in the ditch?"

Pastor Robertson let his smile slide away as he assumed his preacher pose again. "Every man—and woman—has to let his or her own conscience guide in that decision. After prayer, of course. But a funeral does sound to be an appropriate need."

"Yes, some funerals make for many needs." Adria's face darkened.

"Were you close to Mr. Sanderson's family? Is that what is troubling you?" The preacher's forehead wrinkled in concern as he looked at Adria. "I would be more than happy to pray for you if you want to share your concerns."

"I'm sure Adria doesn't want to bother you with her worries," Ruth spoke up quickly.

"But that's why I became a pastor, Mrs. Harmon. To help people in times of trouble as well as in times of joy. The Lord is ever ready to hear our prayers and is a stronghold of dependable strength when we have problems in life."

"I do have a question, Pastor." Adria gave Ruth a quick look and then turned back to the preacher. "About prayer."

"Who better to ask than a preacher?" A flicker of something flashed across the man's face, as though he had worries of his own in need of prayer.

"It says in the Bible that the prayer of a good man availeth much. I know a good man like that. He's always done right by everyone and lived with trust in the Lord."

Adria's lips were trembling. She was obviously near tears. Ruth scooted over closer to her on the couch and took one of her hands. Perhaps it would be good to have the pastor pray for her. While he might not share her abolitionist views, he could still surely pray for a man like Louis.

"And now he's in trouble and in need of prayer himself?" Pastor Robertson leaned toward Adria. "Can you share his need? Whatever you share with me will not be repeated without your permission."

Adria looked at Ruth, seeking permission to speak of Louis. What could Ruth do but nod? She didn't know if the preacher could help Louis in any way, but Adria needed to ask. Needed the prayers said.

"It's Louis Sanderson. He's a member of your church."

"Louis Sanderson." The preacher thought a moment before he shook his head. "I don't think I've met him. Is he a relation of the George Sanderson who died? I understood the family was of the Catholic faith."

"He's a slave, but he shouldn't be. No person should be a slave." Adria's voice was harsh.

Ruth tightened her hold on Adria's hand. "Don't get distracted, dear. Tell the pastor about Louis and why you're so upset. Why we're all upset." Ruth hadn't really let herself think about Louis, but now her heart sank as she knew what it might mean if he were sold.

Adria moistened her lips. "Louis stayed in Springfield when the cholera epidemic came in 1833. Mr. Sanderson gave him the keys to his hotel and told him to take care of things. Other shopkeepers also gave Louis their keys. Then all with the means to do so left town to escape the cholera. My parents didn't get away from the bad air soon enough. Neither did Aunt Ruth's husband. Over fifty people died. Louis dug their graves and buried them all. He found me here beside this couch where my mother and little brother died. I was sick too, and he carried me to the hotel, where he and another slave named Matilda nursed me back to health. Then they found me a home with Aunt Ruth after the epidemic ended."

Pastor Robertson's face saddened. "I'm so sorry. For both of your losses. It is difficult to lose those you love." It was evident he spoke from his own sorrow.

"Yes, well." Adria swallowed and then sat up stiff and straight on the couch. "The town owes much to Louis. It's wrong to let the Sanderson family sell him down the river as though they owe him nothing. Sinfully wrong."

"I can see why you believe that."

"Believe." Adria echoed his word. "When I talked to Louis today, he said that Jesus told his followers that if they prayed believing, they could make a mountain pick up and move to a different place." She stared at the preacher. "What I want to know is how to pray like that. Believing. I don't want to move a mountain. I just want to find a way to give Louis his freedom."

Pastor Robertson stood up and came over to kneel on one knee beside the couch. Not directly in front of Ruth and Adria but to the side. He reached for Adria's other hand. After a slight hesitation, she surrendered it to him.

"There are many verses in the Bible that speak of prayer. Here's one that might be of help to you from Philippians. 'Be careful for nothing; but in every thing by prayer and supplication with thanksgiving let your request be made known unto God.' The Lord wants to hear our prayers. He asks for our prayers."

"But does he answer them?" Adria asked.

"God always answers, but we must remember there are many answers." The pastor's voice deepened as though he were beginning a sermon.

"But Louis needs the right answer."

"We can only look to the Lord for that right answer." His eyes were intent on Adria.

"But—"

"Shh, Adria. Let Pastor Robertson speak his prayer." Ruth squeezed Adria's hand. "Answers to prayers can't come if those prayers are merely examined and not offered in faith."

"Your aunt is right." The pastor looked up toward the ceiling instead of bowing his head. "Lord, we come to you with a burden upon our hearts for this man, your child, Louis. Please help him, and if you have work for us to do in order to bring an answer that will touch hearts and further your kingdom, reveal such to us. Amen."

"Amen," Ruth whispered the word after his. His voice had wrapped around her and made her feel the presence of the Lord as she hadn't since Peter died. Since then, she had gone to church and said many prayers. Dutiful prayers for Adria and for her students. Bless this child. Bless that family. But she hadn't asked the Lord to show her work to do since she'd taken in Adria.

Even then she had merely said a passing prayer that the Lord would lead Adria to someone else for care, but Louis, who surely did let the Lord guide his footsteps, had brought Adria to her. Perhaps she feared another challenge she didn't want to face. Yet, now she felt the preacher's prayer waking something inside her. If there was a way to help Louis and in so doing, help Adria, she was ready to surrender to the Lord's will and step out in faith. Louis deserved that from her. Adria deserved that from her.

Adria kept her head bowed an extra moment, obviously intently trying to pray a believing prayer that would free Louis. But hadn't Ruth prayed such prayers over Peter to no avail? She pushed that thought aside. She must pray as Adria said. Believing with faith in the Lord's providence.

When she looked at the preacher, the sad memory of his own loss was evident on his face. Somehow she sensed he had prayed the same sort of desperate prayers for his wife as she had for Peter. What had he said moments ago? That there were many answers. Neither of them had received the answers they sought. Would the same be true this time?

But she had no reason to anticipate an answer that would bring sadness. Not yet. Adria was right. Louis was a righteous man. If the Lord showed them a way, they needed to be ready.

Adria opened her eyes and looked first at Ruth, then settled her gaze on Pastor Robertson. "We've prayed. Now what do we do?"

The preacher looked a little taken aback by her direct question. Perhaps praying was all he had expected to do, but it was evident Adria wasn't ready to sit back and await miracles from heaven.

Pastor Robertson released Adria's hand and stood up without answering. Ruth wondered if he might be saying another prayer for guidance. Adria's gaze didn't waver. Her face radiated belief, a look that made Ruth remember that day on her doorstep when Adria, as a child, had laid down her rag doll and reached for Ruth's hand. Trusting. Believing Ruth would help. Ruth felt a new prayer rise up inside her that the preacher wouldn't say something to disappoint. Not only Adria. But Ruth too.

He pulled in a deep breath. "You are right, Miss Starr. We have prayed. Believing. But very few prayers are answered with a lightning bolt. Let us continue to pray and be open to the Spirit throughout the day and even in our sleep this night. I have found it is often after sleeping that we awaken with ideas we can pursue with appropriate fervor. The Lord will inspire our thoughts if we will be still and await his guidance. Do you see the wisdom in that?"

Adria looked ready to reject the preacher's logic, so Ruth spoke up. "Pastor Robertson is right, dear. We don't have to have an answer today. Mr. Sanderson's funeral isn't until tomorrow, and then it will take his family some time to prepare a sale of any property. Nothing is going to happen to Louis overnight."

Tears filled Adria's eyes as she looked down at her lap where Ruth still held her hand. "I suppose you're right."

A tear dropped on Ruth's hand. Adria sometimes shed tears of anger, but rarely did she allow anyone to see her sadness. Even when she first came to live with Ruth and so missed her mother and father, she hid her tears from Ruth. So this tear burned into Ruth's skin.

"We will find a way," Ruth said quietly.

"Yes," the preacher added. "I shall come to call again tomorrow after the funeral. I won't be leading the service but feel I should make an appearance there."

"The whole town will be there. Mr. Sanderson was a leading citizen here in Springfield." Ruth looked up at the pastor. She hoped he was sincere about wanting to help Louis.

Adria pulled her hand free from Ruth's, dashed her tears away, and stood up. "Thank you, Pastor, for listening and for your prayers. But if you will excuse me, I have cakes to bake."

Ruth stood up too. She watched Adria out of the room and up the narrow stairs before she said, "Thank you for coming to call, Pastor. I hope you will find your pastorate at Mount Moriah fulfilling. And I do apologize for burdening you with our worries for Louis."

"He is one of my sheep too. Jesus is the shepherd, but I am the under-shepherd of the church. I want to help every member."

"But many of your members are slaveholders. We would not want to embroil you in a situation that would cause division in the church. Adria is strong in her abolitionist views and I can't say she's wrong. Slavery does seem to be an unsightly stain on our hands."

"Don't concern yourself, Mrs. Harmon. I will let the Lord lead me." The preacher smiled again and clasped Ruth's hands between his. "I trust he will not lead me astray."

She liked the strength of his hands around hers. Her cheeks warmed again as she struggled to remember he was her pastor and not simply a man come to call. She slipped her hands from his and cast about for something to say. Her gaze fell on the cake. "Would you like to take some of the cake home for your supper?"

"I couldn't." He waved his hand. "I quite made a pig of myself already enjoying too much of your delicious cake."

"Nonsense. Wait a moment and I'll wrap up a few pieces for you." Ruth picked up the cake and went out to the kitchen. Slicing and wrapping up the cake steadied her.

By the time she carried it back to Pastor Robertson, she was in control of her emotions again. She smiled and saw him on his way. It was only after she closed the door that the color rose in her cheeks again as she thought about him promising to return on the morrow.

Nineteen

Pray believing. The words circled through Will's head as he drove his buggy home to get ready for the evening services. Had he prayed believing with Mrs. Harmon and her niece? Sometimes he worried he was merely playing at being a preacher these days. Saying the words with no faith that his prayers would reach the Lord.

No, he couldn't think that. He was girded about by the Word of the Lord. He knew the Bible. The Lord had blessed him with a good memory to allow him to hide many Scripture verses in his heart where he could call them up in answer to whatever need was presented to him by one of his congregants. He had done that today with the passage about prayer.

And yet he had felt something of a hypocrite. Not that he hadn't prayed with great sincerity. He had. He understood Adria Starr's worries. Such concern was valid for this man, Louis. A slave was considered no more than property in this state. Valuable property in most cases. When money was involved in right and wrong, often those judging let money sway their decisions and their actions.

Will even agreed with Miss Starr's anger over the injustices of slavery. By choice, his family had not been slaveholders, but at the same time they had never publicly protested the lack of freedom for men and women loved by God the same as he and his family.

In the pulpit, Will had preached that one should always treat servants with kindness. Such was plainly spoken of in the Bible. Plus it was not to be forgotten that one was advised to be a servant for God. Hadn't Jesus himself taken the basin and towel in order to wash his disciples' feet and demonstrate the need to have a servant's heart? Will wanted that heart. But then his very human heart had been wounded until he felt as though he merely limped along helping others.

He unhitched and brushed down his horse. That was necessary whatever day it was. Then he put the mare out in the small lot behind the house. He hoped the grass there would last through the summer. Else he would have to pay to have the horse kept at the livery stable. Each penny mattered for a man in his position. He might need to find some way to add to his income. After all, he promised to send money to Hazel for Willeena.

His heart constricted when he thought about Willie. He had done the right thing leaving her with Hazel, but had he done the right thing to run away to another town? He could claim the Lord's leadership. He did claim the Lord's leadership. The Lord could use him wherever he was sent, and perhaps he was here in Springfield just for the purpose of helping this righteous man, Louis. On the morrow, he would seek out Louis to assess the situation and need.

He went back out to the shed where he kept his buggy to fetch Mrs. Harmon's delicious cake. Whoever married that woman would soon be round as a barrel. But the fact she had been a widow since the cholera epidemic in 1833 indicated she had little interest in marrying again. The same as he. Still, should he ever consider a new wife, a woman such as Ruth Harmon would certainly be a fine choice.

He turned from the thought. He had no desire to remarry. Instead he needed to focus his energy on getting deep into the Word in order to find his way back to the confident faith he had once possessed. A preacher trembling on the edge of faith was little help to his church. But then had not David often cried out to the Lord when he obviously felt as low as a worm?

Will pushed it all aside. He had an evening sermon to deliver. Perhaps he would preach about that righteous man's prayer this night. Let each person who heard determine in their own mind which righteous man had inspired his message.

But first he'd have a piece of Mrs. Harmon's cake. As he sat at his table, his Bible unopened in front of him, and enjoyed the spicy taste of the cake, he thought of how pleasant it had been to converse with her. He smiled when he thought of her eyes, the color of a summer sky. A lovely woman not only in looks but also in spirit. Taking in an orphaned child with no husband to help her had required an abundance of both courage and faith. The thought of returning to see Mrs. Harmon the next day was not in the least distressing.

こめ◯◯つ

Ruth Harmon was right about George Sanderson's funeral. When Will arrived at the hotel where the family had elected to have the final service, there was hardly room to squeeze into the spacious lobby. Chairs were set up in every available spot, and men stood two deep against the walls. Several black people gathered outside at one of the open windows, while a cluster of white men stood at one of the others. The town had indeed turned out to say goodbye to one of their own.

Will stopped inside the door to survey the gathering. He wondered if Ruth Harmon and Adria Starr were in the group or still baking the promised cakes for the Sanderson family. From the back, many of the women looked the same in their black dresses and hats. Everything in the room was dark as the gloom of death shrouded the room. Black crepe hung across the windows and around the coffin. Even the large bouquets of roses situated around the casket looked faded, as though the black in the room cast a pall over them.

Such was how funerals were to be. Serious. Dark. Final.

Here and there, Will picked out a member of his church. Leoda Gregory sat on the second row, directly behind the family members. She must have staked her claim to that chair hours ago. Mr. Manderly stood on the other side of the room, casting his eyes about, perhaps for an organ to offer his services. Just as well, no such instrument was in sight. Father Jeffers had taken up a position beside the casket with the daughter, who was dabbing her eyes with a handkerchief. One son sat on the front row with a woman and several restless children. The other man paced in the small area between the casket and the chairs.

The air was stifling with so many crammed into the space. It would hardly be surprising if some of the less hardy women wilted and perhaps fell from their chairs in a faint. At last Will picked out Ruth Harmon by the tilt of her head and her blonde hair that contrasted so dramatically with the mourning black. Adria Starr sat beside her but without the calm demeanor of Mrs. Harmon. The younger woman kept peering over her shoulder, perhaps trying to see this man, Louis, she wanted so desperately to help.

Will stepped back out the door to surrender his bit of space to those who knew George Sanderson as neighbor and friend. After a deep breath of the outside air, Will felt better in spite of the way the sun was hot on his back. Thank goodness the family was sensible enough to schedule an early service. No amount of roses or any kind of flower would mask the body's odor with the kind of heat the day was promising.

Without trying to edge near a window, he found a place in the shade of the building to wait with respectful silence for the service to be done. It hardly mattered if he heard what Father Jeffers might say. Prayers sent heavenward would be of more use than his attention to words about a man he didn't know. He did hope the service would be a comfort to the grieving daughter.

A deceased person should have at least one person who sincerely grieved his or her passing. George Sanderson's daughter seemed to fill that role today. Would his own daughter someday grieve his passing or had he relinquished any hope of that when he left her behind?

To keep from thinking about Willeena, he looked out at the multitude of buggies waiting in the road. Will had not brought his buggy. The walk through town was not that far, and if he should decide to go to the cemetery to see Mr. Sanderson to his final resting place, that too could be accomplished on foot. The funeral procession would proceed slowly, and Will was certain many would walk behind. Especially the blacks gathered around the far window. They would be expected to show their owner respect. Perhaps they were ordered to do so.

He couldn't read their faces to know what they might have honestly thought of the man who kept them in servitude. One man stood apart, head bent in an attitude of prayer. He was a strong-looking man in the prime of life. If a slave, one of value.

As Will watched, several of the black men and women left their places near the window to come stand around the man, as if drawn by his strength. Could this be the man, Louis, who so concerned Miss Starr? He did not appear to be agitated but instead seemed to possess that peace spoken of in Philippians that passed understanding. Will had prayed for such peace many times in the last months, but it eluded him. Now he watched the man, the perfect picture of that peace, and wondered if his impression was true.

"You're the new preacher in town, aren't you?"

Will had been so intent on the man in prayer that he didn't realize another person had stepped up beside him until he spoke.

"That I am. Will Robertson at your service, sir." Will turned toward the man, who was short with a girth that strained the buttons of his coat.

The man pulled out a handkerchief to wipe sweat off his face. "Good to meet you, Reverend. Haskell Abshire here. I work for the druggist, J. C. Moffett, down the street a ways. Town all but closed down for the funeral so thought I'd come pay my respects too. Didn't expect to be standing around out in the sun though." The man held out a hand for Will to shake. Then he took his hat off to reveal his bald head and fanned his face a moment. "It's too hot for a funeral. Better to die when winter's coming or going."

"One can't choose the time for his parting." Will kept his voice low. He didn't want to show disrespect for the funeral proceedings inside.

"True enough. Pity about old George. I figured he'd make it a few more years. He wasn't all that much older than me and I'm healthy as a horse." He put his hat back on. "Folks say that, but horses up and die too. All the time."

"Did you know George Sanderson well?'

"In Springfield, you know everybody well. Not all that many people to know, but I can't say that George and me were close or anything like that. I'm not in his league, seeing as how he owned the hotel and all those slaves over there. Me, I own a hat." The man touched his hat again with a smile. "That isn't entirely so. I do all right, but I have to chop my own wood and my wife has to mop her own floor. No servants around our house."

"I see." Will looked toward the hotel, uneasy with the man's barrage of words during a time for silence, but no one seemed to be paying any attention to their conversation.

"I saw you eyeing them over yonder." The man nodded toward the black man Will had been watching.

"Yes, the man there in the middle appeared to be praying."

"That wouldn't surprise me. That's Louis." Abshire shook his head. "George didn't do right by him. Should have taken steps to free the man before he died. Would have only been right after what Louis has done for George over the years. But then, maybe death sneaked up on George before he got around to doing what he ought to have done. That happens to a man from time to time. You know what they say where that road paved with good intentions leads. I'm guessing you come across that often enough in your preaching profession. Folks aiming to do good but never getting around to it."

"Man has a proclivity to sin."

"Yes, sir. Ever since Adam let Eve talk him into biting that apple." Abshire pulled out his handkerchief to mop his face again. "It's hot as Hades out here. Be nice if a breeze would spring up to mark George's passing."

"It is hot for June." Will kept his voice extra low and looked toward the front door of the hotel in hopes the other man would take the hint and stop talking. That didn't happen.

"That Louis, he goes to your church, doesn't he?"

"I've only been here a couple of weeks, so I still don't know all the members."

"Well, I know he's one of them. Maybe hasn't been to any services since you got here, what with George dying and all."

"Perhaps not."

Abshire looked from Will toward where Louis stood, his head up now as he talked quietly to those around him. "Could be you should say some extra prayers for him, seeing as how you're his preacher and all. I hear those boys of George's are anxious to turn their father's property into cash so's they can carry it away from Springfield. They're going to put everything on the auction block and waste no time about it. Nothing right about it, but that's how it is."

"I will certainly pray for him and for all of Mr. Sanderson's family. I hope you will too, Mr. Abshire."

Will bowed his head in an attitude of prayer and was grateful when the man drifted away to bend somebody else's ear. But it was good to know other Springfield citizens besides Mrs. Harmon and Miss Starr were upset about Louis being sold. That gave Will more hope of finding a way to obtain this man's freedom.

He would go with an open mind and a listening ear to Ruth Harmon's house after the funeral. If they all three could pray believing, as Miss Starr claimed this man standing a few feet away did, then the Lord might smile upon their plans, whatever those plans turned out to be.

The prayer of a righteous man availeth much. He wanted to believe he could be that righteous man praying. He wanted to be that man, had thought he was before Mary's death brought him low. Now he tossed on a sea of uncertainty.

He looked back over at Louis. His shoulders were squared, his jaw set as he stared toward the hotel door. A righteous man whom Will felt called to help, no matter the consequences. And there could be consequences to stand up for the slave of an influential Springfield family.

"Thy will be done." Will softly whispered the words as men carried George Sanderson's body out of the hotel and down to a funeral carriage.

Will waited as people streamed out behind the family. When he saw Ruth Harmon's slight figure, he made his way through the people to step up and walk with her and Adria Starr. His heart lifted when she gave him a look of welcome.

Twenty

The funeral was awful. Absolutely awful. Adria would have gone outside to stand with Louis, but Ruth gripped her arm and insisted she stay in the seat beside her. She was right, of course. Ruth was always right. Adria couldn't go stand with the Sanderson slaves. Not without causing upset and problems for Louis, for Ruth, for herself.

Not that she would have made any kind of scene. She could have just stepped out into the open air where at least she could breathe and not feel as though she might melt in a puddle of mourning sweat. Why couldn't white be the color of mourning? Angel colored. But no, everything had to be black. Black soaked up the heat. Stored it against your skin. Made you wonder which would happen first—you fainting dead away or the priest finally concluding his elaborate praises of the deceased.

Adria felt damp with sweat. Even her head was sweating under the black hat kept solely for funerals. Many of the ladies around Adria looked every bit as miserable. Several pulled fans from their reticules and waved them back and forth while others glared at them with disapproval. Adria envied their bit of stirred air. Better a bit of disrespect than a second funeral featuring you.

Ruth meanwhile sat perfectly still except for the moment she had grasped Adria's arm to keep her in her seat. Ruth's face barely glistened and no sweat drops ran down past her eyes as they did on Adria's face. If Adria lived a hundred years, she would never be the lady Ruth was almost effortlessly.

Carlton sat with his family close to the front, as befitted their position as a family of wealth in the community. Carlton had glanced back at her once without a smile. In fact, she wasn't even sure he was looking for her and not Janie Smith. Not that she cared, she tried to tell herself. She had other things to worry about.

But she did care. Whether she wanted to say yes to marrying Carlton or not, she did love him. At least she was pretty sure she did. Some. And she'd always been positive he loved her. Maybe not exactly the way she wanted to be loved as an independent woman able to think for herself. Even so, there was a certain amount of comfort knowing a man like Carlton wanted to marry her. Now maybe he didn't. Perhaps he had glimpsed the real Adria and was ready to give up on her ever being the wife he dreamed of her being.

It was all so confusing. Thinking she didn't care whether Carlton loved her when she did. Then what about Logan Farrell with those remarkable eyes? The very thought of him was enough to make her heart speed up. Steady, comfortable Carlton or dangerous, unknown Logan Farrell. Why dangerous? He'd done nothing to make her think outlaw, but a woman knew a dangerous man by instinct.

She pushed thoughts of them away. She could simply spurn them both. Take Abigail up on her suggestion to come east and stay with her. Fight for freedom for the slaves and for women. What better freedom than shrugging off the idea that marriage and family was a woman's most important goal in life? And yet, hadn't she always wanted family?

If only Aunt Tilda were still alive. Then, in spite of sitting ramrod straight with sweat running down the inside of her dress and the priest's incomprehensible words floating over top of her head, a smile sneaked out on her face.

She dabbed her upper lip with her handkerchief to hide that smile as she could almost hear Aunt Tilda speaking in her ear. "Missy, you're over-thinking it all. Worryin' a freckle into a canker sore. Just give it time. The right answer will most likely occur to you. And whether it does or not, another worry is sure to come along to push that worry right out of your mind."

She already had that worry. Louis. Everything else could wait. Not that worrying would help anyhow. She needed to be praying. With belief, the way Louis prayed.

When they followed the crowd out of the hotel, the preacher stepped up beside Ruth. Adria was surprised when Ruth almost smiled before she remembered she was at a funeral. But she definitely had a welcoming light in her eyes. Obviously the man's love of poetry had made an impression.

They didn't speak. Just gave each other a little nod of acknowledgment. Then Pastor Robertson shortened his stride to match Ruth's as Adria was accustomed to doing as well. The carriage carrying George Sanderson's body moved slowly down Main Street. Those few who hadn't been at the funeral stepped out on the street to stand quietly as the procession passed. If Logan Farrell was among them, she didn't see him. Some of those walking behind the procession dropped out to join those on the sidelines.

If the preacher hadn't been walking with them, Adria and Ruth might have done the same, but once he joined them, they seemed to have to finish the course with the Sanderson family. At least the carriages and buggies were moving so slowly they only stirred up a little dust. The sheriff had blocked the street so no wagoners or drovers could come through during the funeral procession.

At last the ordeal was over. The coffin was lowered in the grave and the family dropped in their symbolic handfuls of dirt. Carlton looked across the grave directly at Adria while the priest spoke the final prayers. He didn't smile. Neither did she. A graveyard wasn't a place for smiles or the words necessary for them to mend their relationship.

The preacher returned with Ruth and Adria to their house, where they carried chairs out into the backyard to sit under the shade of the oak tree that had to be over a hundred years old. Strong with deep roots and shade a person could count on all through the summer.

Was that how she was in Springfield? Depending on those roots and the shade that not only Ruth provided but Louis as well. The thought of stepping away from that shade started up a tremble inside Adria. Even if she merely stepped away to take Carlton's hand in marriage.

She would have to leave this house, this life, for something totally different. Perhaps Ruth could tell her how she should feel. Ruth had made that step into marriage, and from the way she appeared to welcome the preacher's admiring glances today, it could be she was softening toward the idea of a suitor. The pastor, a widower, was a very eligible prospect.

The church members had much discussion about calling a pastor without the helpmate of a wife. Many were against it, but others suggested an unmarried man would have more time for ministering to the needs of the church. Then a few suggested the Lord would supply the man with a wife if he were meant to have one to help him in his ministry.

Adria looked at Ruth and then the pastor sipping the lemonade Ruth made before they left for the funeral. She had set the pitcher in a pan of cool water from the well to be sure it would be fresh and reviving. They needed reviving after the long ordeal of the funeral.

She and Ruth had shed their black jackets when they reached the house. The white blouses underneath were of a summer material, which, along with the bit of breeze in the oak tree's shade, made the long skirts bearable. Dust rimmed the hem of Adria's skirt, but Ruth must have found a cleaner path to walk or had found a moment to brush her hem when she went in to fetch the lemonade. Adria wasn't concerned with her soiled hem as she helped Ruth carry out bacon sandwiches and cucumber slices. A raisin pie was waiting for dessert. Ruth must have risen before dawn to have time to bake that before the funeral.

When Adria had commented on the trouble Ruth had gone to, Ruth waved away her words. "He's our preacher. If he's here at lunchtime, it's our duty as church members to offer him a meal."

The blush that rose in Ruth's cheeks told more than her words. A blush that still lightly tinged Ruth's cheeks now and made her even lovelier than usual.

But whether or not romance was awakening between Ruth and the preacher, Adria couldn't let them forget the purpose of their gathering.

She was just about to tell them so, when Pastor Robertson put his plate back on the small table they had moved out beside the chairs and said, "I didn't speak with the man you are concerned about today, Miss Starr, but I did take note of this Louis. A man worthy of help. Even a Mr. Abshire was in agreement of that."

Ruth looked a bit alarmed. "You didn't tell Haskell Abshire about our efforts for Louis, did you?" She hesitated, then went on. "Haskell has a tendency to talk overmuch."

"What Aunt Ruth is trying to nicely say is that if Haskell Abshire knows about something, everybody in town will know before nightfall," Adria said.

The preacher chuckled. "I have no doubt that is true, but not to worry. I listened. He talked."

Ruth smiled with relief. "Yes, I can imagine that to be so. Haskell would have been happy to have a new ear for his many words."

"But the interesting thing about those words was that he gave voice to the opinion George Sanderson had done his servant, Louis, an injustice by not giving him his freedom before death took him." Pastor Robertson looked thoughtful. "If that is the general consensus of the townsfolk, perhaps that will help your campaign to free Louis."

"I don't think the son I met yesterday in the hotel kitchen is going to be swayed by public opinion. Bet says he is counting the worth of everything." Adria looked over at Ruth. "You said you have a little money saved. Do you think we could buy Louis?"

"We wouldn't have nearly enough." Ruth looked sad to have to say that. "Not even close. You know what prices they put on slaves."

"Even if we get a loan from the bank? Our house could be collateral." Adria leaned forward toward Ruth. "And maybe I could get Carlton to help."

"Or perhaps you could get Carlton's family to buy him?" Ruth suggested. "His family treats their slaves well."

"No." The word exploded from Adria. "I want Louis to be free. He deserves to be free."

"Do you think you could convince Carlton of that?" Ruth looked doubtful of that being possible.

"I don't know. Perhaps with the proper encouragement." A yes to Carlton's marriage proposal in exchange for help in securing Louis's freedom. That wouldn't be a terrible exchange, since she had been considering that yes anyway. If only she could be sure that yes was the right answer for her.

Pastor Robertson held up his long slender hand. "Wait, ladies. Let us give this more thought and prayer."

"We prayed yesterday." Adria wished the words back as soon as she said them. A Christian should always be ready to pray. Believing.

"Yes, indeed we did." The preacher only smiled. "And we will need to continually pray for the Lord's intervention. But consider this, ladies. If others in town feel as Mr. Abshire did, it could be that they, these others, would be willing to contribute to a freedom fund for this man, Louis."

Adria felt a ray of hope at the preacher's idea. "Do you think so?"

"No, I don't *think* so, I *believe* so, and I'm going to keep believing so as I pray this week."

"Who would ask for the money?" A worried frown wrinkled the skin around Ruth's eyes.

The preacher blew out a long breath. "I doubt I would be well received in that role."

"I'll ask." Adria was already making a list of shop owners in her head.

"I'm not sure that would be seemly. A woman asking businessmen for money. Especially a young woman like you." Ruth shook her head slightly at Adria before she went on. "Perhaps if I went with you."

"But you would hate that, Aunt Ruth." Adria knew how hard Ruth tried to stay away from any kind of controversy.

"True, but sometimes a person has to do hard things."

"You would do that for me?"

"For you." Ruth reached to touch Adria's hand. "And for Louis. You aren't the only one in Springfield or in this family who owes a debt to Louis."

"If there are many, then that bodes well for our plan," Pastor Robertson said. "Plus, you might be surprised at the help you may get. Even from the young man you mentioned. Carlton Damon. A man anxious to impress a certain young lady." The preacher smiled. "And there was another young man Sunday who appeared to want to win your favor. Someone told me he was a newcomer to town. Rather like me, I suppose. He slipped out before I had a chance to say anything to him yesterday morning. What was his name?" The preacher's brow wrinkled as he thought. "Oh yes. Logan Farrell."

"I don't think—"

Before Ruth could get any cautionary words out, Logan Farrell came around the house.

"Did somebody say my name?"

He was smiling and his eyes zeroed in on Adria. Something about the man just seemed to pull the light to him. Or perhaps he brought the light with him, because suddenly everything around Adria seemed brighter.

"Miss Starr." Logan nodded toward Adria and then turned his smile on Ruth and the pastor. "Mrs. Harmon. Reverend."

"Mr. Farrell, to what do we owe the pleasure of your company?" Ruth gave him the look she used to freeze misbehaving students in her classroom. It was obvious she didn't welcome him showing up without an invitation, and that invitation wasn't likely to come from her.

Logan looked so surprised at Ruth's cool tone that Adria had to cover her mouth to hide her smile. He recovered quickly. A man quick on his feet.

"I came by to thank you, Mrs. Harmon. That sawbones you directed me to was a right fair doctor. Stitched me up neat as anything." He touched the cut above his eye. "He should have been a tailor he's such a hand at stitching. But then I come around your house to hear somebody calling my name."

Pastor Robertson stood up to shake Logan's hand. "I had commented on you being at church yesterday, Mr. Farrell. We were glad to have you there."

Ruth relented then. "Adria, why don't you get Mr. Farrell a glass of lemonade and a piece of pie?"

"I wouldn't want to put you to any trouble, but that does sound good." Logan leaned back against the oak tree.

"I'd be glad to," Adria said. "But I did promise Mr. Billiter I'd come in to work after the funeral." She should have already headed for the store. They couldn't activate their plan today anyway. People wouldn't be ready to contribute to a fund to buy Louis until they were absolutely sure the family intended to put him up for sale.

Logan pushed away from the tree. "Then forget the lemonade. I'll walk you to the store."

"You're not walking my girl anywhere." Carlton burst around the corner of the house and glared at Logan.

Logan didn't flinch. "How many girls do you have, Damon? Seems you were with someone else Sunday morning."

Pastor Robertson stepped between the two men. "Come, gentlemen. Best keep your wits about you in front of the ladies. Ladies who have the privilege of deciding with whom they keep company."

Logan's smile didn't waver while Carlton looked like a storm about to happen.

"It was nice of you to stop by, Mr. Farrell." Adria flashed an apologetic smile at Logan as she stepped over to take Carlton's arm. "And you too, Carlton. If you have a few minutes, we can talk while you walk me to the store."

Carlton gave Logan a look. "It appears the lady has made the wise choice."

"Perhaps so." Logan laughed with no indication he was bothered in the least. "But I'm no sore loser. I'll see you on down the road, Miss Starr. Mrs. Harmon. Reverend." With a nod, he was gone.

Adria had the sudden urge to drop Carlton's arm and run after Logan. But she needed Carlton's help with their plan for buying Louis's freedom. She couldn't afford to alienate him now. Not to run after a man she barely knew.

Twenty-one

Will had stood up ready to intervene when young Damon came around the house with his angry words. Love could make a man do foolish things, especially when green-eyed jealousy took control of him. Will was thankful that was something he'd never known personally, since Mary had never given him the first reason to doubt her faithful love. From the time they met, they had been sure the Lord was instrumental in their paths crossing.

Things didn't seem the same for young Miss Starr. Not with the way her face had brightened when the first young man appeared. She might have walked away with Carlton Damon, but her eyes had lingered on Logan Farrell at the same time. Much better to be sure of one's romantic path, as he had been with Mary.

"I apologize for that, Pastor." Ruth Harmon wrung her handkerchief in a knot as she peered after the departing young people.

"No need, Mrs. Harmon. It's not the first time I've seen a man angry at another man he feared might steal his sweetheart's affections."

"Yes. Adria can't seem to make the commitment Carlton wants." Ruth sighed and started stacking up the dishes. "He is a wonderful young man from a fine family. She would never want for anything if she married him."

"When one is choosing a life partner, I would advise considering more than simply the prospect of a comfortable life." Will handed her his empty plate.

She looked surprised at his words as she took the dish. "But there are necessary things in life. Shelter. Food. Clothing."

"Indeed. But would you consider those more necessary than love?"

"You must be a romantic, Pastor." Her smile lightened the blue of her eyes. "I should have guessed that about a man who loves poetry."

"I do think the Lord intends us to be happy. Don't you agree, Mrs. Harmon?"

Interestingly enough, Will noted a lightness of his own spirit when the woman in front of him smiled. No doubt she was expecting him to follow the others and be on his way, but he really didn't have anywhere to go except to his house. While he could certainly profit from more study of the Scriptures, the empty house with its deafening silence wasn't appealing. Hadn't he just said the Lord wanted his people to know happiness? So Will made no move to leave as he waited for Ruth's answer.

Her brow wrinkled as she considered his question. "I don't know. I've always been sure he wants us to be good, or at least as good as we humans can be. Then obedient to his will and with generous hearts to care for others. That's part of loving our neighbors. But I've not seen a command about being happy."

"All those things you mentioned, if we do them, can lend to happiness. In Proverbs 17 a verse says, 'A merry heart doeth good like a medicine, but a broken spirit drieth the bones.'"

"A merry heart." She echoed his words. "Sometimes I wonder if the cholera epidemic took my chances for merriment."

"Are you never happy?" Will studied her face. He asked her the question, but at the same time, he wondered if he had let his broken spirit dry up his joy.

"Am I happy?" She paused a moment before going on. "While

I have walked through some dark valleys, there has always been the promise of light ahead. Yes, I am often happy." She tilted her head and stared up at him. "What about you, Pastor? I know you've experienced grief, as I have. And if I may be so bold to speak, sometimes your smile seems reluctant to lift from your lips to your eyes."

Then before he could fashion an answer, she appeared to lose her boldness as a blush warmed her face. She lowered her eyes. "Forgive me, Pastor. I don't know what came over me. I don't normally speak so recklessly."

"Nothing to forgive, Mrs. Harmon. I am pleased you feel comfortable enough with me to speak so plainly. Many don't, you know. They seem to think a preacher is somehow not a normal person, but rather someone who doesn't face the same challenges as they and thus does not feel the same grief and disappointments. But we are men far below saints and in need of grace the same as those in our congregations."

"Even so, that's no excuse for my rudeness." She kept her head down as though embarrassed to look at him.

He wanted to tip her face back up so he could look into her eyes. He shoved his hand in his pocket. "Actually, you are right in what you've surmised. I do often let my broken spirit overpower my merry heart. My Mary, that was my wife, she was the one with the merry heart. A smile ever ready on her lips. One that shone from her soul, if you know what I mean."

She looked up at him then. "I do. My Peter was the same way. So generous in his spirit. Much more than I."

He stared down at her, and though Mary smiled in his memory, he was glad to see Ruth Harmon's smile in front of his eyes. His next words rose up inside him almost without conscious thought. "If you don't have a busy afternoon planned, I would appreciate you taking a ride with me."

She looked more than a little surprised by his invitation. Truth be told, he was surprised by his words. He rushed on before she could refuse. "Merely to help familiarize me with the area around Springfield. That would be of immeasurable help in my service to the church."

She frowned slightly. "But you don't have your buggy with you."

"That could pose a bit of a problem." He had gotten so carried away by her smile he forgot about walking to the funeral. Certainly if he had looked down at his dusty shoes, he would have remembered.

"You didn't misplace your horse and buggy at the hotel, did you?" A smile twitched the corners of her lips. "They are rather large, after all." The smile won out. "I do once again apologize, Pastor, but you have to realize I have taught school for many years. My students have lost almost everything you can imagine, including a horse from time to time. But so far none of them have ever lost a horse attached to a buggy."

"I can understand why," he said. "One would have to work hard to accomplish that."

"It would take proper talent." In spite of the fingers she pressed against her lips, a giggle bubbled out. That seemed to break down her rules of propriety and laughter spilled out. A merry heart indeed.

Merriness that must be contagious, for he started laughing with her. Laughter that surely burst from every line of his face, and it felt good. After a moment, he said, "A talent I lack, thank the Lord. But I can walk back to the parsonage and get my horse and buggy and return if you would consider showing me around the town."

She was no longer laughing, but her eyes were still definitely merry as she looked up at the sky. "It does look like a lovely afternoon for a buggy ride should you wish to return with your found buggy."

"Barring unforeseen circumstances, I shall do so."

It had been a long time since his feet felt so light as he hurried back toward his house. At the same time, he walked purposely without making eye contact with those he passed, for fear they might want to engage him in conversation.

⁘

Now why had she agreed to go riding with him? Lovely afternoon or not. She had cakes to bake and a book she longed to read once she finished her chores. Ruth stared at the place where the preacher had disappeared from sight.

What would it hurt to go for a ride with her preacher? The baking could wait a couple of hours and a church member was obligated to help her pastor. That's surely all it was. His way to learn about the town. Just as he said. But she had noted a certain jauntiness in his step as he left. And the laughter.

A smile came back to her face now as she carried the dishes into the kitchen and placed them next to the dishpan. She'd felt like a schoolgirl overcome by the giggles. And had acted like one too. What must the man think of her? But he had laughed with her. Both of them finding amusement in something as nonsensical as him forgetting he hadn't come to her house in his buggy.

The cake pans were lined up on the cabinet. The fire was banked awaiting more wood for her baking. But the afternoon stretched out in front of her and she was feeling younger than she had in years. She turned from the pans and hurried to her bedroom to change out of her funeral clothes. A summer dress would be more appropriate for a buggy ride. And a hat with a blue ribbon.

She'd wait to put on the hat until the preacher returned. After all, he might not. Something unforeseen might delay him. A pastor had to deal with the unexpected happening among his church members at any time. His job was to be there when they called upon him. But as she slipped on the light blue dress and tied the ribbon sash, she hoped no one was at his house waiting for his help. She hadn't taken a buggy ride with a gentleman since Peter died.

That thought gave her a moment's pause as she remembered showing Peter the area when he was a newcomer to Springfield just as Pastor Robertson was now. She picked up Peter's Bible from her desk and opened it to Proverbs to find the verse the preacher had quoted. Proverbs 17, he had said. She ran her finger down the page and there it was. *A merry heart doeth good like a medicine.*

She closed the Bible and hugged it close. Perhaps it was time to let her heart be merry again. Peter would understand. His merry heart had brought happiness to those who knew and loved him. And oh, how she had loved him.

But love was like a candle, he had told her once. No matter how many candles you light from the first candle, the flame never goes smaller unless the wick is faulty. She didn't want anything to be wrong with her wick to lessen her flame of love, and sometimes in the years since Peter died, she wondered if that might be the case.

Even with Adria she had always held something back. Not that she didn't love Adria. She did, but taking in an orphaned child hadn't been how she planned to have children. Could she yet have the family she had once so desired?

The very thought made her cheeks burn. The man had merely asked her for a buggy ride and that only to help him learn about his church field. She needed to rein in her imagination. Nobody was thinking anything about love. At least nothing more than Christian love for one's neighbors.

She busied herself in the kitchen, measuring out the ingredients for her cakes and trying not to listen for the clock on the mantel in the next room to strike the hour. She was just deciding on how much longer to wait before she started mixing the eggs and milk into the dry ingredients when a horse whinnied.

She moved to the sitting room doorway to look out the front window. The preacher was stepping up on the porch. In spite of her stern words to herself earlier, her heart gave a little jump. Oh dear. Perhaps she should claim a headache and send him away. People would see them together and imagine all sorts of things. None more far-fetched than the ideas trying to sneak into her head.

She jumped at the knock on the door. "Pull yourself together," she whispered as though she were talking to a recalcitrant student. "He's a preacher. Not a suitor."

But hadn't he just told her earlier how preachers were men like any other with the same hopes and dreams? Same griefs and sorrows too. He could be a friend as well as her pastor. A friend first. If the friendship grew, then would be the time to pray for answers about love.

She grabbed her hat off the hall tree and opened the door. His smile was as warm as hers radiating out to him. "Give me a minute to put on my hat, Pastor, and I'll be ready."

She turned to the small mirror on the hall tree and adjusted her hat quickly. She glimpsed him in the mirror behind her and her cheeks warmed yet again at the way his smile lingered as he watched her.

"There." She stuck in a hat pin and turned back toward him. "I'm ready."

"You look lovely," he said. "Like a fresh breath of spring."

She wasn't sure how she should respond and simply nodded a bit in acknowledgment. Then as he continued watching her, she decided he must be waiting for words. "Thank you."

"Could I ask you a favor, Mrs. Harmon?"

"Certainly."

"I know you may think it forward of me, but I really would consider it a favor if you could bring yourself to call me by my given name. Will."

"Will?" Her heart sped up. Surely that wouldn't be proper.

"Yes. Most people assume my full name is William or Wilhelm, but that's not the case. My mother had some interesting ideas and one was that what she named me would serve as inspiration in my life. Will. As in 'please, Lord, give this son of mine a strong will.' She had hopes the name would give me an advantage."

"Does it?"

He laughed. "Not really. Just makes me have to explain again and again that, no, I am not named William. But I treasure the name anyway, since it was a gift from my dear mother."

"I can understand why."

"But do you think you can bypass social formalities while we enjoy our ride together? Let me be Will and you Ruth. Just two people exploring the town and becoming friends." After the barest of hesitations, he added, "Ruth."

She threw caution to the wind. "I don't see why not, Will."

"Excellent."

When he held out his arm, she tucked her hand through his elbow and walked with him outside and down the walk to his buggy. He matched his steps to hers, even though his legs were surely twice as long as hers. That was what a friend would do.

Twenty-two

The first notices about the sale of George Sanderson's property, including his slaves, went up at the hotel before the week was out. The talk at Billiter's Mercantile was that the Sanderson sons were in a hurry to divest themselves of their father's property in Springfield in order to return to their lives in other towns. Neither they nor the daughter had any interest in keeping the hotel going.

Adria listened to all the talk at the store but kept her silence. Ruth and Pastor Robertson both thought it best to wait until the town was sure Louis was going to be sold before starting a campaign to buy his freedom.

She had talked about it to Carlton that day he'd walked her to the store after George Sanderson's funeral. He had been on his best behavior after showing his jealousy in front of Pastor Robertson. So he hadn't spoken against the truth that the town owed Louis his freedom for what he'd done during the cholera epidemic, but she feared he was merely indulging her. He probably thought trying to procure Louis's freedom was simply a bizarre idea she would eventually forget. Sometimes Carlton acted as though he didn't know her at all.

Perhaps no one could really know a person completely. Even

Ruth looked at Adria at times as though she wondered about the woman she had become. But at least Ruth had gathered her courage and stopped worrying about what the townspeople might think. She was ready to stand up for Louis. The pastor's support had made a difference there. Pastor Robertson didn't know Louis, but he was willing to risk his pastorate at Mount Moriah to help this worthy man.

"We need to make it all about Louis," Ruth insisted at breakfast the day after the notices were posted. She put her teacup down and gave Adria a steady look across the table. "If you flaunt any abolitionist ideals, people might be turned against helping Louis."

"But slavery should be abolished." Adria looked up from the bread she was buttering. "It's a blight on our state. On our country. Our very constitution proclaims all men created equal."

"I don't disagree with any of that." Ruth held up her hand. "So spare me the lecture. But if we want this to work and find a way to free Louis, we have to be realistic in our thinking. While we may believe slavery is wrong, there's little we can actually do about it when the laws in our state make such legal."

Adria put her bread down and clenched her fists. "We can fight those laws. Overthrow them."

"I admire your passion, Adria. Really, I do." Ruth ran her finger around the rim of her cup. "But what do you think would happen if we did go stand on the courthouse steps and demand the laws change? Two women with no brother, father, husband to support us in our fight. First, we couldn't be assured of support if we did have those men in our lives. Secondly, we would be roundly condemned for speaking out in public." Ruth looked over at Adria. "You do remember telling me about the strong resistance the women in the East encounter when they dare speak openly, don't you?"

"You're right, of course." Adria sighed. "My friend Abigail says any woman courageous enough to step beyond the privacy of her parlor to speak out is roundly condemned. Not so much for what they say about abolition but simply for daring to speak in public.

Even men in the abolitionist movement are ready to shout them down." She picked up her bread and took a bite. She chewed slowly and stared at the wall, seeing nothing. After she swallowed, she said, "I sometimes wonder if I could be as brave as those women."

Ruth reached across the table to place her hand on top of Adria's. "You are brave. You were the bravest little girl I ever met and you haven't lost a bit of that courage."

Adria looked at Ruth. "I want to believe that, but sometimes I wonder."

"You're at a wondering stage in your life. Wondering about decisions for your future."

"I just don't know what I should do, Aunt Ruth. I don't mean about Louis. I'm absolutely certain I must do anything I can to help him be free. Whatever the cost." She dropped her gaze back to the bread on her plate. "It's what I should decide for myself that I don't know."

"Follow your heart."

"That sounds good, but what if your heart is confused?" Adria slowly raised her eyes back to Ruth's face. "Did you feel confused when you thought about marrying Peter?"

"Not at all. I felt as though I'd been waiting for him all my life. I was a little younger than you when he came to Springfield, and I knew at once I wanted my future tied to him."

"That sounds so romantic."

"I suppose it does." Ruth squeezed Adria's hand before she turned loose to pick up her teacup again. She took a sip. "I was very happy when he seemed to enjoy settling his eyes on me too."

Adria raised her eyebrows a little at Ruth. "I think there's a certain preacher who likes settling his eyes on you now."

Color flashed in Ruth's cheeks. She was so fair she could never hide a blush. But she didn't try to deny it. "You might be right." She stood up and began gathering up the breakfast dishes. "Whether anything comes of that remains to be seen."

"But you're not worried about it?"

"Worried? I'm not sure that's the best word for what you mean. There's no reason for me to be worried. Apprehensive? That might be more descriptive."

"Don't try to avoid an answer with a word study." Adria shook her head a little. "Worried. Apprehensive. Concerned. Whatever word is best. Are you?"

"It never hurts to exercise our minds to come up with proper words, but I'm not sure I'm any of those. I've made my way as a widow for many years. If the Lord intends that to continue, then I am content with my lot. But it's different for you, Adria. You're young. You need to embrace the opportunities of life."

"You think I should marry Carlton." Adria didn't make it a question.

"He would give you a good life." Ruth turned from setting the cups and saucers in the dishpan. "Is the attraction not there for you?"

"I thought it was, but now I'm not sure." Adria pushed away from the table. She needed to go to work.

"Logan Farrell has turned your head."

"He does make me wonder." Adria brushed crumbs off her skirt. "I don't think I should wonder, do you? Not if I love Carlton enough to marry him."

Ruth didn't answer Adria's question. Instead she said, "You don't know anything about Logan."

"That's just it. I don't, but I think I might like to."

Ruth shook her head. "You have to make your own decisions." She turned to pour water from the teakettle into the dishpan. "You best be on your way or you'll be late. Oh, and it could be you should find Louis and tell him what we're planning before we start asking around town for funds to buy his freedom. Pastor Robertson plans to mention it in church on Sunday."

"What if we don't get enough?" Adria felt the worry of that deep in her heart.

Ruth's mouth tightened. "We will not even consider that. We're praying. You and I and Will. The Lord will hear our fervent prayers."

Will. Adria sneaked a look over at Ruth, who didn't seem to realize she had spoken the preacher's first name. That must mean the name had come easily to her lips. Teasing words sprang up in Adria's mind, but she held them back. If the preacher was courting Ruth and she hadn't slammed the door in his face, Adria didn't want to do anything to spoil that. Ruth would make an excellent pastor's wife should the two of them decide to join hands on that path.

Adria positioned her hat on her head. The straw hat was plain except for a deep blue ribbon that made her think of Logan Farrell's eyes. He did have remarkable eyes, and the most remarkable thing about them was that simply thinking about those eyes made her heart speed up a little. Did she feel the same when she thought of Carlton's hazel eyes that could change color according to his mood? And that mood hadn't been so good lately.

Perhaps that was what was wrong with their relationship. Carlton seemed to always be two, sometimes only one, word away from anger. Weeks had passed since they had done anything fun together. No picnics. No sitting in the swing on his porch holding hands while watching the lightning bugs blink on and off. No walks with the moon and stars for lights after she and Ruth finished baking. That was more her fault than his. She kept putting him off, afraid he would insist on an answer to his proposal. An answer she did not have.

Ruth had said she felt no confusion at all about pledging her love and life to Peter. If Adria loved Carlton enough to marry him, shouldn't she be as sure? She shouldn't be thinking yes, then no, as though she were plucking the petals off a daisy. Perhaps she needed to break it off completely. Let Carlton know she loved him as a very dear friend, but that wasn't enough for her to consider marriage. She needed more, even if she couldn't exactly put her finger on what that more was. But if she did that, what about their campaign to raise money for Louis? Then again, it surely wasn't right to string a man along simply to accomplish a purpose, even if that purpose was a good one.

She didn't have time to figure all that out right now. After a glance at the clock on the mantel, she called a goodbye to Ruth and headed out the front door. Wednesdays were slow mornings, so Mr. Billiter wouldn't be upset if she happened to be a few minutes late. Ruth was right. Louis had to know they were working for him. She didn't want him to despair. Not that he would. Or at least reveal that to her.

Louis still treated her like she wasn't much older than the little girl he'd found next to her dead mother. Careful for her feelings. Wanting to make things easier for her. That included sparing her sadness if he could. Maybe he was the one she needed to ask advice about Carlton. But no, she knew what he'd say. He'd tell her it was the Lord she needed to be asking for guidance.

Aunt Tilda was the one she wished she could ask. That thought made her smile. She knew what she'd say too. *Child, you were born free. I ain't denying you done seen your share of trouble, but you still free to live the life you want to live. Long as you is brave enough.*

"Or wise enough to know what life I want," she muttered under her breath.

She looked around hoping nobody noticed her talking to herself. Lately she was never sure when Logan might pop out of a doorway or around a corner. He had to be watching for her, but last time he appeared beside her on the street, he said he had a job with Walter Byrd's wagon-making establishment on the east end of town.

"Not what I intend to do forever," he'd said. "But it will do for the time being to put some coin in my pockets."

"What do you want to do forever?" Adria had asked.

"I don't know about forever. Best not tie up a fellow's life that long, but I intend to go west. Clear to California. They say that's where a man can find a new start."

"Do you need a new start?"

"Every man does." Logan flashed such a smile at her that her knees went a little weak. "That is, if I don't meet a woman so beautiful she takes the wandering right out of my feet."

"Maybe you'll find a woman who wants to wander just as much as you do."

"Then all the better." He gave her a considering look. "You wouldn't happen to know a woman like that, would you?"

Adria was saved from coming up with an answer by a man shouting out to Logan from a line of wagons going through town. With relief, she had smiled a goodbye to Logan and ducked into Billiter's Mercantile.

Ruth would have been aghast if she'd overhead that conversation. Adria herself was a little amazed at her brazenness. Logan had a way of making her throw caution to the wind. Not that she was ready to chase after him on an unknown adventure. But what would it be like to see California?

Adria gave herself a mental shake. She must be out of her mind to even consider the idea of going west.

At the hotel, she didn't go to the kitchen door. She couldn't face Bet with no way to help her find freedom. Besides, she had to remember Ruth's advice about not firing up the town about abolition right now. People would shout her down. Was she courageous enough for that? Perhaps. But she wasn't willing to risk Louis's freedom or have the town turn against Ruth, who would be condemned along with Adria by association.

Nor did she search out Louis in the buggy house or wherever he might be working. Instead she went in the front entrance. As Ruth continually cautioned her, she needed to do things the proper way. The son she'd met in the kitchen after George Sanderson died was at the front desk.

He looked up from the account book he was examining. "Miss Starr, have you brought us more cakes?" He smiled. "Those you brought last week were delicious. I intended to send a note around to thank you, but it's been hectic trying to get Father's affairs in order." His smile faded as he glanced down at the books and papers scattered across the desk. "Father had his own unique bookkeeping system."

"No thanks were necessary, and unfortunately I didn't bring a cake today. We'd be glad to bake something for you if you have a request, however."

"I'll check with Bet about what we might need." He gave her a curious look. "But if you don't have cakes to deliver and I assume you have no need of a room, what can I do for you?"

She made up something on the spot. "My aunt is in hopes she can hire Louis to fix one of our windows that's difficult to open." They did have to lift the kitchen window just so in order to open it. She smiled at the man. "Your father was always kind enough to allow Louis to help her with such repairs since she's a widow. She lost her husband in the cholera epidemic, you know. Of course, she always paid your father for whatever work Louis did."

Those words about paying someone else for work Louis did nearly choked Adria, but she got them out and even managed to keep a smile on her face.

He frowned a little and let his gaze slip to the books in front of him. It was obvious he was ready for the conversation to be over. "I'm sure that can be arranged. I think Louis is helping the blacksmith over on Walnut today. I can send somebody to tell Louis to go by your house later today to fix your window."

"That's kind of you, Mr. Sanderson. But I'm on my way to Billiter's Mercantile where I work. I pass right by that blacksmith shop. With your permission, I can ask Louis if he'll have time to look at it."

"Fine." The man almost smiled as he waved Adria on her way. "Tell him he's free to help you."

If only he were really free. She turned toward the door and then looked back at the son. He'd already shut out everything but the numbers in front of him again.

She considered telling him their plan to purchase Louis for what he'd done for the town. That might make the man lower the price, but then the way he was studying those account books, he appeared to want every penny possible from his father's estate. She'd ask Pastor Robertson to talk to him. Maybe the preacher could appeal to the man's Christian generosity, if he had any, and it was wrong of her to assume he didn't.

She liked Elias Brown's blacksmith shop. He was a gentle giant of a man, something like Louis, with broad shoulders and strong hands for swinging his hammer to shape the hot metal. Years ago he had twisted a piece of metal in the shape of a star that still hung on her bedroom wall. He had never minded her stopping by to see if Louis was working with him. Even if Louis wasn't, Mr. Brown always greeted her with a smile as big as he was.

Ruth had insisted she stop going to his shop once she reached the age of twelve. That was when a girl had to start acting like a lady, and ladies had no business hanging around a blacksmith shop. So many things were forbidden a lady. To please Ruth, Adria reluctantly accepted the rules of society and practiced ladylike behavior.

But when she reached eighteen, Adria gave up on ladylike occupations and found a job at Billiter's Mercantile. Definitely not something a lady should do. As Carlton continually informed her. Marriage is what he recommended to change her wayward behavior. What everyone recommended. Probably even Mr. Brown, should she ask him.

"Well, if it isn't Miss Starr," Mr. Brown said now when she stepped into the shop. "It's been a while since you came by to see the metal glow. Like a star, you used to say."

He laughed and she laughed with him. She was glad to see he and Louis were the only ones in the shop. "And you used to say, glow like me."

"Since you were a Starr. What can I do for you this day?"

"I came by to see if Louis might stop by our house later to fix a window. I asked Mr. Sanderson at the hotel and he gave his permission." Adria looked past Mr. Brown to where Louis shaped a white-hot piece of metal with glancing blows of the hammer.

"Let me ask him. Can you help the ladies out, Louis?" Mr. Brown called over to Louis.

"Later, sir, after we finish this gate you is making." Louis smiled over at Adria and then quickly back to the job he was doing. A man couldn't let the metal cool unless he wanted to start over with whatever shape he was making.

Mr. Brown looked back at Adria. "I don't know what I'd do without Louis to help." He held up fingers that were twisted with arthritis and then rubbed his shoulder. "Not with how the rheumatism got into my shoulders. May have to close the forge down after they sell Louis." His smile was completely gone. "Can't see how those Sanderson boys can do that, but I ain't got no say in it all."

Louis kept hammering the metal as though he couldn't hear what the blacksmith was saying. Adria glanced over at Louis and back at Mr. Brown. "Aunt Ruth and I, with the help of Pastor Robertson, have a plan to change things for Louis. Almost everybody in Springfield owes Louis for what he did during the cholera epidemic. I do, for certain, and Aunt Ruth too."

The blacksmith frowned. "What you got cooked up?"

There was no reason to keep it a secret now that the sale posters had gone up. She looked straight at Mr. Brown. "We're going to raise money to buy Louis and give him his freedom."

The hammer stopped pinging on the metal, but Adria kept her eyes on Mr. Brown, who gave a low whistle. "That's going to take a pile of bills. A fellow like Louis won't sell cheap."

"No, but I believe enough people in Springfield will know it needs doing." Adria kept her shoulders squared and didn't break eye contact with Mr. Brown.

"Have you collected any money yet?"

"Not yet. You're the first person I've talked to." She still didn't look at Louis, even though she knew he was watching them.

"I see." The man reached under his blacksmith apron and pulled out a couple of bills. "Then let me be the first to give toward the freedom of this man."

Adria took the money and at last looked over at Louis. He had turned from the anvil, the hammer in one hand and the tongs holding the metal turning from white hot to a dull glowing red in the other.

He stared at the blacksmith. "I'm mighty beholdin' to you for that, sir." And then he looked at Adria and a tear slid down his cheek through the gleam of sweat before he turned and thrust the metal back in the coals of the forge to reheat it.

Twenty-three

The money started coming in. Practically without any effort on their part. Ruth hid her amazement each time Adria reported a new donation. After all, she had claimed to be praying believing and she had hoped fervently their plan to raise money for Louis's freedom would be successful. At the same time, she had been wondering how to help Adria through the disappointment when it wasn't. Perhaps in spite of her talk of believing in prayer, she didn't. Not the way she should. Maybe she should ask Will to recommend Scriptures to bolster her faith.

Sunday, Will chose the Bible passage about the Good Samaritan for his sermon and then claimed the Good Samaritan title for what Louis did during the cholera epidemic. The fifty-five graves he had dug. The fifty-seven cholera victims he had buried. How he'd helped others too sick to care for themselves. He had stayed in the town guarding property and life when everyone else able to do so deserted the town to escape the sickness.

Ruth had been one of those who fled the town as Peter begged her to do before he died. But the guilt of not staying with Peter's body to see he had a proper burial still scratched at her heart. It didn't bear considering the macabre scene that might have greeted returning townspeople, if not for Louis burying the dead.

That was the reminder Will impressed on the people two days ago. *Remember when fear clutched your hearts and death stole your loved ones away. Remember how you were too afraid or too sick to do what needed to be done for those loved ones. This good man, with God-given strength, stepped into that gap, and now that man needs our help.* The special offering taken up at the end of the church service gave Ruth hope. Not that they had nearly enough, even with the money Ruth had saved for Adria to go to a finishing school. Not something Adria wanted to do anyway. Perhaps that was a dream Ruth had more than Adria, who chafed at the idea of being a lady with servants to do her bidding. She wanted nothing to do with any of that.

The desire to elevate Adria to a more privileged position in society could have come straight from Ruth, who had never had the opportunity to be a lady. Even if Peter had lived, she would not have had a life of ease. Not on a schoolmaster's pay. But she would have had a completely different life as a helpmate to Peter and mothering their children. Perhaps she could have raised one of those imagined daughters to embrace the gentle life of a lady.

Instead, she had Adria, whom she had treated more as a sister than a child. Matilda had mothered Adria. Dear Matilda, who had desired freedom more than food and water but had never tasted it here on earth. Ruth, in many ways, owed her own freedom to Matilda. Without learning to bake bread and cakes to sell, she would have had to marry one of the suitors who showed up at her door, whether she could bear the thought of living with one of them or not.

But she had learned to bake in the old chimney ovens and then had invested in one of the newfangled cast-iron stoves. What a wonder that stove was turning out to be, especially in the summer when a lesser fire was concentrated to heat the oven chamber.

She lightly ran her fingers over the scrollwork on the top warming oven. Simply looking at the stove made her feel rich. A strange thing to think, when she had to spend hours in the kitchen baking every week to satisfy orders. No lady of leisure with naught to do but toy with writing poetry. Any time for poetry writing had to be chiseled out of her day.

Now she banked the fire in the side chamber. More bread was rising to bake later. But Ruth needed to take some raisin cinnamon bread to Mrs. Gregory, who had cornered her at church on Sunday and insisted she couldn't wait until Friday for the bread. When Ruth had suggested Adria deliver the baked goods before work, Mrs. Gregory insisted that wouldn't do at all.

"Gracious, no. I wouldn't be up to answer the door at that hour."

"Sally will be there, won't she?" Ruth had not looked forward to having tea with Mrs. Gregory more than once a week, and she knew the woman would still expect a pie on Friday.

Mrs. Gregory put her hand on Ruth's arm and ignored her mention of her servant. "Oh, you must come and sit awhile to talk. You can't imagine how very lonesome it is when no one takes time to visit an old lady."

She had pulled a sad face, but the twinkle hadn't disappeared from her eyes. The old lady was up to something. Still, what could Ruth do except smile and agree to bring her the bread? She was one of Ruth's best customers, after all, and generous with her payment. Besides, with the hotel in flux with the sale pending, Ruth hadn't received any orders from Bet. She didn't like thinking about the cook, one of the listed slaves for sale.

All her life she had been around people who owned slaves and had never looked askance at the institution until she knew Matilda. Even then, because Matilda had an owner who gave her a great deal of freedom, she hadn't really understood the black woman's unhappiness with her state.

Some things were too hard to think about. Slavery was one of those. Ruth couldn't change things. She had no vote. No power. She simply had to tend her little corner of the world and try to keep Adria from doing something foolish to endanger her future. Perhaps her life.

Ruth packed three loaves of the bread in her basket. The parsonage wasn't far from Mrs. Gregory's. Ruth wouldn't go into his house. Not with him there alone. It wouldn't be proper, but she could step up on his porch to offer him a loaf of bread the way she had taken him a pie that first week. She'd truly had no ulterior motives then. She was simply a church member welcoming a new pastor.

But now when he came to mind, he was Will, not Pastor Robertson. And she liked hearing her given name fall from his lips. The very thought of that warmed her cheeks. She gave herself a mental shake. Best not to get carried away. As she had truthfully told Adria, she wasn't worried or apprehensive about what might come of their friendship. The right word for how she felt hadn't surfaced in her mind, but it was not a bad feeling.

Even so, she needed a purpose to knock on his door. And more reason than bringing him a loaf of bread. She wouldn't want him to think she was plying him with baked goods to gain his favor. No, but she could ask him about the money collected for Louis and whether he had approached the Sanderson family to see if they might lower the five-hundred-dollar price.

Five hundred dollars. An amount that sounded beyond hope. Not hope. Prayer. Pray believing. That was what they had decided at the very beginning. She had prayed, but belief had lurked on the edge of her prayers. Perhaps now with such a good beginning, she could grab hold of belief and pray with confidence the Lord would reward Louis's faithfulness.

Mrs. Gregory came to the door herself. "Oh, my dear Ruth. I am so pleased to see you. Come in. Come in." She reached out and pulled Ruth into the hallway. "Having you here brightens up my day."

"How kind of you to say that."

"I'm afraid I must impose on you to come into the kitchen and get the tea tray. You can slice some of that delicious bread for us too. I'm guessing you rarely eat any of it yourself since you stay so slender." The old lady beamed at Ruth as she led the way down the hall to the kitchen that was in a state of disarray, with dishes sitting on every surface.

"I do apologize for the untidiness." Mrs. Gregory brushed a scattering of crumbs off the table.

"Where's Sally?" Ruth asked.

"The dear girl is ill. Dreadfully so." It was odd to hear Mrs. Gregory call Sally "girl," as she wasn't that many years behind the old woman in age.

"I'm sorry to hear that." Ruth set the basket down on one of the chairs and lifted out a loaf of bread. "Do you have a knife?"

The old woman looked in several drawers before she found one. "I fear I have forgotten any domestic skills I once knew. At least I can make tea." She indicated the tray with the teapot. "After Charlene from next door came to manage my fire. You have one of those new stoves, I've heard. You wouldn't be interested in selling it, would you?"

"I'm afraid not. It makes my baking so much easier."

"I suppose it would." She looked over at the fireplace with the pothooks over the coals. "I used to be a fair hand at cooking, but then I got Sally."

"What seems to be her trouble?" Ruth arranged the slices of bread on the plate Mrs. Gregory handed her. "Is she up in her room? I could take her a plate."

"Oh, dear, if only you could, but you see, I had to call in the doctor for her, and he prescribed bed rest for days, perhaps weeks." Mrs. Gregory glanced toward the door that opened to the stairway leading to servant's quarters. "Some sort of lung ailment, he said. I couldn't take care of her. Not and climb those stairs. So there was nothing to do but send her to my cousin's farm, where they have people enough to spare someone for Sally's care. Of course, I'll have to pay the cost. But one does have to be responsible for one's servants."

"I hope she recovers soon."

"Yes, that would be good, but Dr. Adams says that even if she gets better, he doubts she'll ever be useful again. Rather like me, I suppose. But at least I'm still afoot." She reached for the plate of bread. "Here, let me carry that and you can bring the tea tray. When I tried to carry it earlier, I set the cups to clattering in their saucers."

"Certainly." Ruth picked up the tray. "You have three cups. Are you expecting someone else?"

"You never know who might drop in. Always best to be prepared," the old lady chirped as she headed back toward the parlor.

After Ruth sat the tray down on the small round table in the parlor, she poured a cup of tea to hand to the old lady. "What are you up to, Mrs. Gregory?"

Mrs. Gregory sat down and reached for the cup. "My dear girl, you make me sound as mischievous as a child. But I've long since left those years behind. That's why I must find a new girl to hire or buy."

Ruth perched on the edge of a brocade chair near the tea tray with her own cup of tea. The tea was weak and already losing any semblance of warmth. "You could see the Sandersons about Bet, the cook at the hotel. She's always been so helpful when we dropped cakes off there. Quite capable, I'm told."

"That's certainly something to consider, even though an experienced cook will surely fetch a good price."

"But you wouldn't have to teach her to cook." Ruth took a sip of tea.

"Are you wanting to set her free too?" Mrs. Gregory peered over her cup at Ruth. "The way you do Louis?"

"I don't think I said that."

"No, no, you didn't." She sat her cup down and took a piece of the raisin cinnamon bread. "You've never had servants, have you? Even when you were a child?"

"I have not."

"Then you don't understand that those people can't make it

on their own. They need someone to give them a place to work. To feed and clothe them. To see that they are cared for when sick, as I am doing for Sally. I fear that your plan with Louis, although surely a grand idea thought up with well-meaning intentions, might very well be a disaster for him."

"Louis will be able to find work here in Springfield. There are other free blacks in the town."

"Perhaps so. But enough about that." Mrs. Gregory waved her hand as if to clear the air. "Tell me about dear Adria. Has she finally said yes to that sweet Damon boy? She really should, you know."

A knock on the door saved Ruth from making up an answer.

Mrs. Gregory's smile got brighter. "My dear, would you mind terribly to see who that might be? I do struggle so getting up from this settee."

"Of course." Ruth set down her cup and went out into the hallway. She didn't see how Mrs. Gregory would be able to manage without a servant.

Ruth was surprised when she opened the door and Will was standing there, his hat in his hand. She shouldn't have been. She knew Mrs. Gregory was up to something and the old woman loved to play matchmaker. She had tried similar tricks with Ruth in years past, but this time Ruth didn't mind.

"Pastor Robertson. I assume Mrs. Gregory invited you to tea." Ruth was smiling almost as much as the old lady no doubt was back in the parlor.

An answering smile lit up Will's face. "That she did, but she didn't tell me it was going to be a party, Mrs. Harmon."

Thank goodness he followed Ruth's lead to stay formal with Mrs. Gregory's sharp ears listening. "Mrs. Gregory does enjoy her tea. Won't you come in?"

"With pleasure." He stepped across the threshold, his gaze not leaving her face.

Warmth flooded Ruth's cheeks. Something Mrs. Gregory's sharp eyes would notice and gossip would soon be circulating the town that Ruth was attracted to the preacher. But was it gossip if it was true?

When he turned to hang his hat on the hall tree, Ruth blew out a soft breath to pull herself together. While he did appear to be as attracted to her as she was to him, they had only known each other a very short time. The idea of letting this feeling grow was definitely reason to pray. But should she pray believing? Sometimes it was difficult to know if your heart's desire was best for your life.

"I'm so glad you're here, Mrs. Harmon. When Mrs. Gregory invited me on Sunday, she said she wanted to talk about our campaign for Louis." He spoke loudly, obviously wanting to be sure Mrs. Gregory heard every word. "I feel sure she summoned us both here to assure us of her support. I've heard so much about her kindness."

Ruth feared he might be laying on the praise a bit too thickly, but when they went back into the parlor, Mrs. Gregory was beaming. "Ah, Reverend. It is so nice of you to come. I know you must be busy out hunting souls to win, but it's good at times to tend those sheep already in your flock, is it not?"

"Indeed, Mrs. Gregory." He went over and leaned down to put his hand over hers for a moment. "Tending my sheep is an important part of my ministry, and I am blessed to have you as one of them. So what is it I can do for you this day?"

"Don't be in such a rush. Sit down and relax a moment, Pastor." Mrs. Gregory looked at Ruth. "Pour the man some tea and give him a slice of that delicious bread. You did know Mrs. Harmon was an accomplished cook, didn't you, Pastor?"

"Actually I do know that. Her pies are delicious." He took the cup of tea from Ruth. It was cold now, but the day was warm. Perhaps sipping her own cold tea would keep her cheeks from flushing again.

"Oh yes, you did take him a pie once, didn't you, dear?" Mrs. Gregory peered over at Ruth with her face practically aglow at having orchestrated them both being in her parlor.

"A welcome to the community gift," Ruth murmured.

"And a very appreciated one." Will didn't seem bothered at all by the old lady's obvious matchmaking.

Ruth sipped her tea and realized she didn't mind either.

"Yes, yes, I can see it was," Mrs. Gregory said.

"But I thought you had something about which you wanted to speak with me." Will put his cup on the table and leaned toward the old lady.

Ruth started to stand up. "I can go straighten up your kitchen while the two of you talk." She looked at Will. "Her servant is ill."

Mrs. Gregory waved her back down in the chair. "Don't worry about that. Mrs. Minton next door will send her servant back over later. Charlene will have it all straightened up in no time, but I do need to find a replacement for Sally. Perhaps I will talk to the Sandersons." She nibbled on the raisin bread. "But I hear Bet lacks some when it comes to making desserts and you know how I love my sweets."

"Should you decide to rescue Bet, I will bake you a pie or cake every week." Ruth stood up to refill the woman's cup.

"You already do that."

"Free of charge." Ruth couldn't believe she promised that, but she didn't try to take the words back. Sometimes a person had to put feet to her prayers.

"That's a proposition I will have to consider." She raised her eyebrows at Ruth and then turned back to Will. "I think our dear Ruth is becoming an abolitionist. What about you, Reverend? Do you think we should free the slaves?"

"It is an issue that needs much prayer. However, I have no doubt at all we should work for the freedom of our fellow church member, Louis. You are going to help us with that cause, aren't you, Mrs. Gregory?"

She put down her plate with a little laugh. "Will that get me into heaven?"

"No price we can pay will achieve entrance into heaven, madam.

The Lord has already paid that price for us all and requires only belief in that truth, as you surely know." Will's smile didn't waver. "However, we often have the opportunity to be used by the Lord and become an answer to prayers."

"I think you're preaching to me."

"Not only to you, but to myself as well. The Lord expects us to be his feet and hands at times to help our fellow man. Don't you agree?"

Ruth heard the echo of her thought from moments ago in Will's words. The Lord did have a way of reinforcing his messages. She watched Mrs. Gregory over the top of her cup to see how she would respond. She was not a woman who liked being told what to do, but it seemed she was more open to what a preacher might suggest.

The old lady's smile didn't waver. "A very convincing sermon." She slipped her hand down into a pocket of her skirt and pulled out several bills to hold out toward Will. "I do hope we are doing the right thing for Louis."

Will took the bills and handed them to Ruth, which brought a frown to Mrs. Gregory's face. "I thought you would safeguard the money collected, Pastor Robertson." She hurried on as though she realized how that sounded. "I know Ruth would keep it well too, but if it becomes known two women alone have cash hidden in their house it might put them in danger."

"You are right." Ruth spoke up. "I'm just keeping a record of the money given and by whom in the unlikely event we are unable to raise the amount needed. Should that happen, we would return the money to those who gave it."

Ruth counted the bills quickly and handed them back to Will.

Will tucked the money into his coat pocket. "Very considerate of you to be concerned about Mrs. Harmon and Miss Starr. We agree completely. I will keep the money donated by our church members, and Mr. Billiter has agreed to accept donations at his store and keep them in his safe until we can deposit the money at the bank."

"Oh, well, it seems you have it planned out." Mrs. Gregory picked up her teacup again. "Except what might become of poor Louis once you give him his freedom."

"I feel assured the Lord will have a plan for him as he has for all of us," Will said.

Ruth hoped it was true. No, not only hoped. She would pray believing for that truth.

Twenty-four

Will carried Ruth's raisin cinnamon bread home. He tried to pay her for it, but the roses had bloomed in her cheeks as she insisted the bread was a gift. He hadn't argued. In the Bible, Paul told his followers the Lord said it was more blessed to give than to receive. But in order to have the blessing of giving, someone must receive and not turn away the giver's blessing.

He would have felt especially blessed if the giver had allowed him to walk her home, but Ruth had seen him to Mrs. Gregory's door and sent him on his way. At least she did promise to come early to prayer services the next day at church to tally up the money collected for Louis. The thought of seeing her again so soon had his step light as he went toward his house.

While Mary still lived in his heart, he had to admit to feeling something new when he was with Ruth. And from the way her cheeks turned rosy if his gaze lingered on her face, he thought she might be feeling something new too. It was surprising she had been a widow so many years. A lovely Christian woman. Intelligent. Well read. And a good cook. What more could a man want?

She'd surely had chances and had instead chosen the single

life. Hadn't he thought to choose the same after Mary died? And now here he was wondering if the Lord was giving him another chance at love.

Whether that was true or not, his confusion over his own walk with God had eased over the last days. He felt more confident in his calling and that his prayers weren't simply empty words bouncing back at him. The prayers he faithfully lifted up for Louis Sanderson might be the reason. And the testimony of the man's life.

The effectual fervent prayer of a righteous man availeth much. Not that Will was claiming that title for himself. He wanted to be a righteous man, but he knew his sins of doubt and struggling faith since Mary died. But Louis, though a slave, appeared to be that righteous man. A man who prayed believing.

Will had sought out the man after Adria Starr revealed she'd told Louis about their efforts to raise money to free him.

"Miss Adria has been a ray of sunshine in my life ever since the cholera spread dark o'er our town, but I never expected her to do nothin' like this." To speak to Will, Louis had stepped out of the buggy house where he was polishing and cleaning things for the Sanderson sale. A sale that included him. The black man kept his head down as slaves were conditioned to do, but then he raised his eyes toward the sky as though looking for those rays of sunshine. "And Miss Ruth too. I've been blessed to be able to help them out from time to time."

"I hear you helped many people out during the cholera epidemic."

"Those I could. Those the good Lord put in my path." He brought his eyes away from the sky and looked at the ground again.

"How did you know the cholera wasn't going to affect you?"

"Wasn't no way to know that till it didn't. But I prayed and the Lord showed me what needed doin' and give me the strength to do it."

"You prayed believing."

"Ain't no other way to pray, is there, Reverend?" Louis looked up at Will then, as though searching his face for an answer he already knew.

"No, but sometimes prayers aren't answered."

"I ain't meanin' to disagree with you, sir, but I'm thinkin' different on that. To my way of thinkin', prayers is always answered but sometimes not the way we be thinkin' they should be. Like now." His gaze went toward the sky again. "Miss Adria, she's prayin'. I'm prayin'. You probably prayin' too that this idea she got is gonna work the way she wants, and if you are, I thank you for that. But it's the Lord what has to make it work. If'n it be his will. If'n it ain't, then maybe he don't want ol' Louis to be free. Maybe he's got other plans for me, and if that be true, then who am I to say the Lord don't have the best plan?"

Who am I to say the Lord don't have the best plan? The black man's words echoed in Will's head as he turned down the street toward his house. If only he had the same powerful faith. To pray not just believing, but believing that whatever happened, whatever answers came, the Lord would somehow turn it to good.

And we know that all things work together for good to them that love God, to them who are the called according to his purpose.

According to his purpose. But even with that verse stored in his heart, Will still couldn't see what good had come of Mary's death. It wasn't God's purpose. Will couldn't believe it was. The fever had just come upon her and stolen her away from this world the same as the cholera had taken so many away all across the country in 1833.

He shook his head a little. That wasn't what the verse said. It was to them called according to his purpose. Will was the one called to the Lord's purpose. It wasn't good that Mary died, but since it did happen, then the Lord could take that, as he could take whatever happened in a man's life, and find a way to make something good come from it. Because Mary died, Will had entered a valley of sorrow and doubt.

Not doubt in the existence of God, but whether his own faith was strong enough to be the under-shepherd he thought he'd been called to be. And yet somewhere even in the darkest moments of doubt, the Lord was always there. Not condemning but knowing and sharing Will's sorrow. Will was broken, but the Lord lovingly put the pieces back together. While Will had come to Springfield to escape his unhappy memories, that didn't mean the Lord couldn't make good come of that too. Perhaps the good was in helping this man, Louis.

He would put away Ruth's raisin bread, more good to consider, and then pay a call on the Sanderson family. Perhaps they could be convinced to lower the price of Louis's freedom. But first he would delve into the Scripture and ask the Lord's blessing on his purpose.

He had just settled down with his Bible when someone knocked on the door. Perhaps Ruth had followed him home for some reason, but no, this knock was no gentle rap but a sturdy pounding to be sure to get his attention. Someone must have a pressing need.

When he pulled open the door, Will wasn't sure he was seeing right. His brother-in-law stood there with Willeena clutching his neck and hiding her face in his shoulder.

"Andrew." Fear that the man brought bad news gripped Will. "Is Hazel all right?"

"She ain't dead, if that's what you mean."

"Praise God." A breath of relief swept through Will. He stepped back from the door to let Andrew come in. He wanted to reach out and touch the wisps of taffy-colored hair curling down on Willeena's neck, but he stayed his hand. She'd grown in the time since he'd seen her.

"Hello, Willeena," he said softly.

Without raising her head off Andrew's shoulder, she peeked around at him.

"The girl's been asleep. She's a mite timid when she first wakes up. Usually won't have nothing to do with anybody but Hazel. That's the trouble." Andrew patted the child's back.

"What trouble? Is something wrong with Hazel?"

"She's not well. She's in the family way again and it's dragging her down. She don't have the energy to run after the little ones. My ma took our little Ginny for a spell, but she's getting on up in the years. Wasn't no way she could handle the both of them. Willie too. You understand that, don't you?" Andrew looked worried Will might not understand.

"I'm sorry to hear Hazel is feeling poorly."

"Well, Hazel didn't want me bringing her to you, but I didn't see no way around it. She's yours to do with as you think best."

"I can't take care of a little girl." Will didn't want to say that, but it was best to face facts.

"Hazel said you'd say that. But it ain't all that hard. They just need watching and feeding. She don't wear nappies no more. And what with you having a church, you're bound to know some woman willing to help you with the watching whilst you're doing your preacher duties."

Will must have still looked doubtful because Andrew's face hardened as he went on. "She's yours to take care of or to find another place for. Hazel done her best for you, but she can't do no more. About broke her heart to admit it, but till she gets back on her feet, there ain't nothing else for it but to bring her back to you. Could be down the road, Hazel will get to feeling better once the baby gets here, and if you still feel like it's too much for you, you can come talk to her then. But this is how it is now. No changing it."

"I see." Will hesitated to reach for Willeena. The child's body had stiffened while Andrew talked. She had heard and understood too much. He never should have said he couldn't take care of her, even if he did feel that way. He reached for her now. "Come here, Willie."

She burrowed her face deeper into Andrew's shoulder and tightened her arms around his neck. "I want Mama Hazie." Her voice was muffled but the words were plain.

Andrew shut his eyes. This was obviously not easy for him.

He took a deep breath, opened his eyes, and very gently lifted the child a little away from him so he could look in her face. "Now, Willie, we talked about this with Mama Hazie and then on the ride over here. You're gonna have to stay with your daddy for a while. He's gonna take good care of you just like me and Mama Hazie have been doing."

"But I won't get to play with Ginny." Tears were in the little girl's voice.

"Not for a while. But your daddy, he has a whole church full of people. I'm guessing there will be some little girls for you to play with come Sunday." Andrew's eyes were too full. "You know Mama Hazie and me love you, but your daddy loves you too. Just as much."

"That's right." Will put in. There was nothing for it but to accept the child. Hazel wouldn't have let Andrew bring Willie to him unless it was necessary. He needed to think about her and not himself. "We'll find some new friends for you and you can help me take care of my horse."

She looked around at Will then. "Can I have a puppy?"

"I don't know. We'll have to think about that." Will couldn't keep from laughing. That was exactly how her mother had been, always ready to negotiate. If there wasn't money for a new hat, was there money for a new ribbon? But this time when he looked at Willie and saw Mary, it didn't stab his heart the way it had before. He was glad to be reminded of her through their child. Perhaps Hazel had been right. He had just needed more time and more acceptance of what couldn't be changed.

Andrew smiled too. "Sometimes it's hard to remember this one is only a little over two the way she talks. Way better than our Ginny, who is already three. Hazel says it's not all that common how Willie never did much baby talking at all. Just started putting sentences together in words a man could understand, but I guess you knew that. It hasn't been all that long since you last saw her."

He handed her over to Will and this time she didn't try to cling to Andrew. Instead she kept her eyes on Will's face as though trying to figure him out. She was a sweet, warm weight in his arms. A strand of hair slid down over her forehead and Will blew it back. That made her giggle. He had forgotten her giggle, or maybe he had never noted it when he made his quick stops at Hazel's to see the child. Those visits had been too infrequent and he hadn't tried to be a daddy. Only a dutiful father or, even more truthfully, a dutiful brother, thankful his sister was caring for the child he couldn't. Couldn't or wouldn't. Whichever, that was about to change.

Again Andrew's eyes looked too watery as he touched the little girl's head. He abruptly dropped his hand back to his side. "I'll get her clothes. She should have plenty, till she grows out of them. That won't take long. Kids this age grow fast. Hazel told me to tell you that, so you'd know to find somebody to make her more in a few months. I expect that won't be hard in a town like this." He turned to go back out the door to his buggy, then looked over his shoulder at Will. "But the easiest thing is for you to find a wife. A preacher, well, any man, needs a wife. I don't know what I'd do without Hazel."

"I'll pray for her to regain her health and for the baby she's carrying too."

Andrew blinked and gave a quick nod. "I'll be beholding to you for that."

The child's possessions were few. Several dresses. Socks and underwear. A sweater. A coat that might not be too small come wintertime. Shoes for church. Gowns for sleeping. A child-sized quilt Hazel had made for her and a rag doll with yarn hair and a patched knee.

"Hazel was aiming to make her a new doll. Could be she'll still get that done, what with having to rest so much right now. Sewing will give her something to do. She can send it to you when she gets it made."

"I'm sure Willie will like that." Will said the words, but he had no idea what Willie would like or not like.

Andrew stooped down in front of Willie, who had stood in the middle of the sitting room and watched the transfer of her things from the buggy to the house. Now instead of Andrew's neck, she clutched the doll. She had a lost look on her face that made Will's heart hurt.

"You be good for your daddy, you hear?" Andrew's voice was gruff with feeling.

The girl nodded. A tear slid down her cheek.

"Now don't you be getting all teary-eyed. Mama Hazie and me, we'll come see you when we can, and you and your daddy can come see us too."

"Ginny too?" Willie said.

"Of course, Ginny too." He leaned toward her and kissed her forehead. "That was for Mama Hazie." He touched his cheek. "Now you give me a kiss right here that I can take home to her."

She brushed her lips across his cheek and then stepped back. "Goodbye, Daddy A."

Andrew stood up and looked at Will. "That's what she calls me. Just seemed easier than teaching her Uncle Andrew. We weren't thinking on having to give her up then. Figured she'd be with us a while. Maybe forever. But this is better. She needs to be with you and you need to make a home for her."

Then with a handshake, he was gone out the door and climbing into his buggy to drive off down the road. Will stood at the doorway and watched till even his buggy's dust trail disappeared.

Behind him, the child started talking to her doll. "Don't cry, Maysie. I'll take care of you."

Lord, help me. The prayer slipped through his mind as he turned back to Willeena. What in the world was he going to do? He had no idea how to take care of a child. What was it Andrew had said? He just had to watch her and feed her. He doubted it would be that simple, but feeding her would be a start.

"Are you hungry?"

She looked at him with big green eyes so like Mary's and nodded.

"What do you like to eat?" He didn't know why he asked. It wasn't as though he had that much to offer. Bread and cheese. Eggs and sausage. Beans. Apples. His larder was far from full.

"Mama Hazie's biscuits." Her lips trembled.

"I'm sorry, but I'm not good at making biscuits." He pushed a smile out on his face and hoped his lips weren't trembling to match hers.

"Mama Hazie's sick." She wasn't crying, but somehow that simply made her words sadder. Her head drooped as she squeezed her doll tight against her chest.

"I know she is." He stooped down beside her. "The two of us, you and me, we'll pray she gets better so she can make you some more of those biscuits. But until then, I do have some raisin cinnamon bread." Thanks to Ruth Harmon. Wonder what she would think of his little girl. She'd taken in a child once. Would she do it again? Or would she step back from Will?

He couldn't worry about that now. One day at a time. That was how he needed to think. Maybe one hour at a time here in the beginning. He stood up and held his hand out to Willie.

She looked at him a long moment and then put her hand in his. It was enough. Somehow he would find a way to take care of her.

Twenty-five

"You don't really want to marry that hayseed, Carlton Damon, do you?" Logan Farrell fell into step beside Adria when she left the store on Tuesday afternoon.

"Good day to you too, Mr. Farrell." She looked over at him without a smile. The man could at least say hello when he waylaid her on the street.

"No need wasting words is how I think about it, Miss Starr. Best to get right to the point."

"I thought you had a job now."

"Even wagon makers have a quitting time, but I can prove I've been working." He took off his hat and brushed some sawdust out of the hair curling down over his forehead. "I've been sawing and sanding all day. I'd have gone back to my room and cleaned up a mite, but I didn't want to miss walking the prettiest girl in Springfield home."

"You do have a silver tongue, Mr. Farrell." She couldn't quite stop a smile from tickling her lips. "Except for not properly greeting a person and asking rude questions that are none of your business."

"But I want to make it my business." He put his hand under her elbow and turned her toward the road. "Why don't we take the long way to your house? Down the street, I met a man who says he has some money for you. For the slave you're trying to buy."

"I'm not buying a slave." Adria shuddered at the thought. "I'm— we're setting one free." She slowed her steps. They were headed toward the tavern area. Not exactly the place a lady should stroll, with or without an escort.

"Either way it takes money, right?" Logan must have noticed her hesitation. "You aren't afraid to go down this way, are you?" He didn't wait for an answer. "You don't have to worry. I'll protect you."

"Are you going to protect my reputation too?" She stopped walking.

"Sorry. I probably already wrecked that for you when I started walking with you." He stared down at her with a daring smile in his eyes. "But I understand if you don't want to go get the money. A lady's reputation is important. And you can probably raise enough for poor Louis in the highfalutin neighborhoods, but I have to tell you—" He shook his head a little. "It's been my experience that poor folks are way more generous than those other folks. I guess when you don't have much, you don't mind getting down to even less by giving to somebody what needs it worse."

"Are you speaking from experience?"

"I've been both places, that's for sure. With plenty and with little of nothing." He moved a couple of steps on down the street. "Generally preferred the taverns to the ballrooms."

"Interesting." She started walking with him. When had she ever worried about her reputation anyway? She left that up to Ruth. "I've never been to either. I must be stuck in the middle."

"Not a bad place to be. The middle. Churchgoing, hardworking, God-fearing folks in the middle." He gave her a sideways glance. "I've even heard some of them are abolitionists."

"Not many of those in Springfield." She stared straight ahead. "If any."

"Must be a few the way this scheme you and the preacher cooked up is drawing in the money. All to set a slave free."

"People want to help Louis."

"I've never been able to count on people helping me." A hint of bitterness tinged his words. He made a sound something like a laugh. "I learned that early on. Had to figure out how to take care of myself."

"I'm sorry."

"No need for you to be sorry about that. If you want to be sorry about something, be sorry I didn't come to Springfield before you got engaged to that hayseed."

"Carlton is far from a hayseed and I'm not engaged to him or anybody." Adria kept her voice firm. This man took far too many liberties.

"I'm guessing if you asked Mr. Damon, he'd give a different opinion on that."

"Carlton is a fine man. We've been friends forever."

"Forever friends. Not a bad way to start a forever life together." He was quiet a couple of seconds, then went on. "If that's what a person wants. To be forever without adventure or anything new. To be stuck here, knee-deep in kids."

"You don't want to have a family?" She wasn't sure she'd ever met anyone who spoke against the joy of a family.

But then there was Abigail in the east ready to give up her chances for love and family to fight for a cause she believed in. Just thinking about that made Adria feel guilty. What was she doing? Reading all the material. Writing anonymous letters. Afraid to even admit to wanting to fight for the abolishment of slavery. She was such a coward.

"Family." Logan echoed her last word. "Sure, I want family when the time is right."

"When will the time be right?" Adria had often wondered about the answer to that question for herself. Would she know when the time was right or would she let that time, perhaps her only time, slip right past her? Plenty of people in Springfield thought she was already letting that happen by not accepting Carlton's proposal.

"I can't name a date, but I figure I've got some more life to live first. Places to see. Things to do." Logan looked off down the street as though trying to see some of those places from where they stood.

"You make settling down to have a family sound like the end of life. Not the beginning, the way I've often heard."

"Trust me. It's more an end than a beginning. No more chance to chase adventure. Got to work to bring home food for the family. Can't hear about a wagon train going west and drop everything and go. Not with a wife and babies."

"Whole families go west," Adria pointed out.

"So I've heard, but then a man is tied to a wagon, ever worried about protecting that family. No chance to ride off and be free." Logan shook his head a little.

"Well then, I suppose it's very good that you don't have a wife to curtail your freedom."

"I have yet to meet the woman who might like adventure as much as I do. A woman with dreams of more than grubby little hands clutching at her apron while a man sits at her table demanding supper."

Adria laughed. "You do paint a sad picture. I don't remember family being like that at all before my parents died. My mother was always happy and singing."

"Must have been because she had such a delightful daughter." He flashed Adria that smile again. "But here we are at Sam's."

Adria looked at the door. She'd never been in a tavern. Ruth would be appalled that she was even standing in front of one. "Perhaps I should wait outside."

"Don't worry, Miss Starr. People are people wherever you meet them. In church or in a tavern. Some good. Some bad. But Sam is one of the good ones." He held the door open for her.

Sam might not be the only man in there, she wanted to say, but she kept quiet and stepped through the door. It was simply a place of business like Billiter's Mercantile. A bawdier business perhaps, but as Logan said, people were people wherever.

Inside the light was dim in spite of the front windows and lamps attached to the walls here and there. The smell of the burning oil mixed with that of fried food and something else. A sharper odor. Alcohol. But the men around a few of the tables didn't appear to have imbibed too much of the stuff.

Logan noticed her looking around. "See, nothing going on. I'm guessing you see these fellows at the store all the time. Just regular Springfield folk. The drovers looking for a good time will be out later to get things hopping." He winked at her. "Wouldn't be the best place for you then. I'd have to fight a dozen men to keep them away from a pretty girl like you."

The short, stocky tavern owner stepped out from behind a counter and hurried toward Adria. Logan was right. She did see Sam Hoskins at the store all the time. She'd had no need to get the gossips talking and Carlton upset by going into the tavern to see him. But that was likely Logan's purpose. To make trouble between Carlton and her.

"Miss Starr, welcome to my tavern." The man socked Logan's arm. "I never thought you'd get her in here, lad." He turned back on Adria. "Not a lady like this one."

Adria smiled at him and shook her head. "I may have given up any claim to being a lady when I went to work at Billiter's."

"No truth to that. It's the heart that shows the lady," Sam said. "What can I do for you? Something to drink or eat?"

"Not right now, Mr. Hoskins, but thank you." She hesitated a moment to give Logan the chance to speak up about why they were there, but for a change, he didn't seem to have anything to say. It was up to her to ask. "Logan said you might be willing to contribute to our fund to buy Louis from the Sanderson family. To buy his freedom."

"A good thing. I'm glad you and Mrs. Harmon came up with the idea. Matter of fact, I left some money with your boss yesterday." Sam frowned a little. "Didn't you get it?"

"Oh, Logan thought I needed to come pick it up." She frowned at Logan, who shrugged a little before he stepped over to one of the tables to talk with the men there. "Mr. Billiter is keeping some of the money in his safe. We were busy today, so he probably forgot to tell me about it."

Sam's smile was back. "I know how that can be, but busy is good for merchants like us."

"Yes. And thank you so much for giving toward Louis's freedom."

"How much have you collected? Enough?"

"I'm not sure, but it's adding up. People are donating at the church to Reverend Robertson and also at the store. Plus, the pastor plans to talk to the Sanderson family to see if they might lower their price."

"They should. Or just write up his manumission papers themselves, but some people see a dime behind every penny."

"We'll get enough."

"I hope so." Sam lifted a corner of his apron to wipe his face. "Louis is a fine man. He buried my little son when I was too sick to lift a finger to do what was needed. Lad was only three years old. Had no chance against the cholera. Louis came and took him out to the cemetery." Sorrow deepened the lines on his face. "Carried his little body like it was the most precious thing in the world. It was to me, but Louis didn't even know the boy. He just had that much compassion flowing out of him for us who were sick."

"I'm sorry you lost your son." Adria's throat tightened as she blinked back tears, remembering her little brother. She hadn't seen Louis pick Eddie up, but she had no doubt he had carried him in the same gentle way.

"My dear mother died too. It was a bad time, for sure. I sent my wife and daughters away at the first sign the boy was sick. The wife hasn't ever forgiven me for that." He pressed his lips together for a moment. "But she and the girls didn't die."

"So many sad stories," Adria said.

"I hear them all the time in here. It's a confessional. Not one in a church with a priest and all. This one is right here where people

221

live." He looked past Adria to the men at the tables. "In fact, I'm thinking some of these men might owe Louis a coin or two. Let me gather a little more for your hopper."

He stepped away from Adria and slapped his hand down on one of the tables. "Gents, this little lady here is taking up money to buy Louis Sanderson and set him free after all he done for us here in town during the cholera epidemic a few years back. Burying our folks when everybody else was too sick or too scared to do it."

A couple of them shuddered at the mention of cholera. Adria knew how they felt.

Sam reached behind the counter and pulled out an empty pan. "So drop in some money and your next drink will be on the house."

Logan took the pan and carried it around among the men in the tavern as though he was passing the offering plate at church. Every man reached in his pocket and pulled out something to put in the pan, even the men Adria didn't remember ever seeing in Springfield. Sam was to thank for that with his offer of free drinks.

Or maybe it was Logan with that smile. He seemed able to get people to do what he asked. Wasn't she standing here in a tavern? She looked across the room where the serving girl leaned against a doorway that must lead to a kitchen. A smile played across her face as she watched Logan, and then she reached into her apron pocket to hold out a few coins for the pan.

Sam spoke up beside Adria. "You know that Farrell fellow well?"

The question surprised her. She turned to look at Sam after watching the girl's smile brighten when Logan stepped toward her. Sam was watching the girl, too, with a little frown scrunching the skin between his eyes.

"Not well. He hasn't been in town long."

"Right. A drifter. He comes in here to eat some." Sam nodded toward the girl. "That's my daughter. I done warned her about the likes of him." Sam looked directly at Adria then. "That kind has sweet words on his tongue and a smile to shove aside a girl's good sense, but little else. Best keep that in mind, Miss Starr."

She did have it in mind already from Ruth's warnings, but still when Logan turned back toward her with that smile, her heart did beat a little faster. She had no doubt Sam's daughter's heart was doing the same as she watched Logan move across the room toward Adria. But smile or not, Adria did not plan to lose her good sense, no matter how her heart fluttered. This man was not the kind of man to settle down and raise a family.

Then again, didn't she wonder if there was more than what Carlton promised her? So perhaps she wasn't the type of woman to settle down and raise a family. That very thought made her heart beat even faster.

"Here's more to add to your Louis fund." Logan handed her the collection pan.

Adria gathered up the bills and coins. Not a lot of money, but every cent counted.

"If I collect more from them that aren't here now, I'll bring it by the store." Sam took the empty pan from her.

"Thank you so much, Mr. Hoskins." She turned and held out her hand toward the others in the tavern. "Thank you all. This means so much."

Once back out on the street, Logan kept step with her. "Now that you've got money in your pocket, you'll have to let me escort you home. For your safety."

"Nobody but you knows I have money in my pocket."

"And all the men back there." Logan nodded his head toward the tavern.

"They wouldn't give the money and then try to take it back." Adria frowned over at him.

"You're too trusting, Miss Starr. Some men will do most anything to put cash in their pockets."

"I prefer to be trusting, but I don't aim to take chances with this money. I'll let Mr. Billiter put it in the safe with the other money we've collected." She stopped to cross the street. "I appreciate your help, Mr. Farrell, even if you weren't entirely honest with me when

223

you said Mr. Hoskins wouldn't give the money unless I came to get it. He'd already given money at the store."

"I must have got that mixed up." Logan shrugged. "But you ended up with more anyway. So all is good, right?" He flashed his smile at her.

"I suppose. It's always interesting talking to you."

"I'm getting the feeling you don't want me to walk you home. Afraid Damon will see you smiling at me?"

"Not at all. Carlton doesn't tell me what to do."

"He wants to." Logan's smile got broader.

"My wants are what matters, and now I want to go home after a very long day at the store without having to verbally spar with you." Adria was tired, but mostly she didn't want to upset Ruth by having Logan show up at the house with her.

Logan laughed. "Are we sparring? It might be more fun to be sparking."

"Good day, Mr. Farrell."

"All right, I'll go peaceably." He put his hand under her elbow. "After I get you safely across the street. You do have a tendency to not watch for the horses."

"I'm quite capable of making it across the street by myself."

"I'm sure you are, and I have scars to prove it." He touched the still red cut over his eye. "But I need to pick up something at Billiter's anyway, so surely you can put up with my company a little longer."

There was nothing for it but to give in gracefully. It was a public walkway, after all. Mr. Billiter was just turning over the closed sign when they got to the store. He left the closed sign on the door, but let them in.

"Did you forget something, Adria?" He looked from her to Logan with a little frown. "Is this man bothering you?"

"No, no." Adria smiled over at Logan. "This is Logan Farrell."

"Pleasure to meet you." When Logan held out his hand, Mr. Billiter took it a bit reluctantly, as though Adria's words hadn't reassured him.

"You're one of those drovers, aren't you?" Mr. Billiter pulled his hand back and narrowed his eyes on Logan.

"I was, but I'm working down at Byrd's wagon shop now." Logan didn't seem bothered by Mr. Billiter's less-than-friendly welcome. "I've been in your store here a few times. Best place in town for bread or just about anything a man might need."

Logan's compliment about the store made Mr. Billiter's frown ease. The man knew how to charm a person. Mr. Billiter jerked on the ends of his vest and stood up a little straighter. He wasn't a young man. The cholera had taken his wife, and he hadn't remarried. His children were all grown with no interest in taking over the store. Mr. Billiter claimed not to care. He wasn't ready to sit down and do nothing anyway. He might be getting up in years, but he had more energy than Adria. Always busy.

"Mr. Farrell helped me collect some more money for Louis. I was hoping you could put it in the safe." Adria reached into her pocket for the money.

"Certainly." Mr. Billiter led the way across the floor to the storeroom where he pushed back the curtain that covered the doorway. A square safe sat just inside the room.

Adria and Logan watched as the storekeeper knelt down in front of it, worked the combination, and pulled it open. He handed Adria an envelope already fat with contributions. She stuffed what she had inside and handed it back.

He put it in one of the cubbyholes and shut the safe before he brushed his hands together and stood up. "Who would have ever thought that our town could come together and do such a thing?" He shook his head. "Give money to set a slave free."

Adria bit her tongue to keep from saying all slaves should be freed. Mr. Billiter didn't share her abolitionist feelings.

Logan spoke up. "This lady right here thought it and she's making it happen."

He casually put his arm around her shoulder and gave her a half hug. She couldn't deny that she liked it, even as she quickly stepped away from him. But like him or not, she still wasn't going to let him walk her home. Ruth wouldn't approve. Carlton would be angry yet again. It seemed nobody approved of her walking or talking with Logan Farrell. Not Mr. Billiter, if his frown was any indication, and not even Sam Hoskins.

The question was, what did she think about Logan Farrell?

Twenty-six

Weeping may endure for a night, but joy cometh in the morning.

That Bible verse circled through Ruth's thoughts as she stepped out the back door to lift her face toward the morning sun. No cloud was anywhere to be seen as warm light spread across the yard behind the house. A thunderstorm had swept past in the night, washing the sky until now it was the perfect blue. A tendril of smoke curled up from her kitchen chimney where the blue swallowed it at once.

She already had four loaves of bread in the chimney oven and two cakes in the stove oven. As wonderful as the stove was, the oven was small. When she had more orders, she had to use both ovens even if the kitchen did get stifling hot. Bet had sent over an order for the Sanderson family. Somebody was supposed to pick up the bread and cakes at noon.

The air was pleasant out on the porch with the damp smell of the grass and the leaves shaking down leftover drops of rain when a breath of air moved through them. From the top of a nearby tree, a mockingbird ran through its repertoire. Every song one of cheer.

A poem was there somewhere if she could only pull the words together.

When the morning brings joy, the heart sings.

No, that wasn't quite right.

When joy comes with the morning, the heart can sing.

Better. But what could she pair with *sing*? *Ring*? *Bring*? *Everything*?

That was how she felt—as if everything was singing. To her. She wanted to spin off the porch and whirl in the yard with her arms flung out to the side as her young students sometimes did when they were released from their studies. Joy in motion.

And what makes you so joyful this day, Ruth Harmon? That thought brought back a memory of Peter. He was always ready for joy and happy to share that joy with anyone and everyone. Especially her. He would want her to embrace the joy she was feeling. He would tell her to go ahead and whirl until she felt like she was floating.

He wouldn't mind at all that her joy was coming not only from the beauty of the morning but from thoughts of another man.

Your love for me isn't made any less by your love for another. The heart has room for a multitude of loves.

She could almost hear him whispering those words to her on the breeze, and that made her heart feel even lighter. She would scatter her worries like dandelion fluff in the wind. Adria was of age. She must decide on her own whom she loved. If that turned out to be Logan Farrell, nothing Ruth could say would change that.

Love had a way of battering down every barrier. Hadn't it done so when her mother was unsure at first about Peter, a stranger in town? She couldn't run after Adria and shield her from every hurt. She'd never been able to do that. The child had come to her knowing how sorrowful life could be. Perhaps that was why Adria wanted to help others who were hurting. The downtrodden. The slave.

Then again, all the stories and poems they'd read together may have given Adria a dreamer's heart. But didn't all children

ANN H. GABHART

look beyond and wonder about what might be? No, Ruth knew that wasn't true. Some children were dreamers. Others wanted to try their wings and find adventure, and then there were those who huddled in safety under the wings of the familiar. Through all her years of teaching, she'd watched many children grow up and settle into good lives. Adria might yet do the same. Ruth had to give her the freedom to do as she wished. She threw out her hands as though releasing those worries. Best to change them into prayers.

She worried too much. Perhaps she was one of those who wanted to rest in the familiar even when life pushed the unfamiliar her way. Widowhood. Then a child to raise. A living to make. Yet she'd found a way to do it all. With God's help. And the help the Lord had put in her path. Louis. Matilda. The families who trusted her to teach their children. Even Adria, who gave her reason to get up in the morning in those first months after Peter died.

And now the Lord had put Will Robertson, Pastor Will Robertson, in her path. She couldn't deny she liked the way the man settled his eyes on her as though he could look at her forever.

Forever. Such a good word when it came to love. Love. That the word had come unbidden to her mind shocked her a bit, but then she smiled. Yes, love. That was the perfect word for how she was feeling this day as she looked forward to being at church tonight. Will would be there with his serious eyes that could sometimes look so sad. Not simply sad, but lonely.

And the Lord God said, It is not good that the man should be alone.

Or perhaps the woman either. Humming, she turned to go back in the kitchen to check on her cakes. The words of the song escaped her, but the tune was there. A happy sound rising from a long-forgotten memory. The sweet smell of the cakes mixed with the bread baking lifted her spirits even more.

She had enough orders to take care of their needs. Mrs. Gregory would surely buy Bet. While that wouldn't give Bet her freedom, it would guarantee her an easier life than she might find in some other situation. The money was coming in for Louis much faster than Ruth dreamed possible. Good things were happening all around. No wonder she had a song in her heart.

The bread loaves were cooled and the caramel on the cake when she heard something and stepped out on the back porch. Louis was chopping a chunk of wood into the right-sized pieces for her stove. The farmer who sold her firewood didn't split it small enough to fit in her stove's firebox. When Louis saw her, he gathered up an armload of wood.

"Thank you, Louis." She stepped back as he came up on the porch to drop the pieces in her woodbox on the end of the porch.

"Looked like you might be gettin' low on stove wood, Miss Ruth." He took off his hat and looked down at the porch.

"I was. Adria usually splits some for me before she goes to work, but she didn't have time this morning." Ruth smiled at the man. "She has liked splitting wood ever since you taught her how."

"Missy Adria will try most anything." He chuckled. "But I recall being some concerned for her toes when she first started swinging that ax. The missy does everything whole hog."

"That's for sure." Ruth laughed along with him. "I guess you're here for Bet's order. I wasn't expecting you. I thought one of the girls would come."

"I had a few extra minutes." He shuffled his feet a little but kept his eyes downcast as a slave was supposed to do.

Others sometimes asked Ruth if she wasn't afraid to have Louis working around her house with no man to protect her. The question always surprised her. She would trust Louis with her life. Now she watched him twist his hat into a spiral. Something was bothering him. Perhaps the upcoming sale. That would be enough to make a man worry.

"Is something wrong, Louis?"

ANN H. GABHART

"Not exactly wrong, ma'am." He looked up at her and quickly back down. "I's just wantin' to thank you for what you and Missy Adria are tryin' to do for me. I wasn't never expectin' nothin' like this."

"It's no more than you deserve after what you did for all of us twelve years ago."

"I just did what needed doin'."

"And that's what we're doing now." When he twisted his hat into a tighter wad, she went on. "Are you worried about it? About being on your own."

"That ain't it. I know the Lord will be with me whatever happens." Again he shot his gaze up to her and then back to the ground. "But I'm some worried 'bout the young missy if her plan don't work for me. I's just askin' you to let her know I'll be all right whether you get the money or not. I done told her, but she was too full of hopin' to listen."

"I understand, Louis, and I will be sure to tell her should that happen." She touched his arm lightly. "But I don't think Adria or you have to worry. The Lord is blessing our efforts after you told Adria to pray believing."

"I ain't sure I'm believin' this." Louis shook his head slowly.

"Believe it, Louis. It's no more than you deserve, and it is going to happen."

"If it does, I has you to thank for it, Miss Ruth."

"Me?" Ruth frowned a little. "No, it's Adria you need to thank."

"But without you takin' her in as a little girl, ain't no tellin' where she might have ended up. Could've been anywhere and someplace not so nice for her as this place here." He waved his hand around to take in the house and yard. "Or with somebody so lovin' as you. If the Lord is rewardin' what I done like as how you say, then he's sure to reward your kind heart too. Couldn't have been easy for you there in the beginnin'."

"I've been rewarded time and time again, Louis. Knowing you and Matilda. A house to live in. And Adria. I can't imagine not

231

having her in my life now in spite of the doubts I admit I did have that first day you brought her to me."

"The good Lord works in ways we can't know nothin' about."

"That makes me think of the hymn we sometimes sing at church. God moves in a mysterious way his wonders to perform."

"That's a good one." Louis stepped off the porch to pick up the basket he'd left on the bottom step. "Here's Bet's basket for whatever she asked you to make."

Ruth took it and went inside to pack up the bread and cake and cover it with Bet's dish towel. Voices drifted in through the window. Will's voice. Ruth's heart did a happy little skip. She hadn't expected to see him until she went to church. She slipped off her apron and smoothed back her hair. She dabbed the perspiration off her forehead with the underside of the apron and was tempted to go check how her hair looked in the hall tree mirror.

She shook her head at her vanity, picked up the basket, and stepped back out the door. Will was there on the stone walkway beside Louis. With a young child in his arms. Louis was talking to the little girl, making her smile without effort. Will was smiling too. Until he noticed Ruth on the steps. Then his smile faded and his face tightened a bit as though the sight of her made him nervous. Certainly not the look she had been feeling so joyful about earlier in the day.

"I knocked on the front door, but when you didn't answer, I came on around here. Hope you don't mind." Will sounded as though he feared she might.

"Of course I don't mind. I'm sorry I didn't hear you knock. I must have been out here talking to Louis."

The child took one look at Ruth and buried her face in the curve of Will's shoulder.

"Yessir, Preacher Robertson." Louis spoke up. "We was talkin' about how the Lord can move in mysterious ways and work wonders for us. I am thankful to you both for what you're doin' for ol' Louis."

"You're not old, Louis," Will said. "You have many good years of freedom awaiting you."

"That would be a wonder." Louis glanced up at the sky with a smile spreading over his face. "If'n that comes about, I'll be praisin' the eternal Master the rest of my days, but right now I'd best be gettin' on back. Bet will be needin' these." He took the basket Ruth held out toward him.

After he left, they both seemed hesitant to break the silence between them. Not the comfortable silence they had shared watching the sundown the day she had gone buggy riding with him. This silence was so taut the air almost twanged with it. The child must have sensed their uneasiness, because she peeked around at Ruth and then hid her face against Will's shirt again.

She had to be Will's daughter even if she looked nothing like him. With her soft, honey-colored curls and round face, she must take after her mother. Perhaps that was why Will seemed so ill at ease. The child in his arms brought the memory of his wife to stand between them. The joyful promise of new love that had lifted Ruth's spirits earlier that morning gathered in a hard knot in her chest as she waited for Will to speak.

A few more seconds ticked by. This was ridiculous. He was standing in front of her like one of her older students afraid to confess not doing the work she'd assigned. She wasn't Will's teacher or his judge or his anything. A promise was only that. A promise and not reality. Reality was the child in his arms, and if he couldn't face that, she could.

She pushed a smile out on her face. "Who is this sweet young lady?"

He moved closer to the porch where she stood. "Meet my daughter, Willeena, but we call her Willie." He shook his head a little as though he'd said something wrong and went on. "That is, my sister and I do. Did."

"After her father." Ruth went down the steps, making sure to keep a smile on her face. She leaned to the side to try to catch the girl's eye. "Hello, Willeena. I like your name. My name is Ruth."

The child sneaked a look over at her and then quickly hid her eyes again. Will rubbed his hand up and down her back. "She's had some upheavals and she's not too sure about things yet. My sister is in the family way and having some difficulties. Her husband brought Willie to me yesterday afternoon after I saw you at Mrs. Gregory's."

"I see."

"I didn't know she was coming."

"So I assume she's not the only one to have some upheavals." Ruth reached to touch the child but stayed her hand.

"No, I fear not." A smile slipped across Will's face.

Ruth's own smile felt easier. She had no trouble imagining some of the difficulties Will may have encountered with the sudden care of such a young child thrust on him. Hadn't she experienced something the same once herself? Of course, Adria had been seven. That was a lot different than a toddler.

The child lifted her head away from his shoulder. "What's a heaval?"

"Upheaval," Will repeated for her. "That's when everything changes."

The child frowned a bit as she considered her father's answer. She was a pretty child with wide, expressive eyes and a sweet bow mouth. Her mother must have been a lovely woman. Mrs. Gregory said the woman died of childbirth fever. So sad to think she never got to mother her child.

The girl started squirming in Will's arms. "Want down." Where moments before she'd burrowed down against his chest, now she pushed against him to get away.

He put her down with a warning. "You can't run away."

She peered up at him but didn't say anything.

Will looked over at Ruth to explain. "At the house while I was hitching up the mare, she got away from me. I was fortunate to catch her before she got out of sight." He settled his gaze back on Willeena. "She can move faster than I thought."

As if to prove his words, the little girl ran across the yard to snatch at a dandelion fluff. When the seeds came off in her hand, she giggled and knelt down on the ground beside the stem.

"She appears to have a curious mind for such a young child," Ruth said.

"Indeed," Will said. "I've been answering questions all morning. What are we going to eat? What's the horse's name? Why are you so tall? Where are we going?"

Ruth had to laugh at the look on his face. "Did you have answers?"

"Not enough." He laughed too, but then the smile completely vanished from his face as he looked from the child to Ruth. "Not nearly enough. I don't know anything about taking care of a little girl." He kept his gaze locked on her face. "I need help, Ruth."

Ruth's heart gave a little lurch as she waited for him to say more, but he just watched her as though waiting for her to answer a question he hadn't asked. Did he want her to take in another child the way she'd taken in Adria? Again another woman's child and not her own. Or did he mean more? They barely knew one another.

"Of course we'll help you. Everyone in the church will be ready to help." She kept her voice light. Best not to assume more than was meant by his plea for help.

He glanced toward the child, entranced now by a bird singing in the oak tree. Then he stepped closer to Ruth. "I don't want everyone's help. I want yours."

"I . . . I . . . ," she stammered, not sure what to say as her heart started racing.

He softly touched her face with the tips of his fingers. "I'm asking a lot, Ruth. Willie needs a mother." He traced her cheekbone with his finger. "I need a wife."

"I don't know what to say." Her skin tingled where he touched her cheek as the answer yes rose unbidden from her heart. But she pushed it aside. Instead she said, "This is all very sudden."

235

"Yes." He dropped his hand back to his side. "I will understand if you tell me to leave and never come back."

She didn't want that. But at the same time she'd never been impulsive. "I need time to think about it. To pray."

His face lightened then. "I'll pray as well. That the Lord will send you a sign. Send us both a sign to show us his will."

Twenty-seven

Why had he said that about a sign? For months Will had despaired of his prayers rising above the ceiling and now he was asking for a sign from the Lord. Next thing he'd be laying out a fleece like Gideon in the Bible. And then doing it again, as though he couldn't be sure of the Lord's answer the first time.

But a little help from the Lord would be good. Will had been about to jump out of his skin ever since he stepped into Ruth's yard. It was good Louis was there to give Will time to settle his nerves. But then he'd been tongue-tied about introducing Willie to Ruth. Even in his worst moments, he generally had no problem spitting out words. But having Willie in his care changed everything for him, and he feared it would change the sweet beginnings of the attraction between him and Ruth. Not for him, but for her.

She had been so lovely standing there, her cheeks flushed by the heat of her kitchen, her lips curled up in a smile that became a bit hesitant as she looked at Willie. Then perhaps it was only his doubt that had put up the wall of silence between them after Louis left with his basket of baked goods. Will was relieved when Ruth spoke first.

That had brought words from him he'd had no intention of

speaking. A proposal, of all things. Not that he wanted to take it back. Instead he wanted to see yes in her eyes. He wanted to know how she felt in his arms. To touch his lips to hers.

He had raced ahead like a runaway horse with no thought of the fences he might crash into.

Instead of yes he'd seen surprise, followed by uncertainty in her eyes. He imagined the same might be reflected back to her from his own eyes. Even if he was the one doing the asking. It was something he had never planned to ask again. Ever. After Mary's death, he pledged to live a single life. Loving someone the way he loved Mary opened up a man to too much pain.

For over two years, he had been satisfied with his solitary life, muddling along helping others if he could, studying the Bible to share the gospel and to attempt to strengthen his wavering faith. But then he met Ruth and his life became a lonely desert. Perhaps he was meant to be alone, but could it be the Lord had brought him to Springfield for other purposes? What was it Louis had said? That the good Lord could work in mysterious ways. Had the Lord brought Will here not only to help free Louis but to start a new life with Ruth?

That might be up to the woman standing in front of him, slight furrows between her eyes as she considered his words.

"What sort of sign?" she asked, as if she really wanted to know what he, as a man of God, meant.

"I don't know," he answered honestly. "I probably shouldn't have said that."

"You don't think the Lord sends signs?" Her frown grew more pronounced.

"Not every time, any more than he answers every prayer as we wish." He wanted to pick up Willie, go back out to the street to start over. Knock on Ruth's front door again and hope he didn't make such a mess of it all.

"But we continue to pray and hope for guidance."

"We do."

She looked away from him, then toward Willie, who paid them no attention as she happily ran about the yard.

After a long moment, Ruth turned back to Will. "Peter saw signs in everything. As much preacher as teacher, he was attuned to whatever the Lord wanted to speak to him. I leaned on his faith and then he died. His death seemed wrong, as though the Lord had somehow played a cruel trick on us. On me." She rushed on as though worried he would take offense at her words. "I know that's not right, but it was a desperate time for me."

"I understand desperation and loss."

"Of course you do." Her eyes softened on him. "But then the Lord did send me signs. Louis brought me Adria. I was encouraged to teach at the school in Peter's place. Life went on. I couldn't stop living. Or believing."

"But you never married again. I'm sure you had opportunities." Many opportunities, he thought. It would be good to know why she turned them aside, even as he hoped she would not as summarily turn him aside.

"None I wanted to entertain. Adria and I were all right on our own. With the Lord's help, of course."

"I'm not all right on my own. I thought I would be, but even before my sister's husband brought me Willie, I wasn't all right. I need a helpmate. Willie merely made that need more acute."

"What sort of helpmate?" Ruth lifted her eyebrows in question. "Are you proposing a marriage of convenience?" Her cheeks reddened, but her gaze didn't waver.

"That would not be my first choice." He'd gone this far, he might as well be truthful. Still, she might not have the same feeling, so he went on. "But if it is a choice that suits you, then we could have such an arrangement. If you have a couch."

"I rather doubt it would be long enough for you." A little smile sneaked into her eyes.

"I am rather used to that. I haven't had a bed long enough since I was fourteen."

The smile spilled out of her eyes down to her lips. "What did you tell Willie when she asked why you were so tall?"

"That the Lord made me that way." Her smile gave him hope. "The same as he gave me a heart that needs to love again."

Her smile faded. "Then perhaps we should wait and pray for that sign."

"If that is what you want. I can wait and pray." He could give her time. As much as she needed if the answer turned out to be yes. He wouldn't think about any other answer. Not after baring his heart to her. "But meanwhile, would you have a loaf of bread I can buy? Willie says she likes biscuits, but I fear my cooking skills are lacking. So I am hoping bread and butter will be an acceptable substitute."

Her smile came back. "Of course. Let me get that and I'll add a few cookies as a treat for you both." She turned to go back in the house.

"Ruth." The sound of her name surprised them both. It was Willie calling out as she ran straight toward Ruth across the yard with a few dandelion blooms clutched in her hand. "Ruth. Dandy flowers."

Ruth stooped down in front of Willie. "For me?"

Willie nodded and held out the flowers. The heads of a couple of the dandelions were already drooping and another barely had a stem to hold. But Willie looked very pleased with her bouquet.

"Thank you." Ruth opened her hand to receive the flower gift.

"I like dandy flowers." Willie looked from the dandelions to stare at Ruth's face as only a small child can. "Do you?"

"I do." Ruth smiled at her.

"Mama Hazie likes flowers. She got sick, so Daddy A brought me here. He told me not to cry, but I miss Mama Hazie."

Willie's bottom lip jutted out and a tear slid down her cheek. Will wanted to go comfort her, but he stayed where he was. It seemed a moment between Willie and Ruth he shouldn't disturb.

"Sometimes it's hard not to cry." Ruth's voice was soft and a little shaky, as though she were near tears herself. "But God gave us tears because he knew that sometimes we would need to let out some of our sadness."

Willie's lips quivered then and more tears came. Will started to reach for her, but Ruth opened her arms to the child first. Without a second's hesitation, Willie stepped into Ruth's embrace. Ruth sat back on the steps and pulled her up into her lap as the child sobbed.

"It's going to be all right, Willeena." Tears wet Ruth's cheeks as she kissed the top of Willie's head.

Will gently touched Willie's back. His heart seemed to be swelling too big for his chest, and then his own eyes were awash with tears.

Ruth looked up at him. "Sit with us, Will."

He settled on the steps beside her and his child. It seemed the most natural thing in the world to put his arms around them both and hold them.

Perhaps shared tears were the sign he'd asked from the Lord.

❧

Ruth watched Will and his daughter leaving. The little girl's head was barely above Will's knee as she clung to his hand and took three steps to his one. She was smiling again, her tears forgotten in an instant, as only possible for someone that young. Two and a half, Will said. Her language skills were advanced for her age.

Just before they turned the corner out of sight, Willeena twisted around without letting go of her father's hand to wave. Her face was still tear-streaked, but her smile was as bright as the dandelions she'd brought Ruth.

She gathered up the little flowers that she'd dropped on the porch while she held the sobbing child. The yellow petals were curling in, already losing their brightness.

The child calling her name and running toward her with the little bouquet had seemed the sign Will said they needed. But then, perhaps the wilted flowers were the sign instead. Fading so quickly. Even if she put them in water, which she would, they wouldn't regain the beauty they showed blooming amid the green grass of the yard.

Other dandelions were scattered about like sun drops in the yard. They bloomed low to the ground, but then their fluff balls shot up in the air for the wind to catch their seeds. Nature's way of ensuring the cycle of life continued.

That could be her sign. She shook her head. Was she going to see signs in everything? Bright flowers. Wilted flowers. Flower seeds. Or perhaps she didn't need to see signs like that. She could simply remember the good feel of Will sitting beside her, his arms encircling both her and his child. The tears they'd shared. The way her heart had bounded up in her throat when he had said he needed a wife. He needed her.

Yes had been on the tip of her tongue, but she hadn't let it out into the air between them. She had to be sensible. She needed to think. Watch for signs. Wonder what those signs meant.

Inside, the kitchen was still stifling, even though she had finished her baking for the day and the fires were dying out. She would keep a few coals banked in the ashes in order to heat the ovens again come morning for the next batch of baking. The same routine every day when school was not in session. Up early to bake and then other chores or sewing in the afternoon. Sometimes she had to fetch supplies or make deliveries. Now and again, she gave herself the gift of reading or writing poetry.

She and Adria had long been settled into that routine. Just the two of them. As she told Will, they had managed. Without a male presence in their house. Did she want to change that now? Whether she chose to or not, change would come. Adria would marry and start her own family. Perhaps with Carlton. Perhaps with someone else.

Then Ruth would be alone. A woman widowed for many more years than she'd been married. That made her feel old. Yet that morning she had welcomed the joy that was awakening in her heart. A new love in the offing. What about the promise becoming a reality made her tremble? It was so sudden.

He needed a mother for his child. But that hadn't been all. He said he needed a helpmate. For himself as well as the child. The thoughts circled in her head as she washed her baking dishes.

After she finished cleaning up the kitchen, she hung up her apron and went into the sitting room. Her eyes went to the couch. She couldn't keep from smiling at the thought of Will trying to sleep there. No way could he fit.

But could he fit in her bed? Could she after twelve years of widowhood welcome a man back into her bed? The thought sent a tingle through her. A not completely uncomfortable tingle. She was only thirty-two.

Are you proposing a marriage of convenience? She'd asked the question. He'd answered, his eyes saying more than his words. Not his first choice, but if it was hers . . .

She looked at the couch again. She would fit. Easily. Will and his daughter could have her bedroom. She pulled in the reins of her runaway thoughts. She hadn't said yes to any sort of marriage. Or to being the mother of yet another motherless child.

But the very memory of the child cuddled in her arms brought a sweet smile. She went into her bedroom to her desk. Perhaps she could still capture a bit of the poem that had wanted to spring from her thoughts as she looked at the morning sky. But before she picked up her pen, she laid her hand on Peter's Bible. Through the years his Bible had continually been a comfort. She never opened it without remembering how Peter depended on the Lord, using the Scriptures to guide him in all he did. In all they did. Even at the end when every word became a struggle, he had spoken the words from Psalm 23. *Yea, though I walk through the valley of death, I shall fear no evil.*

As she had many times since Peter died, Ruth opened the Bible and leafed through pages. She stopped at Isaiah 30, where Peter had marked verse 21.

And thine ears shall hear a word behind thee, saying, "This is the way, walk ye in it, when ye turn to the right hand, and when ye turn to the left."

"But I don't hear your voice."

The words ran through her mind. *Did you not hear me in that child speaking your name? And catch a glimpse of me in the flowers she brought you?*

"Doesn't your word also say to wait on the Lord?" she whispered.

Ruth stood still and listened. Maybe not for an audible answer, but she didn't doubt the Lord could put that word in her mind. Or in front of her in the Scriptures. She ran her hand across the Bible page as though she could absorb the verses' wisdom through her fingertips.

She closed the Bible and then hugged it against her breast. How many times had she done so since Peter died? Perhaps too many times. Was she still leaning on Peter's faith? It could be she needed to step up to the Lord's throne on her own as a beloved child of God and trust him to direct her steps.

She put down the Bible and pulled a straight chair up to the desk. She picked up her pen and dipped it in the pot of ink.

Joy cometh in the morning. She wrote the Scripture words that had come to her that morning with the sun. She stared at those words of promise until they blurred on the page. Could she open her heart and her arms to that promise?

She turned to look at her bed. She couldn't help but smile. Will was right. It wouldn't be long enough for him either, but he could adapt. She could adapt. More telling, she wanted to find ways to adapt.

Suddenly she could hardly wait for the afternoon to pass for it to be time to go to church. So that she could see Will. And Willeena. Another woman's child, but such a very sweet one. Had not Adria been a blessing sent to Ruth from tragedy? Willeena was the same. A child without a mother.

This is the way, walk ye in it.

Twenty-eight

When Adria left the store after work, she looked around. She wasn't sure if she was glad or disappointed when she didn't see Logan Farrell stepping out of some doorway or shadow to join her on the walkway. She had to admit she was attracted to him, but at the same time she was sure a sensible girl would run the other direction at the first sight of him.

She had intended to go to church, but several customers right at quitting time kept her late. Then she had counted the money collected for Louis. She could hardly believe they had enough to purchase Louis's freedom even without whatever had been collected at the church. Some had been left at the bank too. Perhaps enough to help Louis get started on a life of freedom.

She couldn't quit smiling as she put the money back in the safe. In the morning, Pastor Robertson could take the money to the hotel to purchase Louis. He'd be free after years of slavery.

The thought put a spring in Adria's step as, instead of going home, she turned down Walnut Street. Elias Brown had sent word to ask her to come by his shop. She had no idea why. Perhaps he wanted to order a cake.

Elias was banking the forge's fire to leave for the day when she got there. No one else was in the shop.

When he heard her behind him, he turned around. "Miss Adria, glad you got here before I left for the day."

Adria stepped closer to Elias. "What do you need, Elias? Some baked goods?"

It was warm in the shop, but welcoming somehow. His hammers were all hung along the wall, and the anvil was smooth and dark, waiting for more metal to be pounded into shape on it. A place where things were made.

"No, no. The missus does all her own baking. She's a right fine cook, as you can see by the size of me." He touched his broad middle, but it was more muscle than fat. "What I'm wanting to talk to you about has to do with Louis."

"You don't need to worry about giving more," Adria said. "We've collected enough to buy him from the Sanderson family."

"But what is he goin' to do then? A man, any man, needs a job."

"Louis will be able to get work. Mr. Sanderson has hired him out to half the people in Springfield."

"No need to tell me that. I've given George Sanderson a fair share of coin over the years for Louis to swing his hammer here. That's how I kept the shop going after my rheumatism got bad." He rubbed one of his shoulders. "Truth is, I'm ready to lay down my hammers and sell my shop."

"So do you want to put up a notice at the store?" She wasn't sure why he was telling her his plans.

He shook his head. "I've been hearing folks talk about how everybody was giving to buy Louis, and I figured you might get more than his price. That got me to thinking maybe you could use any extra money in that collection of yours to buy my place here and turn it over to Louis. He's a fine smithy. I'll price it better than fair. For Louis."

Adria could hardly believe her ears. That was exactly what Louis had told her he would want to do. The Lord was answering prayers she had been too timid to even voice.

"That would be wonderful." She wanted to hug Elias, but a

look at his smithy apron kept her at arm's length. "If we have enough."

"Long as it's some. Then Louis can pay off the rest over time. When you know what you've got, send that new preacher of yours by and we'll figure out a deal."

Adria was practically dancing when she stepped back out on the street. She couldn't wait to tell Ruth and Pastor Robertson. She wanted to run and tell Louis, but best not do that until it was a sure thing. Even if he wouldn't be surprised. Not after he told her to pray believing. But she could hardly believe this.

Everything was working out. Earlier that day she'd heard Mrs. Gregory had bought Bet. Maybe in time she would set the cook free. Maybe in time all slaves would be freed. Adria had just received a letter from Abigail talking about how the abolition movement was growing in the east. As she did in every letter, she offered Adria a place to live in her home if Adria wanted to more actively join the fight. But Boston seemed as far away as the moon.

Then there was the truth that she did want to marry and have a family. If not tomorrow, then someday. She'd written that to Abigail, who had written back to suggest she might meet forward-thinking men in Boston who not only believed in freedom for slaves but spoke up for the rights of women. What a wonder that might be! Even if there were such men, that didn't mean Adria would fall in love with one of them or him with her. But simply thinking about the possibility seemed to open new ways of thinking for Adria.

Here in Springfield, she had always assumed that someday she would take the expected path and marry Carlton. She would, as Ruth had pointed out, not want for anything. Carlton claimed he loved her, but Adria couldn't help thinking he might love the woman he hoped she was instead of the woman she was. Long ago, she should have been honest with Carlton. Made him understand marriage was not going to change how she felt about slavery. She would not, could not, have slaves in her household.

As if she had summoned him with her thoughts, Carlton was waiting in front of her house when she turned down Elm Street. As soon as he saw her, he started up the street toward her. Even before he got close, she could see he was upset. When had they lost the fun of being together? She liked him. She really did. But when he got that frown in his eyes, he changed from the boy she once thought she might love enough to marry to a man she didn't know.

"Carlton." She smiled as if she didn't notice his frown. "You didn't go to church."

"I came to go with you and Ruth, but now the service will be half over." He stopped in front of her, nearly blocking the walkway.

"I'm sorry. You should have gone on with Ruth. Some people came in right at closing time." She did her best to look genuinely sorry in hopes of appeasing him.

Instead his frown got darker. "You always have an excuse, don't you?"

"Not an excuse. A reason. You have a job. If you need to, don't you stay late to finish whatever needs to be done?"

"I work for my father. I can leave whenever I want."

"But your father doesn't, does he?" Adria raised her eyebrows at him as she eased past him to move on toward her house.

"No, he's probably still working." He turned to walk along with her. "Mother says he's going to work himself to death. That he should hire more people or teach some of our slaves to work at the shop. Father says he'd rather pay his workers. He thinks that makes them have more pride in making a good hat."

"Do you like to make hats?" It wasn't something she had ever asked Carlton.

"I hate making hats. I've surely told you that." Carlton sounded cross that she had to ask.

Adria stopped at the front gate and looked toward the small house that was in need of paint. A little feather of smoke rose from the chimney where Ruth must have been baking earlier. She wanted to go on inside, sit down, and take off her shoes, but she couldn't

ANN H. GABHART

invite Carlton into the house. It wouldn't be proper without Ruth there to chaperone.

"Maybe you did. I don't remember." Adria leaned against the gate. "So what do you want to do?"

"After we marry, we'll move out to my grandfather's farm. He's getting too old to take care of things there. I aim to make it profitable. Have cattle. Pigs. With the slaughterhouses and pork processing places here in town, that will be something good to get into."

"Sounds harder than making hats."

"Grandfather's slaves do the work. I'll just have to see that things are done and take care of the business end of buying and selling the stock."

"And buying and selling slaves?" Adria kept her voice soft.

"That is part of running a successful farm. I know that bothers you, but Grandfather's slaves are well cared for. Grandmother doesn't have to lift a finger in the house. All she has to do is keep the servants in order and doing what they should."

Adria stood up a little straighter and braced herself for whatever might follow her words. "You do know, don't you, that I believe all slavery should be abolished. I could never own a slave."

He waved his hand as though her words were of no consequence. "You'll change your mind after we're married and you see how things are out on the farm. We have to have slaves to get the work done. Those people in the north think we can just set them all free. That's insane. They don't know what they're talking about. Our people would have no idea how to survive if we didn't feed and take care of them. And they are happy that way."

"I don't believe that."

"That's because you've filled your head with stories from books." He tapped her hat with his finger and gave her an indulgent smile. "And now this with Louis has got you all confused on how life really is. You could be right about the town owing Louis his freedom. Father agrees with you completely and gave a big chunk toward

249

your campaign. But all slaves aren't like Louis. Nobody wants to set them free."

"I do."

"And that's a charming thing about you, but you'll have to forget those crazy ideas after we get married."

"And be a proper wife who does what her husband wants, I suppose." Adria's smile hurt her face.

"That's what a wife is supposed to do. And raise our children. Tell me you'll stop putting off our marriage. We could say vows in front of the preacher next Sunday."

He reached for her hand, but she hid it in her skirts. She wanted to be angry with him, but instead she simply felt sad. Deeply sad. "I'm not going to marry you."

"All right, if Sunday is too soon, we can wait until next month. July is hot, but so is August. That doesn't really matter anyway. Once we're married, we'll spend every day the rest of our lives together, no matter the weather."

"I'm not going to marry you, Carlton." She made sure she said the words distinctly and firmly.

Confusion flashed across his face, but then he was smiling again. "You've simply got the vapors. You'll change your mind in a few days. As soon as all this with the Sanderson sale is done and things settle back down." His smile disappeared. "And that Logan Farrell moves along. You can't depend on a man like that. No roots. Nothing but a smile that doesn't mean a thing when he's promising you the moon."

"He hasn't promised me anything. And this isn't about him. It's about you. The two of us." She kept her eyes locked on his face. "I have never had the vapors and I mean what I say. I like you, Carlton. Very much. We've been friends forever, but I can't marry you." She shook her head a little. "No, 'can't' isn't the right word. I won't marry you."

Carlton stared at her for a moment, as though he wasn't sure he heard her right. "You don't know what you're saying. We've known we were going to get married for years. Everybody knows that. Of course you are going to marry me."

Adria just looked at him without saying anything. What more was there to say?

His confusion turned to anger then. He grabbed her and pushed her back against the gate. "Whatever game you're playing, Adria, I'm tired of it. You need to come to your senses and realize I am your only hope of a decent marriage after you've ruined your reputation with that drifter. Going into a tavern with him like a common woman of the night. Not to mention dealing with the lowest of men in that store every day. But because I love you, I am willing to overlook all that." He stared down at her, his eyes fierce as his hands tightened on her arms. "But once we're married, things will change. People will respect you because you're my wife."

Adria wanted to jerk away from him, but instead she stood very still. While she had argued with Carlton many times, she'd never seen him this angry. She took a slow breath to keep her own anger in check. "You're hurting me, Carlton."

For a couple of seconds he kept his grip tight, as though he wanted her to know he was stronger and could impose his will on her. Then his face changed and he was again the Carlton she knew and sometimes thought she loved.

He loosened his hands but didn't turn her loose. "I'm sorry, but sometimes you push me too far, Adria."

"I am simply being honest with you."

His eyes narrowed on her. "So next are you going to tell me you love that scoundrel Logan Farrell?"

"Not at all. I hardly know the man."

"Well, at least you are using your good sense there." His voice softened and he rubbed his hands up and down her arms in a caress now to perhaps make up for his roughness. "You're just not thinking straight, Adria. Eventually you'll see things more clearly. We can have a good life together. I'll give you everything you ever dreamed of having."

Except the freedom to be the woman I want to be. The words threaded through her mind, but she didn't speak them aloud. Carlton wouldn't understand. He had never understood. She would have to convince him that she couldn't marry him, but right now she just wanted him to go away.

"It's been a long day, Carlton, and I'm tired."

"Poor dear." He touched her face with his fingertips. "You'll never have to work again after we marry."

"I know." She smiled a little as she pushed him back and stepped through the gate before he could lean down to kiss her. Perhaps if Ruth talked to him, she could make him understand that Adria meant what she said about not marrying him. Or she could get Pastor Robertson to talk to him.

"I love you, Adria." He leaned across the gate toward her. "Nobody could ever love you like I do."

"Goodbye, Carlton."

"I'll see you tomorrow, won't I?"

"I'm not going anywhere," Adria said. Then she thought of Abigail's letter telling her to come to Boston. While that seemed like somewhere in another world, suddenly her world here felt too small.

She turned to go up the steps onto the front porch. Relief swept through her when she looked back to see Carlton walking away.

The house felt empty when she went in the front door and took off her hat to hang on the hall tree. The scent of fresh-baked bread and cakes lingered in the air. A sweet, homey odor. Adria stood still and listened. Even now, all these years later, she sometimes imagined she could hear the echo of her mother's laugh and her father's voice. They had loved each other so much. Both had been content with their lot in life. Her mother to care for Adria and her little brother. Her father to provide for them.

How different Adria's life surely would have been if not for the cholera. Perhaps then she would have been happy to marry Carlton. She would have never known Aunt Tilda's burning need to be free that had colored her every word. Louis might have been only another slave to barely notice as she walked along the Springfield streets.

But the cholera had raged through the town, stealing that past from Adria and giving her a different future with Ruth, a woman who showed Adria the world through books. A woman who had been strong through every difficulty and had cared for Adria in spite of her hesitation to claim her as a daughter. It could be that, if not for Adria, Ruth would have long ago remarried and had a different life too.

There was no need to think about what might have been. Better to consider what was and decide on her tomorrow with a clear eye.

She went in the kitchen to find something to eat. The room was still warm from the morning's baking.

A soft, almost timid knock on the back door made her look around.

"Missy Adria, are you in there?"

A woman's voice. Not Louis, who still called her "missy" as he had from the time he first carried her away from this house after her family died. But a familiar voice all the same.

Adria pulled the door open. "Bet. What are you doing here?"

"I's needin' your help." The black woman looked behind her and around.

Adria reached out and pulled her into the kitchen. Fear stepped inside with her.

Twenty-nine

S hut the door, Miss Adria, 'fore I get seen." Bet stepped over in the corner out of view of the window.

Adria glanced out the door. No one was there, but she did as Bet said. Her palm slid on the doorknob. She rubbed her damp hands off on her skirt and, like Bet, moved out of sight of the window. "Tell me what's wrong."

Bet's eyes were open wide and she was breathing too fast.

"Has something happened to Louis?" Adria's fears raced ahead when Bet couldn't seem to come up with any words.

"No, miss. Louis be fine far as I knows. It's Twila."

"Twila?" The name didn't mean anything to Adria.

"You likely don't know her. She didn't never work in the kitchen. Helped the maids in the hotel from the time she was a bitsy thing. But she's my girl. Turned fifteen last month, best I can reckon."

"I didn't know you had a daughter, Bet."

"White folks, they don't think nothing about black people's families." She looked sorry for her words then and held out a hand toward Adria. "I ain't meanin' you, Miss Adria. I knows you ain't like that. That's how come I'm here. Hopin' and prayin' you can help me. Help Twila."

"What can I do? Mrs. Gregory is going to take you. You know that, don't you?"

"I do know that. Right now Mistress Gregory thinks I'm still at the hotel and them at the hotel think I've gone on down to Mistress Gregory. Don't nobody know I'm here. And I ain't botherin' you on account of myself. I be fine with that. But it's Twila."

Bet's face screwed up and she looked ready to cry. But then she pressed her lips together and pulled in a deep breath before she went on. "They're done plannin' to sell her to a man from some-where off. I seen him. I knows what he wants with my Twila. She's a pretty child. Light skinned. Could pass for white if folks didn't know she was a slave. I been where they's wantin' to send her and I's willin' to do anythin' to stop that from happenin'." She looked directly at Adria then. "Even put you in trouble's way."

"Did Louis tell you to come here?" Adria's mind was racing, but she had no idea what to do.

"Oh no, miss. Louis wouldn't never do nothin' that might hurt you. I wouldn't neither 'cept for Twila. You is my only hope. You understand, don't you?" She looked as though she meant it, but then she was standing there in the kitchen asking Adria to do something. But what?

"I'm trying, but I don't know how to help you. Or Twila." All her letter writing to newspapers meant nothing in the face of Bet's desperation.

"She just needs to get to this house over in the next county. It ain't all that far. The people there, they has ways of getting her on north where she'll be safe." She pulled a piece of paper out of her pocket. "Louis would have done it, found a way to get her there, if I'd asked him, but I didn't want to risk him losin' his chance for freedom with it just needin' a few more sunrises. But this map shows where the house is. As long as no chair is turned upside down on the porch, they take in folks runnin' to the north."

Adria looked at the map. The paper was old and the lines on it traced over again and again. "Where did you get this?"

"Matilda give it to Louis. He showed me where he hid it."

Adria frowned at Bet. "But Matilda died years ago. How do you know the house or the people are even still there?"

"I knows." Her face tightened as she nodded. "White folks think us slaves don't have ears, but we hear things. People come through. Some racin' for the free states. Others headin' back to try to lead family out. The people is still there."

Adria pulled in a breath. "Where's Twila now?"

"She's out back in your shed. Scared silly, but this is her only chance. You is her only chance."

Adria's hands trembled as she folded the map back up and started to put it in her pocket.

"You can't keep that." Bet reached for it. "You has to memorize the markings. If you got caught with the map, it wouldn't just be you in trouble, but all them others marked there too. Then nobody wouldn't never find the way."

Adria unfolded the paper again and stared at it, but what good would it do if she did memorize it? She had no way of getting Twila there. Or anybody to help her. Ruth might try, but it would frighten her too much. Carlton would drag Twila back to whoever was buying her. The preacher might be moved by compassion, but if he was found out, he'd be run out of town. Perhaps Logan Farrell would be foolhardy enough to help, but she didn't even know how to find him.

She handed Bet the map and then reached for her hands. "Pray with me, Bet. That the Lord will show me a way to help you."

Bet took her hands. "I been prayin' hard, like as how Louis tells me to. Pray believin'."

The words echoed in Adria's head. Louis had told her the same. Bet went on. "The Lord's the one what led me to you."

"Then he'll show us a way." Even as she was shutting her eyes, an idea came to her. She'd go to the store, get some men's clothes. She could pretend to be a stranger in town, rent a buggy at the livery stable, and be on her way with Twila hidden away. It wasn't a great plan, but it was something.

Bet squeezed her hands as they prayed, neither one speaking aloud.

Lord, if you know a better way . . . She didn't finish. The Lord knew what was needed. She would believe that. She had to believe that.

She told Bet her plan. They both wanted to believe it would work. Twila was to make her way from shadow to shadow to wait just outside of town where Adria would stop for her. Bet said Twila had studied the map too, so that if something happened she could try to make it on foot to the house with five chairs on the porch. But it was a long way on foot, with many chances of getting caught.

Adria was taking chances too. It didn't do to think what would happen if she got caught helping a runaway slave. After Bet and Twila disappeared into the gloaming, Adria continued to stare at the gathering darkness for a long moment. She thought about leaving Ruth a note, but what would she say? *I'm about to break the law.* No, it was better if Ruth knew nothing about this.

As she headed up Elm toward Main, Adria's mouth was dry and her heart already beating too hard when the fire bell began clanging. Smoke was rising from the middle of town. Near the store. *Please, not the store.* But no, it was farther to the east. Perhaps one of the pork-packing houses or the lumberyard. Whatever was burning, fire could spread quickly through the frame buildings and race through the town.

On Main Street, people were running from every direction toward the fire. She ran along with them until she reached the store, where she slipped around to the back and reached in her pocket for her key. She didn't need it. When she touched the door, it swung open. Mr. Billiter must have come back to protect the store from sparks carried by the wind. If so, she still might be able to grab the pants and a hat without him seeing her. She'd put the money for them in the till tomorrow. If she wasn't in jail.

She pushed that thought away. She could do this. She had to do this. Not just for Twila but for herself. If she truly believed slavery was wrong in the sight of God and man, then she couldn't refuse the girl help whatever the risks.

Adria moved toward the front of the store, careful to step over the creaky boards. The front door was closed and the shade pulled down the way it always was when the store was closed. Strange. She expected the door to be open if Mr. Billiter was there. The glow of the fire down the street edged in around the shade to light up the store. She'd have no trouble finding the pants even without a lamp.

A noise stopped her in her tracks. A man was crouched just inside the storage room in front of the safe. The smell of sulphur was strong as he struck a match to light a candle. It wasn't Mr. Billiter. Adria's heart gave a funny stutter beat.

Dear Lord. The prayer started in her head and then froze there as the man must have heard her gasp and looked around. Logan Farrell jumped to his feet, obviously as surprised to see her as she was to see him.

"What are you doing?" Adria demanded.

He didn't answer her. Instead, in two steps he was in front of her, still holding the candle. "Do you know the combination? I thought I did, but I must have missed one of the numbers."

"How would you know the combination?"

"I watched your boss open it yesterday. No trouble to read the numbers over his shoulder."

Adria was still confused. "Why are you trying to get in the safe?"

He actually smiled, the same easy smile as always. "There's money in there."

"The money for Louis."

"Right. A goodly sum. Enough to get me to California."

"You'd steal Louis's freedom?" Adria's head was spinning.

"You can collect more. Folks seem right fond of old Louis here in town, but either way, what with always being a slave, he wouldn't know what to do with freedom anyhow. Not how I do." Logan nodded back toward the safe. "The money in there means my freedom. You can help me get it."

"I don't know the combination."

"I don't believe you." Logan's smile disappeared.

"That doesn't make it any less true." Adria stared at him. "I do not know the combination. Mr. Billiter said I was safer that way from anybody who tried to steal from us when he wasn't in the store."

"His money was safer anyhow." Logan frowned. "I thought I had the perfect chance with the wagon shop on fire. Get the money. Go."

"You set the fire."

"Purely an accident, but I've never been one to look askance at an opportunity." Logan shrugged. "I did manage to save a small wagon. A bonus for my work there. Got the horse I bought yesterday harnessed to it ready to go. All I need is some cash in my pocket."

"You have a wagon and horse? Ready to go?" The Lord could make good come from the worst happenings. Like maybe now.

"There's room for two. Just open that safe and we'll be on our way."

"I told you I can't open the safe, but I do know where some petty cash is stashed. In case I needed extra to make change when Mr. Billiter wasn't here."

"Well, get it. Some is better than none." Logan was almost smiling again.

"But you have to do something for me first. Take me somewhere."

He moved closer to Adria. "I've already told you I'd take you all the way to California."

Adria stepped back. "I don't need to go that far. Just to a place in the next county. I have to take a friend there."

"Uh-oh. I sense trouble brewing. Your friend wouldn't happen to be a slave by any chance?"

"What's that matter to you?"

"Only some jail time if we're caught and lucky enough not to get shot by the slave trackers."

"Arson is a crime too." She stared at him without wavering.

"I told you that was an accident. A lamp turned over on a pile of scrap wood. Nothing intentional about it at all. The place went up too fast to do anything about it."

"Mobs don't need much proof. Just a name whispered in the right ears."

"You play a tough hand, Miss Starr." Logan actually laughed. "But find the cash and let's go chase trouble." He handed her the candle. "What's going to be our story if we meet anybody on the road?"

"I'm running away with you to California, of course."

Another laugh. "Your boyfriend isn't going to like that."

"No, he isn't. But maybe we won't meet anybody."

"You're a woman of many secrets." He reached to touch her face, but she stepped away from him.

"And you're a man I shouldn't trust."

"I'm a scoundrel for sure. I'm betting your aunt warned you about me from day one."

Adria didn't bother answering him. Ruth was right about him, but getting Twila away was all that mattered right now. She got the cash out of a jar on a bottom shelf, then grabbed a wool blanket off one of the shelves. She'd have to find a way to replace the money tomorrow.

Logan blew out the candle and loaded up a cloth sack with food. "For the trip. It's a long way to California."

They made their way through town under the cover of smoky darkness. If this was the Lord's better plan, Adria prayed it worked. Pray believing, she reminded herself. She had a lot to believe. That they'd get Twila to a safe place. That nobody would see her with Logan. That he wouldn't betray her. That the town wouldn't burn down. The fire looked like it had jumped to a couple more buildings.

The church wasn't far from where she saw flames. She hoped Pastor Robertson had the money for Louis in a safe place. At least the money at the store would be all right even if the men couldn't stop the fire. The safe wouldn't burn.

They didn't talk as they climbed into the wagon and headed out of town. Thank goodness the road where Twila was to wait for her wasn't blocked by the fire. When she told Logan to stop the wagon and softly called Twila's name, the girl slipped out from the trees.

The moon peeking through clouds lent enough light to the night so that it was easy to see Twila was as pretty as Bet had said. Her fear was plain to see too, but along with it was that same determined set of mouth Bet had.

"Thank you, Miss Adria." She looked from Adria to Logan. "Is that one safe?"

"He's what the Lord sent us," Adria said.

"That's the first time I've been accused of being an answer to prayer." Logan flashed his smile. He watched Twila climb into the wagon. "She's a stunner. Must be worth plenty."

Twila hesitated, ready to jump back out of the wagon. "He don't sound safe."

"Feel easy, girl." Logan held up the blanket for her crawl under the wagon seat. "Not much I won't do to put money in my pocket, but selling people isn't one of them. You're safe as long as we don't run afoul of some hunters hot on your trail."

"They won't be missin' me 'fore morning. By then, Mam says I'll be halfway to freedom and Miss Adria safe back at her house." The girl looked at Logan. "I ain't knowin' what Mam would say about you."

"I'll be headed to California. Fine place, I'm told."

Twila scrambled under the wagon seat then, and they pulled the blanket over her.

Logan flicked the reins to start his horse moving. "I'm no common horse thief either. Bought this beauty for a fair price. And the wagon was there for the taking. It was going to burn anyhow."

"You don't have to convince me, Mr. Farrell. God is the one to hear your confession." Adria kept her eyes straight ahead.

"I suppose so, but if I'm the answer to your prayers, then maybe I'll have some good points on my ledger to balance out the bad." He drove the horses on in silence for a moment. Then he said, "If we're running off to get married, don't you think you should sit closer to me?"

"There's nobody here to see."

"Me. And you." Again he was quiet for a moment. "I wasn't just blowing smoke when I asked you to go to California with me. We could hunt up a judge in the first town we come to. Get married legal and all. I figure that would be important to a girl like you. Raised proper. Then again, I was raised proper too. At least my mother tried. She'd be happy as a catfish in the river if she could know I married a girl like you and started having little Farrells."

Since she didn't move toward him on the wagon seat, he scooted a little closer to her. "I think I could fall in love with you with the least little bit of encouragement. The two of us would make quite a team. We could have a good time together."

"Life is more than a good time."

"People say that, but I've never understood why. What's wrong with having a good time?" He didn't wait for her to answer him. "There aren't any 'thou shalt not have fun' rules in the Bible that anybody has ever been able to point out to me. My opinion is the Lord had a good time now and again while he was down here. Fishing with his buddies. Walking on water. Going around healing folks. That had to be good."

"Then they put him on a cross."

"Well, there is that. Not something I aim to let happen to me or anything like it. I intend to stay one step ahead of the authorities, and I'm pretty sure there aren't a lot of those authorities out West. A man like me will be right at home." He looked over at Adria. "A woman like you, well, you'd be right at home too. With me."

"I'm not in the marrying mood today." Who would have thought she would have the opportunity to turn down two proposals in one day? One from a man who wouldn't believe she didn't love him, at least not enough, and another from a man who didn't seem to care whether she loved him or not.

"You might change me. Set me on the right tracks. Turn me into an upstanding citizen."

Even without looking at him, she knew he was smiling. "With prayer, anything is possible. Even you changing. But right now I'm praying for Twila. And that we can recognize the place we need when we see it."

"Better pray we don't stumble across any slave hunters too. Talk about people who need religion."

And so she did bow her head and pray just that. She had the feeling that under the cover, Twila was doing the same.

Thirty

R ejoice evermore. Pray without ceasing. In everything give thanks: for this is the will of God in Christ Jesus concerning you." Will read from 1 Thessalonians 5 to the faithful few scattered out in the Mount Moriah church pews.

The worshipers didn't come out on Wednesday the way they did on Sundays. But Will liked gathering with those serious about the need for prayer. At his previous church, the people had prayed for Mary and the baby through the months of her confinement. They had come together and stood around Mary's bed and prayed for the fever not to take her.

That if two of you shall agree on earth as touching any thing that they shall ask, it shall be done. That Scripture from Matthew 18 had chipped away at his faith when Mary hadn't been healed.

He still didn't understand. He might never understand until he stood in front of the Lord's throne when all would become clear. But he was ready to accept the Lord's will concerning him. Concerning all of the people who were hearing the Scripture and lifting prayers up for the sick and those in need.

Earlier, at the beginning of the service, smiles bloomed on every face in the church when Will revealed their progress in raising money for Louis. The people had come together with prayer, and this prayer the Lord was answering abundantly. But Will had no bitterness in his heart when he thought about that prayer answered and his prayers for Mary not. He was turning loose of his questions and once more grabbing hold of faith in the Lord's will over his.

Rejoice evermore.

His eyes settled on Ruth sitting straight in front of him, three rows back. With a smile lighting up her face, Willie had run to Ruth when she came in the church. Ruth had stooped down to talk to her and pulled her into a hug when the child told Ruth she'd forgotten her doll.

Willie had been sniffling about not having the doll since they got to church. It could be he should have gone back and fetched it for her, but that would have made him late to start the service. That didn't seem necessary when they would be going home in a little while. She could get the doll then. A spoiled child was a ruined child, or so his mother used to say.

Still, the child's sad face made him wish he hadn't worried about the starting time or what his mother once said. What would a slight delay in the starting time matter if the doll would give his little girl some comfort when everything was so new and different for her?

Perhaps that was why she had run to Ruth. Someone she recognized in a sea of strange faces. Now Willie leaned against Ruth, her eyelids drooping as people spoke various prayer requests.

For more rain. The fields were dry in spite of the shower the night before. For healing. Several had family members in failing health. For spiritual growth. Who among them didn't need that? For more believers in the church pews. Will didn't speak the prayer of his heart aloud, but the words were there in his mind as he watched Ruth gently smoothing back Willie's hair.

Please, Lord, let Ruth be a new beginning for me. And not just for me, but for Willie too. She's lost so much.

He had worried too long about his loss without thinking enough about his child. *And a little child shall lead them.*

Will pulled his mind away from Ruth and Willie to listen to Mr.

Martin asking for prayers for a son who had fallen away from the church. Mrs. Martin dabbed her eyes as Mr. Martin spoke of the son's waywardness.

As the congregation bowed their heads to pray with the Martins, a man Will didn't know burst though the church door.

"Fire!" he shouted.

Alarm rippled through the people as several men jumped to their feet. A couple of the younger children began to whimper, but not Willie.

"Is the church on fire?" Will couldn't smell smoke, but if the church was on fire, they needed to waste no time exiting the frame building. He stepped down from the pulpit toward Willie.

"Not the church. Byrd's wagon shop, but the wind's spreading the flames this way." The man's eyes were wide and his voice loud. "Two other buildings done caught. The sheriff told me to come warn you that your parsonage and the church could be in danger, Preacher." He looked around. "And to get as many men as we can to fight the fire before the whole town goes up in smoke."

The women stepped back to let the men leave. Then they shushed their children and hurried after them. Will took Willie from Ruth and followed them outside where the smell of smoke was strong. Night had been settling in, but the flames licking up into the sky cast an eerie light over the town. Perhaps they should have stopped for a moment of prayer before they left the church, but they were all surely sending up prayers as they ran toward the fire. He supposed he should chase after them, but he had to consider Willie. He tightened his arms around her as she burrowed her face into his shoulder.

"Is the money the church collected for Louis here or at your house?" Ruth looked worried as she stared toward the fire.

"I took it to the bank yesterday. It's safe."

"Pray we all are." Ruth's voice was soft as she stared at the glow that seemed to have moved closer just while they were standing there.

"I best go get my mare out of the shed just in case." He had put the horse up for the night before coming to church. He looked at Ruth. "Will you be all right?"

Ruth seemed ready to say something, but then she merely nodded.

Halfway down the hill to the shed, Willie raised her head off his shoulder. "Are we going to burn up?" She was trembling.

He stroked her back. "No, of course not. The Lord will take care of us."

"Will he take care of Ruth too?"

"Yes, Ruth too." He slowed his step. He should have left the child with Ruth. He looked back up the rise toward the church where Ruth stood watching them. He could take the child back to Ruth, but he was already almost to the shed.

"And Maysie?"

"Maysie?" Will frowned before he remembered that was what Willie called her doll. "I'll get it for you as soon as I can."

"I want Maysie." Willie whimpered, but Will didn't have time to think about a doll. The fire was getting closer. He could hear it crackling through the wooden structures. When he opened the shed door, the horse was neighing, restless in its stall.

He put Willie down next to the building. "You stay right there with your back against the shed and don't move. Do you understand?" He bent down and looked her in the face.

Her wide eyes glistened with tears, but she stood still.

"Stay there," Will repeated as he stood up and pointed a finger at her.

The mare was kicking the stall and tossing her head. Will had to work to calm her enough to attach a lead to her halter. He glanced at his buggy in the other side of the shed, but no time to harness the mare to it. He had to take care of Willie.

He led the mare out to her pasture field behind the shed. He looked back, but the open shed door hid Willie from view. He'd wanted her safely out of way of the nervous mare's hooves. As soon as he unhooked the lead, the mare kicked up her heels and took off for the far edge of the field. Good. No buildings close there.

Not as true with the shed and the house. Even as he thought that, a whoosh of flames rose up from a building only a couple of houses away. Fiery sparks flew up into the sky.

He ran back to the shed and pulled the door back. Willie was gone.

His heart bounded up in his throat as he looked around for his little girl. The smoke was getting thicker, burning his eyes and making it hard to see. Overhead, sparks swirled in the updrafts from the fire. Then a flame flickered to life on the shed roof.

"Willie!" he shouted, but no answer came back to him. The child was nowhere to be seen.

Ruth's throat tightened as she peered toward the smoke rising from the town. A sense of foreboding had settled on her as she watched Will carry Willeena down the hill toward his house. Ruth should have kept the child with her there by the church where it seemed safer, but she had hesitated to be so forward. Besides, from the way the little girl clung to Will, it was obvious she was scared. She needed her father.

The fire was fearsome. Flames licked up from the buildings down the street with sparks flying high into the air. Black smoke gathered above it all to hide the moon that earlier had peeked out between clouds. But the fire hadn't reached the middle of town and was nowhere near her own house on Elm. Adria would be home from Billiter's by now. A breath of relief whispered through Ruth at the thought of Adria safely away from the rushing flames.

Looking back toward where Will and Willeena had disappeared into the smoke and shadows around the shed, she wished she had gone with them. Found a way to help.

At a noise behind her, she whirled around to see Mr. Manderly setting a bucket of water down by the church steps. "Oh, I didn't think anyone was still here," she said.

He straightened up and squared his shoulders. "I don't intend to let that fire have the church building or my organ."

"Perhaps the fire won't reach this far." She saw no need in pointing out the futility of one bucket of water against the raging inferno coming toward them. The church was up on a little hill apart from any other buildings. That gave more hope of the church building surviving than Mr. Manderly's bucket of water, but at least he was doing something and not merely standing and watching.

"We can pray so, Mrs. Harmon, and for rain. That might be all that saves the town." He looked from her toward the fire. "You best go home and see to your own place."

"Yes." But instead of heading toward her house, she started down the hill into the smoke gathering around Will's house and shed. It was hard to see, but something pulled her that way. Will and Willeena pulled her that way. She had to be sure they were all right.

The horse's frantic nickering added to the alarm. She hesitated as, not far away, a new burst of flames lit up the yard and she spotted Willeena running toward the house.

Where was Will? What if the horse knocked him down? Her heart pounded in her ears. But even if he was in need of help, she had to take care of the child first. She chased after Willeena, who was on the porch, trying to turn the doorknob.

"Willeena." Ruth kept her voice soft to keep from startling the child. "What are you doing?"

When Willeena looked around, tears streaked her cheeks. "Gotta get Maysie."

Of course, the doll she'd been crying for at church. "Did you tell your father you were coming to the house?"

She shook her head, and in the wavering light from the fire, Ruth could see her bottom lip trembling. "Don't want Maysie to burn up."

Ruth kept her eyes on Willeena, even as the crackling sound of the fire sounded closer. Too close. Still, how long could it take to get the child's doll? Will would understand, and Willeena would be inconsolable if she lost her doll to the fire. Ruth opened the door and they slipped inside. The fire wasn't close enough to light up the dark room. Thank goodness. But that made it hard to see. She needed a candle or a lamp.

Willeena stopped just inside the door and sniffled. "Don't like dark. It might swallow me."

"No, sweetie. I'm right here with you." Ruth reached for Willeena's hand. "In a minute you'll be able to see better and then you can find your doll. Do you remember where you left it?"

"Uh-uh." The little girl sounded near tears again.

"Shh. Don't cry. You'll find her quicker if you don't cry."

Willeena sniffled but didn't let out any wails.

Ruth squeezed her hand. "Come on. Let's look in the kitchen first."

Surely she could find a taper in there she could light from a live coal in the fireplace where Will had cooked supper. But the ashes were cold. So even if she found a candle, she would have no way to light it. She ran her hand over the surface of the table. A bowl. The loaf of bread she'd given Will earlier. No doll. She checked the seat of each chair and peered under the table. She couldn't see any shapes that might be Willeena's doll.

Smoke was drifting into the house through the open windows. Ruth stopped still. She thought she heard something, but it must have only been the wind. Wind that was relentlessly pushing the fire toward them.

Ruth kept a tight hold on Willeena's hand and went back into the sitting room where she could make out the shapes of a desk and chair. A daybed in the corner. A narrow settee and a table. The doll could be anywhere. She touched a Bible on the desk and picked it up. Perhaps it belonged to Will's wife, a treasure like her Peter's Bible.

When the child sniffled again, Ruth kept her voice cheerful.

ANN H. GABHART

"Maybe we need to call Maysie so she'll know we're looking for her. Then when she answers, we'll find her. Maysie, where are you?" Ruth shook Willeena's hand a little. "Come on. You have to help."

The little girl's whimpers turned into a giggle. "Maysie, stop hiding from me!"

"Does she do that? Hide from you," Ruth asked.

"Sometimes. We play hide. Together."

"Where do you hide?"

"Under Mama Hazie's quilt."

"Well then, let's look there. Maybe she decided to hide without you."

Again the giggle, but this time it ended in a cough. The smoke was getting thicker. A spark must have landed on the roof. If they didn't find the doll in the next few minutes, she'd have to pick Willeena up and take her outside. She yanked the quilt off the little bed and Willeena gave a happy squeal and grabbed her doll.

Ruth felt light-headed. Not enough air. They had to get outside. She draped the quilt over her head and dropped down on her knees beside Willeena. The smoke wasn't as thick low to the floor. She tucked the Bible in her skirt waistband. "Let's play like we're dogs and crawl to the door."

Willeena grabbed hold of her doll's dress with her mouth and took off on her hands and knees. Ruth yanked her skirt out of the way and crawled along beside her. And then Will was there, somehow picking them both up.

He carried them away from the house before he put Ruth down. Her legs felt so shaky she sank to the ground. Still holding Willeena, Will dropped down beside her and reached to pull Ruth close, while behind them, flames spread across the house's roof.

"Are you all right?" Will asked.

"I will be." Ruth managed to get out the words between coughs. She already felt all right with Will's arms around her and Willeena.

Then out of nowhere came a clap of thunder, and rain showered down on them. Ruth lifted her face to the sky and laughed as the drops wet her face. Will tightened his arm around her and laughed too.

Up on the hill, the church stood untouched. Mr. Manderly must have prayed believing.

Thirty-one

The clap of thunder surprised Adria. In spite of how the moon had dipped in and out of clouds, she hadn't given the first thought to storms. Now the thunder gave them fair warning to take shelter. But no time for that. They would have to take their chances with the storm.

Logan gave no notice of the thunder. He had lost his easy manner and sat straight and stiff on the wagon seat. Adria felt every bit as tense beside him. She wondered if they were both ready to leap off the wagon and make a run for it at the first sign of trouble. But the woods beside the road didn't look very inviting, especially with dark storm clouds rolling in to hide the moon.

The only person they'd met so far was a farmer driving his cows home along the road. He gave them a curious look, but Logan grinned and switched the reins to one hand so he could wrap his free arm around Adria. When he pulled her close, the farmer chuckled and saluted them with his walking stick.

Adria waited until they were well out of sight before she scooted away from him.

"Did you recognize him?" Logan asked.

"No."

"Good. It'll be better if nobody knows we traveled this road.

273

Our passenger isn't the only one who needs to disappear without a trace."

After that, neither of them had anything to say, and the only sound was a muffled gasp from Twila now and then when they hit a bump in the road. Adria's ears tuned in to every snap of a twig or whisper of brush along the road that might mean someone was waiting to ambush them. She was almost as jumpy about the man sitting beside her. She had no idea what he might do. She tried to reassure herself with what he'd told Twila about never stooping to selling people, but at the same time, he obviously didn't have a very sure relationship with the truth. As Ruth had warned.

Ruth would worry about her, but Adria was still glad she hadn't left a note. Ruth was better off knowing nothing about any of this. The only one back in Springfield who could implicate Adria was Bet. Adria wasn't worried about her. Only about the man beside her. And the rain that suddenly came down in sheets.

The horse whinnied and balked, but after Logan snapped the reins, it trudged on through the rain.

"You could crawl under the blanket with the girl." Logan looked around with water dripping off his hat.

"No need. I'm already soaked." Adria pushed her wet hair back. She hadn't grabbed a hat when she left the house since she had planned to get a man's hat at the store for her disguise. But the Lord had opened up a different way. She prayed it turned out a better way. "We need the rain."

Logan laughed then. "You are one interesting girl, Adria Starr. Shame you have to be such a stickler for the law." After a few seconds, he went on. "Well, some of the laws, anyway, right?"

She chose not to respond to that. Instead she said, "Are we about there?"

"Hard to say when I don't know where there is." He kept his face forward. "The question is, do you know where there is?"

Adria shut her eyes and pulled up a mental picture of the map. But all the roads were unfamiliar to her. She'd never been farther than Carlton's family farm outside of Springfield. Now here she was, lost with a thief, ferrying a slave to hopeful freedom in the middle of a storm.

She repeated the names written on the lines of the map that indicated roads and then asked, "Are we where we should be?"

"Not where we should be, but where we are."

Adria's heart sank. "So we're lost."

"Don't sound so low. I didn't say we weren't headed where you say we need to go, but that sure isn't where we should be. The two of us are playing with fire."

"You've already done that today."

"I told you that was an accident. An opportune one to be sure, but I didn't set out to burn down the town. I liked your little town and the people in it." He gave her another look. "Especially one of them. You know I could just keep driving this wagon and not take you back. Once you got used to the idea, you might be excited about heading west. With me." He put his hand on her leg. "I'd get you a rain slicker first thing."

She had the craziest urge to laugh and wondered if she was easing toward hysteria. She pulled herself together and pushed his hand away. "I wouldn't go across the river with you, even in the sunshine."

He laughed and flicked the reins to keep his reluctant horse moving. "You know if this little escapade of yours ever does get any light shined on it, you'll have the dickens to pay."

"I'll worry about my reputation after we get Twila to safety."

"Sounds fair. I'll wait till then to figure out if I'm going to hog-tie you and take you with me. The long trip across the country to California would be more fun with a girl along."

"I'm sure you can find a willing girl in your next town."

"Maybe I could." Again he laughed a little. "Looks like the rain is easing up, and if I've got things figured right, we should be seeing some houses along the road. So best we slide along like a shadow. Quiet like. No need inviting folks to wonder."

It was even scarier riding past farmhouses than it had been through the woods. Some showed a light in the window. Others were dark and little more than bulky shadows in the black of the stormy night. Her throat tightened as she feared they might ride past the right house without seeing the porch with stone posts and five chairs. Then, as if the Lord heard her worry, the moon slid out from behind a cloud and bathed light down on a small white house with those very porch posts and the five chairs. No chair was turned upside down.

"That must be it," Adria whispered.

Logan didn't pull in the reins to slow the horse. "Best go on up the road a ways. No need drawing suspicion to them with a strange wagon in front of their house."

The horse kept up a steady pace past another house. "In fact, it might be best if we don't stop at all," Logan said. "I'll slow down in the next bit of road with no houses and plenty of shadows. The girl can slide out and walk back to the house."

Twila began crawling out from under the seat.

"But what if it's not the right house?" Adria asked.

"Better pray it is."

"Pray believing," Adria murmured more to herself than Logan.

"I's afraid, Miss Adria," Twila whispered.

"You'd be crazy not to be," Logan said. "But there's no going back, girl. Not now."

"What if I go to the wrong place?" Twila's voice was shaking. "I was hid down under that blanket and didn't see the house."

"Look, girl, I risked plenty getting you here." Logan sounded angry. "You're going to get out of this wagon and go."

"I'll walk back with you," Adria said. "I saw the house."

"Didn't you hear me?" Logan shook his head. "I just told you it would be better if we didn't stop."

"Then don't stop." Adria looked straight ahead. "You'll have to turn the wagon around to go back to Springfield. You can pick me up then. Without stopping."

"I guess I could, but I was thinking on taking a different road."

"Is there a different road?" Adria asked.

"There's always a different road." He pulled back on the reins to stop the horse. "This looks a likely spot. Nobody around. Tell you what. I'll pretend my horse has a rock in his hoof. So be quick about it."

He jumped down from the wagon and reached up to help them down, but Twila had already slid over the far side of the wagon and crouched in the shadow of the wagon out of sight. Adria's wet skirts clung to her legs and hindered her easy movement out of the wagon. She practically fell into Logan's outstretched arms.

He held her a little tighter and longer than necessary after her feet were on the ground. His eyes glittered in the dim light as he stared down into her face. "You're one entrancing girl, Adria Starr. That California offer is still good."

"I've never dreamed of California."

"Maybe that's because you are afraid to dream."

"I'm not afraid."

"Then why is your heart beating so hard?" Logan's lips turned up in a smile. "If you're not afraid, it must be because I'm holding you. To be honest, my heart is hammering a little faster too."

"I thought you wanted us to be quick about it." She wasn't about to admit that being so close to him was awakening feelings better not felt.

"So I did." With a little laugh, he turned her loose. "Go quiet and don't let anybody see you. Either of you." He glanced over toward where Twila still hid. "Good luck, girl."

Adria took Twila's hand and they started back down the road the way they'd come, slipping from shadow to shadow. The trees along the road showered raindrops down on them, but they didn't dare walk out in the open. Neither of them spoke, but Twila's breath came fast and hard.

It was farther than Adria thought. So far that she began to wonder if somehow she'd taken a wrong turn or missed the house.

Clouds overtook the moon again and darkened the night. That was good to keep them from being seen, but not if they couldn't find the house. Then it was there in front of them with only one stretch of open ground between them and the door promising Twila the chance for freedom.

They stopped in a line of trees and studied the house.

"Are you sure this is it?" Twila's whisper was barely loud enough for Adria to hear.

"It's what the map said and Bet said the map was right. Said she knew."

"Maybe I should just go back." Her words sounded shaky. "Leastways I'd know what might happen there."

"No." Adria kept her voice firm. "This is your chance, Twila. Others have gone this way and made it. You have to go on. For you and for Bet." She squeezed Twila's hand. "Be strong and of good courage."

"That's in the Good Book, ain't it?"

"It is. Now run before the moon comes back out."

"Tell Mam I love her." Then without another word, Twila stepped out of the trees and slipped across the open area and up to the house like the shadow of a bird. Adria held her breath as the girl climbed the porch steps and tapped on the door. The door opened. Two seconds later, Twila was inside with the door closed, and the night settled back undisturbed over the porch.

"Be with her, Lord." Adria whispered the words. "Help her across that river Aunt Tilda talked about. The freedom river."

Somehow it helped Adria to not be so afraid when she imagined Aunt Tilda smiling down on her. She had done the right thing. Even if she got caught and had to pay the price for breaking the law. She pushed that thought away. It could be she might get back to Springfield with nobody the wiser except for Logan Farrell, who would be long gone to California.

She hurried along the road toward where Logan waited. The sooner she got home the better. But when she reached the place where Logan had stopped, the wagon was gone. She shut her eyes and opened them, but that didn't change the yawning emptiness of the road.

Maybe she was wrong about the place, but no, she remembered that stump beside the road. She stared at it while tears stung her eyes. Would he have waited if she'd told him she'd go to California? She almost laughed. What a silly thing to wonder. The man was a thief. Out for no one but himself. That she had been able to convince him to smuggle Twila to the beginning of a freedom trail was amazing. It had taken threats, but he hadn't betrayed them. At least not until now.

What she should be wondering was how to get back to Springfield before Ruth raised the alarm about her being missing. Perhaps the havoc of the fire might keep that from happening for a little while. In fact, it might be suspected she was lost in the fire. Adria trembled at the thought.

She wasn't dead. She wasn't running from slave catchers to find freedom. And she had two good feet. Adria brushed away her tears. No need to panic. She could simply walk back to Springfield. It would take hours, but the way was clear. The rain had stopped, at least for the moment. She would pray the fires had been put out and her house wasn't a blackened shell. She would pray no one had been hurt in those fires. She would pray to stay unseen along the road, but just in case she did meet someone, she needed a story.

The truth was best or at least a fragment of truth. She could say she was running away to California with Logan Farrell before she came to her senses and jumped out of his wagon to find her way home. No one ever had to know the whole truth. Not even Ruth.

She eased past the houses. The one where Twila had been pulled inside looked just the same as the others. Dark and quiet. Adria was relieved when trees again took the place of the houses alongside the road.

She had no idea how much time had passed. The clouds were so thick overhead she could barely make out the road, but she kept moving even when more rain dashed down on her. With a crash of wings, an owl swooped out of a tree in front of her. She shrieked, then clamped her lips shut while holding her breath to listen for signs someone might have heard her. Nothing but a rumble of distant thunder, the dripping trees, and a few night insects not bothered by the rain.

"I am not afraid of the dark." She whispered the words with a bit of defiance as her heart began to slow its racing. True words. She wasn't afraid of the dark. She was afraid of what might be in the dark.

The Scripture she had quoted to Twila came to mind. This time she pulled more of its words out of her memory. *Be strong and of a good courage; be not afraid, neither be thou dismayed: for the Lord thy God is with thee whithersoever thou goest.*

Out in a dark night. In the midst of a storm or a raging fire. In a wagon with a thief and a runaway slave.

Whithersoever. That was a good word. One of those exactly right words Ruth liked to come up with for her poems.

Thirty-two

Will raised his face to the rain. The beautiful, glorious rain. It wasn't going to save his house, where flames continued to flicker up from the roof, even with the deluge of water the Lord was sending down. Showers of blessings. A Bible passage came to mind that he'd preached on more than once. Often enough that he had no trouble remembering the words Ezekiel had written so long ago.

He spoke them aloud into the wind. "There shall be showers of blessing. And the tree of the field shall yield her fruit, and the earth shall yield her increase, and they shall be safe in their land, and shall know that I am the LORD." It was a blessing to know the Lord was in control even at a time like this.

Lightning streaked across the western sky, followed by a clap of thunder that made Ruth start a bit. He tightened his arm around her. He never wanted to let go of either her or Willie. When he had caught sight of them crawling out the door of the burning house, his heart almost stopped. He should have known that was where Willie would go. After her doll. Even now she clutched the rag doll tight to her chest.

He supposed he should fuss at Willie for not staying put where he'd left her by the shed. But that could wait for another day. Now he was just thankful to hold her close under the quilt Ruth draped over the child to protect her from the rain.

When Ruth touched his cheek, he looked down at her. Over the noise of the rain, he could barely hear her. "We need to find shelter from the storm."

Shelter from the storm. Somehow even there in the midst of the pouring rain and rumbling thunder with the smoke of his burning house settling around him, he had already found shelter from the storm. From his inner storm. The Lord was with him. He had been all along. Will had simply been blinded by his own storm of grief.

Any paths he had to walk through whatever storms, the Lord had already walked through worse. And yet the Lord had conquered them all. Even death.

He bent down and spoke close to Ruth's ear. "The Lord has already given us shelter."

In another flash of lightning, he could see her frown. "Yes, and we're not in it."

Will couldn't keep from smiling then. "For a poet, you are very practical, Mrs. Harmon." The rain slacked off a little, so they no longer had to shout to be heard.

"Lightning doesn't care if I'm practical or foolish. It just does what lightning does. With that in mind, the Lord gave us the sense to get out of a storm if we can."

Willie peeked out from under the quilt. "I like rain." She stuck out her tongue and tried to catch a raindrop.

That made Ruth laugh. "So do I. Tonight everybody in Springfield likes rain, but I would rather not dodge lightning bolts."

"I seriously doubt if you can," Will said. "Dodge lightning, I mean."

That made Ruth laugh even more. He liked hearing her laugh, but she was right. They should seek shelter. He held Willie closer as he got to his feet. Then he reached down to help up Ruth. Her hand in his was so small, and yet strength was in her grip.

"We can go to the church," he said.

"Do you think we can find a preacher there?"

"I am the preacher there."

"So you are."

The lightning flashing in the distance gave enough light for him to see her smile, but it still took a moment for him to realize what she was telling him.

"Are you saying yes?" He stared down at her face. Where was another flash of lightning when he needed it?

"Maybe we should review the question."

When he started to say something, she put her fingers over his lips. "Not yet. First shelter from the storm. Then questions."

"And answers?"

"And answers."

His heart bounded up with joy. *Rejoice always.* Wasn't that the Scripture he'd been reading earlier? Pray without ceasing and rejoice. The smoke from the fire burned his nose and throat, and he was soaked to the skin. He had lost all his possessions and was left with nothing but the clothes on his back and the Bible he'd left on the pulpit at the church. None of that mattered. He would find new clothes. A house could be rebuilt.

Even the church building, had it been taken by the fire, could be replaced. Buildings didn't matter. People mattered, and his arms were tight around the two people who mattered most to him. His child and this woman who had somehow stolen his heart in mere weeks. That had to be of the Lord.

∞

As she climbed up the rise to the church, Ruth wondered if she was doing the right thing. She had the same as told this man, this preacher, that she was ready to say yes to his proposal of marriage. Of course, she could still opt for the convenience marriage. She could, but if she did, oh, how she would miss the feel of his arm strong around her the way it was now.

It was true she barely knew him, but how well had the Ruth in the Bible known Boaz when she went and lay at his feet?

This was not Bible times. Things were done differently now. People took time to get to know one another before they stood in front of a preacher to say vows of faithfulness and obedience. She had known Peter for a year before she married him. She had been so young then. So full of hope. Not even as old as Adria was now.

A shiver of worry swept through Ruth, but she had no reason to think Adria wasn't safe. The fires had been in the east end of town. A good distance from Elm Street. More likely, Adria was concerned about Ruth's welfare. A smile slid out on Ruth's face. And perhaps with reason, as she was ready to plunge into a completely different life after years of widowhood. As a preacher's wife besides. Everybody knew a preacher's wife had an ongoing challenge to please a church congregation.

Ruth certainly wasn't going to worry about that. Not yet. One step at a time. First the question. Then the answer. After that, the hows. Or the whens. Ruth's heart began to hammer a little faster in her chest. Not tonight. She had been silly to ask about a different preacher at the church.

A week. That was what she would tell him. But then the man had no place to stay. He might manage at the church, but Willeena would need more than a church pew for a bed.

Willeena's head drooped down on Will's shoulder as they walked through the rain. The child had to be exhausted.

At the church, raindrops plopped on the water in Mr. Manderly's bucket at the bottom of the steps, but he was no longer standing guard with it. He must have decided the church building and his organ were no longer in danger and hurried home to see about his own house.

Ruth was glad he was gone and they were alone. But who knew how long that privacy might last? Others might climb to the sanctuary of the church to pray for those who had suffered losses. It was a time for prayer.

Willeena barely murmured when Will gently laid her on one of the pews. After Will stepped back, Ruth tucked the quilt around the little girl even though it was damp. Perhaps it would provide some warmth. With her face streaked with grime and smoke, Willeena was so precious lying there, holding her doll. Ruth smoothed a stray strand of hair away from the girl's face, and then brushed her lips across her forehead.

Will had already returned to the open church door. Ruth stepped up beside him to stare down toward the street, where flames were still evident here and there amidst the smoke hanging over the buildings. The rain was defeating the fire, but darkness hid how much of the town had burned. Morning would bring that tragic truth.

When Will spoke, his words surprised Ruth. "Did you hear the Lord's voice in the fire? Or in the storm?"

"Or in a still small voice like Elijah?" Ruth said.

"Yes."

"No." Ruth couldn't imagine the Lord speaking audibly to her, but she didn't doubt he might to others. "Is the Lord speaking to you, Will?"

"I think he speaks to me, to all of us, in every way, but sometimes we close our ears." He glanced over at her and then turned back toward the night.

Light flickered out to them from the lamps left burning in the church when everyone rushed out to the fire. Ruth wished one of the lamps nearer so she could see his face, but perhaps it was better for them to talk in the shadows. To let their words be what mattered more than smiles or frowns.

"Have you closed your ears?" she asked softly.

"Ever since Mary died, I've only gone through the motions of listening. I kept searching through the Scriptures, kept saying the right preacher words, but I was empty inside. I knew nothing could bring Mary back. Not after she died, but before she died, I fervently believed God would heal her. Then he didn't."

"I prayed for Peter with like fervor. I thought my faith wasn't strong enough."

"I didn't think it of my prayers. I was sure of it." Will let out a long sigh. "What kind of preacher couldn't even pray down healing on his own wife?"

Ruth put her hand on his arm, but he continued to stare out at the smoky night as he went on. "On a good woman who had forever loved the Lord with a purer heart than my own."

"I felt the same about Peter. He was such a good man. I've taken much comfort over the years reading his Bible and trying to walk a path as faithful as his." That made her remember the Bible still stuffed in her waistband. She pulled it out and handed it to him. "I found this on your desk when I was searching for Willeena's doll. I picked it up because I thought it might be your wife's. I don't know why. Perhaps because I've always kept Peter's Bible on my desk."

He turned from staring out into the darkness to rub his hands over the cover of the Bible. Even though she couldn't see his face clearly in the flickering lamplight, she had no doubt tears were in his eyes when he spoke. "It is Mary's Bible. The one possession I hated to lose in the fire and now you have brought it out for me. Someday it will be Willeena's. A gift from her mother."

"Something she will surely treasure."

"Mary would have loved her so."

"As you love her." Ruth hesitated, but the words rose up from her heart. So she let them come out into the air between them. "As I will love her."

He took both her hands then and stared down at her. "I can profess to be nothing more than a flawed man, struggling to follow the Lord's calling in my life. Now my few earthly possessions have gone up in smoke, leaving me little to offer you but my devotion and my name, but will you do me the honor of accepting that name?"

"Let me ask you a question before I answer."

"Ask anything you want."

"We've known each other for such a short time." Ruth kept her eyes on his. "I fear not long enough, but do you think there is room in your heart for me? I don't want to push Mary out. Or Willeena. They belong there forever just as Peter and Adria do in my heart, but I have space that needs to be filled."

"Then let me have the blessing of filling that space, because I don't merely think I have room for you in my heart, I know it. The Lord led me to Springfield. To you. I love you already, but I will love you more with each passing day. Will you be my wife, Ruth Harmon, and let love for me grow in your heart?"

Ruth didn't hesitate. "Yes, Will Robertson, I will."

He turned loose of her hand and ran his fingers over her cheeks, as though memorizing her face with his touch. "May I kiss you?"

In answer she lifted her face toward him.

His lips touched hers gingerly. She felt just as unsure, but the warmth of his lips spread through her and she slid her hand around behind his neck. His arms tightened around her for a moment before he raised his lips away from hers.

"I'm a bit out of practice," he said.

"As am I." She smiled as she touched his face. "But we'll figure it out."

"Yes, I think we will."

"Come. Get Willeena and go home with me so I can tell Adria. She will be worried." Ruth shook her head a little. "She may be even more worried about me when we tell her I accepted your proposal."

The smell of smoke trailed along with them as they walked through the rain to her house. With so much destruction behind her, Ruth felt a little guilty at how light her heart felt. But a woman didn't decide to get married every day. She reached for Will's hand even as he was reaching for hers. They would work things out one step at a time. With the Lord's help.

Adria was going to be very surprised, but she would be overjoyed for Ruth too. Overjoyed. That was a word to consider. That morning she had been ready to write a poem about joy in the morning. But sometimes joy could flash into the midst of darkness the same as with the rising of the sun.

Thirty-three

A dria tried not to think about how dark the night was as rain kept peppering down. At least the thunder was only a faint rumble now as lightning flashed in the distance, but even if the storm blew back toward her, she would keep walking.

She had to get back to Springfield before she was missed. Enough people might know about her abolitionist leanings to suspect her once Twila was discovered gone. Pray God she was really gone. Safe and on her way to freedom.

How many miles away could Springfield be? She tried to figure out how long it had been since Twila crawled in the wagon and they set out, but this night, the minutes and hours hadn't seemed to tick away in the customary manner. When she had watched Twila slip up to knock on the door of that house, those moments had stretched out to take forever. Then when Adria had returned to the place where she thought Logan would be waiting, time had the same as stood still while she stared at the empty road. Since then, time had rolled on too fast with her need to hurry each step.

The road was either rough with rocks or rife with mud puddles pulling at her shoes. One of her soles flopped loose at the toe, making walking fast even more difficult. As she moved doggedly on, she kept an ear cocked for the slightest noise that might warn her of danger approaching. Logan was right that it would be better if no one saw her here where she had no reason to be.

When her sodden skirts kept dragging at her legs and slowing her steps, she tucked her skirt hem into her waistband to show an indecent amount of her legs, but no one was there to see.

She counted her steps to calculate if she had walked a mile, but she lost count. The night was taking a toll on her. The fires. The danger. The fear. She gave up on numbering her steps and started reciting Bible verses.

"Yea, though I walk through the valley of the shadow of death, I shall fear no evil."

She said the words, but she couldn't push away the fear that stalked her. If Louis had been there walking with her, then she could. His faith would bolster hers. Tomorrow—no, more likely today, since midnight had surely already come and gone—Louis would be free. That thought lifted her spirits. The Sanderson family would take the money. They would have to. No matter what they thought about Twila running away. They would have no reason to suspect Louis. Or her if she could get back to Springfield before she was missed. She tried to walk faster, but the rain drained her energy.

A noise caught her ear. Behind her, the road curved, but the creak of a wagon and jangle of harness was unmistakable. Someone was coming. She ran toward the trees alongside the road but tripped over her loose shoe sole and slid down in a mud puddle as the wagon came around the curve. She stayed low and crept off the road in hopes the wagon driver would not see her in the dark. She breathed a little easier after sidling behind a tree.

The wagon kept coming, but then instead of rolling on past her hiding place, it stopped.

"Adria. Are you all right?"

"Logan." She stepped out from the tree and stared at the man climbing down from the wagon. While she couldn't see his face, it had to be Logan. No one else knew she was out here on this road. She stayed where she was. "What do you want?"

"What do you think?" His voice sounded strained. "I came back for you."

"To do what?" She couldn't trust him. Not now.

"To help you. What else?" He motioned toward her. "Come on."

When she stayed where she was, he made a sound of disgust and stalked off the road toward her. "For heaven's sake, what do you think? I'm going to attack you or something? If I'd wanted to do that, I could have already. So hurry up. No time to waste." He grabbed for her arm.

She jerked away, balled up her fist, and punched him in the face. Her hand hurt, but she felt better.

He rubbed his jaw and then surprised her by laughing. "Is that any way to treat somebody trying to help you? Somebody risking jail or worse. Somebody who could have been halfway to free and clear by now."

"I'm sorry. You're right." She dropped her hands to her side. "You want to hit me back?"

"Hardly. My mother taught me better than that." He stepped closer to her. "A kiss sounds better."

In spite of everything, she almost hoped he would kiss her. She was glad for the dark to hide the warmth flooding her face. How could she still be attracted to him, knowing what he had done? But he wasn't all bad. He helped Twila escape and he came back for her. She didn't move away from him and his teeth flashed in a smile.

After a couple of seconds, he said, "But no time for fun. Come on."

She let him take her hand then and help her across the mud to the wagon. "Smart to hike up your skirt like that."

More heat flashed in her face. She'd forgotten about her skirt. "It made walking easier." After she climbed up into the wagon, she jerked the skirt hem free to let the wet cloth properly cloak her legs.

"The white flash of your legs as you ran across the road is why I spotted you." He laughed again as he got into the wagon. "Are you sure you don't want to go to California? The two of us could have some fun."

"I'm not going to California."

"Might come a day you'll wish you had."

"It might, but that day isn't now."

"Oh well. Then best you crouch down out of sight and not let anybody see you with the likes of me." He took up the reins.

She did as he said and huddled down under the blanket the way Twila had earlier. It wasn't a very comfortable ride, but it was better than walking. And faster, although she still had no idea what time it might be. At least the rain seemed to have nearly stopped or was so light she couldn't feel the drops under the blanket where everything was black and way too steamy. She pushed back the edge to get some air.

At last, when Adria didn't think she could bear another minute under the blanket, the wagon stopped.

"This is as close as I dare go."

Adria threw off the cover and sat up. The gray light of dawn was turning night to day. "How far to town?"

"Probably less than a mile. You can see the smoke." He pointed at a dark cloud hanging on the horizon. "I told the truth when I said the fire was an accident. Not my fault."

"You were still going to steal Louis's freedom money."

"I guess saying I'm sorry isn't good enough on that one."

"No." She stood up.

He grabbed her hand before she could climb out of the wagon. "You could do your good deed and reform me. Make me into the kind of man you could love."

"I appreciate what you chanced to help Twila and then me." She gave him a long look. "You could come back to town with me and explain what happened to the sheriff. I won't say anything about you trying to break into the safe."

"Guess I'll have to pass on that." Logan shook his head. "I'm afraid I might have the smell of smoke on me, and being a stranger in town, folks would be glad enough to have somebody to blame for their troubles."

"Then goodbye, Logan. I hope you make it to California."

"No worry about that. I will. And I hope you make it to wherever you want to be." He squeezed her hand. "But trust me on this. There are better men out there than Carlton Damon."

"Or you?"

"Or me." He laughed and raised her hand up to his lips before he turned her loose. "Good day, Miss Starr. It has been a pleasure. Perhaps I will long live in your memory as the man who saved you not only from getting trampled by a team of runaway horses but also from the disaster of marrying the wrong man."

After he disappeared back the way they'd come, she headed toward town with an odd mixture of regret and relief. Smoky fog settled down around her as she walked. That was good. Better for her to smell like smoke than the mud of the road.

When the town's buildings came into view, she did her best to smooth back her hair and brush off her skirts. She needn't have bothered. The people wandering about in the streets looked every bit as bedraggled as she did. Here and there, a few men and women stood and stared at the smoking ruins of their homes or businesses where flames still flickered among the ashes.

Three hogs ran past her. Nobody was chasing them. The stock pens must have been opened for fear the fire would take the sheds and warehouses around them.

She was glad to leave the destruction behind and move on through town to where the buildings stood untouched. The bank. The hat factory. The drugstore. Billiter's Mercantile, closed and shuttered. She needed to get home and cleaned up so she could show up for work like any other day. But ashes drifting past her in the air proved it wasn't any other day.

A tremble swept through her as she thought about catching

Logan trying to steal Louis's freedom money. She whispered a thankful prayer that he hadn't known all the numbers of the safe combination. The petty cash had been enough to satisfy Logan, but she needed to replace it before Mr. Billiter discovered it missing. She could always say she'd changed the hiding place.

More lies. Dear Lord, forgive her. That was all she had done since Bet showed up at the kitchen door. Lie. Right now, her whole life felt like a lie. Writing her abolitionist letters and sending them out under fake names. Thinking she could find a way to marry into a family of slaveholders. Pretending to be someone she wasn't. She felt like a shell of a woman, something like the burned-out buildings she'd just walked past.

She looked up. The sun was burning off the fog and leaving only the drifting smoke behind. *Did I do the right thing, Aunt Tilda?*

No words came down from heaven, but the words were in her ears. *The only thing.*

At times, a person had to put feet to her prayers. They'd done that with Louis. The whole town had. And she had done that with Twila. The only thing she could do, and the Lord had made a way. Perhaps he was showing her a way too. Out of Springfield. To the East where people fought against the injustice of slavery. She would telegraph Abigail to see if the room in her house was still available.

"Missy Adria. You is a sight for sore eyes."

Adria turned to see Louis hurrying toward her, his face creased with worry. But then everyone she'd seen since she got back to Springfield had that look. A day to be concerned for the future of their town. But not for this man's future. Before the sun went down again, he would be his own man and not have to answer to any master other than his Lord.

"Are you all right? Miss Ruth is some concerned about you." He must have been fighting the fires since his clothes were covered in soot and ashes. "She was ready to set the sheriff to huntin' for you, but I tol' her to let me see if I could find you 'fore she did that. Seein' as how the sheriff is so busy with the fires and all." Louis looked off toward the part of town still smoking. "That you was prob'ly just out here somewheres fightin' fires."

"Yes, fighting fires." There were all different kinds of fires to fight. "But I'm all right."

"That's good to know. I sure am happy to see you. Miss Ruth was some afraid you'd done run off with that drover."

"No, I wouldn't do that."

"I knowed you wouldn't. Leastways without tellin' Miss Ruth. I tol' her whatever you was doin' it had to matter. We been prayin' that you weren't in trouble." Louis looked straight at her. She could tell he knew where she'd been, but neither of them wanted to speak the words aloud.

"Sometimes prayers are answered." She hoped he would know by those words that she had been able to get Bet's daughter to the first house to start her journey to freedom.

He nodded. "All the time prayers are answered if you pray believin' the Lord is there with you. He can get you through some hard times like them we've had here tonight."

"Did anybody get killed in the fire?"

"Not so far as we know, but plenty is gonna have to find new places."

"Including you, Louis. Today is your freedom day."

A smile slipped across his face but didn't stay, as though he thought it wrong to be smiling with the smoke of the fire lingering around them. "It don't hardly seem true, but the reverend, he done tol' me he's payin' the price for me soon's the bank opens. And more than that. Makin' a payment to Elias Brown. Mr. Brown done fixed me up a room in the back of his shop with a bed and ev'rythin' I be needin'."

"I know. It's wonderful."

"A miracle for certain. Now we best hurry on to let Miss Ruth knows you made it through the fires."

"That I have."

A smile stole across his face and settled in his eyes. "You gonna be some surprised when you get there."

"Why's that?"

"The reverend and that little girl child of his done took up residence in your front room. Lost his house in the fire, but the church is still standin'."

"Pastor Robertson? I thought his sister had his child." Adria frowned a little.

"I'm supposin' things must've changed. Things has a way of doin' that."

"So they do." The strong smell of smoke in the air proved it, but nothing looked that different here with the hotel behind her and the houses clustered on Elm Street safe from the fire not that many steps away. The sun was up now, shining down on the tatters of the night. The lost buildings behind her. But it wasn't only the buildings. The night had changed something inside her, made everything different.

Louis trailed along behind her as she started toward her house, talking now of the change she was going to find there.

"Appears Miss Ruth is done ready to take in another motherless child. The child is a pretty little thing. Some younger than you when Miss Ruth took you in after the cholera."

"But I didn't come with a father."

"That you didn't. Could make things some different this time for Miss Ruth, but from the way they was standin' together, even while deep in worry 'bout you, seemed to be a best thing."

"A best thing," Adria softly echoed his words.

"That's all we can hope for, missy, when troubles come our way," Louis said. "For the Lord to take whatever happens and help us to find some of those best things in the midst of it all."

She stopped and turned to face Louis. "'And we know that all things work together for good to them that love God.' Aunt Tilda taught me that verse a long time ago."

"The truth in Scripture words is one of them things that never changes."

Adria kept her gaze on Louis, their unspoken words loud between them. "Did I do the right thing, Louis?"

"That's not for me to say." Louis met her look without wavering. "But sometimes when fires is burnin' out of control, then a body has to do whatever he can to put 'em out."

Thirty-four

A person's life could roll along the same for years and then overnight that life could have an earthquake upheaval. Ruth hadn't been born yet when the New Madrid earthquakes in the western region of the state heaved up the earth and made the Mississippi River run backward, but she had heard a few eyewitness accounts and read even more. Those earthquakes had changed the landscape. Even filled up a new lake where there had been no lake the day before.

That was how she felt. As if she had started out the day yesterday considering joy and had ended the day amidst smoke and flames, one hand firmly clasped by Will and the other holding his daughter's hand. Her daughter now. Another daughter of the heart.

Years ago, after the cholera epidemic, she had shied away from Adria calling her mother. Aunt Ruth seemed more appropriate. But Ruth's reluctance about the title "mother" hadn't kept Adria from finding a forever place in Ruth's heart. That was why Ruth had to fight off panic when she and Will got to her house last night to find Adria gone.

She's gone to fight the fire, Will said. *Perhaps,* conceded Ruth.

Or to guard the store against the flames or those who might take advantage of the confusion to break a window and lift some of the merchandise. But Mr. Billiter wouldn't expect Adria to do that. He had always shielded Adria from the riffraff that showed up at the store from time to time.

Riffraff. That brought Logan Farrell to mind. The drover entranced Adria. His good looks. His easy smile. His lust for adventure. As much as Ruth didn't want to believe Adria would let the man talk her into running away with him, the worry that it might be true kept poking her. Love could make a woman do foolish things.

Just look at her. Ready to join her life with a man she barely knew. She'd heard him preach. She'd seen his care for Willeena. And she did know Will was a man who appreciated books and poetry. That knowledge might explain why she had put her hand into his with so little hesitation. Some things were simply meant to be. The Lord's providence in a person's life.

She didn't believe Adria and Logan Farrell were meant to be, but all through the long night the sick feeling Adria might not realize that had churned inside Ruth. She hadn't slept. How could she while not knowing where Adria might be or if she was safe?

Will hadn't slept either. He had come to the house but then went back out along with Louis to look for Adria. Somehow Louis had feared Adria might be missing. He had come to the house to look for her and then, in spite of the worry creasing his face, told Ruth it might be best not to call in the sheriff's help to search for Adria.

When Ruth asked why, Louis kept his eyes down as he answered. "Lots of happenings goin' on this night. The fire and more. Let me and the reverend do some lookin' first. The sheriff, he's bound to be extra busy anyhow."

Louis knew more than he was saying, but Ruth hadn't pushed him to tell her what he was thinking. She wasn't ready to have this new worry awakening in her out in the open air. Perhaps an even more fearsome thought than Adria going off with Logan Farrell. One more dangerous for Adria and perhaps for them all. What was the girl doing?

After Will and Louis left, Ruth checked on Willeena again. The child was so small, curled there in Ruth's bed, sound asleep with her doll still fiercely clutched to her chest.

Ruth remembered how Adria had clung to her doll, Callie, when she first came to Ruth. A connection to her mother who'd made the doll. Willeena's doll was made by Will's sister, the only mother the child had ever known. And now Ruth would have the chance to mother her. Her heart softened as she leaned down to brush a kiss across the little girl's hair.

Then she went back to stand watch at the front window. A little after sunrise, her prayers were answered when she saw Adria coming down the street with Louis trailing her, almost as though herding her home. Dear Louis. He had once more brought Adria to her.

A dirty, disheveled, exhausted Adria.

Ruth stepped out on the porch to wait for her. Even before she was close enough for Ruth to look into her eyes, she knew Adria, like Ruth, had experienced a seismic upheaval in her life since she'd last seen her yesterday. The droop of the girl's shoulders spoke of more than exhaustion.

"Here she be, Miss Ruth. I found her comin' home," Louis said as Adria stepped up on the porch. "I best be huntin' up the preacher to let him know."

Adria turned back toward Louis. "Don't say anything to anybody else. You don't want to chance messing up your freedom day."

"Can't nothin' mess that up, missy. Not now that I know you're safe. But you know I ain't never been one for talkin' unless'n I had somethin' to say and I ain't got nothin' to say about the fires." He settled his gentle eyes on Adria for a few seconds before he turned back toward town.

Ruth wanted to ask where Adria had been, but instead she took her hands. "I'm glad you're home."

"Home." A smile slipped across Adria's face but didn't stay. "I'm glad it's still here. I'm glad you are here."

300

"I'll always be here for you, Adria." Ruth tightened her hold on Adria's hands.

"I know." Adria looked near tears. "You were the answer to a little girl's prayer."

"And you were the answer to a prayer I didn't even know to speak." Ruth blinked back tears of her own. "I was so afraid I wouldn't know how to take care of you. I think that was why I was hesitant to claim the title of mother to you."

"But you have been a mother to me." A few tears leaked out of Adria's eyes. "I love you and I never wanted to bring you trouble."

"I don't know what trouble you mean, and it's probably better I don't. But the town has plenty of trouble to think about with the fire. Whatever else has happened may be lost in those ashes." Ruth let go of Adria's hands to put her arm around her and turn her toward the door. "Come. You need to clean up and then hear my news."

"The preacher?" Adria's eyes showed more life then. "Louis says his daughter is here."

"She is. Their house burned." Ruth hesitated, but it was time to say it aloud. "I'm going to marry him."

"When?"

"As soon as we can post the bond." Ruth felt a thrill at the words. Anticipation with a tickle of fear.

"Are you sure?"

"He needs a place to live. His little girl needs a mother."

"Is it only for a house?" Adria's frown showed her concern. "Or for his daughter? A marriage of convenience for him?"

"No. He wants me to be his wife." Ruth's voice softened. "I want to be his wife."

Adria's frown vanished as her face lit up and she grabbed Ruth's hands and danced her in a circle. "That's wonderful!"

Ruth couldn't keep from laughing at her excitement. "I can't believe I'm getting married again—before you. I always thought you and Carlton—" Adria's stricken look stopped Ruth from finishing her thought.

The girl's shoulders drooped as she let go of Ruth's hands. "I sent Carlton away. I can't marry him. And it's not only the way he thinks about slaves. I don't love him enough. Not nearly enough. And he has never loved me. Not the real me. He only loved who he hoped I could be."

"I'm sorry." Ruth looked at her for a long moment before she asked, "Is it Logan Farrell?"

"You don't have to worry about him." Adria looked sad. "I turned down his proposal too. No marriage bells in my future."

"The Lord will send you the right man someday."

"If it's meant to be," Adria said.

"Ruth." Willeena was standing in the doorway to the bedroom, still holding her doll. Her voice wavered a bit as she edged into the room.

"Come, Willeena." Ruth held out a hand toward the little girl. "Adria wants to meet you and Maysie."

Adria squatted down in front of the child. "I'm very glad to meet you, Willeena. Would you like to be my sister?"

Willeena's face crunched up as she thought about that. "I have a sister at Mama Hazie's, but she's not big like you."

Adria smiled. "Sisters come in all sizes and I think it would be fun to have one your size. Don't you think it would be good to have one my size?"

Willeena looked up at Ruth and then back at Adria. "I have to ask Daddy."

"I think you should," Adria said. "And ask Maysie too. I used to have a doll like that. Her name was Callie."

"Where is she now?" Willeena looked concerned. "Did you let her burn up?"

"Oh no. She lives in a special place in my heart where I can never forget her."

"Mama Hazie said I had a special place in her heart."

"That's good," Adria said. "And now you will have a special place in Ruth's heart and my heart too. The more love we gather, the better."

Willeena looked as though she wasn't sure what Adria was talking about. So she skipped to another, easier place. "Your dress is dirty."

"Very dirty." Adria laughed a little. "I fell in a mud puddle."

"We got rained on."

Ruth had to laugh then. "That we did."

"Well, that probably cleaned you up." Adria stood up. "I guess I better clean up and go to the store."

"Maybe you should stay home and rest," Ruth said.

"No time for that. It's freedom day. For Louis. For you. For me." Adria looked ready to say more, perhaps another name, but then she didn't.

"What's freedom?" Willeena looked up at Ruth.

Adria answered before Ruth could. "It's when you can dance when you feel like dancing. It's when you have a song to sing and nobody can stop you singing it. It's when you can decide to marry or not to marry. It's when life is good."

"It's when joy comes in the morning." Ruth picked up Willeena and held her tight. It felt so good when the little girl put her arms around Ruth's neck and hugged her back.

"Pray it's so," Adria said.

"Pray believing," Ruth added.

Thirty-five

Will wasn't sure he should feel so happy with part of the town in ruins, including his own house and all he owned but his horse. Still, a few clothes, books, and tools, even a buggy, could hardly compare to the blessings the Lord had been raining down on him. His daughter in his arms. Ruth looking at him with love in her eyes. A church family ready to help with whatever he needed. A town that loved a slave enough to buy his freedom. That man with his unshakeable faith.

Louis looked up and praised the Lord when they handed him his manumission papers. A small group of townspeople had come along with Will to see Louis freed and then to walk him to his new home, where Elias Brown handed him the deed to his blacksmith shop. Ruth held Willie's hand and walked alongside Will. Adria was there too with tears coursing down her cheeks. Ruth had explained all Louis had done for Adria when she was a child orphaned by the cholera epidemic. Plenty of reason for the happy tears, but Will suspected more to her tears than happiness.

The young woman had not revealed where she was during the fire, but then confusion had reigned. Talk had circulated through town about one of the Sanderson slaves disappearing in the night amidst that confusion. A teenage girl.

Logan Farrell seemed to have disappeared in the night too. Since the fire had started at the wagon shop, some suspected him of being the cause. But no one had proof, and whether they did or not, he was nowhere to be found. No one had any reason to make a connection between the runaway slave girl and Logan Farrell, but stranger things sometimes happened.

Will simply hoped neither of them were caught. For the slave girl's sake. For the town's sake, and especially for Adria's sake, because he feared Adria's absence through the night was not completely innocent. A matter for prayer, but not questions.

Better for Will to rejoice in the freedom of this good man who this day was being rewarded for a faithful life of walking whatever path the Lord laid out in front of him. That was how Will should be. Faithful in whatever each day brought his way. He had struggled with that, but the Lord continued to bless him anyway. And now Ruth was going to stand in front of a preacher and pledge her life to him as he pledged his to her. His heart was comforted by the thought that Mary would bless his union with this woman. She would want him to be happy, her child to have a loving mother.

His gaze rested on Ruth, and as though she felt his look, she turned toward him with a smile. Tomorrow she would be Mrs. Will Robertson. The thought of their future together filled him with hope. Hope that her smile showed she shared.

Then they were all smiling as Elias Brown handed Louis Sanderson a pinging hammer. A couple of women clapped their hands together and one of the men laughed.

The biggest smile was on Louis's face as he took the hammer. "The Lord, he done good to me."

∽⬚∾

"Ruth Harmon, wilt you have this man, Will Robertson, to be thy lawfully wedded husband to live together after God's ordinance in the holy estate of Matrimony? Wilt thou obey him, and serve him, love, honor, and keep him, in sickness and in health; and forsaking all others, keep thee only unto him, so long as you both shall live?"

For just a moment, Ruth wanted to hold up her hand and ask to slow things down. Everything was happening too fast. She could barely breathe. She had never been an impulsive person. Never. And yet, here she stood in front of a preacher who was asking if she would speak two words that would change her life's direction forever. Two small words that would join her to the man beside her. A man of God.

Her throat felt too tight to speak. Next to her, Will shifted uneasily on his feet. He had already answered that he would take her as his wife, to love, comfort, and honor. That was what she wanted to hear, and yet now she hesitated. They should have found a way to wait. To get to know one another better.

That morning before they came to the church, Will had promised her all the time she needed to get used to the idea of being married. "I only want to hold you if you want me to hold you."

The thing was, she did want him to hold her, but that didn't keep her from feeling as though she'd climbed into a barrel to roll down a bumpy hill. Once when she was a child, she had done that very thing and been thrilled and scared at the same time. Then the thrill had won out over the dizzy bumps and bruises. Instead of fussing at her foolishness, her father had laughed and helped her back up the hill with his arm strong around her. Just as Will's arm had been strong around her during the storm.

Silence fell over the church as they waited for her to speak. It wasn't a question a preacher asked more than once. Beside her, Adria eased closer to touch her hand, to lend support whatever her answer. On her other side, Will waited for her answer with one hand on Willeena's shoulder to keep the child quiet in front of him. To help her understand what they were doing, Will had explained the marriage ceremony before they came to the church.

So now Willeena tugged on Ruth's skirt and whispered, "You have to say you wilt."

A laugh bubbled up inside Ruth to open up her throat. She glanced down at Willeena. "You're right. I do." She reached to take Will's hand then as she looked at Reverend Collins. With no quaver in her voice, she spoke the necessary words. "I will."

Will smiled over at her, relief more than evident on his face. He squeezed her hand as he said, "Are you sure that's not supposed to be I wilt?"

He didn't appear to be bothered in the least about interrupting the words of the marriage ceremony. And why should he be? It was their wedding. A few extra words would just make it better.

"So true. The right word can mean the world." Ruth smiled up at Will. She loved the kindness in his eyes and maybe even better the understanding she saw there as though he already knew her. "Then I wilt."

Willeena giggled. Adria put her hand over her mouth, but she couldn't hide her smile. Even the Reverend Collins appeared to be struggling not to smile as he intoned the final lines of the ceremony and pronounced them man and wife. He was surely right that a marriage should be a solemn undertaking and not something to be taken lightly.

But that verse in Proverbs did claim a merry heart worketh good like a medicine. Ruth was glad for the smiles as they left the church to walk back to their house with their two daughters. Her hand in Will's felt natural and right.

Life didn't stop rolling along because vows of marriage were spoken. The day was young and much work remained to be done. Will went back out to help clear away debris from the destroyed buildings. Ruth built up the fire in her ovens to bake bread for those in need, along with the cakes and pies her customers expected. She was glad for the return to routine. Kneading the bread dough and stirring up the cakes gave her hands something to do while her mind considered the idea of being Mrs. Robertson and all that meant. Willeena happily settled under the table with spoons and a couple of old pans to pretend cook for her doll.

When Adria came into the kitchen wearing her baking apron, Ruth frowned. "What's wrong? Aren't you going on to work?"

"Not today." Adria didn't look directly at Ruth. "I'm going to help you today. In fact, you should let me do it all and you go find Pastor Robertson to go on a picnic or something to celebrate your marriage. Seems odd to just get married and not do something special." She sprinkled some flour on the biscuit board and turned out a bowl of dough on it. "Not that I know anything about getting married."

"These are not normal times." Ruth shrugged a little. "Not with so many of the church people in need of help."

"I suppose you're right." Adria pressed the dough down and then flipped it over. She worked the dough a moment before she went on. "Actually, I told Mr. Billiter I wouldn't be back to work at the store."

"Oh?" Ruth stopped beating the cake batter and studied Adria's face. "How come?"

Adria stared down at the bread dough as her hands went still. After a moment, she looked up at Ruth. "I hope you won't be upset or disappointed with me." She dropped her gaze back to the dough and began slowly kneading it again. "I suppose I've already disappointed you by refusing Carlton."

"I only want you to be happy." Ruth started to lay her stirring spoon down and step around the table to Adria, but something about the girl held her back. She didn't need hugs. She needed a listening ear.

"I know." A smile flitted across Adria's face as she raised her eyes from the bread to stare at the sunshine flooding in the window. Under the table, Willeena banged her spoon on a pan, but Adria hardly seemed to notice. "Happiness can be like a butterfly you chase after. Always one flutter of wings ahead of you, but then if you stop chasing what you think should make you happy, you can feel the warmth of the sunshine on your shoulders, and the fragrance of your favorite flower is in the air. That butterfly might even drift close enough to let you feel the flutter of its wings."

Ruth reached across the table to touch Adria's arm. "That's lovely."

"I like butterflies." Willeena crawled out from under the table and began circling the room pretending to be a butterfly.

Adria smiled at her and this time the smile didn't slide away but stayed as she looked at Ruth. "I suppose some of that poetry you used to read to me burrowed down in my brain. I'm glad, very glad, you have a new daughter to read to now."

"I can still read to you too."

"I'll wait for the poems in the mail." Adria's smile faded. "I'm going to Boston. I telegraphed my friend Abigail. She has a room where I can stay as long as I need to, and she'll help me find suitable employment." Her eyes begged Ruth for understanding. "I can no longer hide how I feel about slavery. I don't know how much I can do to make a difference, perhaps nothing, but I have to try. If I stay here, I might get you and even Pastor Robertson in trouble simply by association with me. I could even end up in jail. You know the abolitionist message is not welcome here and it's considered a crime to help anyone to freedom."

"It wasn't a crime to help Louis." Ruth's heart felt heavy.

"But we can't collect enough money to free every slave. And even if we could, some would refuse to release their slaves. You know that."

"You're probably right. They would resist losing their property."

"But that's just it. Men, women, and children shouldn't be anybody's property." Adria leaned closer to Ruth as though to make her point clearer. "Our country needs to make slavery illegal instead of making helping some person escape a dreadful life illegal."

"Would you do that? Break the law?"

Adria met Ruth's gaze. "I would."

She didn't say she had already done so, but even though the words didn't pass between them, Ruth knew. She thought of the posters tacked up around town describing the young runaway slave girl. Ruth wasn't sure whether she knew the girl or not. Slaves stayed in the background, a nearly invisible part of life in Springfield. Once you knew the people the way she knew Louis and Matilda, the way she knew Bet, then it was harder to ignore the injustice of slavery.

Ruth started beating the cake batter again and Adria shaped the bread into loaves to rise. An uneasy silence grew between them in spite of the noise of the spoon against the bowl, the thump of dough into the loaf pans, and Willeena back playing with her pan and spoons.

Ruth counted one hundred strokes and then poured the batter into the greased and floured pans. She gave her spoon to Willeena to let her lick the remaining sweetness out of the bowl. When she straightened back up, she let her hands rest a moment on the table. She wasn't sure she should ask, but she did anyway. "Did she make it?"

Adria didn't shy from the question. "I pray so."

Ruth reached across the table to take Adria's flour-covered hand in hers. "I join my prayer to yours. And I will pray for you as you do what you think you must."

Tears floated in Adria's eyes. "I'll miss you, Aunt Ruth."

"If you don't think it's disrespectful to your mother, I'd love to hear you call me 'Mother.'" Ruth blinked back her own tears.

"You've been mother in my heart ever since I put my hand in yours the day Louis brought me to your doorstep." Adria stepped around the table then to hug Ruth. "Thank you for giving me a home, Mother."

The word sounded right in Ruth's ears. Then Willeena was pulling on Ruth's apron. "Mama Ruth, I sticky."

"I think you are." Ruth laughed as she picked Willeena up. The child must have put her face down in the bowl to lick it. She even had batter in her eyebrows.

As Adria got a wet cloth for Willeena's face, she was laughing too. It was good to have the sound of laugher in the kitchen. Tears might follow on the morrow when Ruth had to say goodbye to Adria, but now the laughter felt golden.

Thirty-six

The next morning, Adria was up before the sun. She could hardly believe that at tomorrow's sunrise she wouldn't be waking up here in this house where she'd spent her whole life. First with her parents and then, after the cholera epidemic, with Ruth. But her packed case sat next to the door, ready to be loaded on the stagecoach. Tonight she would stay in a traveler's inn in Louisville before boarding a steamship to Boston.

Excitement warred with trepidation. She wanted to go. She wanted to stay. She had no idea what her future would hold in Boston, but she had no doubt she needed to leave Springfield. Someday she might return, but it was best not to think of somedays. One day at a time.

She dressed and tiptoed down the stairs and out of the house to keep from waking the newlyweds or sweet little Willeena. She did regret not having the chance to get to know the little girl better, but her leaving would open up a room for Willeena. And who knew? Perhaps Ruth would finally have the blessing of bearing a child after adopting two motherless girls. Adria smiled as she imagined a new little boy running through the house the way her little brother had once done. When she'd dreamed of marriage and children, she'd thought to name her first son after her father and Eddie. But now, she'd turned her back on marriage. At least the marriage everyone had expected for her with Carlton. She considered finding him to say goodbye. After all, they'd been friends forever, but his angry words were too fresh in her mind. Best to avoid another confrontation. He would be fine. Janie Smith would happily take Adria's place in his life and make a better wife for him.

But there was one person she did have to tell goodbye. Louis.

He was at the forge, already building up the fire, ready to shape metal into nails, plowshares, horseshoes, or whatever might be needed. Even before she made any noise to let him know she was there, he turned toward her.

"I thought to see you today, Missy Adria."

Adria looked around the blacksmith shop and couldn't help smiling. Louis already had it in better order than it had ever been with Elias there. "You've got it looking good."

"I can't hardly believe this is for real. That the Lord and me can start up the day with no worry about what the massa might want done." He looked around too and then back at Adria. "All because of you and Miss Ruth."

"No, because of the whole town, or really because of you. Just you."

"Whatever the cause, 'tis a mightier blessing than any I ever imagined the Lord sendin' down to me." He ran his fingers over the hammer handles that hung in easy reach. "But what brings you out so early? You ain't been gone all the night long again, have you?"

"No."

"I didn't tell Bet to come to you." Louis's smile turned to a frown. "You know that, don't you?"

"I do. Bet told me you wouldn't do that."

"If'n she'd a come to me, we'd have found another way without puttin' you on danger road."

"It worked out." Adria kept her voice low. "The Lord made a way."

"He has a knack for doin' that. Makin' a way outa no way."

Louis settled his gaze on Adria. "He'll be goin' to do that for you too. Show you a way."

"He already has. I'm leaving Springfield today. Going north to Boston." She felt less shaky saying it this time. Maybe by the time she climbed aboard the stagecoach to begin her journey, she'd be sure of her path.

"I ain't surprised. You was always a child with an overabundance of derring-do."

"You and Aunt Tilda taught me how to be courageous."

"Mostly Matilda. She'd be right proud."

"Of you too."

Louis shook his head. "Not sure that's so. She weren't never happy that I didn't try to find that river she kept talkin' 'bout."

"I have the feeling you pointed some others toward it."

"Them what was braver than me, but some things is better not talked about." He glanced toward the street that was empty in the early morning light.

He was right. In fact, she needed to slip away from his shop before very many people began stirring. If somebody did suspect her of helping Twila, her being here talking to Louis might bring suspicion down on him too. Another reason to be gone from Springfield before anybody came forward who saw her leaving town in the wagon with Logan. The fire grabbed everybody's attention that night, but in a place the size of Springfield, hardly anything went completely unnoticed.

"I'll miss you, Louis."

"Don't you be thinkin' 'bout ol' Louis. I done know you is goin' to have a fine life up there in the north."

Adria smiled. "How do you know?"

"The good Lord, he tol' me so."

Adria's smile got wider. "Did he tell you whether I'll ever meet the right man? One who will love me without wanting to change me?"

"With the Lord's blessin', 'bout anythin' can happen. 'Specially with my prayers runnin' along with you. And yours and Miss Ruth's and that new pastor husband of hers." Louis laughed. "Just look what them prayers done for ol' Louis. Made him a free man with his own blacksmith shop. So ain't no tellin' what them kind of prayers might do for you."

"As long as we pray believing."

"The only way to pray, missy. The onliest way."

Later that morning, Adria walked to the hotel to meet the stage with her excitement beginning to push back her apprehension. She had derring-do. Louis had said so. Then at the house, Ruth had hugged her and told her once again she was the bravest girl she'd ever known. The pastor laid his hand on Adria's head and prayed for a safe journey and blessings to await her in Boston.

They walked to the hotel with her. Pastor Robertson carried her case. Ruth had a parcel of bread and cheese and Adria's favorite sugar cookies. Adria carried Willeena piggyback. The little girl's giggles took some of the sadness out of the goodbyes.

At the hotel, Adria promised Ruth she'd write. She put Willeena down and smiled at her. "And I'll draw pictures to send you, Willeena."

"How about some sermon prompts for me then?" Pastor Robertson said.

Adria shook her head at him. "You wouldn't want to preach the sermons I'd suggest."

"You could be right," Pastor Robertson said. "Springfield might not be ready for those."

It was easier climbing aboard the stagecoach and leaving Ruth behind with her standing there holding the preacher's hand and with Willeena clinging to her skirt. She would not be alone. Adria was the one setting off alone.

She leaned out the window and waved until she couldn't see them waving back at her anymore. Then they were passing the blacksmith shop where Louis was out front, obviously watching for the stage. He didn't wave. Somehow Adria knew he was too busy praying.

She sat back in her seat and looked at her fellow passengers. A man and his wife. Two other men. All going somewhere. And so was she.

She didn't know what the road in front of her held, but she knew the one who paved those roads with hope. The Lord would show her the way. One step at a time. One day at a time. As long as she prayed believing.

Author's Note

When the 1832–33 cholera epidemic swept across the nation, little was known about the disease except that one might feel fine in the morning and sometimes die before night once symptoms of cholera appeared. So it's easy to understand how the report of a case of cholera could incite panic in a town. Before the late 1850s, when the source of the disease was first suspected to be unsanitary drinking water, people thought "bad air," perhaps produced by rotting fruits and vegetables, caused cholera. Millions died all around the world in the 1827–35 pandemic, including 250,000 Americans.

In 1833, Kentucky was hit hard by the epidemic, with many victims all across the state. In Springfield, Kentucky, one-tenth of the population died of cholera that summer. The first day one person died, but by the third day, ten died. People fled the town, including the owner of the local hotel. He gave the hotel's keys to his slave, Louis, and told him to continue running the business. Louis did more than that. Unaffected by the cholera, he, along with a cook, Matilda Sims, took care of the cholera victims still in town. During this time of crisis, Louis passed up what might have been a good opportunity to escape to the north and find freedom.

Instead he stayed in Springfield and did what he could for those affected by the disease. Many died, and Louis dug fifty-five graves to bury the victims.

Twelve years later, when the hotel owner died, the town of Springfield purchased Louis's freedom and set him up in business with a blacksmith shop in gratitude for his service to the town. When another cholera epidemic hit in 1849, Louis once more cared for those stricken by the disease and buried those who died. A memorial monument in the Springfield cemetery honors Louis's memory.

When I came across the story of Louis and the town that bought his freedom, I decided to write a story about how that might have happened. I took the nugget of truth in the historical facts of what Louis did and invented characters and events to surround it. I sincerely hope my story does justice to this man who served others so selflessly.

Read on for an excerpt of another story from *award-winning* and *bestselling author*

Ann H. Gabhart

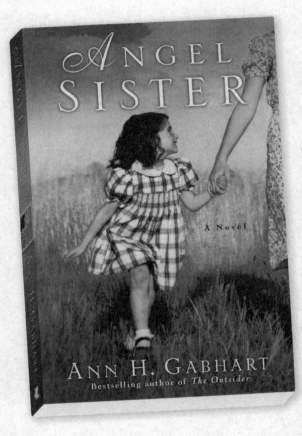

Something woke Kate Merritt. Her eyes flew open and her heart began to thump in her ears. She couldn't see a thing. Not even a hint of moonlight was filtering through the lace curtains at the bedroom window. The dark night wrapped around her like a thick blanket as she stared up toward her bedroom ceiling and fervently hoped it was nothing but a bad dream shaking her awake.

Next to Kate, Evie's breath was whisper quiet. Her sister obviously hadn't heard whatever it was that had jerked Kate from sleep. Slowly Kate's eyes began adjusting to the darkness, but she didn't need to see to know how Evie's red hair would be spread around her head like a halo. Or that even in sleep she'd have a death grip on the top sheet so Kate couldn't pull it off her. Kate always woke up every day with her pillow on the floor and her hair sticking out in all directions. The total opposite of Evie, who got up with barely a rumple in her nightgown.

Just a couple of mornings ago, their mother had laughed as she smoothed down Kate's tangled dark brown hair. "Don't you worry about not being as ladylike as Evangeline. Your sister's going on seventeen. When you get older, you'll be more like her."

Kate jerked away from her mother. "Like Evie? I don't have to be, do I? That would be awful. Really awful," she said before she thought. Kate was always doing that. Saying things before she thought.

But she didn't want to be like Evie. Ever. Evie wouldn't climb trees or catch frogs down at the creek. She even claimed to prefer reading inside by the oil lamp instead of playing hide-and-seek after dark. The truth was she was scared of her shadow.

Evie wasn't only worried about things in the dark. Day or night she shrieked if anybody so much as mentioned Fern Lindell. True, Fern—who lived down the road—was off her rocker, but Kate wasn't a bit afraid of her. At least not unless she was carrying around her little axe. Then anybody with any sense knew to stay away from her.

One thing sure, Kate had sense. That was because she was the middle sister, and the middle sister had to learn early on to take care of herself. And not only herself. Half the time she had to take care of Evie too, and all the time Tori who turned ten last month.

In the cot across the room, Tori was breathing soft and peaceful. So Tori hadn't been what woke Kate, but something had. Kate raised her head up off her pillow and listened. The middle sister had to make sure everything was all right.

Kate didn't mind. She might be only fourteen, but she knew things. She kept her eyes and ears open and did what had to be done. Of course sometimes it might be better to be like Evie, who had a way of simply ignoring anything that didn't fit into her idea of how things should be, or Tori, who didn't worry about much except whether she could find enough worms to go fishing. Neither of them was holding her breath waiting to see if the bump in the night might be their father sneaking in after being out drinking.

Victor Merritt learned to drink in France. At least that's what Kate overheard Aunt Hattie telling Mama a few months back. They didn't know she heard them. She was supposed to be at school, but she'd run back home to get the history report she left on the table by the front door. Kate tiptoed across the porch and inched the door open to keep it from creaking. She aimed to grab the paper and be in and out without her mother hearing her. That way she'd only be in hot water at school and not at home too.

They didn't know she was there. Not even Aunt Hattie, who just about always knew everything. After all, she'd delivered nearly every baby who'd been born in Rosey Corner since the turn of the century thirty-six years ago. A lot of folks avoided Aunt Hattie unless a baby was on the way or they needed somebody to do their wash, but not Mama. She said you might not be able to depend on a lot in this world, but you could depend on Aunt Hattie telling you the truth. Like it or not.

That morning last spring when Kate had crept back in the house and heard her mother and Aunt Hattie, it sounded as if Kate's mother wasn't liking a lot of things. She was crying. The sound pierced Kate and pinned her to the floor right inside the door. She hardly dared breathe.

She should have grabbed the paper and gone right back out the door. That was what she should have done, but instead she stood still as a stone and listened. Of course she knew her father drank. Everybody in Rosey Corner knew that. Nothing stayed secret long in their little community. Two churches, one school, two general stores—the one run by Grandfather Merritt had a gasoline pump—and her father's blacksmith shop.

"But why?" Kate's mother said between sobs.

Aunt Hattie didn't sound cross the way she sometimes did when people started crying around her. Instead she sounded like she might be about to cry herself. Kate couldn't remember ever seeing Aunt Hattie cry. Not even when she talked about her son dying in the war over in France.

"Some answers we can't be seein', Nadine. We wasn't over there. But our Victor was. Men right beside him died. He got some whiffs of that poison gas those German devils used. He laid down on the cold hard ground and stared up at the same moon you was starin' up at but without the first idea of whether or not he'd ever be looking at it with you again. He couldn't even be sure he'd see the sun come up."

"No, no, that's not what I meant." Kate's mother swallowed back her tears, and her voice got stronger, more like Kate was used to hearing. "I mean, why now? I grant you he started drinking over there, but when he got home, he didn't drink all that much. Just a nip now and again, but lately he dives into the bottle like he wants to drown in it."

"It ain't got the first thing to do with you, child. He still loves his girls." Now Aunt Hattie's voice was soft and kind, the voice she used when she was talking to some woman about to have a baby.

"The girls perhaps. Me, I'm not so sure anymore." Kate couldn't see her mother, but she knew the look that would be on her face. Her lips would be mashed together like she had just swallowed something that tasted bad.

"You can be sure. I knows our Victor. I's the first person to ever lay eyes on him when he come into the world. And a pitiful sight he was. Barely bigger than my hand. His mama, Miss Juanita, had trouble carryin' her babies. We lost the two before Victor. You remember Miss Juanita. How she was prone to the vapors. She was sure we would lose Victor even after he made the journey out to daylight and pulled in that first breath, but no how was I gonna let that happen. Raised him right alongside my own boy. Bo was four when our Victor was born."

Kate heard a chair creak as if maybe her mother had shifted to get more comfortable. Everybody knew it wasn't any use trying to stop Aunt Hattie when she started talking about her boy. "My Bo was a sturdy little feller. Stronger and smarter than most. Soon's Victor started walking, Bo took it upon hisself to watch out for him. Miss Juanita paid him some for it once he got older." Aunt Hattie paused as if realizing she'd gone a little far afield. "Anyhows that's how I knows Victor hasn't stopped carin' about you, girl, 'cause I know our Victor. He's just strugglin' some now what with the way things is goin' at his shop. Folks is wantin' to drive those motorcars and puttin' their horses out to pasture. It ain't right, but a pile of things that happen ain't right."

Kate expected Aunt Hattie to start talking about Bo dying in France, but she didn't. Instead she stopped talking altogether, and it was so quiet that Kate was sure they'd hear her breathing. She wanted to step backward, out the door, but she had to wait until somebody said something. The only noise was the slow tick of the clock on the mantel and the soft hiss of water heating on the cooking stove. Nothing that would cover up the sound of her sneaking out of the house.

Kate was up to fifty-five ticks when her mother finally spoke again. "I don't believe in drinking alcohol to hide from your problems."

"No way you could with how your own daddy has been preaching against that very thing since the beginnin' of time. Preacher Reece, he don't cut nobody no slack."

"There are better ways of handling troubles than making more troubles by drinking too much." Mama's voice didn't have the first hint of doubt in it.

"I ain't arguing with you, Nadine. I's agreein' all the way."

"Then what am I supposed to do, Aunt Hattie?"

"I ain't got no answers. Alls I can do is listen and maybe talk to one who does have the answers."

"I've been praying."

"Course you have, but maybe we can join our prayers together. It says in the Good Book that where two or more agree on something, the Lord pays attention. Me. You. We's two."

"Pray with me right now, Aunt Hattie. For Victor. And the girls." Her mother hesitated before she went on. "Especially Kate. She's picked up some of the load I can't seem to make myself shoulder."

In the front room, Kate pulled in her breath.

"Don't you be worryin' none about that child. She's got some broad shoulders. Here, grab hold of my hands." Aunt Hattie's voice changed, got a little louder as if she wanted to make sure the Lord could hear her plain. "Our holy Father who watches over us up in heaven. May we always honor ever' living day you give us. We praise you for lettin' us have this very day right now. And for sending us trials and tribulations so that we can learn to lean on you."

She fell silent a moment as if considering those tribulations. Then she started praying again. "Help our Victor. You knows what he needs better than me or even your sweet child, Nadine here. Turn him away from the devil's temptations and bring him home to his family. Not just his feet but his heart too. And strengthen that family and watch over them, each and every one. Increase their joy and decrease their sorrow. Especially our Katherine Reece. Put your hand over top her and keep her from wrong."

Kate didn't wait to hear any more. She felt like Aunt Hattie's eyes were seeing right through the walls and poking into her. Seeing her doing wrong right that moment as she stood there eavesdropping on them. Kate snatched her history paper off the table and tiptoed out of the house. Once off the porch she didn't stop running until she was going up the steps into the school.

The prayer hadn't worked yet. At least not the part about her father resisting the devil's temptation to go out drinking. Kate worried that the Lord hadn't answered Aunt Hattie's prayer because Kate had been listening when she shouldn't have been. As if somehow that had made the prayer go sideways instead of up toward heaven the way Aunt Hattie had intended.

Now Kate stayed perfectly still to keep the bedsprings from squeaking as she listened intently for whatever had awakened her. The front screen door rattled against the doorframe. That could have been the wind if any wind had been blowing, but then there was a bump as somebody ran into the table beside the door. Kate let out her breath as she sat up on the side of the bed and felt for a match. After she lit the small kerosene lamp, she didn't bother fishing under the bed for her shoes. The night was hot, and her father had made it through the front door.

"Please don't get sick." She mouthed the words silently as she adjusted the wick to keep the flame low. She hated cleaning up after him when he got sick. From the sour smell of alcohol creeping back into the bedroom toward her, she guessed he might have already been sick before he came inside.

She looked back at Evie as she stood up. Evie looked just as Kate had imagined her moments earlier, but she didn't fool Kate. She was awake. Her eyes were shut too tight, and Kate couldn't be positive in the dim light, but she thought she saw a tear on her cheek. "No sense crying now, Evie. Daddy's home," Kate whispered softly.

Evie kept pretending to be asleep, but tears were definitely sliding out of the corners of her eyes. Kate sighed as she turned away from the bed. "Go on back to sleep, Evie. I'll take care of him."

Kate carried her lamp toward the front room where her father was tripping over the rocking chair. She wondered if her mother was lying in her bed pretending to sleep and if she had tears on her cheeks. She wouldn't get up. Not even if Daddy fell flat on his face in the middle of the floor. She couldn't. Not and keep cooking him breakfast when daylight came. Kate knew that. She didn't know how she knew it, but she did.

Acknowledgments

Each time I am fortunate enough to have a new book to send out to readers in hopes they will walk down the story paths with my characters, I have many people to thank. That includes you, the reader. I appreciate each of you who open my books to make my writing journey complete by letting my story spring to life in your imagination.

I am also blessed to have a great publishing team at Revell. My editor, Lonnie Hull DuPont, has worked with me on all my inspirational novels and always points out ways I can improve the stories. Barb Barnes has made me a better writer with her careful edits. It's great working with Karen Steele and Michele Misiak, who are both always ready to help in so many ways. Cheryl Van Andel and her team have a way of coming up with eye-popping covers. Many more workers behind the scenes at Revell, from proofreaders to the sales team, do their part in getting my books out to readers in the best shape possible. I thank all of you.

Thanks also to my wonderful agent, Wendy Lawton. Her encouragement and advice are always exactly what I need. She's the best.

And of course, I have to thank my ever-patient family as I take these periodic trips with imaginary people into story land.

Last, but never least, I thank the Lord for giving me words and answering my prayers when I prayed "believing" that I would get this story told. As Louis says in the story, "The Lord, he done good to me."

Ann H. Gabhart is the bestselling author of more than thirty novels for adults and young adults. *Angel Sister*, Ann's first Rosey Corner book, was a nominee for inspirational novel of 2011 by *RT Book Reviews* magazine. Her Shaker novel, *The Outsider*, was a Christian Book Awards finalist in the fiction category. Ann lives on a farm not far from where she was born in rural Kentucky. She and her husband are blessed with three children, three in-law children, and nine grandchildren. When Ann's not coming up with new stories, she loves reading and hiking on her farm with her grandkids and her new dog, Frankie.

Ann enjoys connecting with readers on her Facebook page, www.facebook.com/anngabhart, where you can share her popular "Sunday morning coming down" feature or laugh with her on Friday smiles day. Find out more about Ann's books and check out her blog posts at www.annhgabhart.com.

Love Ann H. Gabhart?

Be transported to Rosey Corner where love, hope, and the sacrifice of both will grip your heart and have you longing for more.

Revell
a division of Baker Publishing Group
www.RevellBooks.com

Available wherever books and ebooks are sold.

Cozy up in Hidden Springs where things are sweet, sentimental— and a **little sinister**

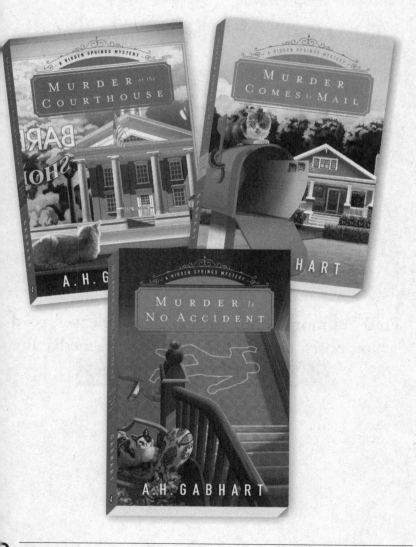

Revell
a division of Baker Publishing Group
www.RevellBooks.com

Available wherever books and ebooks are sold.

Meet

Ann H. Gabhart

Find out more about Ann's newest releases, read blog posts, and follow her on social media at

AnnHGabhart.com